HELL COMES TO HOLLYWOOD

HELL COMES TO HOLLYWOOD

**An Anthology Of Short Horror Fiction
Set In Tinseltown
Written By Hollywood Genre Professionals**

**Produced, Directed And
EDITED BY ERIC MILLER**

Big Time Books™
Los Angeles, California
www.BigTimeBooks.com

HELL COMES TO HOLLYWOOD

Dedicated to Brian Muir

Taken from us too soon,
with many tales yet to tell

CONTENTS

ACKNOWLEDGEMENTS

To borrow a line from Alice Cooper, welcome to my nightmare. "Hell Comes To Hollywood" is the end result of years of dreaming on my part, followed by a lot of good old-fashioned hard work. But I didn't do it alone. Many people contributed along the way, and this book would be nothing but blank pages without them.

So in no particular order, I'd like to thank:

The Writers. Too often in Hollywood other people get credit for what the writers do. But this is *Hellywood*—so credit where credit is due. Thanks for the great tales, and for putting up with my often annoying notes.

Travis Baker and Jed Strahm, who knocked some sense into me when I proposed making this book a collection of stories about mushroom farming in Maine (or something like that) rather than a horror collection. They reminded me of the oldest writing rule in the book: "Write (or in this case, edit) what you know." I don't know anything about mushrooms or much about Maine, but I do know Hollywood, and I know horror. And here we are. Thanks, guys. The Mushroom book will have to wait.

The Horror Community in general. You will never meet a nicer bunch of sick and twisted people. It's an honor to be part of the business I grew up dreaming about.

Charles Muir and the Muir family, for not only letting me dedicate this book to our departed friend Brian, but also letting me include one of his stories. In some small way I hope this helps keep his memory—and his talent—alive.

Shane Bitterling, for being my sounding board and partner in crime, and also for being that nagging voice repeating "get the damn thing done already." I couldn't have done it without you—and wouldn't have wanted to.

And finally thanks to my wonderful wife Wendy, for catching all the typos and for putting up with the long nights alone while I was working on the book. Thanks for understanding. Again.

So now, without further ado: Lights! Camera! Oh, you know the rest...

Eric Miller
Los Angeles, California
January, 2012

FOREWORD

When Eric Miller told me he was doing an anthology of horror stories set in Hollywood, I thought he was crazy. I mean, we make horror *movies,* not books. In fact, Eric and I have made a ton of horror films since we first met in Hollywood, ripping people apart in crazy ways (on set of course) and trying to scare the pants off audiences for more years than either of us wants to admit.

Sure, there was always a *script,* so of course there was *writing*, but the end result after months and years of fake blood and real sweat was always a movie or TV episode—not a *book.* So what the hell was he thinking?

But the more I thought about it, the more a book made sense. No matter what the format, we're storytellers first and foremost.

It doesn't matter how that horrible image or great character or scary story gets burned into your mind—through a tale told around a campfire, or in a movie you see at your local theatre, or from the words of a well-written yarn leaping off the page of a book and grabbing you by the throat and refusing to let go until you wheeze out your last dying breath—as long as it sticks there, and keeps you up at night wondering what that creaking noise was in the hallway, or if you locked the back door, or what creature might be lurking under your bed waiting for you to go to sleep and let your guard down so it can chew on your toes... we've done our job. We told the story.

In the end, the medium doesn't matter. A great story is a great story, no matter how you devour it.

Or how it devours you.

Roy Knyrim
Director/Special Effects Makeup Artist
SOTA Productions

FADE IN:

Laura Brennan's eclectic career has so far included lopping people's heads off on Highlander: The Raven, *feeding them to dinosaurs on TV's* The Lost World, *and sacrificing them to demons and vampires in her adaptation of the L.A. Banks'* Vampire Huntress *series for PicturePlay Films. But it hasn't all been blood and guts: her web series* Faux Baby *explores the lighter side of motherhood... and if the faux baby loses a limb here and there, well... No, actually, she has no justification for that at all. Check her out at* www.PitchingPerfectly. com.

MESSAGE IN A BOTTLE

Laura Brennan

I'D BEEN DEAD about ten minutes before I started to worry.

In my defense, it was Halloween—Halloween in Hollywood, which is even worse. All those out-of-work set designers and special effects geeks go nuts this time of year. Rotting zombie flesh; mechanical, swooping bats; glaring statues that may or may not be alive—this town puts the peeled-grape-eyeball crowd to shame. But it's all fake. The haunted houses are never actually haunted.

Except of course mine. Now.

You always think of Hollywood stars living in million-dollar homes, and you'd be right—it's just that a million bucks doesn't buy what it used to. My humble—now haunted—abode was worth a million five at the top of the market... and it's a three-bedroom ranch. Ah, but the location—that's what you're paying for. In the hills. Got an Oscar winner down the block, private security patrolling the streets—not that in the end they were worth a damn—and the view out the back... a view to die for. That's what sold me on the place. Well, that and the realtor. Natasha.

That's how we met. She had golden hair and crazy-long

legs, but more than that, she had grace. She had class. I'd just come off my first big film and I was looking to upgrade my image, my life. Natasha fit right in.

Natasha loved Halloween. I got her a Roman Goddess costume our first year together. She didn't want to wear it, but I told her that's how I saw her, as a goddess. We'd go to parties and I'd get a kick out of watching her—watching other men watch her—knowing she was coming home with me. I always wanted her to look perfect—hell, with the paparazzi everywhere, she had to look perfect. It was important, she came to realize that. Everything she did was a reflection on me.

But that was a lifetime ago. Back to getting dead. When the doorbell rang, I thought it was a late trick-or-treater. I got those a lot, teenagers who have spent the night daring each other, working themselves up to knocking on my door. I didn't get many little kids, not many families, not since the trial. Which offends me, a bit, when I think about it. It's not like it was my fault she died. She's the one who decided to leave. Plus I was acquitted. That's supposed to count.

The trial was a joke from the start; that cow of a judge had it in for me. But the jury was on my side. A jury of my peers. So some holier-than-thou freaks forgot that in this country we're innocent until proven guilty, so they wouldn't let their nose-wipes eat my candy, so what? More Snickers for me.

Anyway, the bell rang. I put down my beer, grabbed the candy bowl, silently unlocked the door. I paused for an instant, then jerked it open—give the kids a bit of a fright, you know? Hell, they'd be disappointed if I didn't...

And then I saw the Glock.

I remember thinking, stupid kid, Jason didn't carry a gun. But she lifted up her hockey mask and I saw it wasn't a tall kid after all. It was a small woman. It was Natasha's mother.

And then I was dead. I mean, I must've blanked for the actual dying part, because the next thing I knew I was standing next to my own body—which was on the ground covered in chocolate bars and surprisingly little blood—and the door was closed and she was gone.

So you'll forgive me if it took a few minutes for everything to sink in.

When it did, I ran to the window, threw it open and started screaming, just shouting for help, for someone, anyone. Or at least, it felt like I'd opened the window. But once the screaming jag wound down, I realized I was leaning out right through the glass in traditional ghostly fashion.

There was nobody out there anyway. The cars in the street seemed abandoned. Nothing moved. No rustle of squirrels, not a breath of wind against my face. The fake skeleton propped against the phony tombstone across the street leered up at me. I shivered. Not so funny anymore.

I wish I could remember her name. Natasha's mother, I mean. I'd only met her that once, after the acquittal. It was Adele, or Abigail—something with an A. I'd have paid more attention if I'd known she was gonna kill me. Hell, if I'd known, I would've...

Natasha.

The first coherent thought I had after all this went down was, *Natasha*. If I was here, she was here. All at once dying didn't seem like such a bad idea.

Besides, I figured, hey, *something's* got to happen next, right? Not that I expected archangels, no, but some kind of welcoming committee. My grandma. Some guy with horns and an instruction manual. Natasha. She would show, that was certain. We were meant to be together, that's why I spent so much time working on her, correcting her. I was friggin' Henry Higgins, molding her into the perfect girl. All that couldn't have been for nothing. She would come. I just had to wait.

So I waited. I sat on the couch and turned on the TV. Nothing. I flipped through the channels—I'd done a lot of guest star roles early on, I could usually find myself on something re-running in late-night—but after a couple of minutes I realized the remote was back on the table. The TV was off again. So this is hell, I thought. No TV. Fine. I'd survive.

I picked up a magazine I'd swiped from the gym and started to read about the hot new exercise class I'd never get to try. After a few minutes, the words began to fade. Next thing I knew, the magazine was out of my hands, back on the pile by the couch. And still, no one had come. She hadn't come.

I fought down panic. To hell with her, I thought—and then laughed, as the irony caught me. I'd always had a great sense of humor, an appreciation of the absurd. No one ever got that about me, not even Natasha. No one ever understood. And somehow, as my laugh died away, a laugh no one could hear but me, I knew—she wasn't going to come. Not then, not now, not ever.

That was—what was that? A week ago? A month? You lose track of time. It's still Halloween, you see. It's always Halloween. My body is still by the door; I've tried to neaten things up, but nothing I do seems to matter. Ten minutes later, everything's back the way it was, frozen in time at the moment I died.

So I have to keep this short. I gotta finish typing, gotta hit "Send" before the words start to fade. I can't be all alone in the universe for all eternity. I can't—

Damn. The keys—the laptop—the words. There's no more time. Help me. Answer me. Don't leave me alone like this, forever.

Is there anybody else out there? Anybody else—like me?

Andrew Helm has written for every medium and genre that's come down the pike because he's a writer and that's what writers do... especially if they might get paid. To that end he's helped create a Hong Kong action script for Jet Li's first video game Rise to Honor. *He oversaw the writing staff for the video game* Area 51 *that featured David Duchovny, Powers Boothe and Marilyn Manson. He wrote a sequence for TV's* Flash Gordon *that referenced both Wile E. Coyote and the poop of the dreaded Ice Worm. He wrote a Western feature that won several writing awards. He got murdered on camera by the* Insane Clown Posse *in* Death Racers, *a film he wrote for them. He's written and acted in the long-running sword-slinging internet vampire show* The Hunted. *And two of his upcoming film projects feature a family that needs help staying together during difficult times: One is* Christmas Spirit *(Holiday fun for the whole family!), and the other is* Amityville: The Legacy 3-D *(Mommy, why is Daddy spending so much time in the attic?).*

MUSE

Andrew Helm

THE MONSTER DIDN'T WORK.

This wasn't a surprise to anyone on the set of *Blood Beast From Mars!*; they were used to the titular creatures being less than fearsome. And since the metal rods in three of the beast's tentacled arms had bent or snapped two takes into its close-up, it was left to one lowly arm to reach out and grasp the heroine in its blood-seeking embrace.

"Looks like a lonely, masturbating octopus." Huell Graves was the Director of Photography, his voice gravelly from a lifetime of unfiltered Lucky Strikes. He was a good DP in the sense he'd keep the battered Arriflex in focus and framed out Archie's lazy boom mic, but he knew whatever 'artistic' aspirations he might have had were long over. He rarely laughed at his own jokes as the ensuing coughing fit sometimes found him spitting up blood into the ragged handkerchief he kept in his shirt pocket.

Griffin Charles chuckled from his post at the rickety card table otherwise known as 'craft services.' He knew not to insin-uate himself into the process too much. Griffin was a team player. And on this team, he was holding the spit bucket.

Griffin had moved to Los Angeles eight months before. He had been bequeathed the title of 'Most Likely to be the Next J.D. Salinger' by the Beaverton High School Graduating Class of 1957. He had always been prone to flights of fancy during 'free writing' time in his English classes, often reading his work out loud. Hearing his classmates ask him to read one of his stories filled him with a sense of purpose.

When Griffin said he wanted to be a writer, his parents weren't enthusiastic. They were hoping he would attend O.U. for mechanical engineering—after all, his father had been an inventor of some repute during WWII in the Pacific—but it was not to be. He had written for the Beaverton High School paper, then for the local Willamette Press during his senior year; and the writing bug was in him. But journalism just didn't spark his fire.

Griffin had long loved hitting the ornate lights of the Rose City Cinema every Saturday as a kid. Sci-Fi was his wheel-house. The notion that mankind was destined for flight was tantalizing; the coming space race between the US and the Russkies held so many possibilities it made his head spin. In between stories for the papers, he wrote treatments for the movies he saw in his head, slogging away on a battered Underwood typewriter with a sticky 'Y' key. So, the day after graduation, he loaded up his Nash 'Country Club' and with the money he had saved he headed south. The timing chain broke somewhere near a town in Northern California called Weed. It was all Griffin could do not to laugh every time he saw the name on a sign or awning. Some miles after that, near a dusky farm town called Chico, he had a blowout, followed by a hair-raising spin out into a ditch. And just like that, Griffin's moving fund money was nearly spent and what should have been a three day trip was stretched out into a week.

But when he finally hit the San Fernando Valley, smelling the sweet summer trees—and the exhaust of more cars than he'd ever seen in his life—it was all worth it. Griffin had set up accommodations with a cousin on his mom's side named Bill who lived in Burbank. Cousin Bill worked at the Lockheed Skunk Works facility. When Griffin asked what he was working on, a bleary-eyed Bill mumbled something that sounded like 'U-2,' but didn't or wouldn't elaborate. He would be at work, sometimes for days at a stretch. Griffin would have the place mostly to himself.

The day after arriving, Griffin drove over Laurel Canyon and into Hollywood proper. And there his eagerness was fully alight. The city was sprawling and alive, from Griffith Park and the Hollywood sign, to Hollywood and Vine. Griffin had read in the Los Angeles Mirror that the city was going to install stars into the sidewalk to commemorate Hollywood actors. He wondered if they'd ever include writers.

As he looked for work, he repeated this trek into Hollywood every day, sometimes heading down Sunset Blvd., thinking he was William Holden on his way to see Norma Desmond. Other times he'd head down to Melrose Ave., sometimes driving right up to the gates at Paramount Pictures. Sure, the guards would shoo him away, but he knew one day they'd let him pass with a knowing smile and wave.

It was on one of his forays into Hollywood that a soda jerk at Schwab's asked him if he'd been up to Bronson Caves. Griffin shook his head, but the kid just smiled.

"You like science-fiction flicks, that's where they shot a bunch of 'em." The kid reeled off the names and Griffin had just about died and gone to heaven; *Robot Monster*, *Invasion of the Body Snatchers*, *Killers From Space* and *It Conquered the World*.

It Conquered the World was one of Griffin's favorites. He had a not-so-secret crush on Beverly Garland and had seen the film six times. The fact he could go to the very spot where she made such a heroic last stand against the Venusian... he got shivers just thinking about it.

The next day, he headed off to Griffith Park, enjoying another sunny Southern California day. He followed the instructions the soda jerk had given him and soon found himself walking up a gravel road. Then he saw the truck. A half-ton job, rusted and makeshift. In the back were a couple of Klieg lights and an assortment of grip gear... someone was shooting a movie up at the caves!

He'd been looking for work, but certainly holding out hope of finding the right work. But this was a sign. What else could it be? Griffin started to sweat. How the hell could he parlay this into a script? Or maybe he was getting ahead of himself. What if security would just escort him away? How would he know who to talk to? He just needed a job, maybe they...

"Hey, slack-jaw, grab that C-stand." Griffin looked over at the squat-looking guy, a fedora with a sweat ring all the way around crooked at an angle on his head.

Griffin almost replied, "I don't work here..." But that would have been stupid. So, he picked up what he hoped was a C-stand, threw it over his shoulder, heading toward the set of *War of the Spacemen*. And like that, his career in show business began.

Griffin wasn't paid that first day, or even the second. By then the guy in the sweat-stained fedora asked him how long he was going to work for free. Griffin blushed, but the guy laughed. He was Henry Bromstein, Head of Production for Atomic Pictures. He seemed to do a little bit of everything around set, even while barking orders. Griffin was awestruck. "So, what is it you want to do?" Henry asked him.

"I want to write movies. I want to explore the..."

"That's great, kid, do what I tell you, and don't get in the way. Then maybe we'll talk."

Eight months later, Griffin was still schlepping for Atomic Films, this time on *Blood Beast From Mars!* He'd written a few treatments for potential stories, but they mostly sat unread under a pile of scripts, posters and press clippings about two feet high on Bromstein's desk.

But that day, even as the creature waggled its one limp tentacle, Henry still liked what he saw in the creature. And more importantly what he saw in the sweater of the leading lady.

"Hey, Slack Jaw..." Despite Griffin's half-hearted attempts at a new nickname, Slack Jaw it was.

"Yes, Mr. Bromstein?"

"This is lookin' pretty good. You got any ideas for *The Blood Beast Returns?*"

Griffin got that deer-in-the-headlights look that always tickled Bromstein.

"Um... I think so, sir... sure." Griffin swallowed hard, with not a clue in the world how to have the fearsome 'Blood Beast' return.

"Good, have a treatment on my desk Monday morning. Actually, my desk is a disaster area, put it on my chair. If I don't like it, I'll use it to wipe my ass." And with that, Henry was off to yell at the special effects team.

* * *

Griffin sat at the counter of the Bob's Big Boy on Riverside, his regular mealtime spot when he had a few coins to rub together. He had come in high on a cloud. This was it. This was his big chance. This weekend would make or break him.

"You look happy, Griff." Sandy nodded to him as he had sat down, pouring him a cup of coffee and peering over her glasses. She had started working at Bob's when it opened in '49 and it seemed for all the world like she would be buried here.

"I got a writing job..." Griffin let the words slide off his tongue for the first time and liked very much how they sounded. Sandy smiled. "That's great. Sounds like you're on your way."

And as he dug into his burger he felt she was right.

But then the pickle relish caught in his throat. How did the Blood Beast return? It died at the end of the movie, caught in a cave-in caused by a crate full of dynamite. And the Beast was the last of a dying race...

Griffin put his burger down, his mind going a hundred miles an hour. He took out a small notepad and a pen, wrote *Blood Beast* at the top... then nothing. He left it sitting on the counter, staring at it, when a sudden chill came over him.

Griffin turned toward the front door, thinking he felt a draft. But it was no draft.

It was her.

She was small, perhaps 5'4" but she stood much taller in black heels that seemed impossibly high. Her black hair cascaded in short, curved bangs, which curled inward like daggers. Her waist was cinched in a corset. Griffin could see the outline of it through her silky white blouse. He could also see a black bra as well, the outline of her nipples clear just as she turned, her ample breasts straining against the fabric. The seams in her stockings disappeared into a red skirt that was just above her knee, a bit high for a 'good girl.' But then, clearly she wasn't a good girl.

Griffin turned away, knowing he looked too long, but also to hide his growing erection. Had he looked up, he would have seen every male eye turn a gaze toward the voluptuous brunette. And every female eye as well, some out of spiteful jealousy, some out of a want equal to the men.

She sat down at a booth, sliding effortlessly across the seat. Sandy went to take her order, the same bemused smirk on her face that greeted everyone. The woman ordered coffee, black and a slice of cherry pie.

There was a Coca-Cola clock near the wall above her booth. Griffin checked the time on it no less than a dozen times, his own Timex forgotten. There was something magnetic about the woman. He knew he was being a creep, but he just could not help himself. As she ate her pie, her tongue curling around the fork, her lipstick-lashed lips wrapping around the crust, he was transfixed.

Griffin had only had sex twice. Both times with his off-and-on again high school girlfriend Alice. They both inherently knew the relationship was lukewarm and Griffin never pressured her for tokens of affection, his shyness being a large part of that. But thankfully, Alice was more forward at those private moments, and truth be told she had a massive crush on Chip Garvey, the star halfback for the Cougars. She wanted to use Griffin as 'practice' for when she moved in on his current girlfriend.

By the time Griffin moved to Los Angeles, Alice had broken up with him and made her play for Chip. Whatever research Alice gleaned from Griffin worked; she and Chip were married right out of high school. Griffin was left to his own devices.

In his time in the City of Angels, Griffin had seen a lot of beautiful women; all of them aspiring actresses. And if ever a conversation was struck up, when they found out he was a writer (and an unemployed one at that), they quickly went from cheerful and welcoming to cold and aloof.

The brunette in the booth exuded a natural confidence, that was obvious, but it was coupled with a seeming disinterest in the heads that craned when she walked in. Every actress he ever saw or worked with reveled in that kind of attention; the brunette didn't seem to care or notice.

As she finished her pie, leaving a crisp dollar bill on the table as payment and ample tip, she slid out of the booth.

Griffin turned back to his half-forgotten milkshake, somehow feeling her move behind him toward the door. But then he felt a hand on his back. Her hand. If Griffin had been chewing gum, he would have swallowed it right then and there. And then she spoke.

"I couldn't help but notice you're a writer. Maybe we can go somewhere, and talk about your work? I consider sage advice something of a specialty."

Her voice was like honey, low and smooth, and with his heart beating so loud, he didn't actually hear much of what she said. Just that entreaty; 'maybe we can go somewhere...' It was intoxicating in so many ways.

He turned, looking into her eyes, dark blue with flecks of green. She smelled of wild flowers, her milky white skin flawless. Griffin realized he hadn't said anything or even acknowledged her for what seemed like an eternity.

"I'm... Griffin... I...." But then she placed two crisp dollar bills down on the counter for his meal, touching his hand and pulling him gently toward the door. He noticed her nails, dark red, edges in fine points; probably manicured at one of the swanky shops in Beverly Hills.

"I'm Callie." Callie pulled him toward the door, his face flush. He remained hunched over slightly, trying to hide his excitement. She didn't seem to notice. But the patrons who saw this strange little fantasy tableau would repeat the tale often. The night the gawky dumbstruck kid got picked up—hard—by the pin-up model.

* * *

Griffin's cousin lived five blocks away in a little bungalow off Hollywood Way. So they walked, Callie leading him as if she knew where he lived, her heels clicking lightly on the pavement in practiced precision. Griffin's hands fumbled with the key, but he finally opened the door, hoping against hope Bill was at work. He was; the house was empty.

Griffin stepped inside, but Callie stayed on the threshold. "Are your certain you'd like my guidance?" she asked. "Are you sure you want me, Griffin?"

"Yes, of course, please..." Callie came inside and he shut the door behind her.

Callie never took her eyes off of Griffin, making him even more nervous... and even more excited. "So, Callie..." he started.

She stopped him with a wave of her hand. "What are you working on? I'd like to see you write."

"I don't think it's that interesting..."

"I make it interesting." Callie pushed him over to the desk by the window, the one that held his battered Underwood with the sticky 'Y' key. She put a sheet of paper against the platen, wheeled it around. She motioned him to sit, and as he did, she knelt down beside him, her hand on his back.

"What's your story called?"

"It's a script—*The Blood Beast Returns*." He was stammering, a trickle of sweat rolling down his brow.

"Fade in..." Callie said, leaning into him, resting on her knees, her breasts rubbing up against his leg with the slightest of pressure. Griffin dutifully typed the words. Seventeen hours and 72 pages later, Griffin was spent in more ways than one.

* * *

It all seemed like a dream; one even his imagination couldn't comprehend. And there was much he simply couldn't remember. When he awoke, Sunday afternoon, angry, red nail scratches criss-crossed his body, many of them spotted with blood. He was sore everywhere and yet, he wasn't sure exactly when the wounds had occurred. It was as if he was in a trance.

He vaguely recalled writing *The Blood Beast Returns*; his fingers flying over the typewriter keys; however what he remembered viscerally was the pure sensation instilled in him. Callie had both mentally and physically stimulated him. It was as if one fed on the other, or vice-versa. He couldn't tell.

And clearly she had been more than a little rough with him. But, the fact was, he liked it. Loved it. He didn't want her to stop. He could recall his voice getting higher, more impassioned, begging her to continue, to increase the feeling with each page he wrote, each pleasure center she prodded. She took him higher and higher into the stratosphere, like a rocket breaking free from gravity. At some point he was simply unable to process what was happening to him. There was no room to feel bashful, or worry, or mull over character traits or dialog choices or plot twists. Everything just came.

Griffin blushed at the double meaning, his shyness

returning full force given his complete lack of self during his time with Callie. Griffin was most self-conscious of a large, red birthmark that covered the area of his left pectoral. It resembled a large bird, wings spread wide; like a crow or vulture. (He'd been called 'bird boy' by Sean Finley in junior-high gym class and he plotted Sean's terrible demise in his head for years after.) For that reason he rarely, if ever, took his shirt off. But Callie clearly had no problem with it. She didn't even take off her own clothes, merely lifted up her skirt and...

Griffin blushed again, the memory hitting him like a freight train and he blushed again, even as he noted several bruises across his forearms, stymied as to where they came from. As he moved slowly across the living, he picked up the 72 pages laid at the side of the typewriter. He began to read them over.

He was more than a little surprised to find them good. Really good. The fix for the Blood Beast's return was ingenious. The hero was brave, but empathetic. The heroine had some great lines and a touching arc involving her estrang-ed scientist father. The Beast was actually quite terrifying. Griffin knew he had a way with words, but this was leaps and bounds beyond his abilities. And how he had managed to finish it in this one marathon sitting was beyond him.

As he finished reading the last page, he noted a final piece of paper with Callie's name and phone number for a Hollywood exchange.

Griffin put the piece of paper with her phone number in the desk drawer.

The next day, he put the script on Bromstein's chair, hoping he might read it within the week, but not holding his breath about it.

Around noon, as he was unloading one of the grip trucks, Bromstein approached, an unlit cigar dangling out of his mouth.

"Hey, kid, I took a gander at that script for *Blood Beast*."

Griffin looked up, wiping the sweat off his face, his hopeful look akin to something you might see on a Disney animal.

"It was OK. I'm thinking with a few tweaks, a few cuts, it might be pretty good. We got the Blood Beast suit for another week, so it'll have to do."

Griffin knew this was as good a compliment as Bromstein ever gave anyone, much less a lowly writer. Griffin couldn't help smiling.

For the princely sum of $300, Griffin's first film was in the can and out the door by the end of a month that went all too quickly for him. Bromstein never changed a word. Sure, he still made Griffin schlep the lights and bring him coffee, but he had stopped calling him 'slack-jaw' and moved on to 'kid.' The actors all commented on the nobility of the characters and the thrilling moments of derring-do. Griffin had heard these kinds of compliments before on other productions, movies everyone involved knew were crappy, but this was his baby and he knew they meant it. He relished the attention.

The Blood Beast Returns would be packaged on a double bill with *The Monster Walks*, a dubious title for a dubious piece of celluloid. But Griffin didn't care. He called his parents to tell them the news and while they were happy for him, he did note that both asked if he had any thoughts about returning to college... any college.

It was during this heady time that Henry Bromstein called Griffin into his office. He had a poster; on it was a giant crab, menacing a damsel in distress, a buff hero with a spear gun off in the corner. The title of the picture was *Crab Attack!*

"Whaddya say?"

"It looks good, Mr. Bromstein..."

"Great, get to work. Oh, let's say $400 on completion of the script. And you got a week, 'cause I'm feeling generous, kid." Bromstein smiled and flung the poster back down on his desk. The meeting was over.

* * *

Sandy wasn't working as he sat down at the Bob's Big Boy counter, which was fine by Griffin, as he didn't feel like small talk. He had work to do. He flipped his notepad open, writing *Crab Attack!* at the top, then putting his pen down to take a sip of coffee.

He wrote quick notes, trying to channel some sort of inspiration, wanting to free associate. But even as his food arrived, he looked glumly at what he'd written: 'Giant crab', 'hero with speargun', 'damsel in distress'.

Griffin had a notion that the man with the spear gun was a scientist of some sort. And maybe the girl was a reporter, investigating the sudden disappearance of a group of... what? College students? A bus load of deaf kids? A van full of nuns? At least with *Blood Beast* he already had a basic premise to work off of. And he had had Callie.

Griffin sighed, half-turning to the front door, almost expecting her to walk in at that moment. He frowned, the realization hitting him that he didn't retain any of the magic Callie had somehow tapped into. He had thought about her every day since that night, conveniently leaving out her creative inputs, focusing on her raw sexuality; on the strange electricity she had provoked in him. But now, he just needed some inspiration.

Griffin laid some money on the counter, leaving his food untouched. He returned home at a quick march, almost running. His cousin was working late. He needed this.

He opened his desk drawer, as he had done a dozen times, looking at the piece of paper with Callie's phone number on it. But this time, he picked it up and made the call.

The phone rang, but no one answered.

Griffin sighed, thinking he would make some more notes and start in earnest again tomorrow morning. It was late anyway.

An hour later, there was a knock at the door. It was Callie. She stood in the doorway. She wore a tight white skirt, white stockings underneath. Her blouse was red with white polka dots, unbuttoned to the top of her luscious cleavage, her corset visible underneath.

"Are you sure you want me?" she asked, cocking her head

like the RCA Victor dog, as if his answer held greater significance.

"Yes. Please." He invited her in and she went to work.

* * *

When Griffin woke up he wasn't sure where he was, or what had happened. He did realize the intensity of the experience with Callie felt like it had increased tenfold from the first time. His head was pounding, he was dehydrated and every part of him hurt, including a nasty stinging sensation on his back.

As best he could tell, she wrote with him for almost 22 hours straight. As he tried to get to his feet, the stinging in his back sharpened and he realized his sheets were stuck to him. He did his best to gently peel them off, but they were glued with encrusted blood. He winced when the sheet finally fell away. He had bled badly in the night and the sight of the dark, dried stripes on his sheets made him queasy.

Griffin went into the bathroom. When he managed to turn, to look at his back in the mirror, what he saw caused his stomach to tighten. He threw up in the toilet, each heave cracking open the scabs on his back, causing fresh trickles of blood to run down his sides, landing on the bathroom tiles in dime-sized drops.

Callie had sliced out two, long continuous strips of flesh off his back. The wounds were deep and meaty, about a quarter-inch wide and just as deep. In addition, he had a highway map of nail marks and what he came to realize were deep bite marks all over his body as well, the bruises glowing a dark, angry purple.

He spent the remainder of the week nursing his wounds as best he could. He eventually decided to mail the script to Bromstein with a note, saying he was battling the flu.

The following week when he finally walked into Bromstein's office, the producer still grimaced. "Jumpin' Jesus, kid, you look like shit. You been wrestling cats or something?"

"Something like that." Griffin tried not to move, as he

knew even with the amount of gauze he stuffed down his shirt he'd probably bleed through it all again.

The one thing that gave Griffin solace the past two weeks was the script. *Crab Attack!* was good. Really good. And the look on Bromstein's face told him as much.

"This is a great script, kid, top notch. I've got a proposition. If you can write me another one as good as this, I'll package it to a real studio, with some real money—I'm thinking RKO or even Warner's, with me as producer of course. You get in good with those guys you never have to look back."

"What's the poster?"

"No poster, kid. Write whatever you like, long as it has a monster that reduces men to husks, of course. And a beautiful dame in a tight sweater. You know, kid, you're the writer."

Griffin smiled, despite the pain.

"I need the script next week, though."

Griffin's smile dissipated. "I was hoping for a little more time. I'm kind of recovering still."

"I know, kid, but I'll let you in on another little secret— Atomic Films is probably going to fold by the end of the month. It's been a good ride, but that's the business. Your time is now."

Griffin's face fell. He'd tried so hard and now when it seemed within reach, he was thrown for a loop. It was all so close.

"So, kid, I know you won't let me down. You got a gift, you work fast and you got a future in this town. You just need to dig down deep one more time."

Griffin nodded, leaving the office with his money, offering a slight smile to Bromstein, as he saw the producer for the last time.

* * *

Griffin sat at his desk, staring at the typewriter. At the top of the paper were the words 'FADE IN:'

He had been sitting here staring at the page for nearly an

hour. The one question he kept mulling was, 'How bad do I want this?'

Inside the desk drawer to his right was the piece of paper with Callie's phone number. How bad *did* he want this? What would his parents think? He had to prove to them show business wasn't just a lark, this was his life. Would he ever get another chance like this? Did he want to regret not having rolled the dice the rest of his life? It was his time, Bromstein had said so. He realized with a start he had come too far to turn back now.

He made the call.

Forty-five minutes later there was a knock at the door.

"Are you sure you want me?" Callie asked, her eyes dark.

"Yes."

Callie came in, her heels clicking over the threshold. She was wearing a red skirt and a pink top. She put down her purse, removing her blouse. Despite his worry, he became excited, the sexual electricity overriding his hesitation. She removed her bra, her breasts spilling out over the corset she had worn every time they met. She never took it off. Until now.

He got a good look at the garment as she started to loosen the long laces that held it tight. It looked frayed; some of the eyelets holding the laces were on the verge of snapping. There were spots worn shiny with age. He thought she should probably get a new one, given all her other outfits seemed like they were tailored and made of the finest material.

She continued to strip out the laces from the corset, taking her time.

"Can I help you?" Griffin offered, his politeness second nature.

"You are helping me," she said, finishing the removal of the corset laces and laying the fraying strips of leather on top of her purse. "My inspiration comes from inside; it requires your endeavor... and your sacrifice."

"I... don't understand."

She moved toward him and it took a second for him to notice what was wrong.

The corset, though completely unlaced, didn't fall away from her body. It stayed tightly wrapped around her, as if stuck there.

"What's the title of this one?" She almost whispered the question.

"*She Creature From Beyond*," he replied. The corner of her mouth turned up in a smile.

"Help me out of this, will you?" Callie turned. Griffin gripped the edge of the corset, the smooth leather surprisingly thin. "Hold on tight," she said. He did so, and she twirled slowly, the corset peeling from her body with a sound like wet fabric being torn in half.

Underneath the corset was a sticky, oozing morass of veins and musculature that stretched from the top of her waist to the bottom of her breasts. It was if the skin from her midsection had been peeled away in one continuous sheet.

"Let's get started, shall we?" Callie turned, blood starting to ooze down her waist from the gaping, open wound Griffin had exposed. The blood expanded as it reached the sheer material of her skirt, sopping through it quickly.

And for the first time in his life, Griffin screamed.

* * *

Almost 24 hours later, she left Griffin's house. The boy would survive of course. She had been doing this a long time. Her precision was much envied among others of her kind. The cost was sometimes less, sometimes more, but she always ensured they would be marked forever in some way.

The one variable she always pondered of her scribes; would they call on her again? Of the multitude of writers she'd assisted, they all had a different goal, a different methodology, all bristling with new stories to tell; but so many seemed willing to sacrifice themselves over and over for their work, no matter the toll she exacted. It fascinated her. And there was always someone else, eager to provide her with an offering for her services.

She adjusted her new corset, the night air feeling cool on her skin. The leather almost glowed in the Valley darkness. The material would tan rather quickly of course, but for now it was still almost pale white, except for the patch across her midsection bearing a ruddy marking that looked a bit like a large bird, wings spread wide.

Jeff Seeman is the creator and writer of the comic book Dream Police, *as well as the author of two novels,* Political Science *and* Guns and Butter, *and was a contributor to the humor collection* Lunacy: The Best of the Cornell Lunatic. *He's written several feature-length screenplays (one of which was adapted into the film* American Virgin *starring Rob Schneider and Jenna Dewan) and has written, produced, and directed a series of short films. He's performed stand-up comedy in Los Angeles, Boston, and San Francisco. He is also the writer of the progressive political blog* Ramparts, *found at www.ram partsblog.com.*

THE CUTTING ROOM

Jeff Seeman

"IT'S CALLED *The Cutting Room.*"

Through bloodshot eyes, producer Hal Blechman looked across his cluttered desk at the latest screenwriter desperately trying to seduce him with a pitch. In this case it was a tall kid in his twenties, dressed entirely in black, dark hair and eyes, with a pale, expressionless countenance and an unnervingly intense gaze. *Norman something,* Blechman thought. *Cinder? Schneider? Something like that.*

"It's a horror about a psychotic killer," the kid continued. "Only it takes place in Hollywood. And the killer's a screen-writer."

"Uh-huh," said Blechman. How many pitches had he already heard this morning? Six? Seven? Shit, would this day never end?

"See, he's been struggling to make it in Hollywood. And finally he snaps. And he exacts his revenge on all the studio execs and development execs and producers and agents and managers who've pissed all over him."

"Uh-huh," Blechman repeated.

"Only it's not a straight horror. It's kind of broad. More like a horror-comedy."

Blechman sat up. "Like *Scary Movie*?"

"No, that wasn't a horror movie. That was a *parody* of a horror movie."

Blechman looked at him blankly. "And what's this?"

"This is an actual horror. Only with comedic elements. It's more like a self-referential pastiche paying tribute to the genre."

"A what?"

"What I mean is, it's not so much a parody as a... a satire."

Blechman cringed. "Satire is what closes on Saturday night, kid. You ever hear that? Sam Goldwyn said that."

"Actually, I believe it was George S. Kauf—"

"Look, you seem like a nice kid, so let me level with you. That movie never gets made. You know why? No producer's going to finance a movie about producers getting offed. You see what I'm saying?"

"It's just a... a satire. A satire on Hollywood. I just thought..."

"That's your problem, kid. You think too much. *Satire. Self-referential...* whatever the fuck you called it. No one wants that. You know what people want? Huh?"

Blechman leaned back and tapped the poster hanging on the wall behind him, a garish montage of explosions, guns, speeding cars, and screaming, half-naked women. The title emblazoned across the bottom was *Citizen Kane 2: The Revenge*.

"Uh... yes, I noticed that when I came in."

"*Kane 2*, baby! That's our next big hit. You ever hear of the original?"

"*Citizen Kane*? Of course."

"Of course. Of course, he says. That's the beauty. Everyone's heard of it, but no one's seen it."

"Actually, I'm pretty sure millions of people—"

"Which is great for us. Means we can do whatever we want with the property. I finally screened the original last week. Nothing to work with there. God awful boring. Damn thing's not even in color. Do you know it starts off with a newsreel? It's like a movie inside a movie. And then the lights come up and we're in a different movie. What the fuck is that? Confused the hell out of me."

"Uh... not really sure what to say here."

"Anyway, so we get to start from scratch. Completely reinvent the franchise."

"The franchise?"

Blechman leaned forward, warming to his subject. "See, Kane dies at the end of the first one. So in this one, he comes back. He's a zombie, see? And he can't rest in peace until he gets his sled back."

"His sled?"

"Yeah, it's from the original. The whole stupid picture ends up being about this fucking sled. Anyway, Kane can't rest until he gets his sled. And he kills everyone who stands in his way. Now honestly, does that sound like a great picture or what?"

"Honestly? It sounds... awful."

"What? Fuck you."

"You asked for my opinion."

"What the fuck do you know? You know how many pictures I've produced? How many hits I've had? How many years I've been in this business?"

"You just asked me—"

Blechman grabbed the Academy Award from the bookcase behind him and slammed it on the desk.

"That's an Oscar, you snot-nosed punk! A goddamn Oscar! 1972! Best Assistant Gaffer to the Second Second Assistant Director, motherfucker! What do you say to *that?!*"

And what Norman Sawyer said to that was to stand, pick up the weighty statuette, and bring it down on Hal Blechman's head. Again. And again. And again. Until his head cracked open like an overripe melon, and blood and brains rained down on top of *Death Fist 5000* and *Love Is So Funny* and *Vampire Robots From Hell* and all the other unread spec scripts that littered the top of Blechman's desk.

Norman stood for several long moments, dispassionately looking down at the bleeding corpse. Finally, he walked around behind Blechman's chair, where Blechman had hung his jacket, and unclipped the dead man's studio lot badge from the breast pocket.

Located in Culver City, the Warnamount Studios backlot was a 100-acre labyrinth of offices, sound stages, exterior sets, and various other buildings that housed everything from costumes and props to post-production services and screening rooms. The layout had probably made sense to someone somewhere at some distant point in the past, but to present day visitors it invariably seemed a random jumble of sets and buildings, some in use, others deserted. And although a badge was required to gain access to the premises, once on the grounds a visitor had free rein to go virtually anywhere he wanted.

So Norman strolled about the premises, investigating, wandering past row upon row of non-descript gray buildings, then through a Western ghost town of 1850, then past a line of modern-day shops and restaurants, then through a deserted Manhattan in the 1930's, then past more rows of gray buildings, periodically trying the random doorknob here and there to see if one would open.

And so it was that, after roughly half an hour of exploring, Norman successfully opened the door of Building G19, one of the small, gray office buildings on the Warnamount backlot, and stepped inside. He walked up and down the hallways of the mostly deserted building until he found an unoccupied office with a decent view and a comfortable chair. And that, Norman decided, was his office. He fished some Warnamount stationery out of a desk drawer, found an old fax machine at the end of one of the hallways, and sent a press release to *Variety* and *The Hollywood Reporter* announcing his new position: he was now a development executive with an office at Warnamount.

It was just a matter of days before query letters began pouring in from screenwriters trying to nab his interest in one project or another. *Now I'll finally find out what it's like*, he thought. *Now I'll finally see what it feels like to be on the other side of the desk.* Norman set up some pitch meetings.

The first meeting was with a nervous, balding man with bad skin.

"Hundreds of thousands of people died when the U.S. dropped atomic bombs on Japan at the end of World War II," said the man seriously. "This is the story of their pain and devastation. Only with singing and dancing. It's called *Nagasaki Nights*. It's for people who are concerned about nuclear annihilation, but who also love musicals."

Norman stared at him for several long moments.

And then removed a ten-inch butcher knife from his desk drawer and stabbed him in the face.

Next was a bookish woman in her forties. "*Recipe For Love* is a classic feel-good boy-meets-girl romantic comedy," she practically cooed. "Only she's a professional chef. And he's a cannibal."

Norman split her chest open with an axe.

Then there was an effeminate young man with a nose ring. "It's called *Lube Job*. Two robots arrive on earth and must keep their forbidden love secret from their intergalactic overlord. It's *Brokeback Mountain* meets *Transformers*."

Norman threw him into a wood chipper.

"It's what happens when a famous Mexican painter meets a rampaging serial killer. It's called *Frida Vs. Jason*."

Norman took a meat cleaver to her jugular.

"It's *The Sound of Music*, but with prostitutes."

Norman took his head off with a chainsaw.

By the end of the morning, Norman was exhausted and decided to stroll over to the studio commissary for lunch. The commissary looked like any other cafeteria anywhere in the world, except for the plethora of people in costumes. Cowboys, Indians, soldiers, uniformed cops, intergalactic storm troopers —all wandered about holding their orange cafeteria trays in front of them, swapping stories about the morning's shoot and trying to decide between the cheeseburger special and the tuna surprise.

At the salad bar, Norman saw a strikingly beautiful brunette with high cheekbones and large, almond-shaped eyes. She looked him up and down disdainfully.

"You're covered in blood."

"Corn syrup."

"Looks real."

"Thank you."

The woman paid for her salad and found her way to an empty table. Norman followed her.

"I noticed you're sitting alone," he said. "May I join you?"

She glared at him as if he'd just taken a dump on her croutons. "Are you above-the-line or below-the-line?" she demanded.

"Excuse me?"

"Are you above-the-line talent or below-the-line? Because if you're below-the-line, I can't be seen with you. It's bad for my career." She turned her attention back to her arugula.

Norman studied her carefully. *An axe*, he decided. *Definitely an axe.*

That evening, Norman stood in the shadows of the studio parking lot as the woman made her way to her car. And as she drove through the gates and eased her red Mustang into the perennial traffic on the 405, Norman followed close behind.

It was dark by the time she arrived home, a small apartment complex in Van Nuys. Norman watched as she unlocked the door to her first-floor apartment and entered. Thunder rumbled and rain began to fall as the light in her apartment window switched on. Norman opened the trunk of his car and removed the axe.

He walked slowly towards the door, the rain falling more steadily now, the axe dangling at his side, gravel lightly crunching beneath his feet. Standing beneath a solitary light, he tried the doorknob. The door opened a crack, secured only by eight inches of chain. One swipe of the axe split the chain from the door frame and Norman was inside.

He walked slowly through the small, dimly-lit apartment, following the sound of running water that emanated from within. Slowly through the modestly furnished living room and into the darkened bedroom, littered with discarded clothing. Norman stood silently before the bathroom door, listening to the sound of the running water and of the woman softly humming, the door open just a crack, throwing a sliver of light across the room.

The nude woman spun around as Norman threw open the door, her face a mask of shock and horror. The beginning of a blood-curdling scream was just escaping from her throat as Norman raised the axe high above his head and, in one quick motion, brought it down on—

"Is that it?"

"I think that's it."

"We can't do anything with that."

"I know."

"There's no fucking ending."

"I know, I know."

"Sherm, turn up the goddamn lights!"

The lights in the screening room rose as producers Joel Weisberg and Sheila Kaufman rubbed their eyes.

"That's two hours of my life I'll never get back," said Joel. "Did we finance that piece of shit?"

"Don't know," said Sheila. "We don't even have a record of the project. Sherm found a bunch of unmarked canisters in the back of the storeroom. No indication what they were. Figured we might as well take a look." She shook her head. "Maybe we can fix it in the cutting room?"

"Fix what? Can't create a third act out of thin air."

"No," she agreed.

Joel sipped from his half-empty cup of coffee, long gone cold, and grimaced. "Besides, it's got other problems. The tone's all wrong. It's too gruesome for a comedy and too wacky for a horror."

"No way to market it."

"Exactly. And the comedy's way too heavy-handed. That whole bit with the producer at the beginning? Yeah, okay, the producer's a schmuck. We get it. But he doesn't know from *Citizen Kane*? That's just stupid. Nobody's going to make *Citizen Kane 2*, for Christ's sake. The humor's too broad by a mile."

"Still," said Sheila, her eyes narrowing, "horror's an easy sell on the foreign market. And they won't even get the jokes."

Joel considered her words. "Valid point," he conceded.

"Why don't I at least have Ed take a look tomorrow? Maybe he can find some way to salvage it."

"Knock yourself out," said Joel. "I'm heading home."

They left the screening room and walked towards their offices, down a long hallway decorated with the obligatory framed posters advertising various features they'd released over the years.

"I actually thought that actress at the end was pretty good," said Sheila. "Seen her in some other low-budget stuff."

"Yeah, Veronica something-or-other. Never thought much of her before."

"Want to hear something strange? I swear I've heard one of those pitches. That Nagasaki musical thing? I'm sure I've read that log line. How's that for weird?"

"Serious?"

"It might even be in that batch of spec scripts you took home with you."

"Well shit, *that* gives me something to look forward to."

Driving west on the 10, Joel replayed the last few scenes of the picture in his mind. *Veronica Rice*, he thought. *That was her name.* He'd heard she was difficult to work with, a real ball-buster. Still, he had to admit, she'd given a convincing performance. She was beautiful, she had screen presence. And clearly she was willing to do full frontal. A great combination.

Lately, Joel had been devoting almost all his time and energy to his latest project, *Casablanca 2: Vichy France*

Strikes Back! He'd been struggling with the casting, however, particularly the part of Ilsa, Rick's long-lost love who, in this version, was a space alien. Perhaps Veronica Rice was just the actress he'd been looking for. As he pulled into the driveway of his Malibu home, he resolved to call her agent first thing in the morning.

The following morning, lounging poolside, Joel placed a call to Ted Kiel, Veronica's agent. Kiel told him he was no longer repping Veronica due to what he delicately described as "personality differences." He didn't think she currently had representation, but he offered to give Joel her home number, which Joel gratefully accepted.

Joel punched the number into his cell phone. A man answered.

"Yes?" came a gruff voice.

"Can I speak to Veronica Rice?"

"Who's calling?"

"Joel Weisberg."

"You a friend of hers?"

"No, a producer. Who's this?"

"Detective Larry Doyle. Homicide. I'm afraid Ms. Rice has been murdered."

Joel sat up. "Murdered? When?"

"Last night," said the detective. "Most likely between 8:00 and 10:00."

Between 8:00 and 10:00? That was when he and Sheila had screened the picture. Joel felt a chill rush through his body.

"Was she...? She wasn't killed with an axe, was she?" The words were out of his mouth before he could stop them.

"How the hell did you know that?" the detective demanded. "Mr. Weisberg, where are you? I want you to immediately—"

Joel hung up. *What the hell was going on?*

He rushed inside to his office and began tearing through a tower of unread spec scripts, glancing at the title pages. There it was, just as Sheila had said. Nagasaki Nights. Some idiot had actually written that. Joel dialed the number of the writer listed on the bottom of the page. A woman answered.

"Hello?"

"Can I talk to Jerome Stelzer?"

"He's not here. Who is this?"

"Joel Weisberg. I'm a producer."

"Are you the one he met with last night?"

"Last night? No."

"He had a pitch meeting with someone from Warnamount last night."

"A pitch meeting at night?"

"At 9:00. We both thought it was so bizarre. But Jerome went and I haven't heard from him since. I keep calling his cell, but there's no answer. I called the police. This isn't like him at all. He—"

9:00. That's probably when he and Sheila had been watching that scene.

Joel hung up. His mind was spinning now. *This is crazy. This makes no sense.* The movie seemed to have depicted events that actually occurred last night—and at the very same time that he and Sheila had been watching them. *What the fuck?*

Joel's heart began racing and he broke into a cold sweat. The events in the movie had taken place over the course of several days. But like a dream that seems to go on a long time yet really only lasts a few seconds, the movie appeared to somehow collapse time, depicting events that were actually happening at the exact moment they unfolded on screen. *Depicting* events? Or *causing* them? Joel shuddered. How long had those canisters been sitting in the back of the storeroom unnoticed? Would anyone have been killed if he and Sheila hadn't watched the movie last night? It was if the very screening of the picture had caused the murders depicted in it to happen. *But that's insane. That's not possible. Is it?*

Trembling, Joel dialed Sheila's cell. She answered from her car. His words spilled out in a rush.

"VictoriaRicewasmurderedlastnightwithanaxeatthesame

timewewatchedithappeninthemovieandtheguywiththeNagasaki
pitchactuallyhadameetingwith—"

"Whoa, whoa," said Sheila. "Slow the fuck down, Eminem.
I can't make out a word you're saying."

Joel took a breath. "Victoria Rice is dead."

"Who?"

"The actress. From last night's movie. I think the movie's...
dangerous somehow."

"What? I can't... only... driving through Laurel Canyon...
reception... sucks..."

"Sheila? Are you there?"

"Going to... with Ed... screening room... Ed said... maybe...
meeting... screen... movie again..."

"No! Sheila, don't screen the movie!"

"...can't hear... losing... have to meet... show Ed... talk to
you..."

"Sheila, whatever you do, do *not* screen that movie again!
Sheila? Sheila?!"

The connection was lost.

Joel jumped in his Porsche and took off for the screening
room in West Hollywood, a hundred questions flooding his
mind. Who was Norman Sawyer? Was he really just a
disgruntled screenwriter? Had he made the movie himself?
And if not him, who? How had it ended up in the back of their
storeroom? And, more importantly, how was it doing what it
seemed to be doing?

Joel battled his way through the traffic on the PCH and
the 10, followed by the inevitable crawl down La Cienega. It
was a full ninety minutes later before he finally burst through
the door of the screening room, sweating, panting, and on the
verge of hysteria.

Sheila and Ed were already seated and watching the
picture. Sheila turned to him with a confused look.

"It's not the same movie," she said.

"What?" said Joel. "What do you mean?"

"Must be some mix-up with the reels," said Ed.

"It's the same character," said Sheila. "The same killer.

But it's a totally different story. Like a sequel. The victims are all different."

"No!" said Joel. "God, no!"

"Hey!" said Ed. "Look!"

They turned to look up at the screen.

And there, displayed on the screen, were the three of them in the screening room, looking up at another screen. And on that screen, there they were again, looking up at yet another screen. A movie within a movie within a movie within a movie. And on and on and on into infinity.

"What the hell?" said Ed.

"Is this a joke?" said Sheila. "Is there a camera in here?"

"Oh, shit," said Joel.

And the characters on the screens repeated their words, only with a two-second delay between each movie, creating a weird rippling echo of voices that went on forever.

And then suddenly everything was drowned out by the roar of a motor. And Norman Sawyer—huge, towering, dressed in black from head to toe, his face a white snarling mask of death—stepped onto the movie screens and into the screening room, a whirring chainsaw in his hands.

What followed next was pandemonium. Ed was immediately cut down where he stood as Norman sliced through him, sending blood and bone and entrails splattering across the room. Joel and Sheila sprinted for the door, only to find it locked shut. They pounded on it with all their might, screaming and clawing like animals, to no avail. Until suddenly Joel turned to find the bottom half of Sheila's body had been ripped out from under her. The realization seemed to hit both of them at the same moment and they looked at each other in shock for the split-second before the top half of her torso collapsed to the floor in a pile of gore.

And then Joel felt an intense pain in the back of his head. And everything faded to black.

When he regained consciousness, he found himself seated in one of the aisle seats, bound securely with duct tape.

"Time to wake up," said Norman, towering over him.

"Intermission is over." His words echoed over and over on the screens behind him.

"What... what are you going to do with me?" asked Joel.

Norman grinned sadistically. "Well, I was going to force you to watch all fifteen hours of *Berlin Alexanderplatz*. But I think I'll be merciful and just torture you to death instead." He gestured to the screen behind him. "And you get to watch it all on the big screen."

"No. Please." Joel shut his eyes.

"Oh, no. But you *have* to watch."

Norman pinched Joel's right eyelid between his thumb and forefinger. And with a ten-inch butcher knife, proceeded to slice the eyelid off. Joel screamed in pain as the blood poured down his face.

"No struggling now. Only half done," said Norman.

Joel felt his left eyelid being pinched and then, again, the sting of the blade.

"Very *Un Chien Andalou*, don't you think?" said Norman, as Joel's screams echoed into infinity.

"And now it's time for some movie trivia. Because everyone loves movie trivia, don't they?" Norman pulled out a pair of pruning shears and placed the little finger of Joel's right hand between the blades. "And you know all about movies. So this should be easy for you, shouldn't it?"

"Please," Joel pleaded, "please just let me go."

"Question 1: What two movies are generally credited with beginning the French New Wave?"

"The French—? What are you—? Please! Please let me go!"

"What two movies are generally credited with beginning the French New Wave?" Norman demanded.

"I don't— I don't know! Please!"

Snap. Pain shot through Joel's hand as his finger snapped off in a spurt of blood. He screamed and watched in horror as the scene unfolded on the screen in front of him, over and over and over.

"Wrong. The correct answer is Truffaut's *400 Blows* and

Godard's *Breathless*. Question 2: What film, now considered a classic, was booed when it premiered at the 1960 Cannes Film Festival?"

"Oh, God! Please! Please!"

Snap.

"Wrong. The correct answer is Antonioni's *L'Avventura*. Question 3..."

"Sherm!" Joel screamed at the top of his lungs. "Sherm, wherever you are, turn off the goddamn projector! Sherm! In God's name! In the name of everything holy! Turn off the fucking projector!!"

"Is that it?"

"Guess so."

"I kind of liked it."

"I thought it sucked."

Bob Hertzel and Ray Sternberg sat in Bob's office watching the now blank video screen.

"No end credits," said Bob.

"Very *avant garde*," said Ray.

"No markings on the DVD, either. Where'd we get this thing?"

"Must have been mailed to us. I assume he's looking for distribution. Contact info must have gotten separated from the DVD. Should I track it down?"

"Don't bother. I don't want to distribute the piece of shit anyway."

"No? I kind of liked the whole circular, self-referential thing."

"Seen it. Charlie Kaufman meets Wes Craven. Big fucking deal. You hungry?"

Bob pushed the button on the intercom. "Cheryl, can you order us some lunch?" Silence. "Cheryl?"

"Hey, it's not over yet," said Ray.

And the screen showed Bob's outer office, where Norman Sawyer was slitting Cheryl's throat from ear to ear.

"What the fuck?"
They both turned as the office door opened.

Joseph Dougherty's plays have been produced at Lincoln Center and Manhattan Theatre Club. He blended H.P. Lovecraft and Raymond Chandler to create the occult noir mystery Cast a Deadly Spell *for HBO, receiving a Ray Bradbury Award nomination from The Mystery Writers of America. An Emmy and Humanitas Prize winner for his work on the groundbreaking series* thirtysomething, *he's contributed to several popular shows including* Once and Again, Judging Amy, *and* Saving Grace *starring Holly Hunter. He described his work on the hit ABC Family series* Pretty Little Liars *as creating "Hitchcock for teens." His books include* Comfort and Joi, *the story of a movie fan obsessed with a minor glamour girl, and* Psychopomp, *a very different take on the Greek legend of Charon and The River Styx. You can learn more than you might want to know about Joseph at* www.jarndyce-jarndyce.com.

TOWN CAR

Joseph Dougherty

THE LINCOLN TOWN CAR is the most expensive American luxury sedan made, but it's not made in America. It's made in Canada. In Ontario. It's the longest car built in Canada. The L Edition is eighteen-and-a-half feet long. V-8 engine. Two-hundred-and-thirty-nine horsepower. About fifty inches of rear legroom, sixty inches of rear shoulder room.

Forbes Magazine calls the Town Car one of the best cars to be chauffeured in. Curb weight two-and-a-quarter tons. Nineteen gallon fuel tank. Miles per gallon: Adequate. Consumer Guide rates it above average in the premium luxury segment for comfort and safety. They have problems with the acceleration and steering. I agree it's not the most responsive automobile in the world, but a good driver should be able to make allowances and adjust to any driving situation. That's his job.

I am not employed by a family. I work for a car service.

No more chauffeurs on family staff. Well, very few. Those that remain have additional responsibilities beyond driving. Security. Sometimes they are armed. I don't carry a gun. If I carried a gun it would cause nothing but trouble.

I know a driver who worked for a family and carried a gun. It was part of his expanded responsibilities when the family was in the car. One night he saved the life of the daughter. He drew his gun and a situation was resolved. But the police became involved, because of the gun. The family was shocked that this faithful and trusted employee had a gun. He was discharged. He was arrested. He was deported. He was replaced.

No more liveried servants. No more uniforms. This is the uniform now. A dark gray suit, a light blue shirt, a tie. A dark red tie. Good shoes, polished.

The Town Car is not a limousine, it is a sedan. Which means open containers of alcohol are not permitted in the car. People can drink before they get in the car or after they get out, but they are not allowed to drink in the car. This makes things easier for me.

Largely airport work now. Business men, business women. International flights as well as domestic. Some events. Sometimes I take women from the surgical suites of their plastic surgeons to the recovery hotel. Sometimes I take young girls from the plastic surgeon to the hotel. More girls than ever these days.

Parents give the procedures as gifts. Or they think they're giving them as gifts. The girls don't see it that way. They see it as their due. The surgeries are not an indulgence, they are an entitlement.

Often I drive the children of money. I was driving some of them tonight. These children drink all through the night. They stagger out of dark doorways, laughing, shrieking, clinging to each other.

What do they need to drink for? What have they got that needs to be pushed aside? They are playing at something. They don't know what it is. But I think I do. I think I've started to see the shape of it.

The eyes of the young are moist, almost rheumy. As if they were battling an infection. The surface of the eyes catch pinpoint reflections, but there is also this rim, this trough of moisture at the bottom of the eye that is often smeared with light. A little crescent. They seem to have trouble tracking things with their eyes, they can't seem to focus. They are like glass eyes. Like smooth wet stones in a river bed.

Reach into the water, pick up one of the smaller stones, the smaller dark stones polished by a million years of water. Hold it in your hand, in your palm. It's still wet. The sunlight coming through the leaves strikes the skin of water clinging to the stone. Their eyes, at least the ones I look into, and lately I make a point of looking into their eyes, their eyes have as much life as those wet stones.

From the back the girls have the shape of thirteen-year-old boys, but from the front they have these absurd breasts. Massive. Disproportionate. Great symmetrical orbs that make them look like the figureheads on nineteenth century sailing ships. Round and erectly nippled, like those wooden maidens who sailed from New Bedford and Plymouth. Think of what the cities must have looked like then. Boston. New York. Looking from the Battery to the narrows, the horizon etched by spar and mast.

I drove one of the boy-from-the-back-girls tonight. I drove two of them, in fact. One is still with me, still in the car. Sleeping. Passed out. I took them to a party and then I took them to a bar and they drank prodigiously.

Just one of them left. Just the one girl in the back when I drove north, out of West Hollywood, up Laurel Canyon, down the other side, then the freeway, then off the freeway to where we are now.

Where we are now is a turnoff. The beautiful black Lincoln in the blue moonlight, like something from the bottom of the sea. Glistening.

I stand at the edge of the turnoff and look up at the stars. Mountains all around us, like the sides of a box and me and the car and the girl at the bottom of the box.

A night like this, you look at the stars and you swear you can see them moving. Turning over you.

The rear door of the car opens and the girl tumbles out, clinging to the side, pulling herself along the fender to the back of the car. She throws up on the dusty ground.

Her thin dress is very short. Her shoulders are bare. Her impossible breasts are on the verge of spilling out of her dress. She does not seem to notice or care. Her shoes are vertiginously heeled. When she tumbled out of the car, her small, jewel-encrusted purse came with her and fell on the ground.

When I'm sure she's done throwing up, at least for now, I walk over to her and take her by her shoulders and prop her up against the side of the town car. Then I close the passenger door and go to the trunk, open it and take out this little plastic step-stool I keep back there. I put the stool on the ground by the rear wheel and I bend the girl into a sitting position and put her butt on the plastic.

I have a cooler in the trunk and I get her a bottle of grape Pedialyte. I keep a supply for the drunken teenagers. It's better for them than water or a sports drink. I crack the seal and put it in her hand and she drinks automatically. I open a bottle of water and wet some paper towels and wipe her face.

She looks up at me while I'm cleaning her face. She looks up at me, but she doesn't see me. She smiles because the water is cool on her skin.

Her face is round. Wet blonde hair sticking to her forehead and cheeks. Green eyes. She licks her lips. She's probably starting to dehydrate, starting to move from drunk to hungover.

I know this face. I've known it for years. It's looked at me from the sides of buses and from the billboards that crowd the streets and hide the buildings.

It has changed over the years. This face. I remember her dark-haired and childlike advertising movies about high school girls. She was at the edge in those posters, a pretty little after-thought. Then she was suddenly not a child anymore. She moved to the center, her face dominating the image, crowding out all other details till it was impossible to tell what a parti-cular movie was about. All you needed to know was that she was in it.

But she has been missing from the buses and the billboards lately. She has fallen off the sides of the buildings. The faces there are very similar to hers, the expression, the parted lips, the half-closed eyes, but it isn't her face anymore. I wonder what happened.

There's a blanket in the trunk. I put it around her shoulders then I get a shammy and polish where she smeared her hands on the side of the car.

She suckles on the bottle of Pedialyte like a baby. Like someone pretending to be a baby.

Goo.

I have been reading *Moby Dick* which explains why the images of sailing ships and figureheads and harbors are so close to the surface of my thoughts. *Moby Dick* is fascinating. It doesn't feel like it was written a long time ago. It feels like it was written yesterday. I find that remarkable. I find I have to remind myself while I'm reading how old this story is.

I am very fond of Starbuck. Starbuck, surrounded by all that madness. "In him courage was not a sentiment; but a thing simply useful to him, and always at hand upon all mortally practical occasions."

There is much time for reading on this job. Reading is a solace. It is also a way to keep the mind from going places where it is not wise to linger.

Lately. Recently. There have been unexpected moments in which I have lost charge of my emotions. Or how my emotions play out through my behavior.

I was in the shower, under the hot water, when I felt my face twisting. Twisting into what felt like a fist. And I started to cry. To weep. Weep in the shower. Shaking with sobs. I put my hands against the glass walls and wept. For what, I do not know. They had the feel of funeral tears. Bottomless. The tears that come with certainty: Something is dead. But I'd had no great loss the evening I stood in the shower crying. All my losses happened a long time ago and far from this pleasant land. So why was I crying? What did I have to weep about? What?

I stopped myself from crying. It took some time. It was like falling down a steep and muddy hill. You grab and struggle, but you still slide. You're still falling down the hill. Eventually I gained control.

When I got out of the shower I put on my robe, sat at the kitchen table and drank the last of the coffee from my thermos. The coffee was cold, but I drank it.

I'm afraid something like that might happen again. Happen in front of other people. I don't know what I'll do if that happens. Recently, I find myself losing control of my emotions. And more recently still, losing control of my actions.

"More."

I turn away from the stars, turn away from The Belt of Orion, and I see her sitting on the plastic-stool, her knees pulled up close to her, the empty bottle of Pedialyte in her hand, holding it toward me.

You want some more?

She nods. The nodding makes her dizzy and she shuts her eyes.

I get her another bottle, crack it and give it to her. She doesn't thank me, she just drinks what I give her.

I lock the car doors with the transmitter attached to the keys in my pocket.

I read. Melville. Whitman. Hawthorne. Also Sinclair Lewis and Fitzgerald and Hemingway. Hemingway was not what I expected. "The Snows of Kilimanjaro." The dying man in "Kilimanjaro," considering his death, experiencing his death. Feeling it come to him like an animal. Like an animal settling its weight on him. Slowing his breath. Crouching.

And Conrad. "Typhoon." The Chinese in the hold. Frightened. Being thrown around inside the forward hold by the storm. Thrown around like... like frightened Chinese. Conrad led me to Melville. The sea.

I think about the sea. I think about leaving. About booking passage somewhere. Someplace beyond the curvature of the Earth. Across the Pacific. On a freighter. Many freighters carry passengers. A handful of passengers, along with the containers. Hong Kong. Singapore. I'll do it. But I have to find the right ship.

I've driven people to the harbor in Long Beach. To the cruise ships. Ships that don't look like ships. They look like Las Vegas hotels. Terraces and balconies, the color of toys. Where's the majesty in that?

These hotels crowd the old Queen Mary. Hem her in. Ignore her. Someone built the Queen Mary. Human hands shaped her. These cruise ships were not built. They were assembled. Like lawn furniture from Target.

The hotels sail away. The Queen settles in the silt. Why?

Booking passage.

"Open the door, Trish."

The girl has pulled herself up and turned and is banging on the glass of the passenger door with her little fist. Her gold bracelets chime against the glass.

"Come on, Trish."

I tell her, *Trish isn't in there.*

"Open the fucking door, Trish."

Again, I tell her, *Trish isn't in there.*

She looks at me. She doesn't really remember who I am.

"What do you mean she's not there?"

She's not in the car.

"Then who locked the car?"

I did. I have the remote in my pocket. I locked the doors.

"Well, open it."

I tell her, *no.*

"No?"

No. You might throw up again. I don't want you throwing up inside the car.

She looks at me, then turns and slams on the door.

"Trish, open the fucking door."

Trish isn't in there.

She stops hitting the car and looks at me. Tries to look at me. She's weaving in her silly shoes.

"Where's Trish?"

Trish is gone, I tell her.

"What do you mean, Trish is gone?"

She's gone. She's not here.

She leans her face against the glass and shades her eyes. The car is empty.

"Where is she? Where'd she go?"

I don't know where she went. I just know she isn't here.

The girl looks around. She sees her bag on the ground and grabs it. She starts going through the bag, but she doesn't find what she's looking for.

"Where's my phone? Shit. Where is it?"

You must have lost it somewhere.

"Open the door."

No. You might get sick again. I won't take the chance. This is an expensive car. I'm responsible for it. I'm responsible for its care.

"What the fuck are you talking about?"

I'm talking about the car. The Lincoln Town Car L Edition. The one you're leaning against. The one you've been riding in tonight. You and Trish. Remember? You went to a party. You were at Trish's and I picked you up and I took you to a party and I waited for you. In Holmby Hills.

She tries to think about this and it makes her head hurt. Thought is painful to the unaccustomed mind.

"So, where's Trish?"

Trish isn't here.

"Man, open the door."

Sit down.

"Are you some kind of moron? You're supposed to drive

me in the car. You can't drive me in the car if I'm not in the car. So, open the fucking door and get behind the fucking wheel and do your fucking job. Okay? Clear?"

I'm thinking about you. I'm thinking about your comfort. The road twists. You'd be very uncomfortable. You'd get sick again. So far you haven't stained your pretty dress. If you got sick again I'd have to stop the car. It would end up taking longer to get back. You'd end up feeling much worse. Rest for a little while. If you rest we can leave sooner.

"And do what in the meantime?"

We can talk. Talking will pass the time.

"Talk about what?"

We could talk about you. You could tell me all about yourself. I bet you're a very interesting person. I bet your life is very, very interesting.

"Open the door."

Have you been to college? Did you graduate?

"Fuck that."

I went to college.

"Yeah, and now you're a fucking limo driver."

It's a town car. Not a limousine.

"Whatever."

I found it a transformative experience in many ways. I was the first one in my family to go to college.

She makes a snorting sound. She sounds like a pig. *Have you had anything in your stomach today except for the drinks? Was there food at the party you went to?*

"The party?"

The one in Holmby Hills.

"There were trays going by."

But nothing caught your fancy?

"My what?"

Your appetite was not stimulated.

"We had some grass."

What about later, at the bar?

"Bar?"

The one on Santa Monica. The one in West Hollywood.

"The fag bar? We were there?"

You and Trish. You went there after Holmby Hills. I drove you there. I parked in the alley across the street. I could see the front window. I saw you in the bar. You were dancing.

"Faggots are the best dancers. Fucking trannies leave the seats up in the ladies."

Nothing to eat, though? Nothing to settle your stomach and balance the alcohol?

"Did we leave Trish at the fag bar?"

No, she was with us when we left.

"Shit."

She's trying to remember.

Is Trish your friend?

"I wouldn't go out with her if she wasn't my friend. Why would I bother with her if she wasn't my friend?"

Do you spend much time with her?

"Yeah. Weekdays, mostly. I upgrade on the weekends. Fuck!"

She puts her hand to her forehead. She's miserable. I open the trunk again, and take out one of the chemical ice packs I keep in the first aid kit. You slap it to start a chemical reaction in the pack. A chemical reaction that gives off cold instead of heat. Is that right? "Gives off cold." That can't be right. It must take away heat. But from where?

The pack gets cold and I wrap it in one of the hand towels I keep back there. It's a very well-stocked trunk. I have everything I need for any given situation and still have plenty of storage space for luggage.

I sit Tru on the stool and press the cold hand towel against her forehead. She sighs and puts her hand on mine and presses the pack against her head. I know her name because I looked in her wallet when I took the phone out of her bag.

I'm worried about the potential for mischief in those moments without control. I'm afraid they will lead to some-thing. Some thing.

I picked up a man at LAX. He wanted to go to The Beverly Wilshire. He was on his cell phone the whole time he was in the car. He spoke a foreign language on the phone so I would-n't understand his conversation. But he spoke a language I know. He assumed I was a real American and only knew English. But I know more than English.

He spoke on the phone. He spoke to a friend in the city. He spoke of the age of the prostitute he had recently used in an Asian country he had visited. The girl was no more than twelve. It was, he told his friend, a remarkable experience, one he promised himself to repeat and recommended to his friend as a tonic for the spirit and the body. I got off the 405 at Wil-shire Boulevard and drove east toward Beverly Hills, toward the hotel, and wondered what pleasure there could be in raping a child.

I was walking along a road once. A long time ago. There was shooting. Rifles. Then another noise that sounded like birds, but wasn't birds. Then truck gears grinding, driving away. Then nothing. I kept walking.

I came out from under the trees and on the side of the road, in a ditch by the side of the road, there were three bodies of three girls. Naked. Soldiers had raped them. Then they had thrust the bayonets of their rifles inside them and fired their guns. Then they pulled their bayonets up through the girls, splitting them open up to the sternum. That's how they left them. In the ditch. They were in their early teens, I think. The girls. From the look of them.

Soldiers in a truck, a rich man in the back seat of a town car. I don't understand where these things come from and it frightens me that I don't understand. When people talk to me about God, I just walk away.

Suppose I decided not to drive that man to The Beverly Wilshire. Suppose I pushed the button that locks all the doors and the windows and drove up Beverly Glenn, drove up to one of those abandoned, unfinished houses in the canyon. What would he think was happening?

What if I cut off his dick and shove it down his throat before I kill him. Would he know why it was happening?

Happening to him? Would he understand? Would it make a difference?

If it would make a difference, I can understand the urge, even the action. Otherwise, what am I doing?

Tru groans.

I take the cold pack from her forehead. I put my hand on the back of her head, in all that silky, confused hair, and lean her forward. Then I put the cold pack on the back of her neck.

A fly gets in the car. It's mindless, annoying. You may get angry at it, but you don't hate it. You let it out, or you ignore it, or you kill it. But you don't assign it a motive. You don't credit the thing with an agenda. It's an insect. You kill it or you don't. Your goal is not the killing. All you want to do is stop the buzzing.

She groans again.

Does that help?

"That helps."

She leans her head against my leg as I hold the cold pack to her neck.

"Let's go."

Rest a little more first.

"Fuck."

I have a theory. About young people. Young people today. You can help me with it. That'll make the time pass. Do you want to help me?

"Fuckity-fuck-fuck."

Just listen to the theory. Tell me if it makes sense to you. Tell me if you recognize yourself or your friends in anything I say. It's a theory about innocence. The evolutionary purpose of innocence. The innocence of youth. I believe innocence protects the young from the world, but it's meant to fall away when the time comes to become an adult. It was meant to wear away, to recede, to be pushed aside by curiosity and experience. It wasn't meant to surround you for your entire life. But this shaving away, the sanding down of protective bliss, it's a tricky business. Do it too quickly and you don't get an adult, you get a seven-year-old zombie. Do it too slowly and you get something soft and purposeless. The forces that wear away innocence are unequally distributed on this planet. In some places they are in great concentration, places where the abrasion is premature, rapid, terminal. In other places the forces don't seem to exist at all. Places without friction, where nothing wears away the bubble. So, to test my theory, I have to ask you a question.

She lifts her head from my leg and looks at me. The ice pack is very cold in my hand.

What do you think when you look at people older than you? Older than your friends? People like me. Like your parents. What do you think when you look at them? Or do you even see us? Are we just shadows that bring you food and open doors? What do you see when you see us? Do you see the people you will become? Or do you see an all together different animal, another species, as different from you as you are from a starfish? Is it possible you don't think you will ever change?

"Fuck that." She says this less like a curse, more like a sigh.

Do you think of yourself as timeless? Immortal? What does it feel like? To be immortal. How does the world look to you? Is it just something blurring by outside the windows of shops and the windows of cars? Do you ever wonder? Do you ever question? This is important. This is vital. It's a matter of life and death, for me as much as it is for you, so try to answer.

"I don't know what the fuck you're talking about."

I'm talking about innocence.

"Unlock the car. Let's go."

I don't want to go yet.

"I don't care what the fuck you want. Let's go."

No. I like it here. We'll stay awhile longer.

"Fuck you. I'll walk."

She leans forward, pitching herself into a standing position, her arms going out, like someone doing a drunk act on a high-wire.

If you walk you'll get lost.

"I'll walk down."

Down where? You aren't where you think you are.

She looks around and for the first time sees where she is.

"Where are the lights?"

No lights. No city. No cars. Listen. Just the noise your shoes make on the gravel.

She looks at me. I think it's the first time she's really looked at me all night.

"Who the fuck are you?"

My name is Anthony. I've been driving you all night. Earlier I drove you and your friend, but for the past few hours I've been driving you. You fell asleep in the back. I was feeling tired so I pulled over and got out and stretched my legs. I had some coffee from my thermos and a Powerbar. I was looking at the sky. Then you woke up. I heard Trish call you Tru. Is that your name? How do you spell that?

"Yeah, that's my name. Tru. T-R-U. Tru. Where the fuck are we?"

North of where you thought you were.

She knows something is wrong, but she's not sure what.

"I want to go home. You have to take me home. Unlock the car, okay? Just unlock the car and take me home. Take me back to town, you don't even have to take me all the way home. Drop me off and nobody knows nothing. Deal?"

Answer a question first.

"What the fuck are you talking about?"

If you won't help me with my theory, at least you can answer a question. Answer one question and I'll unlock the car.

"Jesus, all right, whatever. Ask your fucking question and let's go."

Who was the thirty-third President of the United States?

"What?"

Who was the thirty-third President of the United States?

"Are you insane? How am I supposed to know?"

Count them. Count them backwards till you get to thirty-three. I'll get you started: Obama is number forty-four.

"This is bullshit."

When you tell me the name of the thirty-third President, we can move on.

"Fuck that."

The louder she shouts, the calmer I speak. She doesn't like that, it makes her head hurt, and I find that very funny. In the middle of all this, I find that amusing.

It's very important that you answer my question.

"Listen, why don't I just give you the blow job instead?"

What?

"We know what this is all about. Come on. If I give you the blow job can we just go?"

Do you think that's what I want?

"Of course it is, come on. I won't fuck you, but I'll suck you, if it gets me out of here. Don't stand there like you don't know what I'm talking about. That's why you got rid of Trish, that's why we came up to wherever the fuck we are. I won't do it out here. Unlock the car. Get in the back and let's get this over with."

I guess that's easier than thought for her. That's how far she's willing to go to avoid thinking.

"You're blushing. You want it. You planned it, right? Course you did. Me and Trish in the back, you looking in the mirror. It's hot, I understand. But no cell phones, no little cameras; I'm not stupid. I'm not ending up with my ass on YouTube."

She reaches for my belt. I grab her wrist and I twist it.

Why would I want to touch you? What pleasure could I possibly get from that? From you? Why would I want you to touch me? Any part of me? Who do you think I am? Who do you think you are?

I hold onto her wrist, waiting for an answer. She tries to pull free. No chance, but it takes her almost a minute to realize that and she stops pulling. She works to focus on my face.

"You want to know what I see? What I see when I look at

you? I'll tell you what I see. I see a big pile of old newspapers, I see nothing but old paper. Stacks of it, in the gutter all soaked from the rain and rotting. I see how confused you look when we talk because you don't know what we're talking about because what we're talking about is something that has nothing to do with you because you are fucking dead, man. You are over. You are done. You are boring. You're fat and old and boring. And there's nothing you can do about it. And that makes me laugh. You're funny. So I laugh."

That's when the phone in my coat pocket starts to ring. Not ring. These phones play little songs. She hears the song and she recognizes it.

"That's Trish's phone."

I let go of her. She holds the red ring I made around her wrist. She thinks about running, but there's nowhere to go. I reach into my pocket and take out the other girl's cell phone. I hold it in my hand. It flashes green and gold and makes its little electric music box sounds. Then it stops.

"What are you doing with Trish's phone?"

I found it.

"Where is she? Trish. Exactly."

I don't know where she is. Exactly.

I put the phone back in my pocket. She watches my hand when it comes out of the pocket. Then she looks at my face.

There's a sound. The sound of faint bells. Impossibly small bells. At first, I think the sound is inside me, but it's not. The sound comes from her. It comes from her head. From her earrings. She's shaking now, trembling, and her earrings make distant, angelic music. She's vibrating, like a tuning fork. I can't see it, but I can hear it.

I have her full attention.

She swallows and says: "Bush came before Obama."

Obama is forty-four, so Bush would be what?

"Forty-three."

And before Bush?

"His father."

You missed one.

"Clinton. Clinton came between the two Bushes. So, Clinton's forty-two, the other Bush is forty-one."

And before the first Bush? So far we're still in the eighties, that's not so long ago.

She tries to think and ends up guessing, pulling a name she remembers someone saying once.

"Reagan?"

Number forty. See, it's there. In your head. Who was before Reagan?

"I don't know."

Yes, you do.

"I don't know."

She's shaking now. It's cold, but that's not why she's shaking.

"CARTER! JIMMY CARTER!"

Carter was thirty-nine. Who was number thirty-eight?

"Nixon."

I smile and she thinks she's right, then I shake my head and she knows she's wrong.

"Fuck. Give me a hint.

He pardoned Nixon.

"I thought that was Reagan."

No, it wasn't.

"Give me another hint. Please."

Please. She said, please.

His wife has a famous detox facility named after her.

"Ford. Betty Ford. Mr. Betty Ford. Gerry. Gerry Ford."

Number thirty-eight. Next.

"Nixon."

Nixon.

"Finally."

Nixon's number thirty-seven. Three more to go. Who was number thirty-six?

"Kennedy?"

No.

"Fuck."

Think.

"Give me a hint."

No more hints.

"You gave me hints before."

That was before. No more hints.

"That's not fair. You asked me who the thirty-third President was. That was the first question, the real question. Then you said count them backwards to get to thirty-three. Thirty-three, that's the real question. So, it shouldn't matter how I get there. It shouldn't matter if I get clues to the others. You see what I'm saying?"

You're right, that was the original question.

"So it's okay that you give me hints. See?"

Then I'll give you a really big hint. Number thirty-six took office when Number thirty-five was assassinated.

"So, thirty-five was Kennedy! Right? I got thirty-five, so I don't even really need to guess thirty-six. Right?"

Kennedy is thirty-five. Two more.

"The one before Kennedy. Shit. Okay. That's like in the fifties. Shit, the fifties. Okay."

She doesn't know. Then her face opens up and she shouts the answer at me.

"McCarthy!"

Joseph McCarthy?

"Yeah, if that was his name. His first name. But I got his last name."

Joseph McCarthy was never President.

"Yes, he was. In the fifties."

No, he wasn't.

"How do you know he wasn't?"

Because he was never President.

"You could be lying to me, there's no way I would know."

If you knew the history of your own country you'd know.

"You should give it to me."

Because you managed to name somebody from the right decade? No.

Part of her still hopes I'm playing a game. I walk toward

her, she steps backwards and almost falls in those ridiculous shoes.

Get it right. For God's sake, make an effort. Please. Get it right. Two more. Just two more. I want you to get this right, I do. I need you to get this right. Try.

"You're asking me things I don't know. That's not fair. Ask me about something I know."

Thirty-four was a general. He was supreme commander of allied forces on D-Day.

I might as well be speaking Latin.

"I don't know what that is. You know I don't know. You're doing this on purpose. Give me a real hint."

You don't want a hint. You want the answer.

"Then give me a choice. Give me three and let me guess."

Why am I doing this? Why am I giving her even this chance?

A. Thomas Jefferson. B. Dwight D. Eisenhower. C. Woodrow Wilson.

"Okay. It's not A. It's not Jefferson, he's one of the really old ones. One of the founding fathers. Right? Okay, so it's B or C. It's Eisenhower or Wilson. Wilson or Eisenhower. Wilson. Wilson. Eisenhower. Eisenhower. Fifties. Mr. Wilson. Fifties. Fifties. B or C. B or C. I'm going to say... B. Eisenhower."

What if I said you're wrong? How would you know?

"Because it's all over your face. I'm right. It's Eisenhower."

Eisenhower is number thirty-four.

She erupts with "Yes!" Tiny fists pumping in the air. She feels lucky. She thinks she has a chance.

Who is number thirty-three?

"Give me the choices."

No choices this time. This time I have to be sure you know the answer.

"You're changing the rules."

There are no rules.

"Then you have to give me hint."

You already have the hint for this one.

"No, I don't."

Yes, you do. You *are the hint.*

"What are you talking about?"

You are the hint. You are the answer. At least part of it.
You already know the first part of the answer because you
know who you are.

"I don't know what the fuck you're talking about."

Yes, you do. I promise, you do.

"You're crazy."

Think. Just think about it.

She backs away from me till her ass is against the side of
the car.

"I don't know."

You know. You have to know. Please, know.

"I fucking don't know who it is. I don't know anything. I
don't know shit. All right? You happy? I don't know shit!"

She slides down the side of the car and curls up in a little
ball. She starts to cry. To weep. She knows it's over for her.

What I'm waiting for? Really?

All the feeling has drained out through my fingertips.

I turn my back on her and walk to the edge of the turnout.
The sky isn't crisp any more. It's muddy. Like a television
screen when the set is on, but there's no image. Waiting for a
signal.

Things have worked out very differently for me than I
thought they would. I shouldn't even be alive at this point. But
that's not about my courage, my character, my worth. That's
just luck and knowing when to be selfish. Character gets in the
way of surviving.

The Belt of Orion. Three stars in a row. They're not really
in a row. We just perceive them that way because of our
position in space. They're not in a row. They are completely
unrelated.

I hear the gravel behind me and turn to see that Tru has
gotten up from the ground and tip-toed her way over to where
I'm standing. One hand is raised over her head and now it
swings down toward my face. I recognize the thing in her hand

just before it hits me. She's holding one of her shoes, the heel pointed at my face.

I start to turn and the point of the heel catches the side of my nose. If I hadn't moved, it would have punctured my eye, stabbed it like an olive. But it hits my nose and fills my eyes with ragged white light for a second.

Tru pulls the shoe back and takes another whack at my head. My hands are coming up. She's lost her chance, but this is still going to cost me.

She hits my forehead and I feel the blood right away. She hits the side of my head, almost driving the heel into my ear.

She keeps hitting me as I grab for her wrists.

Listen.

She doesn't listen. She keeps hitting me with the shoe, with the heel. The Stiletto heel. Her teeth are clenched. They are amazingly white.

I knock the shoe out of her hand and scoop her up, off her feet, and carry her back to the car. She weighs nothing and I slam her against the passenger door. I close my right hand around her throat.

Your name. Your name is the clue. He was FDR's vice president. He dropped the bomb on Japan. He started the Korean War without congressional assent. Think. Your name. What's your name?

"Tru."

Tru.

"Tru."

She shakes her head. Not to get loose, but because she doesn't know.

I have both of my hands around her neck now. I can feel the cartilage in her throat against my thumbs. I squeeze.

Her eyes are green. Two shades of green. A darker green circling something like jade.

We stay like that for a very long time.

Someone whispers in my ear: "True Man."

Did she say it?

The whites of her eyes are threaded with blood.

Who said Truman? Did anybody say it? Did I say it?

"Tru - man."

She said it. I felt it through my hands.

I hear the air rushing back into her lungs and I realize I've let go of her neck. Her face falls away from my hands and she slips down the side of the car, gasping, crying.

I step back. This is not going well. My vision is blurry. I reach up and touch the blood coming down from the cuts in my forehead and getting in my eyes. I go to the trunk for water and a clean towel. I start to wipe the blood off my face and try not to think about what's going to happen next.

"Truman? Is that right?"

Her voice is croaky, her breathing whistles. It must hurt her to talk. I look around the trunk lid. She's still on the ground. How old is she? Really? She's much younger than I thought.

Yes. That's right.

"Your clue helped. About it being my name."

That's why I picked the thirty-third President. Because it was Truman. Because the answer had part of your name in it. I thought that would make it easier.

"Did I hurt you?"

It's all right.

I go to the trunk and come back with water for her. I watch her drink. It hurts her to swallow.

She looks at me.

What?

"Can we go now?"

I don't see why not.

I reach into my pocket and press my thumb on the transmitter. The doors all thunk open at once. I offer her my hand and she takes it. I help her to her feet. Then I open the rear passenger door for her and hold it. She looks inside the car then she looks at me.

"I won't say anything."

It doesn't matter and I tell her so.

"Okay, but I promise I won't say anything. Honest."

Tru gets into the car. She slides across the rear seat and presses herself against the opposite door, pulling her legs up under her, compressing herself as much as possible.

I close the door and the lights go off in the car. Between the darkness and the tinted glass, the inside of the car disappears. She can see me, but I can't see her.

I pick up the foot-stool, the empty bottles, anything that would indicate anyone had been there, and put all that in the trunk. I suppose I've left behind some of my blood, in the dirt, but there's nothing I can do about that.

To be honest, I don't want to do anything about it.

This is the last place. This country. It is strong and wealthy and surprisingly untested. I thought that meant it would be the place that survives. Now, I don't think so.

You don't know what's coming for you. You don't know, but I do. You won't know what's happening to you when it happens. You'll be surprised when it happens. You won't believe it at first. "This can't be happening. It certainly can't be happening to me." But it will be happening to you. And you'll be alone when it happens. You don't believe me? Look in their eyes. Look in those eyes like wet stones.

I'll throw the cell phones out the window on my way back to town.

Writer, producer and director Ann Lewis Hamilton has work-ed on thirtysomething, Stephen King's Dead Zone, Haven, *and many other TV shows and movies. She is married to a movie producer, has two wonderful kids, throws a mean Super Bowl party every year, and has been known to contribute to the literary webzine* www.Hot ValleyWriters.com.

POOL BOY

Ann Lewis Hamilton

BOTTLE TANS LOOK FAKE. And they smell funny, too, like old vitamins. Jacqui feels pity when she walks by a woman with a bottle tan. "I can see your orange palms or the brown on your cuticles where you thought you wiped off the lotion, but you didn't. Fake fake, *faker*," she wants to say. But she doesn't, because that would be catty.

She knows people admire her tan, they want to ask her what product she uses. L'Oreal? Kiehl's? One of those tanning towels you see on the home shopping networks? Are they sniffing at her, wondering why she doesn't have that strange medicinal scent?

Because I'm *natural*, that's what she'd tell her admirers. No tanning beds or creams, I use the sun and before you launch into one of those—oh my God, what about skin cancer rants, let me tell you—God created sun, didn't he? Did he create dihydroxyacetone, the creepy, stinky chemical in self-tanners that does who knows *what* to your immune system? I go to my dermatologist once a year to get checked out and I'm doing just fine, thanks. S.P.F.? Not for this girl. S.P.F. to me means Skin Perfectly Fine.

But Jacqui keeps those thoughts to herself. She is lucky, she is blessed. In addition to being bronzed and sun-kissed.

When Jacqui decides to rent a house, the most important item on her wish list is the position of the pool. The wrong exposure, too much shade—deal breaker. The stone cottage in the hills of Laurel Canyon only has one and a half baths and the half bath is so small your knees bang against the sink when you sit on the toilet. Not to mention the kitchen floor with checkerboard black and white press-n-stick tiles that curl up at the edges.

But the pool, the pool is the home run. Built in the back yard halfway up the hillside, it sits like a mini-oasis, surrounded by a low brick and metal fence, cypress trees behind it on two sides (not creating shade, only privacy). The pool is oval-shaped, with a flagstone deck, sapphire and bronze glass tiles rim the pool edge. A black bottom pool, the leasing agent explains to Jacqui. They don't make them like that any more, it's against code. Jacqui could care less about the code, she looks down at the water in the pool. Flat and still, deep blue and green.

"The price seems too good, especially for this neighborhood," Jacqui says to Darlene, the leasing agent. But in her mind she's already arranging her new pool furniture around the deck.

Darlene hesitates. She is pale and has freckles, what a curse. "I was going to have to tell you anyway—full disclosure and all that. There were some deaths..."

Jacqui is trying to decide between a striped patio umbrella or a solid—dark green might disappear in front of the cypress trees, but would a multi-stripe be too dramatic? She realizes Darlene has said something about death.

"Somebody died here?"

"The last owner, she was elderly. She slipped." Darlene takes a deep breath. "She drowned. In the pool."

Jacqui looks at the water again. More green now than blue, splashes of bronze reflect from the tiles.

"An accident," Darlene says. And takes another breath. "The man who lived here before her, too."

"*Both* of them drowned?"

Darlene nods.

Why don't more people take swimming lessons, Jacqui wonders. "They investigated," says Darlene. "But didn't find anything. Tragic accidents."

"Were they drunk?" Jacqui asks.

"I don't know," Darlene says. "They could have been."

Darlene wants Jacqui to rent this house, she'll say anything. She only mentioned the two drowned people because she had to. Legally. Do most of the people who look at the house freak out because of the dead tenants?

"I'm not afraid of ghosts," Jacqui says to Darlene. "Everything has a logical explanation."

"That's what I think, too." Darlene smiles, *whew*, you can see the relief on her face.

Jacqui watches light dance on the surface of the water, like silver ribbons. Silver and bronze and gold. It's not as if the bodies are still floating in there. They must've drained the pool. And cleaned it. Twice.

She'll go with the multi-colored umbrella. Bright patches of color against the flat green background. Stunning.

Jacqui never wanted to be an actress, she'd moved to L.A. with a high school girlfriend who had the acting bug. Jacqui figured she'd get a job, marry a nice man. Enough of a reason to get out of Fresno. The girlfriend took acting classes, one night she did a showcase for a group of agents. Afterwards Jacqui was approached in the lobby by one of them who said he admired her performance.

"I wasn't in the show," Jacqui told him.

"You should've been," the agent told her, not missing a beat.

Jacqui married the agent, did a few guest spots on T.V. shows. Nothing memorable. A pretty face, a nice figure, but L.A. was filled with girls like Jacqui. Although Jacqui always had the best tan.

Divorce, alimony. Another marriage, another divorce. Alimony again.

Everything happens so fast, when people say time flies, they're not kidding, Jacqui thinks as she watches the movers carrying boxes into her new house. She's almost forty—forty seemed like a million years old when she was a kid, now it's the new thirty. At least that's what somebody said on "The View."

Darlene has given Jacqui a list of information about the house. How to fix the temperamental water heater, the gardeners' schedule, the best way to clean the hardwood floors (vinegar and water).

There are two gardeners who come on Fridays, the first day they show up Jacqui is poolside trying out her new commercial grade chaise lounge. She's admiring the dark brown weather-resistant aluminum frame when she hears the roar of a leaf blower from the front of the house. Shit. Why do they have to come at prime tanning time? (Those negative people who talk about skin cancer yammer on and on about the most dangerous hours to sit in the sun. Well, *duh*. Who's going to get a tan at five in the afternoon?) She supposes she could ask the gardeners to come back later. But when they appear in the back yard, they do their job quickly, and avoid the pool area completely. Jacqui gives them a polite wave and wonders if they speak English. "Hot," one of the gardeners says to her as he wipes sweat off his forehead with a dirty red handkerchief. She says, "Very," before she slips into the pool to cool off.

The first time the pool boy arrives she's on her stomach. For years lying on her stomach was the least favorite part of her tanning routine. Smushed boobs, too much sweat. But lately she's come to prefer it. Her cushion on her new chaise lounge is comfortable and in this position it's easier to look through magazines and catalogues. When she sits up, she has to squint to read and lately she's noticed lines on the sides of her eyes.

Uh-oh. Bigger sunglasses? Less reading? She'll have to think that over.

The click of the gate makes her turn and she wonders if the gardeners have picked the wrong day, but it's not the gardeners, it's a slim young man in dark slacks and a white shirt carrying a long pole with a net and a plastic bucket.

He nods at her. His cap is pulled low over his face so she can't see his eyes. There's a name stitched on the front of his shirt. Juan. He's Hispanic like the gardeners, does he speak English? Probably not.

"Hot," she says.

He nods at her again and moves to the other side of the pool.

Should she go inside? Is it rude to sit here while he works? But she doesn't want to miss prime tanning time, plus she hasn't flipped over yet. She has ten more minutes on her stomach. The weather forecast tomorrow calls for showers. And possibly the day after that. Miss two days of tanning in a row?

She chooses to stay. Glances at the new Boston Proper catalogue. On some women the slashed-sleeve top would look slutty. Not on her though. She dog-ears the page.

The pool boy is skimming the water with his pole. Like a fisherman, she thinks. There aren't many leaves in the pool. A few sticks, bugs, but it's probably a good thing he's here cleaning. It's not as if she'd enjoy swimming through scum or clods of dirt. She should thank him, instead she checks her watch on the patio table—time to flip over.

The pool boy examines the skimmer basket. Removes some leaves and probably more dead bugs. He pulls out the chlorine float and adds something to it from a white jar.

Cleaning leaves and changing pool filters all day must be boring. On the upside, at least he gets to look at women in bathing suits. Unless he's gay.

Well, he probably sees men in bathing suits, too. Either way, that works. She thinks about saying goodbye to him when he's finished, but the shoes in the J. Crew catalogue are cute, even though the black patent leather strappy sandals might be *too* shiny. So when she hears the sound of the gate closing, he already has his back to her. What would be the point of saying goodbye? He's already gone, right?

She loves her new house. She rarely sees her neighbors, at night she sleeps with the windows open in the bedroom and listens to the coyotes barking, but they never appear in her yard. The gardeners have changed their schedule and come late in the afternoons. The pool boy still hasn't spoken to her, but she knows he's watching her. Out of the corner of her eye she sees the skimming pole moving back and forth, but he's not paying attention to his work. He's looking at her. She feels a flush of pride, I'm probably old enough to be his mother and he's admiring me. But maybe he shouldn't. He's my employee. My rent pays his salary. He's not paid to look at me, he's paid to do his job. I should complain.

Or not. What does he think about, she wonders? Is he trying to guess how old I am? I'm older than I look, Juan, she wants to tell him. Guess how old I am? He'll look surprised, she'll smile at him and put a finger to his lips. No, Juan. It's true. Cross my heart.

Juan is handsome, his black hair curls out from under his cap and almost touches his shoulders. His forearms are thick and strong, Jacqui has always admired muscular forearms. Hispanic skin is pretty, she decides. Like a tan.

She wishes she could see his eyes, but they're always hidden under the cap.

I know what you're doing, she wants to say to him. And it's okay. I don't mind you looking at me. I enjoy being a perk.

She decides to give him another perk. One day when he's there she sits up, doesn't grab her top bikini strap in time and flashes her breast—did he see? She's not sure, she hopes so.

He doesn't say anything. Skims the leaves, the dirt, the pieces of palm fronds. Back and forth, never too fast. The waves slap against the sides of the pool, a pleasant sound. He's a gondolier. In Venice that's the job he would have. Not Juan, but Giovanni the gondolier.

Sometimes she keeps the pool lights on at night so she can see the pool from her bed. The water shimmers, the coyotes howl. She could invite Juan over one night, they'll drink wine at the patio table. Take off their clothes, slip into the silver blue water. "Juan," she'll say, tracing the name on his bare chest.

Maybe she shouldn't have flashed her boob. But it's not as if he's getting too familiar. He still doesn't speak. Only nods.

Is he laughing at her? She imagined herself as Juan's favorite client, now there's something in the way he moves past her, checks the filters—does he think she's ridiculous? Desperate, lonely, trying too hard? No, she won't go there. Like she cares what he thinks. He's the pool boy.

"Hot," she says to him one day. He nods, goes back to his work. She sips green iced tea. Considers offering him some, she could go in the kitchen. Get another glass. But is he expecting her to? That's the feeling she gets from him these days, as if he feels *entitled* to tea. Entitled to see her tit.

The ice cubes clink against her teeth and she frowns. Don't be presumptuous, Juan. Know your place. That's what she should say to him. Except she isn't going to say anything to him. Nothing.

He isn't paying attention to her. He does his job as if she's not there.

On Wednesday Jacqui is sitting by the pool. It must be in the eighties today, the light breeze helps a little. Jacqui watches the tops of the cypress trees wave back and forth. The sun feels warm on her skin. This is the best tan she's ever had. I adore my pool, she thinks, I have found my bliss. This is my perfect spot, my paradise. I can't let anything threaten it. She reaches for her cell phone.

"The house is fabulous," she says to Darlene. "I don't have any complaints. Well, just one. I'm not sure the pool boy is working out. He's doing a great job, the pool is very clean. But he's a little too... mysterious."

A pause on the other end of the line. "What pool boy?" Darlene says.

"Juan. He comes twice a week."

"The house doesn't come with a pool service, only gardening."

The tops of the cypress trees are moving more quickly now, the breeze has picked up.

"I've got another call, Jacqui, hold on a sec..."

She's put me on hold, Jacqui realizes.

The sound of a click.

The gate opens and Juan walks in. He puts his skimmer and bucket down by the fence and walks to the foot of Jacqui's lounge chair. When she looks up at him, she can see his eyes. Large and brown, almost black. Only something's wrong, she can't see any white—that can't be right, everybody has white in their eyes, don't they?

And she realizes she's not looking at his eyes because he doesn't have any—there are holes, caves, empty spaces where his eyes should be.

She shivers, even though the sun is still warm.

Juan is smiling at her.

"Hot," he says. "A swim will cool you off."

And he reaches for her hand.

John Schouweiler began his career in film working as Roger Corman's assistant. After serving as Director of Business Affairs at Hemdale Film Corporation (Terminator, Platoon, and Hoosiers), *he produced his first movie,* Saigon Commandos. *He has produced more than thirty movies since, including the Academy Award winning ode to horror director James Whale,* Gods and Monsters, *which was produced for less than the other nominees spent on their craft service budgets. Take that, Hollywood.*

DOG EATS DOG

John Schouweiler

EVER NOTICE THE WAY people describe their agents? If they love him, it's, "He's a killer." If she gets the client twice his quote, "She smelled blood." And so on.

And when things go bad, the comments run in the opposite, albeit equally evocative, direction. "What happened to his killer instinct?" or "She rolled over and played dead."

I suppose something in all this explained why, after I graduated from USC's Peter Stark Program, I gravitated to a big agency. I had received my B.S. in marine biology at Stanford, where I then stayed on for two more years to get my masters, studying the predation of Great White Sharks. So I was clearly drawn to apex hunters—whether they were in the ocean or sitting down for a business lunch at the Ivy.

When I began work in the mailroom at the Indevour Talent Agency I got to observe the predatory habits of the partners whose ranks I hoped to join. And as I watched them bring producers and VPs in Business Affairs to their knees, I thought that somehow my unique education might someday give me a competitive advantage.

Right. Like I was going to teach a shark to eat...

* * *

Davis Schachter, a 24 year old schlub known throughout our two years at SC for spending more energy pulling up his pants than studying, started in the mail room the same day I did. I immediately tried to put as much distance between us as possible. I figured if the guy was anywhere near the disaster he was at school, his days at a premier agency were numbered. And Schachter did not disappoint. Within two weeks his nicknames included "Beltless in Seattle," "Davis and Butthead," and "The Fat Fuck in the Mail Room."

The agency orientation program included a one on one sit down with one of the partners. So the afternoon of my first day I met with Bryan Lassiter. Depending on the metrics employed, Lassiter was not only the most powerful agent at Indevour, but in Hollywood. And even if you disagreed with that assertion, it didn't matter. Because all that counted was whether or not Lassiter believed it. And he most emphatically did.

He described to me how lucky I was to get the entry level job in the mail room.

"We'll work you like a dog, pay you shit and the chances are you'll be unemployed within four weeks." *Sounds like fun*, I thought to myself. And I remembered that sharks frequently ate their young.

The whole time Lassiter spoke I couldn't help but recall all the stories I had heard about him. He was renowned for lewd behavior designed to shock and scare. When he went toe to toe with a Paramount Head of Production he was reputed to have whipped out his cock and peed all over a papier mache Picasso sculpture. When the client won the best supporting actor award, the studio gave Lassiter the sculpture. And there it was, somewhat wrinkled from its golden shower, perched on his coffee table.

As I left Lassiter's office he introduced me to his assistant, Brigitta Svedberg. Brigitta was on the fast track to becoming an agent. She handled the rigors of Lassiter's desk with calm determination. To the outside world, she was both tough and thoughtful. She handled approximately 400 calls during her 12 hour day, was the gatekeeper to the most powerful man in Hollywood, did much of his shit work both within and outside the Agency, and seemed to not have one detractor. And she was a brick house.

As Lassiter's aide she was white hot in the fraternity of agents' assistants. Davis could recite the names of Lassiter's last ten assistants, eight of whom were already incredibly successful. They were the survivors. For six months they ate, drank, and shit on Lassiter's command. And they didn't just eat, drink and shit like you and I do. They were like the Michael Jordan, Alexander the Great, and Winston Churchill of eaters, drinkers and shitters.

They were responsible for everything that could possibly pop into Lassiter's shallow, yet prodigiously fast moving brain. Flowers for a funeral of a casting director whose former assistant was now casting a movie for which an Indevour client would be perfect? "Already sent over a large bouquet of lilies, her favorite flower, Bryan."

A Chemistry tutor for Bryan, Jr., who was struggling in his AP class at Harvard Westlake? "Nobel Laureate, Professor Overland, has been contacted and is happy to meet with Junior three times a week, Bryan."

Work all weekend doing comparative cumes on the top twenty directors of the last three years, breaking out domestic and foreign theatrical, dvd, cable and pay per view revenue? No problem. Mom and Dad's anniversary can suck my cock, Bryan.

And the other two Lassiter assistants who weren't successful? Speaking of sucking cock, one was supposedly working as a prostitute in Pioche, Nevada, blowing truckers for $20 a pop. And the other one just disappeared which, given the notoriety surrounding the position of Lassiter's assistant, was inexplicable. Such was the scary downside to being awarded the most sought after position in Hollywood. And it only took one fuck up (yours or sometimes someone else's) to destroy everything to which you aspired.

To those of us who dealt with Brigitta directly, she was also utterly professional. She wouldn't be disappearing off the planet without a trace. To the contrary, Brigitta was on a trajectory right to the top of any studio she picked. But in spite of that, mailroom scum like me knew she had our backs. Like nearly every other assistant, she had started in the mailroom. But unlike the rest, she didn't forget or resent where she came from. She had a keen idea of what your job entailed, what you probably knew and didn't know and how you knew it, and with a few well chosen words of advice she could make you look like you knew what the hell you were doing. Lassiter, thinking a line from Mel Brooks made him look erudite, called her his "Teutonic Twat."

The rest of us called her perfect.

* * *

On the Friday of our third week, Davis was called up to the penthouse and returned to the mailroom with a Manila envelope stamped with the word "URGENT." Like the effect of the stamp was somehow going to turn Davis into a combination of Robert Oppenheimer, the dudes who discovered DNA and James Bond. Poor Brigitta. I bet when she saw The Fat Fuck from the Mailroom approach her desk, she took out that stamp, picked the spot on the envelope that would have the most impact on Davis, and prayed to the God of Agents for his divine assistance.

Anyway, Davis came waddling down to the mailroom holding the envelope above his head, looking like a schlubby Neville Chamberlain. "It's the proposal to Steve Jobs! The Apple/Indevour deal!"

I gotta take my hat off to Davis, he kept up with what was happening in Hollywood. If an executive farted at Musso & Frank's, Davis knew about it. He trawled Nikki Finke, LA Times Company Town, Hollywood Reporter (or what's left of it), Variety, and about a million other rags, blogs and personal sources. If you mentioned a crew member's name he'd say something scary like "Wasn't he the craft service person on Corman's 'Battle Beyond the Stars'?"

In what was the only compliment I think poor Davis received his first week on the job, he pulled some obscure crew credit out of his fleshy ass just as Lassiter walked by. Lord Vader stopped and asked, "What the fuck are you, the Rainman of IMDB Pro?" For two days after that, Davis was known as Rainman.

So Davis had a manila envelope, inside of which was a letter to Steve Jobs setting forth one of the biggest Hollywood deals of all time, the deal points of which only Davis, Lassiter, Steve Jobs and Brigitta had any knowledge about. And Davis had been told to personally drive it over to the Four Seasons on Doheny, tell valet parking that he was with Indevour, that he had to run the envelope up to Steve Jobs' room in the Penthouse, and that if anyone so much as touched—much less moved—his car, the hotel would cave in and sink into the earth like Carrie's house did at the end of the worst prom night in history.

Once inside the exclusive hotel, Davis had to run a gauntlet of security, all of whom were to have been informed in excruciating detail by Brigitta that Davis was to go directly up to Jobs' room, present him with the document, wait while Jobs signed it, and return to Indevour with the executed copy.

So in addition to his own bacon, Davis was also carrying Brigitta's. And what followed was absolute proof that either we lived in a chaotic, random and utterly godless world or if a God or gods did exist he or they was or were mean and petty.

Brigitta had made arrangements with Jobs' assistant in Beverly Hills and his secretary in Cupertino. She had alerted the head Valet, the Bell Captain, the Concierge and Head of Hotel Security. She had already ordered a gift basket of rye whiskey, sweet vermouth, Angostura bitters and maraschino cherries for the VP of Sales at the Four Seasons, who was known to love Manhattans. Short of tying a string attached to the steering wheel of Davis's car and unfurling it all the way up to Jobs' thumb, Brigitta had done all a human could do.

Except one thing. When Lassiter said, "Send that fat fuck in the mailroom over to Jobs' room at the Four Seasons," she hadn't looked Lassiter in the eye and asked, "Did your mother drop you on your head when you were a baby?"

After Davis gave me a beautiful summary of the super confidential contents in the envelope (which Brigitta had expressly forbidden him to open and read), I reminded him that he had already wasted ten minutes, leaving him a little over an hour until Jobs had to leave his hotel room for an internationally televised dog and pony show for Wall Street fund investors, where he would be announcing, provided Davis succeeded in his task, the synergistic agreement between Indevour and Apple and the billions of dollars the two corporations would generate together.

Of course, Lassiter would be in attendance. Given his penchant for basking in the limelight, he would join Jobs on stage immediately after the announcement to figuratively (and maybe literally—this was Lassiter after all) poop on the agency pantheon of CAA, UTA, Paradigm, Gersh, APA and any number of ten-percentaries who had been pursuing Jobs with a fervor usually reserved for holy wars or iPhone launches. And by 8:00 P.M., heads would be rolling all over Beverly Hills when they all realized that Lassiter had once again captured another vital beachhead in the campaign to represent—and excise 10% off the top of—everything that mattered in the universe.

"Hey, Dickhead, you better get going if you're going to become part of business history."

"Yeah, yeah," he sneered. "It takes ten minutes to get to the hotel where I'll be greeted like Obama."

God, Davis was a douchebag. He grabbed his keys and wallet, and waddled off toward the elevator, shirt tail hanging out of his 46 inch waist pants.

That was 3:46. I remember looking at the upper right hand corner of my computer (a MacBook Pro, coincidentally) when the elevator bell rang and Beltless in Seattle set off on his mile and a half trip to the Four Seasons.

* * *

At 4:17, I was bragging to everyone about my brush with the incredibly big and supposedly secret deal between Indevour and Apple. Unknown to me, Davis had also told one of the other mailroom schlubs, who had Nikki Finke on speed dial, and she had already called Lassiter's office, causing him to verbally excoriate Brigitta. He railed at her, convinced that she had leaked the contents of the deal to someone and word had gotten out. How could she be so fucking stupid?

And I have no doubt she surmised that because she had, in fact, not mentioned one iota of the deal to anyone, the leak was the work of Davis. Obviously, he had looked in the envelope and blabbed to someone what he had seen. The fact that Lassiter himself had picked the moron for the job was not worth mentioning. She just had to sit there and take it.

Anyway, at 4:17 I felt my phone vibrate in my pocket. I looked down and saw it was Beltless. I was so full of myself, I announced to my adoring public, "Excuse me, Davis is calling from Jobs' suite." Fuck, I was an asshole.

"Yeah, what's up?" I answered just loud enough, so those within earshot could appreciate who the brains of the operation was.

"I am standing at the corner of Clifton and Doheny. Smoke is pouring out of my car. Dude, you gotta get here NOW. Or I'm fucked."

I put my hand over my phone, turned from said adoring fans and walked to the Men's Room. If there had been a hole in the ground, I would have run down it. But the sterility of the Italian marble shitter would have to do. "Clifton and Doheny! How the fuck did you only get that far in half an hour? The whole fucking trip is only 12 blocks!"

Davis may have been crying, "I don't know. I got a ticket for using my cell phone. It's hotter than hell and I kept my air conditioning on while the cop wrote me up. This goddamn fucking car!"

"Fifteen million assholes in L.A., every one of them yak-king on their cell phone while driving, and *you* get caught?"

"I know. I know. You gotta help me out. You have to drive here, pick me up and get me to the hotel before 5:00."

"Okay, okay. Don't panic. I'll be right there. But first, I gotta tell Brigitta what happened."

"No! Lassiter can't know about this! He'll fucking kill me. Just get in your car and get over here. We've still got about 40 minutes to pull this off."

Davis was right. If Lassiter ever found out how FUBAR this simple run had become, he was likely to fire the entire mailroom, Brigitta, and maybe the Postmaster General. Despite serious reservations about partnering with ol' Fat Fuck on anything, self preservation and the possibility that I might be able to spin some of this mess to my advantage demanded that I grab my wallet and keys and make for Davis.

Beverly Hills at 4:30 on a Friday afternoon is not what a man faced with imminent death needs. But if I don't say so myself, getting to Davis in 14 minutes was driving that would have impressed Steve McQueen. I rolled down the passenger side window and honked as I pulled up to his derelict car. He jumped in, and we headed straight to the Four Seasons.

We pulled up to the front door, Davis jumped out, composed himself and took one step toward the Bellman at the large glass doors. And froze. My heart sank when he did the self pat down routine.

"He's fucking lost the envelope!" I said to myself.

I rolled down the window again, not even waiting for Fuckface to explain his latest, greatest fuckup, and yelled, "Throw me your keys and WAIT HERE."

Keys in hand, I screeched out of the Four Seasons' semi circular drive, scaring the shit out of an old Jewish couple. Steve McQueen didn't serve my purposes anymore. I channel-ed Gene Hackman as I tore back down Doheny. I stomped on the brakes and parked in front of a hydrant across from Davis's car. If I had been armed I would have shot the drivers of the cars heading North and South on Doheny to insure my safe passage across the street.

The envelope was laying on the passenger seat. I grabbed it and ran back across the street to my car. The U-Turn I pulled rated a ten on the Dale Earnhardt, Jr. Auto Thrills Index; the rubber I laid, an eleven.

It was 4:49 when I got out of my car at the Four Seasons. And there was Davis sitting in the little closet the Head Bellman called his office with an officer from LAPD pushing him down into a chair.

I muttered to myself, "This can't be fucking happening." Davis had obviously done something very wrong. And if I wanted to pull this piece of fatty bacon out of the fire, I had to carefully consider every move I had to make from here on out. I really didn't want to join the rogue's gallery of Lassiter's fired assistants giving truckers blowjobs.

So, first, I calmly approached the parking attendant, handed him my keys, and courteously explained that I needed the car to be waiting for me in five minutes.

Next, I needed to figure out what to do with the officer. Fuck, his back was the size of card table. And the way he kept putting both his hands out to calm the obviously panicked Davis led me to believe that interrupting their "talk" was out of the question. In fact, I figured that if Davis looked up and recognized me, the Officer was going to unsnap his holster guard and slowly turn toward me with his service revolver pointed at my head. So I adjusted my thinking—and walked directly into the hotel lobby. I was going to pull this off without involving Davis.

I walked right up to the Head Bellman. I took a big breath. Let's see how good Brigitta really is.

"Hi, I'm Stewart Magnussen from Indevour. I have a document for Steve Jobs, who is waiting for it in his suite in the Penthouse. I believe arrangements have been made."

The Head Bellman's name tag read "Carlos Navarro." He considered my words and calmly gave me a once over. Still giving me an inspection, he picked up the phone, "The Indevour guy's here.... No, not really.... Mmm-hmmm."

He hung up the phone. "Take the elevator to Penthouse. You're way late."

I nodded and walked to the Elevator bank. One of the elevators opened instantaneously. Every second was golden now, so when I saw that no one was in the elevator, I practically danced around like Walter Huston in "Treasure of the Sierra Madre."

I punched "PH." The doors closed, and the car rushed up towards the penthouse. I thought to myself, When the Head Bellman was on the phone, what was the question that caused him to reply, "Not really"? The door opened.

Now I knew why more Presidents are assassinated than are corporate moguls. The penthouse was crawling with what looked like two dozen creepy guys in dark suits. Three of them immediately surrounded me, and I presented the envelope to one of them and mumbled, "From Indevour. The document for Mr. Jobs' signature."

Creepy Guy #1 took the envelope and gave me the stink eye, starting from the top of my head he slowly inspected every inch of my body until he reached my shoes. As he repeated the action in reverse, his eyes stopped at my skinny assed 32 inch waist. What was he looking at?

The double doors to 1701 at the end of the hall opened, and another Creepy Guy stuck his head out and looked at the three Creepy Guys around me. And much to my dismay Creepy Guy #1 was slowly shaking his head.

I will never know for sure what the fuck they were doing, but my guess was that Brigitta had been so thorough in her description of Davis—5'10", 210 to 225 pounds, big fat gut, shirt's usually out (God, Brigitta probably gave F. Scott Fitzgerald a run for his literary meal money if Jobs' goons required it)—that when I got off that elevator they figured someone had intercepted Davis and replaced him with the scariest 145-pound twenty-four-year-old the Mossad had on standby.

"Uh, guys, Mr. Jobs really needs to sign this document. It's like really urgent."

Creepy Guy #1 looked at his buddies for a beat. Creepy Guy #2 swiftly put me in a half nelson, put his fleshy hand over my mouth, and started hustling me toward a room, the door of which was pushed open by Creepy Guy #3. I figured this was when one of them would wrench my head suddenly and break my neck. Fucking Davis.

* * *

"...and you think that when they saw how thin you were, they realized that you weren't Davis and they freaked out and subdued you?" surmised Officer Horan.

When he and the hotel staff realized that they had been a party to a pretty amazing fuck up in which an employee from Hollywood's most powerful agency was subdued while trying to conduct business with a guest in the hotel, visions of Harvey Levin and TMZ infamy started dancing in their heads. I had been offered water and medical care. If I had wanted escargot and sourdough bread flown in from San Francisco, I am sure they would have had some poor bellman on a Southwest Airlines jet to SFO. Which was the last thing that was going through my head.

"Does Davis always cry like this?"

"No. It's just this was a really important document that had to be signed. And," I tried to find the words to describe how badly we had fucked up what two hours earlier was the easiest run in mailroom history, "we work for a monster who, if we were in a different culture, would probably castrate Davis, and maybe me and, fuck, who knows what he'd do to his assistant. And when he was done with us, he'd be ready to *really* start opening up a can of whoop-ass."

Officer Horan tried to get me to let up on the self pity throttle, "I doubt it's that bad, Mr. Magnussen."

He was right, of course. This wasn't about self pity. This was about abject terror. I was entering a point on the map somewhere between my head being stuck on a pike and my tongue being cut out as an example to others for what awaits them when they fuck things up like we did. "No, Officer, it's probably worse. We work in an environment where you only get one chance. And because we're so inextricably interconnected with everyone in our industry, if anyone in this delicate web fucks up, we're all presumed guilty." I watched the policeman's face as he took this in.

"Let's say the President is in town. A production assistant makes an important run but gets trapped in the traffic? Fired. The production coordinator who gave him directions? Toast. The production sound crew that got shitty production sound because of all the news helicopters hovering above the set? Canned! The agent whose meeting is cancelled because the studio head is a big shot liberal and blew him off to go to a $10,000 a plate dinner with the President? Leonardo dumps him."

Officer Horan took a deep breath, "Look, I could explain to your boss what happened."

"No, you're now in the web. Don't get taken down, too. But thanks for the offer. If it's okay, I gotta get Davis back to work."

* * *

The drive to the office was quiet. Davis's car had been towed while we had waged our war at the Four Seasons, so he rode with me; that only made the drive all the more pathetic. When I pulled into the garage, I parked in the reserved parking spot of the head of the literary department at Indevour, a position I had occasionally day dreamed about. Wouldn't it be nice to read a book and be able to create a buzz sufficient to float its chances of being adapted as a motion picture? This morning I would never have considered parking in an agent's reserved space. Now it seemed irrelevant.

"Hey, if it's okay with you, I think I'm just going to walk

home," Davis whimpered. "I'm history. I don't need to be humiliated any more."

What I had told Officer Horan stuck in my head. "I understand, Davis. And don't think that I haven't had the same thought. But this fuck up is so colossal that you and I may not be the only ones who get shit-canned. Maybe we should do the right thing and explain how we fucked up and limit the damage. And maybe save what's left of our dignity."

I started to open my car door. Davis seemed to get the message. He slowly opened the passenger door and got out. He looked at me, "Do you really think Lassiter gives a shit about our dignity?"

"No. I doubt it. But ten years from now when you're at a Lakers game and introduce yourself to the douchebag sitting next to you with slicked back hair, and he says, 'Davis Schachter? I work at Indevour, and there's a famous story about an asshole with that name who cost the agency a billion dollar deal.' You'll be able to look him in the eye and say, 'That's me. I'm that asshole. And CAA made me a full agent the next day for making Lassiter look like a dickweed. Can I get you a beer?' And you'll realize, life went on because you didn't care what the fuck Lassiter thought."

Davis looked at me blankly for a beat, and then out of nowhere he said, "Thanks for everything you did this afternoon, Stewart. I really fucked this up for you. I just want you to know I appreciate how hard you tried to save me. I'll never forget that."

He closed the car door and started walking toward the elevators. Somehow Davis had become a man in the underground garage at Indevour. And I felt a little better about going upstairs with him covering my back.

The elevator opened on the top floor. And we walked past the security guard. I wondered if he knew we were dead men walking. The place was a tomb. Which, despite my brave front in the garage, gave me a rush of hope that perhaps Lassiter had departed and our punishment would be something wimpy like a message on the voice mail of my cell phone.

Because no one was around, I was drawn to Lassiter's office. More to the point, I was drawn to Brigitta. As long as I had worked at Indevour, she had never left earlier than 8:00 P.M. And although I didn't harbor any hope that she would comfort me with a hug and express how bad she felt about what had happened, I knew that when she asked, "What the fuck happened?" that it would be the kind of question that a quality person in authority was compelled to ask. As opposed to Lassiter, who wouldn't wait for me to answer and would immediately follow the question with some kind of profanity-laden riff that played well to all his toadies.

When we turned the corner, two things struck me. One was that Brigitta was not at her desk. And, two, sounds were coming from Lassiter's open door, men's hushed voices and the moan of a woman. The men's voices reminded me of the sound that partiers make late in the night. You know, the sound of tired revelers who have way overstayed their welcome, but stay on anyway. And given that it was only 7:30, there was a disconnect between the time and the fatigued tone of the conversation.

The woman's moan didn't conjure up sex or mourning or sadness or pain. Consequently, I don't know what I was thinking. I'd like to think that I was in some kind of "My dreams of a great career are over" shock, and I was just acting reflexively, just walking up to the door where the dream was officially going to be shredded and declared dead. Only, I now know what shock feels like, and that's not what I was feeling.

So, like a dork, I walked to the door, and without even knocking I entered.

And a hush fell upon the room. Except the moans. They didn't change at all.

I guess Davis took in the horrible tableau before I did. For he started hyperventilating. I looked dumbly from the faces of three of the most powerful agents in Los Angeles. They were seated in the low slung sofas in the seating area of Lassiter's beautiful suite. Standing behind each magnate was his assistant. And there was Lassiter, sitting in a beautiful upholstered chair that set him apart from the others.

All of the agents were covered with blood. Hands. And faces. Not bright red movie blood, but the brownish, dirty blood that oozed from...

Brigitta. She lay lifeless, save for pleading eyes and the deliberate inhalation of her last breaths of oxygen, upon Lassiter's 4x6 Italian glass coffee table. Her blouse was torn open. Her bra was still on, but was soaked with her own blood. Her skirt was pulled down to her panties. And her abdomen was ripped open.

I was now living the nightmare where you move at a speed one third as fast as you desire. Why was Brigitta splayed open like that? Why was she moaning? What accident could possibly have befallen her to leave her in this condition? And I looked at Lassiter and it all became clear.

Lassiter, who was the bloodiest of all, held a fist sized piece of Brigitta's flesh in his right hand. Blood dripped from his chin, staining his tailored white shirt. With an incongruous pinky out elegance, he lifted the flesh to his mouth and carefully bit off a piece. The back of the flesh still had Brigitta's pale skin attached, but it offered little resistance to the same teeth that had gutted her.

He took both Davis and me in while he deliberately chewed the meat. After swallowing he said, "At last. The main course and dessert." Lassiter looked to the assistant nearest him and held out his hand. The assistant stepped forward and tentatively took the raw flesh from Lassiter.

And looking at his sycophants, he pronounced, "Eat up. Eat up. There's plenty to go around."

The instinct to survive stirred in both Davis and me. But our respective responses couldn't have been more different. I began to look around, attempting to get my bearings. No one had moved to block our retreat from Lassiter's suite. There were eight bad guys in the room—Lassiter, three agents and three assistants. I assumed that the security guard at the elevators knew what was happening, so escape via the elevator was not an option. And Brigitta was now dead. Her pretty green eyes stared dryly into peaceful non-specific space. Her mouth was slightly ajar, bloody spittle still oozing across her cheek toward her ear.

Davis, never renowned for his discretion, took a different tack than I did. He wanted some answers. "What the fuck are you doing?"

For the first time since I had joined the agency, Lassiter exhibited an interest in explaining his motivations. "Excuse me? What does it look like we're doing? Brigitta here was given the simplest of jobs, organize and coordinate your delivering a document to an address in the same zip code as ours for signature, which document you were to return to me. Time was of the essence. She failed. So we ate her."

I now knew our fate was sealed. I know, I was a little slow on the uptake. Walk into a group of cannibals eating someone whose culpability for a fuck up paled in comparison to your own. Hear someone say, "Ah, at last. The main course and dessert." So shoot me. But at least I wasn't arguing with Lassiter about it. Come on, Davis, arguing with the guy? Really!

"Further," Lassiter said, getting right in Davis's grill, "her failure cost the agency prestige, publicity and financial advantage." Lassiter poked his finger into Davis's fleshy chest, hard enough that the blood on it stained Davis's shirt.

Lassiter turned theatrically to his entourage. "Punishment was appropriate. As was absolute discretion about the details of this colossal fuck up. While Brigitta had always demonstrated discretion, once fired she would be subject to the pressures of gossip, the questions about the agency put to her by our competition and that damned Nikki Finke. So letting her go was not an option. Finally, I knew she worked out every morning before coming to work, so her fit body had a certain appeal that only connoisseurs of lean cuts like my assembled staff here can appreciate. So we brought her in here, held her down and ate her alive!"

Lassiter turned back to Davis, who now stood in a puddle of his own pee, and said, "If it makes you feel any better, she never blamed you, Davis. She just described to me what she had done to insure that you would succeed. Like I was suddenly going to stuff her kidney back into her abdomen and tell her to amend her methodology next time."

"But we're not in a 'next time' business, fellas, are we?" Lassiter was starting to ham it up. I could see his sycophants start to react to his oration. This was probably how Lassiter maintained discipline. I mean, you don't just eat employees, especially someone like Brigitta, "the most powerful assistant in Hollywood," and not have everyone present understand that they were the next course should they ever breathe a word about what happened.

And the key to getting that point across was to convince everyone in the room that they were complicit in the crime. By getting everyone nodding and agreeing and feeling comfortable about Lassiter's insanity, he was insuring that no one would ever go public with this. Let's face it, "Yes, officer, I did eat her flesh. In fact, I held her down while Jamison ate her liver. But Lassiter made me do it," wouldn't play well in Superior Court, would it? I wondered how many of Lassiter's toadies had run a line like that over in their head. And after contrasting the advantages that ran to those in Lassiter's inner circle with a life sentence at a Supermax facility on Pelican Bay, I figured Lassiter had 100% buy in.

No, I was looking at seven (eight, if you counted the security guy out front) people whose souls had been bartered for power, fame and whatever other fucking ghoulish perks made up the Indevour "benefits package." And I was having serious problems figuring out how the hell I was going to survive to ever see the peroxide blonde babe who butchered the ten o'clock news on Channel 5.

Lassiter made my planning easy. "So, Davis, you look well marbled." Now it was Davis's time to descend into a mental fog. He allowed Lassiter's thugs to grab him by the arms and the back of his knees. Evidently, human flesh was energy food, because the two assistants who did this easily swung the Fat Fuck from the Mailroom off the floor. Two agents swept

Brigitta's corpse off the glass table and with a final indignity kicked her under the table. A now struggling Davis replaced her on the table and the carnage began.

As for me, they grabbed and slammed me against the wall. It's hard trying to think when a man, who is bitten just south of his rib cage, screams. That much harder when you can't take your eyes off white fatty tissue while it fills with blood and turns crimson. First one of Lassiter's henchmen went in and ripped away at Davis's abdomen, then another.

I would like to say something about how his fat helped him through this initial attack. But by the time Lassiter ripped a patch of flesh about the size of a kitchen sponge from Davis's abdomen, I didn't know if "survival" was to be wished on anyone.

By that point Davis had lapsed into some type of shock. His screams had given way to sobs. Morbid curiosity caused me to look back at Brigitta. By the time we entered Lassiter's office, she had been ravaged more than Davis had to this point. But her moans were similar to what I now heard from Davis.

I was right when I initially recognized that Brigitta's moans neither resembled the sound a person makes during sex or mourning or sadness or pain. It was the sound a person makes when they are tired of living. I am guessing that humans, the only animal on our planet that contemplates the finality of death—and with it, the culmination of the suffering of life, are the only animals that can actually override the pain and panic that other animals would exhibit were they cast into Davis's present predicament. They would squeal and fight for life. It was what instinct commanded. But Davis was begging for an end.

And with that end would come my turn.

I don't know when I became aware of the voice of the security guard. "Mr. Lassiter, I need to speak with you. It's urgent."

Lassiter, who was in a stupor from the murderous frenzy, suddenly blinked and cleared his head. He grabbed a wet towel, thoroughly wiped his face, and left the office to talk to the security guard, throwing off to his guests a convivial, "Don't stop on my account."

I was near enough to the door to hear fractions of the conversation.

"Cop named Horan." "When?" "What took you?" "No one called." "He can't see us like this." "Just walked off the damn elevator." And, "He wants to know about Davis and Magnussen."

Officer Horan had dropped by to see how we were! I held all the cards, the good and the bad. And when he came back into the room, I could see that Lassiter knew it. The only move he could make without involving me was to add cop killer to his night's activities. And even Lassiter's balls weren't that big.

But mine were.

All the mystery that shrouds Great Whites doesn't obscure certain facts: The resident shark dominates the newcomer, the larger shark dominates the smaller, the female shark dominates the male, and so on. Hollywood had its certainties as well. Audacity, meanness, business advantage and, oh, a little talent were a royal flush in entertainment industry. And right now I was about to give Lassiter notice that he had better follow directions or die.

I looked Lassiter in the eye and said, "Someone shut up Davis! And I mean permanently. I'll go out to Officer Horan, tell him that you shit-canned Davis and he started crying and left. Earlier you did the same to Brigitta. She packed up her shit and took off without a word."

Lassiter was on the same page as I was and asked, "Why tell him about Brigitta?"

"Earlier at the hotel, I told him that she was in for some major punishment from you."

"And what about you, Magnussen?" Lassiter probably knew he didn't have a hand, but he wasn't going down without a fight. "What did I do to you?"

I flashed my best apex hunter smile, "Why, you bumped me up to full literary agent, that's what. Partner, no less. You figured that I was the only person in the whole fucked up mess who kept his head and tried to save the deal for the agency."

Lassiter nodded and turned to the others in the room. He pointed his blood stained finger at me and started laughing, "Standing right there is why I love the Mailroom, gentlemen. That's where you find the *real* talent in this town."

I couldn't resist punctuating his reverie. As the man with the biggest balls in the room, I had to get in the last word, "Shut the fuck up, Lassiter! I have to go out and talk with Officer Horan and save all your sorry asses." And I turned and walked out not knowing what his reaction was.

* * *

So that's how I became a partner at Indevour, driving a black 700 series BMW and wearing Armani suits, tailored dress shirts and, from time to time, a torn Alice In Chains t-shirt and distressed jeans just to show Lassiter that he was no longer King at the agency.

No one ever inquired about Davis. I guess his family disliked him more than Lassiter did. Brigitta, on the other hand, was missed by everyone. Friends, family, police and bloggers, but eventually it trickled off. About eight months later, I handed my assistant a novel that had to go out to a director, and I heard two mailroom fucks talking about the three assistants to Lassiter that hadn't made the grade. One was blowing truckers in Pioche. One had completely disappeared. And about half a year earlier, one had been fired, cracked up and moved to New Orleans where she became a meth addict.

I would have liked to have set them straight. But if I started being nice to mailroom guys, there's no telling what could happen.

Writer, producer, and assistant director James Grayford has worked on the movies Legion *with Paul Bettany,* The Final Season, *for which he received a co-writing credit, Sundance winner* Captain Abu Raed *and numerous other Hollywood film and TV projects. He has a number of scripts in development, and placed three others high in the prestigious Nicholl Fellowship Screenwriting Competition. When not writing or making movies, he enjoys photography, cycling and raising Ms. Fantastic, his daughter Sadie Rose.*

THE BRIDGE

James Grayford

The sun heats up this little room, here I must reside
Rebelling from my demons like a child who won't abide
Without a haven to be found in this tinseled town
I prowl these cinematic streets beneath a bloody crown

    Thirty marks upon the wall since the last reunion
    Thirty days of freedom from a life and death communion

I never cross the bridge by choice nor willingly comply
'Cause morality and circumstance rarely coincide
I feel the fear, it's creeping near, I'm failing in its stead
For each attempt to dull the point gleams a tapered edge

    I'm falling in a chasm of compulsionary sin
    Despite suppresionary means, I've crossed the bridge again

I've killed in Jersey, killed in Berkeley, killed in Darien
Took a young girl on a spree of slayings in the sand
I've killed in Boston, killed in Memphis, killed in San Antone
While a family safely slumbered in their summer home

Over the bridge, instinct rules, calm and cool, collected
Luring me to lethal grounds where prey can be inspected
Life and law have no affect, restraint escapes my grasp
I'm trolling for a proxy to the demons of my past

Unbeknownst the victim strolls, their face an apparition
For they've crossed the bridge to my subconscious affirmation

I've killed in Portland, killed in Stanford, killed in New Orleans
The swamps enshroud the many wraiths who died at my decree
I've killed in Detroit, killed in Tulsa, killed in Chapel Hill
Where it took weeks to cross the bridge and days for blood to spill

I'm haunted by archaic voices, this I won't deny
Accede to your defenses and you may survive
But talk with me incessantly and my beguiling charm
Will shepherd a sacrificial lamb to consecrated harm

My words sustain tranquility until the trammel springs
Seizing you on the bridge to immortality

I've killed in Redlands, killed in Freeport, killed in Lincoln County
Followed a good ole boy into a closed down local foundry
I've killed in Wheaten, killed in Fargo, killed on Interstates
While I cruised the badlands with an unsuspecting waif

Brutal torture purges my emotional entrapments
Cleanses every pore through ritualistic reenactment
Demons scurry in a fury as apparitions plea
For euthanasia or a painless death with dignity

The climax surges through me like a Holy privilege
Leading back to normalcy found across the bridge

I've killed in sunlight, killed in darkness, killed in rain and sleet
But the killing always fails to make my soul complete
I've killed in summer, killed in winter, killed in spring and fall
Killed so many times a count's impossible

The fleeting nature of the ritualistic reenactments
Are reminisced through totems, collected by detachment
Preservation never takes and as the totem fades
The specters of my past echo like a masquerade

Without a haven to be had, no sanctuary either
The only choice wears on me like a bridge across desire

I've killed in Phoenix, killed in Denver, killed in Tennessee
Killed enough to wish the law would imprison me
I've killed in Rochelle, killed in Barstow, killed in Valley Glen
And unless I learn to burn my bridges I'll kill and kill again

Sculptor William Paquet's art for the collectibles field spans tweny years working with comic publishers, movie studios, and private collectors. He is also developing a series of graphic novel projects and Intellectual Properties and is a contributing writer to the literary webzine Hot Valley Writers, where you can find more of his brand of story time fun. He lives somewhere in Virginia and longs for the N.Y. style Pizza of his youth—Virginia style apparently doesn't cut it. Whatever it is. Check out his masterworks at www. quarantinestudio.com.

TRASH DAY

William Paquet

THE CRASH WOKE KIRK from the waning moments of a dream, a dream in which he was screwing the actress he'd seen on set the week before. She was unlike the standard Hollywood silicone sisterhood, more like the girls he'd known back home; naturally pretty with plump breasts and long dark hair. He was just reaching zenith from behind when the noise roused him and deflated his zeppelin. His eyes popped open and he saw 2:12 AM glowing on the clock.

"Damn it!"

The sound that woke him came from the alley behind the Hampton Arms Residence Hotel, but that didn't really matter as a more pressing need arose. He ambled out of his cozy bed and trudged to the bathroom, taking the opportunity present-ed by the boner killing noise to relieve his bladder. As the little waterfall sang a tune of relief in the toilet, he was startled by another sharp bang from the alley. Not a gunshot, but like a heavy object dropped from a height.

He finished his business and went to the kitchen. The short, over-the-sink window there looked out over the alley, and when he leaned to open it, he found that he couldn't. Age was the likely culprit in the hundred plus year old building, age, paint, and oven grease.

The kitchen was dark, with just a little light from the bathroom bending in enough to keep him from stubbing a toe. He was five floors up and didn't expect to see anything in the alley but he tried anyway. Climbing onto the counter he hunkered down, ass on the formica and feet in the sink, and pressed his face to the glass. Even without the darkness the angle he had showed nothing but a small stretch of the far side of the alleyway. He could barely make out some boxes and other assorted trash. With nothing to see, Kirk instead pressed his ear to the glass, quieted his breathing and focused all his senses on sound. He thought he heard quiet voices, but wasn't sure. After a few minutes he definitely heard footsteps fading away.

He sat in the same position for a good ten more minutes, listening and hearing nothing, so he gave up and climbed down from the sink. It was now almost three o'clock and he knew he was done with sleep. For a minute he considered working on the script, *Dead End Road* but he wasn't 'feeling it' as writer types often said, and opted instead to grab a film from his DVD library and veg out. It would be formula slice and dice, but the vintage flare of the period was what Kirk needed to stoke the dwindling fire of his present project. Splattertainment, Ltd., the production company paying him squat to write a story they would ruin, had requested a retro treatment of torture porn film, kind of a 70's version of today's standard fare trash. Fittingly, they had their headquarters in the back room of a taco shack in the eye of the needle, where L.A. gives way to street vermin, and not three blocks from Kirk's place.

The TV flickered bloody mayhem circa 1979, with nubile all-natural girls and a killer wearing a disguise made from a catcher's mask. The horrid man-boy beat his victims to death wielding a baseball bat embedded with razor blades, and before every murder would mutter, "high and inside!" Halfway through the film Kirk drifted off again and had more vivid dreams. But not pleasant ones.

* * *

The next afternoon Kirk got a call from his sometime writing partner Stumpy, informing him that legendary producer Frank Kemper was looking for a writer to reinvent *Frankenstein* for modern tastes.

"Kemper?" Kirk said. "Holy shit! I must have seen *Die Like You Really Mean It* a hundred times. Jeez, the guy is the damn 'Duke of New York' and 'Josey Wales' all in one. Bad ass!"

"Yup. I'd go for it myself if I didn't have so much to do."

"Damn, Kemper. So *Frankenstein* reborn, cool. Any more detail than that?"

"He wants something where the monster ends up eating the doctor in the last scene, and he wants girls with swinging joy jugs in at least five different scenes. The rest is up to the writer," said Stumpy.

"That's friggin stupid," said Kirk, his excitement losing some of its edge.

"News flash, idiot, no one is looking for a rewrite of *Clockwork Orange*, and if they were you wouldn't have a shot. So shut the fuck up and take the meeting, if they'll even see you."

Kirk hung up the phone and looked at the computer screen. *Dead End Road* was nearing completion and even though the premise was nothing to brag on, he thought he put enough good work into it that it would not be a complete embarrassment if the studio handled it with a modicum of taste.

Fat chance.

He worked the rest of the day on the script, then just before six he called the number Stumpy gave him. He spoke to an automaton with a feminine voice who told him, "Tuesday the eighth, two p.m. is your appointment, Mr. Logan. If for some reason you cannot make it, we will not reschedule."

"I'll be there, thanks," said Kirk.

"Goodbye," said the voice.

Kirk penciled in the appointment on the blotter calendar on his desk. A week from today. He turned off his computer, put his pencil back where it belonged and replaced every desk item to its proper place. This was his daily ritual and it was the one thing that never changed no matter what. The small measure of discipline kept a sense of control in place and kept him somewhat sane even when the shit hit the fan, as it often did. After he returned order to his world, he showered, threw on some clothes and went out to meet Wendy, a some-time model, most-time waitress, he had been dating for a couple months.

They ate char-grilled monster burgers at a nameless restaurant and drank too much at a scummy dive bar. Kirk brought Wendy home and they screwed ferociously. He saw the actress with the dark hair from his dream during much of the rutting, but not when he "hit the target" as he was known to say; a gentleman knows where to draw the line.

The next morning they kissed goodbye outside the hotel and Kirk decided he was done with her. Wendy was nice enough and a lot of fun—a *lot* of fun—but the relationship was little more than convenience, and Kirk was feeling like it was time to grow up. He lived every day in the fantasy of the film world; time to think about getting serious in his personal life.

He went back inside the Hotel and saw Jerry manning the front desk. Jerry looked like a cross between a fat hillbilly and a shoe salesman. He always wore a jacket and tie and three day's beard growth with hair that looked like Valvoline spaghetti ringing around a bald dome. Still, greasy or not, the guy had a pleasant manner and a gargantuan vocabulary and he managed the front desk of the Hampton Arms with the utmost professionalism. Kirk loved talking with him.

"Hey Jerry," he said.

"Kirk, Mr. Logan, Hampton Arms' thespian of elucidation and tomes, a fine day, is it not?"

"Fine day, Jerry. You're looking well."

"My propensity to consume an abundance of brown spirits keeps my cerebral cortex in fine tune. I believe bourbon is God's true nectar."

Kirk smiled. "No argument from me. Hey, let me ask you something—who works the night shift since Paul got fired last month?"

"It depends on the day. Presently myself, Mr. Appleton, and Brenda Trevor take our turns. Until the owner removes his posterior from his throne and pries his purse open with the jaws of life, the post is technically vacant. What sparks your query?"

"I heard some noises in the alley, night before last. Loud."

"Tuesday is trash day, Kirk. You've resided in our fine establishment for greater than half a year, you should know when the garbage goes out."

"Yeah, I know. It's not the day, it's the time. Trash is always picked up around six, this was just after two."

"Two Ante Meridiem?"

Even for Jerry, "Ante Meridiem" was a bit much. Kirk sighed silently.

"Yes, Jerry, two a.m."

"Appleton was here then. I'll check with him. Entirely possible he was taking out more refuse. In fact, likely. We have had a spate of tenants coming and going lately. That always means more garbage. Either which way, Kirk my dear friend, nothing for you to worry about. Put it out of your mind."

Another day of writing *Dead End Road* awaited Kirk, so he signed off with Jerry and walked to the elevator. At the last second he bypassed the lift and continued to the end of the hall where he knocked on the door to the janitor's office. There was no answer and after another minute he decided he should get to the writing, but chose to go up the five flights to his apartment by the stairs.

At every floor landing was a window facing the alley, and at every one Kirk stopped and looked out. He saw nothing unusual until the third floor, where the window was slightly open and a rusty brown smear stained the window sill. It was a small mark, maybe a half inch wide and three inches long, running perpendicular to the wood. He turned around and looked down the long hall. The ceilings of the building were vaulted, at least twelve feet tall. The floors were small square tiles, white borders flanking a dull green center that gave the appearance of a long hall rug. Every room door was painted gloss black and had a glass transom hat. Eight rooms on each side of the hall; Kirk's own, two floors up, was directly above the first room on the left. The vintage Otis elevator was at the opposite end of the hall.

He walked slowly down the hall, glancing at each door, noting the numbers, odd left, 301, 303, etc. Even, right. As he neared 308 the sound of a television blared from beyond the door. It was one of the Spanish speaking stations and he could hear fast talking and audience laughter. A fly buzzed near his face and Kirk swatted it absentmindedly. He kept moving and reached the end of the corridor without much suspicion for his effort. Feeling a bit like a phony detective wannabe, he took the elevator the last two stories to his floor. As the elevator doors opened and he stepped into the hall, he saw the ancient Mr. Hammicker was shuffling toward him. They met near the center of the hall.

"Morning, Mr. Hammicker," said Kirk.

"Good day, Mr. Logan," replied the arched sunken man. Hammicker was the Arms' oldest and longest resident. He moved in temporarily when his wife kicked him out of their Burbank bungalow and he never left. That was in 1943.

"It's going to be bad today, hot as hell. The street stinks already," said Kirk

"People always talking about how bad things are getting in society, how good things used to be, way back, but this neighborhood has smelled like sewage as long as I've been here, and if you think all those new drugs, the crack and meth and all that are dragging everything down, you should have been here when liquor was the only drug most folks could get. No romance in the old days, son. No romance with bums and winos, just wreckage and vomit."

Kirk just nodded. The old man could go on for hours if

you let him. When he reached home, room 501, he turned back and saw Mr. Hammicker waiting for the elevator. His body was so deformed that from a distance his silhouette formed a question mark, and Kirk bemused the real question was how long the old man had left in his porous bones.

* * *

Kirk spent the remainder of the work week wrapping up *Dead End Road*. Late on Friday he delivered it and collected a few thousand dollars, which would cover him for almost two months if he was frugal. He called Wendy and officially ended it. She didn't seem to care much, which was a relief. It had been a convenience relationship for both, nothing more.

Kirk decided a minor celebration of his sale was in order, so he met Stumpy and some of their other friends at a hole that served drinks at Bowery prices and attracted the same kind of crowd. They liked the place for both reasons, finding inspiration in the whiskey and the patrons. Stumpy once said the place smelled like "corpses pickled in vinegar" and Kirk swore he would steal that line someday for a story.

Saturday was spent recuperating, which always consisted of movie marathons. Kirk called Stumpy around noon, and two hours later he showed up with a large pizza, and a couple bags of chips and pretzels. Kirk already had the theme for the day chosen, but he gave Stumpy his choice of titles.

"This is all domestic. No euro-trash?" asked Stumpy.

"I got some ideas for that meeting next week. I need to keep my head focused and the dubbing is going to pull me out of the narratives. This is a working marathon."

"Okay then, maestro. Let me look through this pile of delights and find something we can shit on like Stinkel and Eggbert."

Kirk went to the kitchen while Stumpy dug around and found a primo choice about an inbred lunatic living in a basement, starring a guy who once played a frat boy named after a fish. As he put the disk in the player, Kirk came out of the kitchen carrying a pair of frosty diet sodas. He handed one to Stumpy and they took opposite ends of his couch, both putting their feet on the coffee table. Stumpy insisted they watch the trailers before the feature, and he took control of the remote. Kirk was an exploitation fan, but Stumpy was a fiend. No flick until the pump was primed.

They snacked on the crispy treats through two flicks. They watched, but never stopped talking. The conversations ran the gamut of subjects, but the central focus was the films, their structure, the pacing, story and writing. They deconstructed the scripts and discussed what worked, what didn't work, and what would have worked better. Around six o'clock they took a break; Stumpy left the apartment to call his agent while Kirk cleaned up the mess.

Stumpy returned from the hall half an hour later; he looked pissed off but didn't want to discuss it. Kirk knew his friend's moods could be schizoid so he paid little attention. He put the pizza in the oven to reheat it and put the day's last film in the DVD player.

They watched, ate, and talked. Eventually Stumpy blurted out that the studio interested in his zombie script passed on it, citing waning interest in the genre. It was a major studio and the fee would have set Stumpy up for years. His agent had said just the day before, "it's a done deal, Stump, go celebrate."

"Hate to say it, bro, but I told you that Allen fuck was a lying scumbag. When was the last time he got you a job?"

Stumpy slumped. "Been a while."

They watched in silence for a while. A girl was running down a mountain road being chased by a crazy man in bib overalls. He was waving a machete and screaming incoherent blurbs. After the freak caught and decapitated the lovely young thing, Kirk spoke up. "So, you wanna go for the *Frankenstein* gig then? I mean, you turned me on to Kemper in the first place."

"Nah, you got that in the bag. I'll dig up something else.

Maybe I'll try a vampire spec. Everyone wants vampire shit these days."

They finished the movie and Stumpy left around 10:30. Kirk cleaned up the last of the mess then crashed. He slept well, later vaguely recalling dreams of the long haired actress.

* * *

The next couple days were routine. On Sunday Kirk called his mom in Indiana and heard family gossip for an hour. The rest of the day and all day Monday were spent developing ideas and writing two different treatments of the *Frankenstein* story.

Tuesday Kirk awoke to the sound of the garbage truck in the alley. He looked at the clock: Six a.m. Hunky dory.

After showering he went back to work tightening up his ideas for the meeting with Frank Kemper. The producer was a legend, and Kirk wanted to be more prepared than he had ever been before. He printed both outlines and re-read them while sitting on the couch. Writing always looked different on the printed page than on a screen; it became tangible, more real, and in that state was easier consumed and better criticized. He found a couple of glaring screw-ups on the second version, so he did a fast edit and another printing. Satisfied, he put the work in his satchel, grabbed his phone and called a cab.

In the lobby he saw Jerry and waved. Jerry saluted in return. This was a ritual the two developed over the past months. Whenever Kirk was dressed smartly and carrying his satchel he was "on duty" and Jerry "deferred" to the writer's status. Appearances and good humor.

The cab ride took longer than expected, but Kirk routinely gave himself double the amount of time he thought necessary to get to appointments so he arrived with time to spare and introduced himself to the glamorous robot at the front desk.

"You're ten minutes early," said the vacant beauty queen. "Take a seat. Mr. Kemper will be with you shortly."

Kirk sat and sent an obnoxious text to Stumpy, referencing a long running inside joke. Stumpy responded with a picture message of the perfect ass of a young woman he was walking behind near Grauman's Chinese. Her pants rode low enough to display butt cleavage and those awesome lower back dimples some girls exhibit in grand form. Kirk was ogling the image and caught off guard when the receptionist said, "Mr. Kemper is ready for you."

Frank Kemper had been a production powerhouse since the late 60's. He churned out gems and junk in equal measure, giving fledgling artists their first working papers and launching the careers of many future Oscar winners. Kemper worked fast and furious, and even on a shoestring he could make crap look like gold. He made a fortune but still never financed a single project from his own bank accounts. He was a living legend with a ruthless reputation and Kirk's stomach fluttered a little as he walked toward the producer's office.

Once the meeting started, it was amazing. Kirk was on his game like never before. He got along famously with the legend, who oddly, was nothing like the ice queen at the gate, but friendly, affable and generous with compliments. Nothing was written in stone, but he told Kirk he thought he was "the man" for the project and asked for Kirk's agent's number.

"Well, I'm sort of between agents right now."

"No problem, Kirk. I'll have legal draft an offer and fax it to you. Give my assistant Jackie a fax number and we will have something put together by the end of the week."

Late in the day Friday Jerry called from the front desk, telling Kirk a fax was coming in with his name on it. He bolted to the lobby just as the last page was printing. As Kirk requested, no fee was included in the paperwork, just the terms of legality, the deadline and other clauses. If the terms of the contract were agreeable, Kirk was to call Jackie to discuss the fee. He was no lawyer, but Kirk had read enough contracts to understand them and this one looked all good. He called Jackie later but the office had closed for the weekend. Damn.

The weekend was restless, disjointed. The job with Kemper never left the front of Kirk's consciousness and he had a hard time enjoying any leisure activities. He distracted himself with mindless tasks and a marathon of zombie films.

On Monday morning Kirk spoke with Jackie, who was nice, but all business. The development fee was pretty damn good and he had six weeks to complete the first draft. Rewrites would be negotiated on an individual basis. If the film went into production the bonus was nearly phenomenal, but even without, the job would keep him afloat for many months. He signed the papers at the production offices that afternoon, feeling like a seminal moment just occurred. That evening he went to bed on top of the world.

He awoke from a nightmare just after two a.m. The dream was vague. It wasn't even a dream, just an instantaneous feeling of total dread, a sweeping kind of black energy driving toward him at sonic speed, like a freight train from hell, total fear stopping his heart for a brief moment.

He sat straight up, shaken. He went to the kitchen, grabbed a glass and turned on the sink tap. He filled the glass twice and dumped it twice, like his father always did, then filled it again and took a long cool drink. In the night silence, the faucet dripped loudly. Kirk swallowed the last from the glass, then rested his hands on the sink and leaned forward with his head down. He took a deep breath, trying to wipe away the feeling of the dream.

As he reached for the faucet to refill his glass, a muffled thump came from below.

He listened and heard voices in the alley, very low and barely audible. Two weeks earlier he had tried to open the window over the sink, and now he tried again. It still wouldn't budge, so Kirk took a butter knife and used it to scrape the crevice between the window and the molding, around the entire perimeter. The blade scraped and crunched along, slicing through debris, layers of paint and old caked grease. He traced the area over a full three times then tried the window again. It remained stuck, but with a tad more force it popped open, making a loud squealing noise, probably not as loud as it seemed in the quiet darkness, but it was loud enough.

Kirk stood silent for several minutes, listening. The warm night blew a soft breeze through the window. The stench of the city wafted in, a mixture of sour milk and urine, and a touch of car exhaust to round out the recipe: Urban Stew. The only sound was a slight rustling of strewn paper down below, kicked about by the night wind. Kirk was certain he heard voices seconds before, but maybe he only imagined it. Or maybe they scattered at the noise of the window's resurrection. Living in the seedy flanks of L.A. for seven months had been a trial by fire schooling of caution for the Hoosier, and perhaps the most important lesson he learned was to mind his own fucking business. But now that rule was quickly forgotten, and he decided he was going to pop his head out of the window. He waited long enough to be sure that if there was anyone down there, they would have forgotten their suspicions of the screech from above.

The condenser in the fridge kicked on, startling him. It wasn't loud but in the dead silence his mind registered a rifle shot. He laughed at himself, shook it off and waited. Several minutes ticked off the oven clock, and not a sound was heard from the alley. He climbed onto the counter top like before, put his feet in the sink and slowly leaned his head down and through the small window.

It took a moment for his eyes to adjust to the darkness and the odd angle, but then he saw it: A rounded back, a bald head and pale hands. The thing kneeled, leaning forward and slowly perusing the contents of a corrugated box big enough to hold a major appliance. There were several black plastic bags cast aside, their contents spilling onto the pavement and from five flights up and in the darkness it was impossible to tell what was there. Leaning further out, Kirk could now hear the soft crisp sounds of moving plastic, but nothing else until a sudden brief grunt of satisfaction as the hands pulled another bag from the box. The bag was opened, revealing nothing from Kirk's view, but what was found was obviously some sought-after treasure because the bald humped visitor immediately tucked it close to his chest and scuttled out of the alley.

Puzzled, Kirk backed out of the window and slipped off the counter. *What the hell?* he thought, before going back to bed and tossing and turning until dawn.

* * *

The next several days were a blur of phone and office meetings with Kemper's studio on the development of *Frankenstein's Torture Chamber*. Kirk was simpatico with Frank and his team on nearly all elements of the script, and the few areas where he saw things differently he planned to develop script options, hoping they would see that his ideas would make the story better. A major meeting was scheduled for two weeks away and Kirk was expected to have a complete outline and character bible ready.

Jerry was off all week and Kirk didn't care much for Brenda Trevor, the skirt who filled in, so he didn't mention the nocturnal activity. By the time the following Tuesday arrived, the episode was forgotten as the outline for Kemper consumed Kirk's every waking moment.

Tuesday evening Stumpy called to tell him that word was out that the studio was going full bore on the *Frankenstein* concept. They had already lined up Rick Baker for the Special Effects and had a tentative shooting schedule to begin next spring. He also told Kirk that the producer was telling anyone who would listen that he found the perfect writer.

"Get the hell out of here," said Kirk. "Don't bust my balls."

"I'm serious, bro. They think you're the second coming. But just do your usual and they'll piss on that notion in no time."

Kirk stayed up until 1:30 working on the outline. Stumpy's call injected him with testosterone and caffeine and he wrote until his lids were lead. Breaking with routine, he didn't even straighten his desk, just kicked off his shoes and crashed into comatose, dreamless sleep, and heard nothing when the visitor came back for trash day.

* * *

On Thursday Kirk went to make himself a ham sandwich and found his loaf of bread moldy. A quick check of the cabinets and fridge reminded him he had not shopped for provisions in weeks. He ate a couple slices of cheddar from a block and a few crackers to hold him over. "No time like the present" was his motto, so he put on his shoes and headed out.

Jerry was back and as Kirk got off the elevator he meandered over to the desk. Jerry was intently looking through a ledger and did not see Kirk approach, so when Kirk said "hey!" Jerry started like a frightened small mammal and slammed the ledger shut. A look of anger furled his brow, briefly, but clearly. The look soon evaporated and the formula Jerry smile replaced it.

"Mr. Logan! A churlish weeping pardon, for not seeing you sooner, good sir. Work beckons as always, and my poor decrepit medulla oblongata has been tested to the limit. Did you know Ms. Trevor has left our employ? Shame, she was sweet as sugar too."

"Oh, she left? That's too bad, I guess. Looks like you're really short-handed now."

"Yes, I do believe our need for new blood is nearing critical. Pardon the pun. Would you happen to know anyone looking for work, Kirk?"

"No, sorry. Hey Jerry, I've been meaning to tell someone about this. Twice now I've noticed something going on in the alley, someone messing around with the trash."

"Messing around?" said Jerry, looking concerned.

"Or digging around."

"Didn't we already have this conversation, Kirk?"

"Yes, but it's still going on."

"How do you know you didn't just hear Alvin?"

"At two a.m.?"

Jerry smirked, another unusual facade to go with the earlier anger, and Kirk noted it. "Kirk, there is a whole world of business that goes on when the world sleeps. Goodness, is there a set time for when trash goes out to the alley?" He smiled pure Jerry.

"I guess not," said Kirk. "But has Alvin started shaving his head?"

Jerry's smile faded a tad. "As I elucidated during our last conversation on this, your worries are wasted energy. It is very likely a homeless person looking for delectables. Maybe we should move you to the other side of the building."

"No, I'm fine where I am," replied Kirk.

Jerry wore a paternal expression and said, "you let me know if you change your mind, my friend."

"Sure," said Kirk, already forgetting any silly concerns. Jerry was right. "Well, I am low on all the staples of subsistence, Jerry, old pal. I'm headed over to Ferguson's. Need anything?"

"Nothing, thanks. I do believe I gorged myself to the brink last night."

Out front, Kirk looked at the building he called home. For the first time he really saw the old elegance it once displayed. It was natural to miss the hidden grandeur given its present state of disrepair, but the arched doors and fancy brickwork were pure gothic. As he focused for the first time on its nuances and details, he saw that what he always thought was a sculpture of a dog was actually a wolf perched above the double doors.

At Ferguson's Market he ran into Wendy. She told him she was modeling for a photographer in Venice, shooting ads for some bra company and making five hundred dollars a day. She didn't seem the least upset by their abrupt break up, and they parted with a familial peck as Kirk searched the store for the remaining items on his list.

When he arrived back home, neither Jerry nor anyone else was at the desk. Kirk noted the absence but brushed it off after remembering that the place was presently understaffed. Back upstairs he put away his purchases and then settled down to write some more. At seven he made dinner and ate while watching a Naschy werewolf flick and wondered why God didn't make women these days like the Spanish girls of the 70's. He went to bed hoping for dreams of unrelenting sexual deviance but was instead treated to the most horrific nightmare of his life.

A shape, basically human, floated ahead of him as he walked through a dark alley. The figure was rigid, like a flagpole but at the same time it was loose at the joints, like a ventriloquist's dummy that looked like it would rattle hard and thick in a stiff breeze. It rose three feet above the pavement and its feet either didn't exist, or were tucked up into its pant legs. It wore a suit of jet black and its bald head and pale hands glowed white with a slight green cast. Kirk followed, constantly increasing his pace, but never closing the gap. The alley widened increasingly as he walked, starting at a width of perhaps five feet and growing ten-fold. The wider the alley got, the darker the sky turned.

Graphite and steel wool carpeted the sky, and soon the first drops fell. They were heavy and large and made a splat of such nauseating voice that every splat made Kirk's bile rise. He had never before noticed the ability to smell in dreams, but now there was a stench so foul it seemed beyond possibility, and as the scene unfolded the alley morphed into a graveyard. Crypts and headstones flanked both sides as the bald pale cretin floated over lush green grass. The rain continued its slow gorged cadence.

The creature was increasing the distance between them. Kirk jogged, then ran. The rain kept its plodding pace and the head and hands of the floating thing began to bloat. Kirk ran faster, the gap opened more. The thing turned its head slightly to the right as it passed a hearse parked by an open grave, and when it did Kirk saw that it wore a blank smile. As Kirk reached the funeral car he saw the body of a small boy lying prone in the back. There were flowers in his folded little hands and his lips were blue. Kirk stopped, frozen into place by the face he knew. His brother, Kyle, turned toward him and opened his rotted mouth. Kyle's teeth were black like licorice and thick liquid like molasses ran out and oozed down the side of his pale sunken face.

Kirk looked away in time to see the floating thing disappear at a crest in the cemetery landscape. The sound of the wind carried a rattling tune from the distance, like a dancing skeleton. The rain stopped and the sky turned hurricane yellow as the wind picked up, blowing old leaves into a dervish and directing debris and dust into Kirk's eyes. He closed them and rubbed the irritation away.

When he opened his eyes again he was in Ferguson's Market. Wendy stood in front of him wearing a black satin bra. Her cleavage was deep and milky white and Kirk kicked himself for breaking up with her. "I'm modeling bras in Venice," she said. "Do you like my melons?"

He looked at her and wanted to bury his face in her warm softness but only said "I like all kinds of melons."

The image of Wendy became that of a fifty-something male store manager wearing a white smock with a name tag that was illegible. He looked familiar but Kirk was not certain. "Our melons are in the first produce aisle," the friendly manager said.

Kirk found the aisle. There was no one else in the store, and suddenly he found himself surprised that he had not been surprised before. He walked past the lemons, limes, oranges and apples. He found the melons and was picking through them when he noticed a coconut had gotten mixed in with the honeydews. He thought the manager would want to know so he reached for it, and the hairy shell with its coarse husk became smooth and silky in his hand. He raised the orb from the bin and as it turned in his hand, the face of Brenda Trevor looked back at him. The stump where her neck should have been dripped white like coconut milk and a gentle moan escaped her lips. Kirk screamed and threw the horrific thing across the aisles where it collided with a display and exploded in a cloud of frothy red gore.

Kirk awoke sweating and breathing like he had sprinted a mile. Instead of feeling better knowing it was just a dream, he felt very afraid. He turned on the lights and checked the clock; it was a little past four a.m. Back home in Indiana it would be six; his Mom would be up, maybe fixing breakfast or putting in a load of laundry. The maternal draw was insatiable, childlike, and the need to hear his mother was an ache. He picked up his phone and called home. Her sweet gentle voice answered on the third ring and Kirk sucked back all his terror, put a smile on and said, "Hi, Mom."

* * *

Kirk came downstairs around 11 that morning, just in time to catch Jerry giving the standard spiel to a new tenant, explaining the differences in paying daily, weekly or monthly, giving warning of the old elevators which had been known to crap out from time to time, detailing the rules of the laundry room, and finally the method of trash removal. The young woman listened attentively, asking questions when necessary and maintaining all along a pleasant and mature demeanor. Her good looks were genuine, no plastic, even with scant make-up. Her body was fit enough to be a gymnast. Kirk guessed correctly that she was thirty-one.

"Not for nothing, but we at The Arms do try our best to keep the plethora of vermin out of the lobby, and we haven't rented to them intentionally since the new owner came in. This is a safer place to live than the cacophony of dreadful hell holes along the boulevard." He looked over and saw Kirk approaching. "Just ask our resident writer, Mr. Logan here!"

Jerry was back to his normal self and Kirk was happy to see him. "Hi, Jerry."

"Kirk, we have a new tenant. Meet Miss Dana Pelman. Miss Pelman, Mr. Logan." Kirk was not the most on the ball when it came to knowing what women were thinking, but even he knew the look Dana offered meant they would be meeting again. He gave her the same and they shook hands longer than strangers normally do. He noticed a small heart tattoo on her hand, where the meat resides between the thumb and the back of the hand, and the nails which were an unusual shade of blue, almost black but more rich than that.

"You're a writer?" she asked.

"I'm working at it," Kirk said.

"I'm a director," she said. "I'm here working on a documentary about the starving creators of all sorts who come to make it in Tinseltown. There may be room for you in the production if you are interested."

"As a writer?"

"Yes and no. As a guy who is here to write. Your input would be your face on camera, not your scripting ability," she said.

"What makes you think I have anything to say worth hearing?"

"You have a nice face, handsome. You would look good. I guess we can find out if you have anything to say worth a damn after a short interview."

Kirk smiled, "Over dinner?"

Jerry had sat down and was writing in his ledger, half listening to the conversation.

"Sure, but not tonight. I'm meeting a rep from Miramax. Cross your fingers for me. But dinner tomorrow would be good."

They parted after exchanging cell phone and room numbers. She was directly above him in 601.

Kirk left and met Stumpy at a sandwich shop called "The Grindhouse" which specialized in hoagies, subs, hero sandwiches, or as they are known in New England, "Grinders". The proprietor, Sal Napoli came from back east and was a fan of both hoagies and horror and made the best cold Italian sandwich in the city. Between the sandwiches and the cinema the name of his shop was born. He played further off the Grindhouse Cinema motif by naming sandwiches after some of his favorite directors, especially the Italians. There was *La Fulci*, *La Bava*, *La Lenzi* and *La Argento*, along with some lesser known names. Stumpy knew all of them. Each sandwich had a unique twist which cued off the directors' trademarks— *La Fulci*, for instance, included several olives pierced with toothpicks to the outer crust of the roll, in homage to the master's penchant for eye trauma.

Sal's biggest seller though was his own namesake, *Grinder A La Napoli*, which was a typical cold meat and cheese deal drizzled with vinaigrette and fresh herbs. He sold loads of them.

Sal was a big burly and jovial fellow with an accent so thick with Boston it was often hard to understand him when he talked fast; a true character in a town full of clones. His shop was small and clean and had movie posters from his favorite flicks lining the walls. The place smelled like sautéed onions, olive oil and fresh bread. The writers met here at least once a week; the atmosphere was perfection and the food better.

Stumpy was sitting at a small formica table with a soda, talking on his cell. He saw Kirk and waved him over. When Kirk sat, Stumpy put up a finger ("one minute") and was nodding to the voice on the other end of the line. He smiled, nodded harder, smiled more and gave a silent thumbs-up to Kirk.

"What time?" was the only thing he said into the phone. And then, "Right," and he hung up.

"Why do you look like you just got a beaver shot of that chick that does the weather?" said Kirk.

"That was Allen. Lionsgate wants my script. They're sending an offer to him this week."

"Holy shit! Hate to even go there but, you sure this time?"

"Sure as I can be. Supposedly they think the undead still got some juice flowing, but for a limited time, so they want something that's ready yesterday. They claim they are putting the stall on some other projects to expedite this. I think it's happening." He smiled like a fool smiles, no pretense.

"Most awesome," said Kirk.

They ordered *Grinders A La Napoli* and talked until Sal tapped the bell, when Kirk got up and grabbed the sandwiches from the counter. They ate and talked more. Kirk told his pal about Dana and Stumpy acted interested, but was still so high from his own pending victory that his mind was not much in the game.

They met in the lobby the next night at seven. Kirk wore his "professional" duds, khakis and a button shirt. Dana sported hip-hugging denim and a white cotton blouse that hid nothing. Kirk kept a game face as he imagined his hands gliding across her hard ribcage from behind until the soft swell of her breasts met his grasp. He forced himself to think of something else and smiled innocently at her. She smiled back.

For Kirk it was a rare occasion for a real sit down meal in a place that didn't have paper napkins. The joint wasn't five star, but a New York Strip was twenty-eight bucks and he could buy four meals at the Grindhouse for that.

The conversation was brisk and covered the usual background, family, friends, education, ambitions, and of course their present career developments.

Dana said, "You're theoretically perfect for the Doc. Why don't we set something up for next week, a test shoot. I'll set up and plan maybe an hour of shooting time."

"By yourself, or do you have a crew?" asked Kirk.

"I work alone mostly, run the tech stuff, sound, camera.

It's tight shooting but I still use a small boom mike. You can always tell when stuff is shot with camera sound, it's lame."

They talked for hours and Dana did mention that she sometimes worked with a guy named Joey, who knew a little about film tech and a lot about beat-downs. He was a former Mixed Martial Arts fighter who met Dana when she shot a documentary about the sport. Joey lived in Venice and charged her only for his gas and food.

"He took care of me more than once," she said.

"There's a lot of dangerous people, especially in this town. Nice to have some muscle around if you need it," He replied. "So how long have you been working on the film?"

"Two months. I have three finished segments, well, finished meaning 'shot'. No editing yet. I wanted two more, but there might be enough material from you to leave it at that. I should know pretty quickly if you have the same charm on screen as you do eating that steak."

"I knew my Neanderthal attraction would come in handy someday," he said around a mouthful of steak.

They walked back to the hotel near midnight. Kirk wanted to grab her and plant a juicy one on her velvet mouth, but they were now engaged in a professional relationship so he chilled. He did, however, ride the elevator to the sixth floor and walk her to her door. She made a subtle affectionate gesture, touching his shoulder as they parted and thanking him for the meal and for agreeing to the project. She turned to open her door and the view of her from behind burned itself into his eyes. He hoped the picture would return in the wee hours.

It did not.

He dreamed stark and intense visions these days. Good or bad, the dreams were vivid, Technicolor movies of things his mind wouldn't let go of, bastardizations of reality that were beginning to interfere with the rest his body needed. He went to bed with Dana's ass in his mind's eye, and woke up screaming five hours later as the last remnant of Kyle's eyeless, rotting face faded away into his subconscious.

The death of his brother had been all but set aside for over twenty years. It had been tragic, like any family death, but time is the great equalizer and its magical power of healing is like any natural element; you don't need to search for wind, it comes when it needs to come.

Kyle died and was buried in the spring of 1980. Kirk mourned along with his parents, and eventually dwelled on the memories of good times. Not even as a child did he have nightmares about his brother, so why now? He looked at the clock. Even two hours ahead it was far too early to call home right now, and even if he could, Mom would only worry about him afterward; he could tell that she had sensed something beneath the nonchalant exterior he wore during the last call.

He lay in the dark and focused his mind on the *Frankenstein* script. He tapped his anxiety to develop scenes of tension in the story. Kirk had an uncanny ability to write scenes, including dialog, completely finished in his mind and not lose the tiniest morsel by the time he was able to sit down and type. Even when the gap between thought and composition was many days later, once the scenes were set, they were set.

He drifted off again for a couple hours and woke groggy and with a hangover even though he had only drank two beers at dinner.

* * *

Friday morning flew by as he set to writing everything his mind had already composed. Dana called at lunchtime and set up the first filming for mid afternoon. She sounded bright and happy, and during the conversation Kirk fought to keep her ass out of his mind.

He made himself a sandwich and popped open a soda. He clicked on the TV and looked for something that would not annoy him. He found nothing to suit, and picked a random DVD.

After lunch he called Jackie and informed her he was finished with the outline if they wanted to meet before the scheduled appointment they could, but she told him Mr. Kemper was scouting locations somewhere in Canada and would not be back until the original meeting date. Kirk stood for a minute deciding what to do until Dana arrived in a few hours. He called Stumpy to see if he wanted to do something, but he was in a meeting with his agent reviewing the offer from Lionsgate. That he even answered Kirk's call was testament to their brotherhood.

Restless and anxious, Kirk left the apartment.

He took the stairs down to the lobby, stopping at the window on the third floor again. Something was off about this spot but there was nothing to show it. The smear on the windowsill was gone, thanks to Alvin the super janitor, who only stopped cleaning in order to fix something. Kirk looked down the hall as he did weeks back. There was something off in the hall too. He noticed it last time as well; the space was much darker than his floor. Once that fact registered he quickly discovered why. Each hall had three hanging pendant lights, like the old schoolhouse lights, milk glass globes. The lights were spaced evenly to illuminate the entire length of the corridor but the fixture in the center of the hall was out. It stood right at the door to room 308.

Weird, thought Kirk. *Alvin should be all over this.*

As he crept closer to the door there were more flies; they buzzed and hummed and bounced off Kirk's face. A stench seeped out from under the door. It was a rotten odor, under-lying and heavy, and riding clumsily above it was a pungent, flowery stench. The mixture was noxious, like hot day roadkill and old lady perfume from Sears.

Downstairs, Kirk relayed his concerns to Jerry.

"I'll have Alvin take a look," said Jerry.

"Okay, well you might want to do that ASAP. Something is rotten for sure."

"Probably just a dead rat or pigeon."

Kirk shrugged. "I'm surprised none of the neighbors have said anything."

"They didn't. Is that all, Kirk?"

Kirk flinched at Jerry's abruptness. "Hey, Jerry, everything okay? You seem on edge lately, a little short."

Jerry put on a strange face. It appeared to Kirk like he was trying to look concerned, but really it only looked like he had gas and was trying to hold it back in front of a hot chick.

"Sorry, Kirk, it's just all this work and we are really short-handed and the owner cannot seem to decide on applicants to fill the positions. The procrastination of the patriarch is beginning to take its toll."

It sounded reasonable enough to Kirk, and his anxiety faded. He said, "I think I'll take a walk." When he got to the door, he turned back to ask Jerry one more thing, but saw he was on the phone. Jerry was facing the opposite direction, so all Kirk saw was his back when he heard, "Al, we need to talk."

* * *

"You need to look at me when I ask the questions, not at the camera," said Dana.

Kirk smiled. "I've been around sets for quite a bit now. I know how this is done," he said.

Dana checked the digicam's settings, adjusted the boom once more and made sure the tripod was tight, then she held up three, two, one fingers...

"You are from the Midwest. What was the most glaring change when you moved to L.A.?"

He looked into the lens. "What I found—"

"Cut," said Dana.

"Something wrong with the camera?"

"Yeah," she said. "You're looking at it."

They worked for several hours. Kirk looked at the camera on almost every take for the first ten minutes. Finally to get him to look at her, Dana loosened another button on her shirt, giving him a damn fine target for his gaze. That took several takes to get the giggles out, but he finally settled in and eventually even focused on her face. And an amazing face it was.

The interview was smooth sailing from then on.

She left before dinner and told him she would be gone for the weekend.

It was a long weekend for Kirk.

* * *

Monday came and went without any big news. Dana called early in the day, saying she was back and working on editing the tape.

"You could be a star if you ever gave up writing, assuming you can learn to deliver your lines," she said.

"I learned just fine when I was given the right incentive," he quipped.

"The incentives have reached their limit," she replied. "If you think I'm taking my shirt off next time, you're nuts."

"You're right," he said. "We'll save that for when the work is done."

She did not respond right away and for a minute Kirk thought he stepped over the line. He was quickly getting paranoid that Dana would come back yelling at him, or worse, cold and indifferent. He was about to take back his gentle jab, but she spoke up first and when she did her voice was lighter, more girlish. "Don't count your chickens before they hatch," she flirted.

Kirk beamed inside, but played cool. They talked for another few minutes and set another shoot date for Thursday afternoon.

Kirk saw Alvin taking out the trash that evening, like every other Monday. He read a book until he drifted off near midnight, and was soon dreaming what he'd dreamed of dreaming...

He was with Dana, somewhere outside the country. It looked like Italy; they were in a stucco house on a vineyard hillside with a view of the sea. They stood together by an open multi-paned arched window and each had a glass of red wine. Kirk sipped his, then put it down and gently grasped Dana around her waist. She leaned into him and their heads rested next to each other. He could smell her perfume, like honeysuckle. She put her glass down and covered his hands with hers, massaging his, delicately scratching the back of his hand with her blue black nails. Kirk took her hand and raised it up to his face and kissed the small heart inked near her thumb. She settled further into him, exhaling, and he surrounded her with his entire body like a cocoon. A gentle breeze blew salt air and flowers in, and...

A loud thump woke him. The noise came from above, but his mind told him it was the alley. He went directly to the kitchen and peered out the window; the bald cretin was down there again.

Kirk was done screwing around. He threw on jeans and shoes, and didn't even bother to lock his door behind him as he stormed out. He ran down the stairs and paid little attention to the noises from above; it sounded like a domestic squabble anyway, what little he caught of it. Life in the hotel was starting to become increasingly unsettled these days, and Kirk was getting the sense he might be best off moving out soon.

The front desk was vacant and Kirk swore that he would call the owner of the hotel himself the next day to tell him his property was not being managed well at all. He stomped out the front doors and into the stillness of the eerie quiet. The air was stagnant. It stunk the way cities stink in the heat. It was after two but Kirk was soon sweating.

He walked around to the side between the hotel and the store beside it. There was a very slim passage, barely wide enough for a narrow-shouldered person. Kirk had to walk semi-sideways to get through and still he bumped into the bricks numerous times. The stink of urine was overpowering. The little causeway bisecting the buildings was nothing more than a urinal and a drug den. Multiple hypodermic needles bounced off Kirk's shoes and cigarette butts were everywhere. He moved slowly, quietly. Twenty feet ahead the alley inter-sected. He closed the gap with each step, and the closer he got, the louder the rustling in the trash became.

At the entrance to the alley he stopped, listening. The rustling continued as he gathered the courage to take a peek; the rush of anger that had gotten him this far had faded, and he started questioning the wisdom of being here alone at two in the morning. He took a very deep, silent breath and exhaled with great care. With a small nod to his fortitude, he slowly eased his head beyond the wall.

The figure was ten feet away. Bald and pale and bent, just like he had seen from above, but from this perspective it looked smaller, less threatening. Kirk watched the cretin open a bag and toss it aside, then grab another one. He had just mustered the balls to confront the figure, when he saw it open another bag and grunt a satisfied noise. The man removed several items and looked closely at them, setting each aside as he inspected another.

Even in the darkness Kirk recognized two sets of human hands and feet.

His mouth gaped, searching for the vocal chords to engage, but before the slightest sound escaped someone put Kirk's lights out with a solid crack to the back of his skull. The blackness was instantaneous and total, and he felt nothing when his face hit the pavement.

* * *

Kirk dreamed.

He was back in the supermarket, but this time no one was there, not even the manager. He walked aimlessly for a bit, then headed to the produce aisles. He went straight for the melons, looking for a coconut. He found one and again the scraggy husk became silken hair when he raised it. This time, as the item turned in his hand, the face was Dana.

He awoke in a haze and gradually realized he was dreaming, and this time that truth did ease his mind. His bedroom was fuzzy and he vaguely comprehended that it was brighter than it should be. Did he leave the light on in the living room? Still exhausted, he covered his face with an arm to block the light. He thought of Dana and was excited he would be seeing her in just a couple days. He rolled over, and his bed felt strangely hard. His head hurt too, and when he touched where it hurt, there was warm sticky moisture. He gingerly uncovered his eyes, and after a moment his blurred vision gathered focus.

He saw Jerry in front of him sitting in a rigid wood chair, like the kind found in abundance in school libraries. A no nonsense, all business chair. He was making notes in his ledger, stone faced and focused. Kirk was confused, but relieved to see a friendly face. He vaguely heard sawing sounds and hard chopping noises somewhere nearby. Other than that it was quiet. His head throbbed. Was he drunk? Did Jerry invite him to a party? Had he drunk so much that he blacked out?

His eyes slowly focused and his mind along with them. There was no party. He remembered the noises, the alley, then a dead zone.

"Jerry," he called dizzily. "What happened? Where am I?"

"Shut the fuck up. I'm busy here," Jerry snapped as he continued writing in his ledger.

Kirk came to full awareness finally and realized he was chained in a cage, about the size of a small closet. Outside the bars, bare bulbs illuminated the space. There were no windows and only one door in or out. The air was damp and cool, and some easy listening music played softly in the background. Even under the best of circumstances the atmosphere would have been oppressive, strange and ugly.

On the other side of the room, Alvin was cutting beautiful chops from a thigh. The skin was very pale and the flesh was very red, and it looked strangely familiar.

"I was sort of hoping to see you get your break before this part of the story," Jerry said, sounding more like the old jovial Jerry, the Jerry of before, the Jerry of good natured pontifications and verbose communications. But that Jerry wasn't real. This was the real Jerry, Kirk realized with a sudden blast of clarity, and the real Jerry was angry, nasty, and scary. Good God, but he was massive too! His brutish barrel chest and telephone pole arms had been well hidden in his standard front desk attire, but now he wore an old t-shirt and green work pants, and his greasy hair looked even more oily. He looked powerful enough to compete in that bizarre strong man contest where they lift giant tires and piles of rocks, gorilla strong. His eyes were the picture of insanity, gaping pupils, whites showing above the irises, insane but totally focused.

Crazy cool, Kirk thought, and for a brief second he made a mental note to use that in a script, until reality once again crept in. He would never write again, and he knew it.

Kirk quickly added up the pieces of his present predicament. It made no sense, but it was real. He yelled, "Are you nuts? Let me the fuck out of here, you freak!"

"Not a chance."

"You can't keep me here, you fucking ape. What the fuck are you doing?"

"You'll find out soon enough," said Jerry, and his face grew black, almost demonic. The true face of evil, Kirk thought. He shuddered to think this was the man he once saw as a kind of eccentric second cousin.

Jerry focused on Kirk and pointed a meaty finger straight at his face. "Now like I said, shut your fucking mug before I push my fist down your self-righteous gullet, shit head. And I'll have Alvin take care of you without the benefit of you being dead first. Wouldn't be the first time. You get me, fuck stick?"

Kirk could only blink.

"I'll take that as a yes," said Jerry.

Minutes passed. Jerry continued logging information and Kirk sat silently, looking around, adding things up. None of it made sense. He drew a hideous conclusion that he would have rather not, but he was a realist. His dad had a saying: "If some jack-bagged fruit hands you a sandwich that smells like a dog just crapped it out, it ain't liverwurst." Gathering what little courage remained in his confused mind, Kirk mustered the energy to weakly ask, "How do you expect to get away with this? The hotel owner... I mean damn, he must come around sometimes, he'll have to figure it out!"

Jerry laughed. "I'm the owner, Kirk."

Kirk looked incredulous. "You?!"

"Yesiree, bub. I came out here after I was paroled in '89 and worked for the old man, then I inherited the place when he died fifteen years ago." He closed his ledger, put his pencil behind his ear and stared at Kirk.

"Paroled." Kirk said flatly.

Jerry just continued his stare and as Kirk's expression went cold, the big man's head tilted back and he let out a howling laugh. Kirk remained quiet as the guffaws subsided, and he didn't know which was more unsettling; the maniacal laughter or the hollow void left when the shrieks died.

Other than Alvin's butchery, there was silence for a long time.

The cage which held Kirk was barely tall enough for him to sit up and when he did the top of his head touched the bars. His hands were free but his feet were handcuffed together and chained to the bars. He could move his legs side to side about four inches each way. Kirk felt like a groundhog in a Have-a-heart cage, waiting for animal control to come and remove him. He started to zone out, removing his consciousness from the location, digging deep for some subconscious deflection, some place his mind would take him.

Home.

He focused on the little town in central Indiana where he grew up. The broad tree lined streets and cozy downtown were just coming into his mind's eye. He concentrated and the picture started to solidify, kids riding bikes, a big yellow dog chasing a Frisbee, the ice cream truck coming down the street, the sound of a lawn mower, a neighbor taking a hose to his driveway to wash away the remnants of grass clippings in the hot afternoon sun. Kirk was nearly there but...

The sound of water came on hard and fast. Kirk looked and saw Alvin using a garden hose to wash blood and small bits of flesh into a large floor drain. He felt like puking but held it back. His mouth opened wide.

"Make all the noise you want, honey," said Jerry.

"Huh?" said Kirk.

"My paperwork is done, so you may now dispense with fetal wallowings, if that suits you, Mr. Logan. Wails of despair, cries of injustice, et cetera. I defer to your vocal stylings, henceforth."

Kirk could only blink, shock was taking hold.

"Scream, holler, yell, have at it, buddy. Look at the walls," continued Jerry. Kirk looked. The same audio muffling pads he had seen in studio sound rooms covered every inch of wall and ceiling. He just looked at Jerry like he was an alien, and Jerry smiled. "We could blast AC fuckin' DC down here, and no one would hear it."

Kirk sunk further into himself and struggled to maintain his tenuous hold on reality.

Jerry got up and walked over to talk to Alvin. Kirk heard nothing but murmurs from across the room. The ledger in which Jerry had been writing, sat open on the floor next to the chair. It was turned slightly away from Kirk's view, but it was close enough for him to decipher the writing. Each page contained two columns, one titled "Customer," the other, "Cuts." Under the "Customer" section were numbers; 27, 90, 5, 13, etc. In the "Cuts" column were things like flank, shoulder, ribs, etc.

and initials. One such log read: 38... 2lbs shoulder, 1/2 lb filet, B.T.

The initials stood out in Kirk's mind and he shuddered. He looked back to where the men were talking and then rubbed his face with both hands, trying to wash away the thoughts that continued to creep in. When he removed his hands he saw Jerry back at his chair, bent over, and gathering a few items including his ledger.

Kirk mustered enough lucidity to ask, "What the hell are you doing in here? What in God's name is all this?"

Jerry looked up. "You can't figure it out? Smart young man like you? Do I need to spell it out?" He was writing a final note in his ledger as he spoke, barely giving Kirk another glance.

"Yeah," said Kirk, "I think you should."

Jerry straightened up, put his ledger on the chair, and removed a handkerchief from his back pocket. He wiped sweat from his face and bull neck, with a hand as big as a baseball mitt and said, "Tell you what, Mr. Screenplay Man, use your imagination, and then imagine the worst, and you're halfway there."

"What happened to Brenda Trevor?"

Jerry did not respond.

Kirk was trying to hold it together. His father's words tried to creep back in, but he told himself this was all some big prank, he was being *Punk'd* and somewhere in the dungeon was a candid camera. That was it! *Dana had her camera set up somewhere behind a stack of boxes. She was just waiting for him to go all loony bin and pitch fits and then she'd pop out and yell "surprise!" and they'd all laugh. Jerry would hand out frosty crisp Coronas and they'd all yuck it up, on the back of old Kirk "The Punk'd".* Everything finally made total sense.

Except Kirk really was injured. In fact, his head hurt like hell, and there is no way Dana would have allowed that kind of abuse simply to film a prank on a fledgling screenwriter. His mind switched gears quickly and he asked Jerry, "Who's the bald guy in the alley?"

"His name is Shane. He runs a soup kitchen for the local homeless. Ugly mother, and dumb as a goat, but he can cook like an Iron Chef. You know, he has bums coming from all over for his stews and soups. No one can figure out why his food ranks the highest among the vagrant jet set, but there is just a quality of taste no one else offers. We give him a hand now and again."

Kirk puked.

Jerry looked toward Alvin and said, "Hose that down, will ya?" and then left without another word.

Alvin continued to work in silence. Several times Kirk made awkward attempts to engage him in conversation, but Alvin never responded. After packaging the meats in brown butcher's paper and tying them with string, Alvin opened a massive walk-in freezer and put away all the provisions. He hosed down the work area and Kirk's vomit, and put a heavy padlock on the freezer door. He took off his bloody apron and turned off the lights, leaving Kirk alone in the darkness. Alone, unless you count the remains of a dozen or so slaughtered human beings chilling in the restaurant-style freezer.

* * *

The garbage truck did not wake Kirk this trash day. He had no clue how long he was in the pit of hell deli, but since he woke from his head trauma, he had not slept again. He heard muffled banging from the hydraulic compression as the vehicle ate its meals. He tried screaming for help, but like Jerry said, no one could hear. The truck's diesel belched and the gears propelled it to its next stop.

No one returned to the room that day, and eventually Kirk drifted off from total and utter exhaustion, the kind of tired most people never experience in their lives, except perhaps in the hell of war, or some awful civilian calamity like the Donner Party.

There were no dreams.

Sometime later a shape entered the room. It was large.

The lights remained off, but Kirk could feel the being standing and looking down at him. Its breathing was measured and strong. He did not think it an apparition and when it left, Kirk slept some more.

* * *

Time did not exist here. There was no clock, no natural light. The only way to know time had passed at all was the pain in his stiffening legs and the hunger pangs that came even in the hellish surroundings. Kirk awoke having pissed himself in his sleep. The comatose slumber had not allowed his bladder signals to get past his unconscious, and as a result his pants were soaked. Even if he had awoken, there was no place to go anyway. Still, the humiliation came on hard, and he felt like a pathetic child. He cried.

He thought about Dana. She would be worried about him if she called and got no answer. The second shoot was scheduled for two days after trash day. Kirk didn't know exactly how much time had passed, but certainly a day at least, making it some time on Wednesday when Alvin came in.

The janitor/butcher pulled the chains, lighting the bulbs, and as he walked past the cage he tossed two candy bars and a large bottle of water inside. Kirk scrambled for the food and drink, only vaguely aware of Alvin unlocking the freezer and going inside. He was guzzling water around a mouthful of candy when Alvin came out seconds later carrying several brown packages. The janitor closed and locked the door and made a non-stop line for the exit as Kirk continued his sugary feast.

* * *

It was late Wednesday afternoon when an elderly man entered the dungeon. Kirk was shocked to see another person come in the dank space. The man was dressed like a Fortune 500 CEO and his silver hair shone like a full harvest moon. He nodded to Kirk as he walked and kept moving to the giant refrigerator in the back. Kirk wanted to say something, yell out, "hey!" but he was stupefied. Instead, as he watched mutely, Alvin briskly shook the older man's hand and waved him into the pantry.

Minutes later Silver Hair swung back through the lair with an armload of packages in brown paper, and a Cheshire cat's grin. His brisk, bouncy walk was strange, giddy, juvenile. Kirk's voice never found it's mark, as the man disappeared through the door. Alvin followed shortly after, killing the lights and again leaving Kirk alone with only his thoughts.

* * *

With food and water energizing his brain, Kirk considered his predicament logically for the first time; he shoved his emotions (which basically consisted of sheer terror at this point) aside and forced himself to be rational.

Without something to pick the lock, even with free hands he was not getting out of this, and he wasn't going to waste energy in futility. There was no way out and he knew it. He was not Houdini. He took another long drink of the water. It was a little bitter, but still a sweet way to end a thirst. Dana's face painted itself in his mind; where was she? And how the hell could things have turned so completely fucked up? He wondered if he would ever see her again, and thought it unlikely.

Kirk knew life could turn on a dime. Kyle had been running after a ball one minute, and plastered by a blue Ford pick-up the next. His last meal had been Frosted Flakes with milk and a glass of orange juice, and he never knew the PB&J that was on his mind as lunchtime neared would never be enjoyed. He never realized that his last words to his older brother Kirk would be, *shove it, loser*. Joke or not, he would probably have chosen his words differently had he known, but the reaper is a tricky fucker. Watch your back, that shadow has a sling blade.

Suddenly Kirk felt light headed and sleepy. He lay back on

the cold hard cement. Water dripped on the other side of the room as regular as a metronome, and its hypnotic beat played a lullaby. He slept.

His nocturne was full of brief visions, subliminal and disturbing. There was no coherence of dream or nightmare, just muzzle fire flashing—

Mysterious faces, dismembered body parts, dripping blood, meat, insects, rats, then faces he knew; Mom, Dad, Kyle, Stumpy, Wendy, Jerry, Dana, his third grade art teacher, and other forgotten faces bubbling from his subconscious mind.

There was no rhyme or reasoning, no tale unfolding, just pictures like an album, the story of his life in rapid fire. He saw people he'd met only once, or people who meant the world to him twenty years ago, but were then forgotten.

Tears ran down his face, silent sleeping tears. A sadness of profound intensity enveloped him like a cloud of acid rain. His arms twitched, then flopped in angst. He moved with greater and greater fervor until he swung fast and far enough to slam his knuckles against the steel bars and the sharp pain woke him.

The lights cast hard shadows in the dank space, casting the room in a yellow/orange glow, like a warehouse parking lot late at night. Jerry and Alvin stood at the massive butcher's block table. Their backs were to Kirk, and Jerry was pointing and moving his hand in different patterns, like a conductor. He looked at Alvin and said something Kirk could not hear, but Alvin nodded. Jerry was in his dirty job getup again, and his size was truly startling. Alvin looked like a child next to him and Kirk was astonished at how he had never before observed his physical stature when Jerry wore a suit. He looked like a late 60's era Pittsburgh Steelers' lineman. Monstrous the natural way.

Both men wore large rubber aprons and Alvin wore heavy rubber gloves that reached almost to his elbows. They separated a bit as Alvin reached for a large knife, and the gap was filled with the image of a prone nude woman from breast to pelvis. She had pale skin and medium large breasts with dark upturned nipples. Under different circumstances Kirk would have been turned on; the body was exceptional.

Kirk watched as Alvin took the blade and slit the corpse up through the abdomen, like a trout. Blood oozed out and onto the floor and he noticed the men were wearing rubber boots like those used for mopping out flooded basements. An odor unlike any he had ever smelled before wafted into his nose. It was unusual and slightly fetid, but not completely offensive.

Alvin worked as Jerry directed, and soon enough organs and intestines littered the floor, landing wet and heavy. At one point Alvin tossed a kidney high up, over, and back, like a bride's garter, and it landed hard, six feet from Kirk, catapulting a spatter of blood right at him. The fluid had partly coagulated, and it attached itself to his cheek like a wad of crimson phlegm. Had Jerry turned to look at that moment he would have swore he saw a leech on the writer's face.

"Watch the liver," said Jerry as Alvin continued emptying the torso cavity, and it occurred to Kirk that no movie ever got right the sense of total horror and revulsion felt upon seeing such a nauseating display. No, not close. This was real horror. But he couldn't look away. Alvin cut and carved with the greatest of deftness, like a sushi chef, and before long the body was dismembered into its main components, pieces of a puzzle.

A chainsaw jigsaw, thought Kirk.

Jerry pointed again and this time Alvin used a cleaver to hack off the hands, each with one swift blow. Jerry laughed as he looked at Alvin and nudged his side, like they were sharing some inside joke. As Kirk watched, it appeared Jerry was egging on his partner, elbowing him in the side and mouthing the words, "go ahead."

Jerry turned and looked right at Kirk and smiled the broad affable smile that Kirk once knew. Even now, here, in this torture chamber, the smile for a brief second took Kirk off his guard. Jerry, the man who first befriended him here. Jerry, who pontificated like a jocular William F Buckley. Jerry, who took his faxes for him. Jerry, who introduced him to Dana. Jerry, old pal.

Alvin turned. He had something in his hands, an extra hand.

Three hands? Kirk thought. *How odd. I need to write that into a script...*

The 12 point Courier words floated before him:

```
         HANDY MANIFESTATIONS
                  by
            Kirk Logan


A man with three hands uses one to commit
telepathic crimes. The hand has its own
consciousness, its own mind. It can infiltrate
the minds of others and become one with their
own hands as it uses its evil digits to fondle
random breasts and strangle children...
```

Kirk, off in fantasy land, barely noticed Alvin toss the thing. It landed right next to the cage with strange sound: One hand clapping.

Alvin would be a champion at horse shoes, Kirk thought as he came back to the present and looked down. *It's a hand.*

No surprise, he saw the whole routine. Okay, there's a hand sitting on the floor. He could touch it if he wanted. He looked at it. Aside from the present circumstances, purely from an objective viewpoint, it was a nice hand. A delicately feminine hand. Strong and healthy, but sensuous. The kind of hand that might offer a slow sweet tug on a menstrual Saturday night. Maybe that hand once sewed clothing, or baked bread. Maybe it used its nails to give a nice ticklish back rub, or maybe it slapped a screaming child. No telling now, but what was telling was the nails were an unusual shade of blue, almost black but more rich than that. Odd.

Both Alvin and Jerry were watching him closely. Jerry had his massive arms folded into themselves and was leaning back against the heavy table. They watched, as recognition crept onto Kirk's face. A strange light appeared briefly in his eyes, and he almost smiled.

Kirk reached between the bars and picked up the hand. It was heavier than it looked, dead weight. The nails felt like cockroach armor and their tickle gave him a shiver. The knuckles were beautiful. *How could knuckles be beautiful?* he wondered, and yet they were. He massaged the disembodied fingers and felt their cold smoothness. He thought again about what kind of tasks this porcelain hand might have partaken in and he grasped it like one would in a greeting, *pleased to meet you*. A spot of blood was present on the otherwise flawless flesh, and while that was understandable given the present situation, Kirk thought the mark spoiled the beauty so he used his other hand to wipe the stain away. He rubbed back and forth. The skin was so silky, so smooth.

The stain remained. A stubborn stain, he thought, so he licked his finger absently and rubbed it again.

Still there.

Stress, exhaustion and head trauma, all combined to sap Kirk's mental faculties. He was like a drunken imbecile, a retarded child. He regressed, and the state of his once sharp senses dulled. The line between reality and fantasy faded away like hopscotch marks in a spring rain.

The space went dark all around; tunnel vision crowded in and it was like a bright spotlight cast it's beam on the hand. It appeared as a vision of great importance, a holy relic from some grand celluloid master's vision of a quest, an ancient religious artifact from an Egyptian tomb or on a Scottish moor. The benevolent light of God himself, illuminating it for the great mighty searcher of truth, to find, and discover the answers of eternity. He could almost hear the chord of regal trumpets announcing his spiritual victory.

The room again grew bright, and in his peripheral vision Kirk saw the men, still standing and staring at him. Jerry, my old pal, Jerry. Kirk turned and smiled and Jerry smiled back. Kirk returned his gaze back to the beautiful hand with it's terrible bloodstain. Darn stain. He shook his head, stuck his finger in his mouth again and gave that mark a real good rub. When it remained, he cocked his head as a curious dog will, and that refocused his vision. The blood. The damned blood. Right near the thumb, that blood.

The blood, in the perfect shape of a small heart. Kirk screamed, as Jerry had instructed.

And no one heard.

EPILOGUE

The studio developing *Frankenstein's Torture Chamber* found a new writer. There was a two sentence blurb about it in *VARIETY*, stating only that the original writer was unable to fulfill his commitment.

Alvin cleaned up room 308 and it was rented by a waitress/ actress named Brooke who was expecting her big break any day now.

Stumpy sold his zombie script for six figures.

The Hampton Arms celebrated its 95th year in business with a grand buffet style party, which included and open bar and many unusual meat dishes.

Dana's belongings were found in a dumpster by a local bum some time later. He kept some trinkets and a bra, but pawned her digicam for thirty dollars and used the money for wine and a street blow job. The digicam was resold again and eventually the last moments of Kirk's recorded life were taped over when the new owner decided to shoot film of himself drinking a gallon of barbeque sauce and throwing it up onto a painter's canvas. The video was posted on-line and received over a million hits on YouTube. The canvas was auctioned on eBay and a collector from Japan bought the barf art for a little over $200,000. The performance artist went on to star in his own reality TV show called, *Eat, Drink, Puke*, which Kirk's mother never watched.

In his Indiana hometown, Kirk's disappearance was covered by the local news in a series of reports called, "Careful what you wish for." The series was narrated by a lovely young lady from South Bend whose greatest ambition was to someday make her mark in Hollywood.

Edgar Allan Poe was an influence on Alan Bernhoft from a very young age, and Alan could often be found riding his bicycle around his Southern hometown quoting stanzas from The Raven much to the befuddlement of his fellow citizens. It was in his twenties when he became a model for legendary horror and fantasy illustrator J.K. Potter that Alan became aware of such great writers as Steven King, Ramsey Campbell, Dennis Etchison and the late, great Clarence John Laughlin, all of whom had several works published with classic Potter illustrations featuring Alan. Fast forward a few years and Bernhoft is now himself a horror writer of both the page and screen, as well as actor, filmmaker and musician. He wrote, produced and starred in the cult hit feature film The Dr. Jekyll & Mr. Hyde Rock 'N Roll Musical. *He calls Los Angeles home, where he lives with his beautiful wife and two daughters. Get more info on Alan at* www.alanbernhoft.com *and at* www.jekyllandhyderock.com.

THE LEGEND OF SLEEPY HOLLYWOOD

Alan Bernhoft

Inspired by Actual Events

WARM, DARK LIQUID GUSHES from the transient's severed head, steaming in the cool night air as a fountain of blood sprays from the neck, the arms reaching out randomly, as if to complete some futile act. The Creature makes one last slice through the neck flesh with a long, bright machete-like blade, slightly curved as if to suggest a scythe from another dimension. The body rips away from its head and collapses on the urine-soaked cement of the alley with a heavy wet thud. The Creature's cat-like red eyes flash in the pitch black night. A scaly reptilian webbed claw deposits the fresh head in a large black duffle bag, which it then drops haphazardly to the ground and drags along on the sidewalk behind as it limps sluggishly off into the shadows.

Curious eyes watch from above, as the Hollywood Stars of yesteryear observe the scene from a faded mural on the wall of the adjacent building on Wilcox Avenue. The half-a-block wide painting depicts dozens of stars of the silver screen seated in a movie theater viewing the people on the funky side street—the tourists, locals, and other eccentric characters going about their business. The inanimate celebrities stir.

Charlie Chaplin covers Shirley Temple's eyes to protect her from the gory sight. She pushes his hands away impatiently.

"I suppose that's one way of eliminating the poor." W. C. Fields breaks the long silence.

"What a messy way to whack someone. He didn't even know the guy," Bogart chimes in.

"There's a strange, twisted poetry to this night..." James Dean mumbles, slouching even further into his seat.

"I kinda feel sorry for the Creature." Marilyn Monroe contributes sweetly, with an angelic innocence. "He just wants to be loved."

"There's no business like *our* business!" chirps Jimmy Cagney, half humming.

"Hollywood is a cutthroat place." Elizabeth Taylor remarks in a brazen tone.

"Depends on where you're sittin', doll face!" Clark Gable smirks.

"I'm four seats away from you... *that's* where I'm sitting." Liz fires back.

"Quiet. Somebody's coming," warns Rudolph Valentino in a thick accent.

"What the hell did he just say?" quips Groucho.

"Shhhhhhhhhhh!" the others fire back.

From around the corner stumbles a tall, black transvestite, clearly having enjoyed a few too many. A coif of purple hair adorns her head, with a leopard skirt as short as the law allows ... and even shorter. The sparkles on her halter top are stained and tarnished, and her fishnets slightly ripped here and there. She wears large hoop earrings and thick garish makeup that, even in the dark cover of this Hollywood night, looks clownish. Her eight inch purple pumps cobble loudly away on the sidewalk, as she sings to herself, just barely able to keep it together enough to traverse the dimly lit side street. She's seen better days... but not many.

"Now there's something you don't see every day," remarks Paul Newman.

"*We* do," says Richard Pryor.

"Oh yeah, I suppose we do, don't we?" agrees Newman.

"How does a girl like you get to be a girl like you?" Cary Grant comments.

"I'm oddly aroused!" Robert Mitchum adds.

"Quiet!" says Lauren Bacall, "This oughta be good"

From behind a dark doorway, the Creature is perched, waiting, blade in hand. The tall purple-haired lady-man of the night saunters up to the mural, taking in all the faces of the famous, the familiar and the forgotten. She adjusts herself, then suddenly whips out her member like a garden hose and sprays a section of the front row. The Stars barely suppress a unanimous howl of disapproval.

"Now that's what I call talent!" says Errol Flynn.

"When ya gotta go..." answers W.C. Fields.

"Talk about upstaging yourself...!" Carole Lombard laughs.

Again, Chaplin covers Shirley Temple's eyes.

"Fucking movie stars," the tranny mumbles to herself. She opens her purse, produces a tube of lipstick and, barely maintaining her balance, paints it on her thick parched lips. All dolled up, she continues her drunken saunter forward as the Creature waits, watching, breathing deeply with an other-worldly mucus-filled guttural bovine grunt.

"Wuzzat?" quirks the tranny, but it is much too late.

Like lightning, the Creature quickly springs into action, towering over its victim, jumping behind her with one large step, snapping back her head, brandishing the long blade high into the air and WHACK! The head goes spinning through the air as the body kicks about spastically, then falls to the ground.

The Creature lifts the head from the blood drenched concrete when, crawling like a devilish serpent from deep within its mouth, slithers a long, pointed reptilian tongue, which caresses the head, sucking every orifice, in and out the ears and eye sockets, in the mouth and out through the severed neck. It licks the head clean with a slow, deliberate, gratifying motion before depositing it in the big black bag. The clownish head cracks against several other decapitated noggins, settling into the collection.

John Wayne is relieved. "He deserved nothing less, after exposing himself like that right in front of the women."

"*Her*self," corrects Al Jolson.

"Whatever," says Wayne.

"That makes twelve," notes Richard Burton.

"I count eleven," quibbles Burt Reynolds, "are you *sure* it was twelve?"

"Nope. That was twelve alright." Spencer Tracy confirms. "I'm sure of it."

"Twelve and counting, I suspect," says Kirk Douglas.

"Good enough for me!" Answers Reynolds, with a huge shit-eating grin on his face. He is interrupted by a deep rumble. It grows louder and louder, shaking the bricks and mortar of the wall.

"We're tearing apart!" cries James Dean with a melo-dramatic flare.

"Cool it. It's just an earthquake," says Brando.

"I don't think so... not this time!" says Mickey Rooney, pointing at the sidewalk.

A crack appears in the street as the rumble becomes deafening. Suddenly bolts of light shoot skyward from the open hole in the street, streaking high into the night. A thunderous clap explodes as a cloud of bright molten sparks shoot from the opening.

Slowly all the smoke and flashes settle down to reveal a human figure, a man, standing there in the middle of Wilcox. He wears some sort of military style gear, brandishing several other-worldly weapons, with a shiny, leathery suit and gladia-tor-like helmet, wearing thick steel boots. He strikes a match on his chest plate, reaching it up near his face to light the hand-rolled cigar straddled between his teeth, revealing a handsome, rugged, unshaven face. It is the face of a warrior, a soldier, a true hero.

"I like what I see," cackles Bette Davis.

"Hands off, you ole witch," says Joan Crawford.

"Bite your tongue, you old hag!" Davis fires back.

Theda Bara rolls her eyes and yawns.

"Settle down ladies. Please!" Edward G. Robinson restores order.

"If you please, sir, who are you?" asks a wide-eyed Judy Garland.

The stranger takes a long, cool drag from his cigar, spits on the ground, then looks over the mural group with squinty eyes.

"Banyon's the name. Intergalactic Bounty Hunter. I'm on the hunt for a creature from another part of the galaxy. He's on a sort of interstellar scavenger hunt. Collecting heads. Human heads. When he collects thirteen, he'll leave your planet and travel back to our part of the star system. I'm here to bring him in, dead or alive. Preferably dead. There's a price on his head. A high price. Most of his kind are wanted. This is what they do. And guys like me... well, this is what we do. We go after them. Keep the place safe for nice friendly folks like yourselves."

He shoots a wink towards Jane Russell. She blows a kiss.

"Have any of you good people seen anything of a big, ugly, dark, scaly reptilian creature carrying a sack full of heads? Smells pretty awful, too."

"Could that be the fellow you're talking about up the street there?" Gregory Peck gives a nod to the south.

Banyon turns, flips a night-vision goggle attached to his helmet over his right eye and surveys the area. He spots the Creature moving away in the shadows. He moves the cigar slowly to the right side of his mouth as he raises his weapon, a large bazooka-shaped rocket-launching serious killing machine from another world. He aims and fires at the Creature down the street. With a huge fiery explosion of light, a shimmering rocket flies down the street, implanting itself into the unsuspecting Creature's back. There's a bright flash of radiant light and a huge explosion. The entire block at Hollywood and Wilcox lights up like midday.

Banyon stares into the pillar of smoke and debris. He lowers his weapon, searching the thick haze with his sharp, trained eye for any movement. He steps cautiously forward as the smoke clears slightly.

Suddenly, the bright red eyes of the Creature appear right in front of him as it leaps from the thick dark smoke and jumps directly on top of the bounty hunter, knocking him to the ground. His weapon goes flying, shattering into pieces against the mural wall.

The stars almost jump out of their seats.

A large webbed claw swipes at Banyon's face, mauling his left eye and cheek. He pulls free and runs up the side of the mural, back-flipping over the Creature's head, revealing two long glowing light sword weapons in mid air. He stabs one deep into the Creature's chest and slices off the left claw with the other. He lands a few feet away, rolls onto the street, and leaps to his feet.

The Creature lets out an unholy shrieking roar from a large, frog-like mouth filled with rows of hideous jagged teeth, as thick, dark green glowing liquid oozes out its gaping wounds. The claw re-generates in seconds to Banyon's astonishment. Then the Creature falls to one knee, clenches a webbed fist, and turns slowly towards the bounty hunter, raising the other webbed hand and pointing a jagged lizard-like claw right at the bounty hunter. Banyon jumps to his feet, raising the light swords above his head and charges the Creature with a blistering scream. The Creature leans back with a loud grunt. Long, sharp spines shoot out of its shoulders, back and legs.

Banyon dodges the sharp edges at the last second, flying to the right in a midair summersault. The Creature swats the swords from Banyon's grasp, as they slam to the ground and slide into a storm drain with a crash. Banyon turns quickly to deliver a series of flying spinning crescent kicks to the Creature's face and head.

The Creature grabs a leg mid-kick and flings Banyon to the ground, his head barely missing a rusty metal pole that marks a parking driveway. The Creature leaps upon Banyon, claws outstretched. The bounty hunter is flat on his back; he looks to his side, spies a chain hanging from the pole next to his head. Just as the creature is on him, inches from his face, he lassos the chain around the Creature's neck, bounds out from under and around the Creature, and drags it backwards, hanging it from the chain.

The Creature struggles and kicks, howling and spitting fiery slime into the night, as Banyon twists his grip to snap out the last bit of life from the hideous choking monster.

Suddenly a shout comes from the mural. "Hey, Banyon, look out behind ya!"

"What?" says Banyon, temporarily distracted.

This moment is all that the Creature needs to whip out its blade and make a quick clean cut through the bounty hunter's neck. His head flies through the air, flipping again and again before landing with a loud SPLAT in the bloody head-filled duffle bag.

"And thirteen!" shouts Henry Fonda with a giggle. "I knew he could do it."

"It was awful close this time, you gotta admit!" pipes Jimmy Stewart.

The Creature removes the chain from its neck, which has sunk deep into its scaly sliminess, causing more glowing green liquid to ooze forth.

It plops down on the cement with a monstrous sigh, turns to the Stars in the mural, waves a claw with a mock salute and mumbles, in a deep guttural tone, "Thanks for everything, folks."

"Don't mention it," we hear Walter Matthau from the back of the mural.

"How did *he* get in here?" Clint Eastwood remarks, befuddled.

"Safe travels, friend!" Fred Astaire shouts, twirling up the aisle.

"Don't be a stranger." Ginger Rogers chimes in.

The Creature nods, fumbles through its bag, doing one last head count.

"Ollie" says Stan Laurel to his pal.

"Yes, Stanley?"

"Ollie, there's one thing I don't understand."

"And what might that be?" Hardy is perturbed.

"Well, he needed thirteen human heads, right?"

"Yeah... so?"

"I didn't think the bounty hunter was human."

"Why you...!" He slaps his whimpering friend repeatedly on the head with his hat.

"Good luck with the scavenger hunt!" Katherine Hepburn calls after the Creature.

The Creature rises to its reptilian feet, makes a final waving gesture over its shoulder as it steps to the middle of the street. A slight purple ray of morning sheepishly appears in the sky to the east.

It lifts its bag of heads, spreads its huge tattered reptilian wings and shoots off into the night sky and out into the stars towards another galaxy.

"There's no business like *our* business!" chirps Jimmy Cagney, half humming.

"There's a strange, twisted poetry to this night..." James Dean mumbles, slouching even further into his seat.

Elizabeth J. Musgrave is a working writer who has turned her screenplay Farmhouse *into a graphic novel illustrated by Szymon Kudranski (Spawn) and to be published by Asylum Press. She is currently finishing her first novella,* 85 Boys. *Her scripts have placed in Scriptapalooza and Writer's Script Network competitions. Her play* Darwin's Pâté *and short play* The Soundman *were produced in Los Angeles.*

CATTLE CALL

Elizabeth J. Musgrave

ONE BY ONE the girls filed into the room. Blonde. Blue-eyed. Built. C-cups. Beauty queens from small, Midwestern towns who came to Hollywood in search of glamour and glitz. Hoping to be the next Lana Turner discovered in Schwab's Drug Store. How their dear hearts would break when they found out there was no longer a Schwab's and that they weren't the only pretty 4-H County Fair Queen to come to Tinseltown with a dream. A dream to make it big on the silver screen. To be the next Marilyn Monroe. Julia Roberts. Angelina Jolie. Hell, Tara Reid.

Each wannabe flashed Max Fishman a veneered smile and flipped her bleached tresses, telling him how she had read the script and how much she really, really wanted the part of "The Girl" for which he was casting. Max, knee deep in head shots, peered over the rims of his glasses to do the obligatory once-over of the naif standing before him. He noticed her nipples jutting from the halter top she'd most likely purchased for that day's audition. Clearly, she was wearing no bra. Then again, none of them were.

"What makes you think you're The Girl?" he asked, fighting back a yawn.

"Because I can scream." And she belted out a blood

curdling squeal that would make Scream Queen Barbara Steele proud.

Max pushed the glasses further up the bridge of his nose. If it were under different circumstances, no doubt he would offer her the part based on her girl next door looks and eager disposition. She had promise; however, she was run of the mill when he actually considered the dozens of others he'd already seen and prodded on. He would know "The Girl" when he saw her. The problem was he hadn't. And time was running out.

"Thank you," said Max, forcing a smile. "That will be all, ladies."

The remaining girls scanned each other—confused—since they hadn't the opportunity to show off their assets yet. While two or three stormed out in a huff, a few still lingered, hoping for their one last chance to impress.

"You heard Max, girls, that's it for the day," said Justin, herding the hopefuls to the door and crushing their dreams on the way out. Not that Justin was a bad guy. He was just on a tight schedule. It was Saturday, nearing five o'clock. He had places to go; people to see. A premiere or opening somewhere. He didn't have time to dillydally in a twenty-five seat theater that smelled like piss. Even if there had been a bevy of beauties paraded in front of him all day, auditions were over now. It was time they get on home and not waste his time. Although he was known to make exceptions.

As he took the name and phone number of the vacillating blonde, Justin gave her a wink and told her he'd put in a good word to the director. Even without her auditioning, he could tell just by looking at her that she had talent. After all, he had been an assistant casting director for two years. He knew these things. Of course, she giggled and twirled her flaxen hair around her finger, insisting she show him, that night, her audition monologue for a recurring role on *Gossip Girl*. All he had to bring was the wine. He took her number down.

"Red or white?" he asked.

"Red," she smiled coyly, shutting the door behind her.

Justin plopped down in the seat next to Max who throwing him a dubious look. "What can I say? I'm a shit," grinned Justin as he pulled out his iPhone to text his high school girlfriend back home in Oklahoma.

To be young again, thought Max. Although Max was only forty, in Hollywood terms he was over the hill. And he had yet to make his first feature. Sure, he had a couple of award winning shorts to his name, but that didn't mean squat in a town where a middle schooler could make a feature on video, cut on Final Cut, then post it on YouTube to become an internet sensation and land a three picture studio deal. *Filmmaking's no longer an art*, Max told himself. *Why even bother?*

To many, just the idea of still harboring a childhood dream at his age would be enough to drive them into another, more practical, career lane. Not Max. This only fueled his desire more, especially these last few years. So when he finally swallowed all that was left of his pride and the pill of bitterness stayed lodged in his throat, he did what any poor, vanquished soul in his predicament would do: he went to a Black Mass.

"So you found her?" inquired Justin, interrupting Max's reverie.

Max paused. "Who?"

"The Girl, man," Justin said insistently.

"No." Max gathered the headshots, handing them back to Justin. "Here. I never know what to do with these."

Justin stared at the stack of pictures in his hands. "Out of all these girls, you can't find one? Dude, it's not even a speaking role. What the hell?"

Max shook his head.

"What a wasted day," said Justin. "I could've slept in." It didn't seem to occur to him it was because of Max he got the phone number of tonight's lay.

Stupid kid, Max couldn't help but think. *He doesn't have a clue.*

Max certainly didn't have one either prior to his initiation into the Black Mass. He had scoffed at the idea of a devilish exchange between the dark lord and a desperate individual in need of vindication for all his earthly toil. To Max, it was the stuff of scary movies, the folklore behind Robert Johnson, the Rolling Stones, Jayne Mansfield. It was all garbage in his opinion. But that mindset changed once he experienced what many refer to as the dark night of the soul.

It was his fortieth birthday, which happened to be Halloween, when he stumbled home drunk and then shoved a loaded gun in his mouth. He was done; finished with this town. He had nothing to show for the talent that even the suits at the studios said he had. Nothing to show for his sweat, perseverance, and sacrifice. Nothing, nothing, nothing. But a scrap heap of rejection and self-deprecation. He was, in his mind, an abject failure.

That night, as dark as it was, he managed to pull the gun from of his mouth. Not so much out of divine intervention as it was earthly tomfoolery. As his finger had pulsed on the trigger and he bit down on the pistol, he imagined the scene he would leave behind: Blackened blood and brain matter splattered against the wall, George A. Romero style. But before he could execute his plan, his attention diverted to an annoying cackle outside his apartment. It was so irritating, in fact, that it broke his concentration and caused him to go to the window. There, cloaked in shadows under the dim streetlight, Max saw what looked to be a hoofed, horned figure. In his drunken haze, he squinted to focus his bloodshot eyes. On closer examination, the thing looked to have claws and a hunchback, pointed ears. A hideous aura surrounding it that only seemed to captivate Max.

All of a sudden, the creature turned, locking eyes with Max. It was beastly looking. Its eyes like burning embers, its skin covered in pustules. Although the joker-like smile on its face remained frozen, the hysterical laughter it spewed forth seemed to echo throughout the neighborhood, sending shivers down Max's spine. He gasped in horror, running—though more like staggering—to his bed for cover.

Although Max failed to see the trick-or-treat bag at the monster's side, he saw this vision as a sign. And in the next few days, everything seemed to be a sign. Like the screening of *Rosemary's Baby* at the NuArt, hearing that Kanye West admitted to selling his soul to the devil, stumbling across Anton LaVey's tome *The Satanic Bible* at Counterpoint Records and Books. Max may have bought the book out of curiosity, but he devoured the pages in one night's sitting. Why not, a little satanic deal making? It was worth a shot.

Gradually, his determination and tenacity reignited. He vowed never to give up. He was going to make his movie, damnit. To hell with everybody... Literally.

"Make sure you take the trash out when you leave," Justin told Max as he headed for the door. "These assholes charge for everything."

Max heaved a sigh.

* * *

"Coffee," Max requested to the hipster waitress with a bad-ass swagger and an even badder-ass devil tattoo on her forearm. *Another minion*, he thought. He glanced at his watch—8:30— then scratched his two day old scruff and leaned back in the booth. What had he agreed to? A virgin in L.A.? Impossible. This was a town made up of whores, himself included.

Since he was still new to the black arts, the council sent him on a mission to see if he was truly serious about giving himself over. His task was to bring them a virgin. Guidelines: 1.) She had to be in L.A. 2.) She had to be an aspiring actress 3.) He had one week to find her. A mighty tall order, indeed. In return, he would be given a $10 million budget to make his film. One of the high priests was a producer and had connections to Stardance. Max's film would be sure to get in the career-making film festival, just like all the other compliant first-time directors' films before his did. He felt in his bones she was out there. But where was she? He only had until midnight that night—three and a half hours.

Suddenly, sniffles and stifled cries came from the booth behind him. Max craned his neck to see a young woman, no more than twenty, blowing her nose in a hankie. She was wearing a pastel, floral printed dress; her hair tied back in a bow. There was a freshness to her that he forgot still existed. She was pretty. Slender. Her skin almost translucent, as if she had never been out in the sun. She bent over, rummaging through a bag at her feet. He couldn't help but watch her slightest move. She must have felt his eyes on her because she caught his gaze.

Embarrassed, Max raised his hand feigning a wave then quickly turned back around in his seat. He'd been caught. He tried to shake off the encounter and reroute his stare else-where: to the fork on the table, the couple at the counter. Until he heard her blubbering again.

Max glanced back. No one was coming to comfort her. *She must be alone*, he thought. Reluctantly, he got up and stood next to her table at the booth.

"Are you okay?" Max inquired.

By now, she was crying so hard she could barely catch her breath.

"Would you like some hot tea?"

"No. I'm, I'm, I'm okay," she heaved between sobs.

Max couldn't help but feel sorry for her. She was a mess. Poor girl. "Do you want to talk about it? I mean, I know we don't know each other, but sometimes that's best."

She swallowed hard. Then paused. "There is no Schwab's." Again, she burst into a puddle of tears.

He knew it was callous, but it was hard not to chuckle. He persisted further, breaking more bad news. "There is no Cocoanut Grove either."

She was agape. Dumbfounded. But this time she didn't cry. Instead, she sat there, shell shocked from what had been told to her. She took a sip of water then blew her nose.

"Next you'll tell me there's no Brown Derby," she sniffed.

He didn't have the heart to tell her there wasn't. Was she really that outdated? Naïve? Or was she just that stupid? Max hadn't decided.

"You should probably be more up to date on L.A. I'll write

down a few tourist attractions for you," said Max, pulling out a pen and grabbing a napkin. He felt obliged to point her to a few landmarks, but what he really wanted to do was wipe the green off her brow before someone really took advantage of her. Someone like him.

"I just got off the bus. I'm new to the city. In case you're wondering," she said, bowing her head.

Max lifted his eyes and then quickly found himself studying her. There was something about her that he couldn't put his finger on. Something unique. He was intrigued. "Where are you from?" and he was genuinely interested.

"Nebraska." She poked around in her purse, pulling out a compact. "Oh, dear. I look terrible. This mascara was supposed to be waterproof," she whimpered. She wetted a napkin, wiping away the makeup that had run down her cheeks.

The hipster waitress came over to the table with Max's coffee. "So you'll be sitting over here?" she asked him. He glanced over at the newbie, fishing for her consent. He didn't want to assume that she wanted him there. Over the years, he learned not to assume anything.

"I, uh, I— " Max suddenly was at a loss for words.

"Would you? Sit with me?" she asked timidly.

Max mustered a smile. "Sure."

He slid in the booth beside her. As the waitress set down the cup of coffee, Miss Nebraska observed the devil tattoo on her arm. The new transplant sneered in disgust as the waitress walked away. She elbowed Max.

"Did you see that? A tattoo of the D-E-V-I-L." Church lady shook her head, appalled.

What a breath of fresh air, thought Max. "What's your name?"

"Daisy."

Of course it was. She had to be a Daisy. Or a Rose. Some fragile flower.

"I'm Max," he told her.

Daisy's eyes darted over the customers in the diner.

Suddenly, she leaned into Max. Excitedly, she whispered, "Celebrity sighting. John Stamos from *Full House*."

"Oh, he's always here. So he was on that show with the Olsen twins?" Max was oblivious.

"Duh. Like he was only Uncle Jesse. He was my first crush. Shhh." She was almost child-like in her enthusiasm as she jotted John Stamos' name down in a diary she extracted from her bag. "I'm keeping a diary of all the stars I see. How exciting. My first one. I can't wait to tell Maryann. She is going to be so jealous," she giggled.

Max sipped his coffee, quite taken with Daisy's simple charm. "So what brings you to L.A.?"

"Movies. I want to be an actress," she smiled.

Of course she does. Daisy. From Nebraska. *This town will eat her alive*, he thought. She couldn't get on the bus back home soon enough, as far as he was concerned. "There are a lot of actresses out here, Daisy. What makes you stand out?"

"Well, I've got a really good memory," Daisy went on. "I mean, like, I can memorize pages. I don't mean to brag and all, but my grandma says I've got potential if I had the right training. And she does community theater." She sat back in her seat proudly.

Max was thoroughly amused. And then it dawned on him; this could very well be "The Girl." Except how would he know if she were a virgin? He couldn't just come out and ask her. That wasn't Daisy's style. Daisy was prim. Proper.

"You're a long way from home. No boyfriend you left behind?"

Daisy dropped her head. "We broke up," and a stray tear slid down her cheek.

Max knew there was a story there, and he wanted to pry, but he also didn't want to come on too strong. "Sorry to hear. Break-ups are tough."

"And how. We were high school sweethearts. Homecoming King and Queen. We talked about getting married, having a family. You know, stuff like that."

"What happened?" he asked.

Daisy hesitated, only to begin shredding a napkin at the table. "He changed."

"How so?"

"He wanted things," she winced. Obviously, she was uncomfortable with the subject matter.

"Things?" Max was intrigued.

"You know," then in a whisper she spelled out the word she seemed to revile. "S-E-X." She shuddered.

Max nudged her more. "You mean, you haven't? I mean, you didn't?"

And that's when it all started to come together. When Max was fairly certain he had found the girl. Daisy did something that no female since his sixth grade girlfriend Kelly Russell had done: Daisy blushed.

She folded her hands in her lap as if she were protecting her sacred spot. "I'm saving myself for marriage. I know it's old fashioned. But I have morals. Unlike some with questionable values," she said, glaring over at the hipster waitress.

Yes! Ding. Ding. Ding. We have a winner, folks. Daisy. The virginal startlet. Right off the bus from Nebraska. Max felt like the luckiest man on earth to have discovered such an exquisite find. He would phone the council members as soon as he got home.

Max smiled, reaching in his pocket to give her a business card that he created on his PC. It was plain and to the point: "Max Fishman—Filmmaker."

"You're a filmmaker? Like movies?" said Daisy, her eyes lighting up.

Max shifted in his seat, a new-found confidence in his posture. "Yes. I'm a director."

Daisy's eyes widened. "Oh, my gosh. I can't believe it. What have you directed? Anything with Ashley Judd? Because I just love Ashley Judd. I've seen all her movies."

"No. Nothing with Ashley Judd. But I am making a movie. And I'm casting for a role."

"Are you serious?" Daisy beamed. She bit her tongue, trying hard to hold back what she really wanted to say, until she could no longer contain herself. She blurted out, "I know it's forward of me, but is there any way I could audition?"

Max slid in closer to her. "That's just it. You don't need to audition. You're perfect for the part. It's yours if you want it," Max grinned devilishly.

"Mine? The role's mine? Oh, good golly. Of course, I want it. I can't believe you're even asking me. Wow. This is—like, so —Lana Turner. Wait till I call home!"

Max suddenly became very serious in his tone. "Look, I know you're excited, but this has to be under wraps for now. We're still in contract negotiations. Not even all the actors have signed on. This has got to be hush-hush. Understand?"

Daisy nodded. "Got it. Tick a lock," she said, gesturing her lips were zipped.

Max watched Daisy. He almost pitied her naiveté. She was so easy to dupe. She never even asked what the part was. Or what the script was about. She was so trusting, so willing. He was ashamed of himself. It was wrong what he was doing, but he couldn't think about that right now. He had a movie to make.

"Where are you staying?" asked Max.

"At the hotel next door," Daisy replied.

"Tell you what. Call me first thing tomorrow morning. I'm going to start filming as soon as possible. Everything's been on hold because I've been waiting for The Girl. That girl is you, Daisy." And it was true.

Daisy squealed out, wrapping her arms around his neck. "Thank you," she cried into his shoulder. "Thank you."

That night when Max got home he called the council members to tell them he'd found the girl. They told him to bring her to their Hollywood address at midnight the next night. They would conduct the sacrifice then.

Sacrifice? Daisy? Although Max had agreed to find them a virgin, he never imagined they were looking for a sacrifice.

Honestly, Max just never thought. He was too wrapped up in his own vain interests to think of intention. They were committing murder. Max pondered this. All night he was racked with guilt. He was an accomplice in something heinous. Criminal. Unforgivable. And for what?

Ten million reasons, that's for what. He couldn't give in to his moral conscience at this point. He was far too close. The deal was done. Daisy was to be sacrificed. And he was going to make his movie, damnit. Max thrust the pillow over his head to smother any scruples burrowing their way into his psyche.

Max picked Daisy up at 11:30 the next night. He told her he was doing a night shoot first. She didn't ask any questions, not even anything about the character. She was just so excited to begin her first day of shooting.

When Daisy got in the car, the first thing Max noticed was her smell. She smelled clean. Pure. Although she wore another floral printed dress, this time she had her hair down. It hung past her shoulders and the ends were curled. Max imagined how many hours she must've painstakingly prepared. Not one strand of hair out of place.

"We don't have to do this, if you don't want to," said Max, the car idling in front of the ominous building where she was to be sacrificed.

"You're joking, right? You don't understand, I've been waiting my whole life for this. A way to get out of Nebraska and off that dairy farm. This is a dream come true. I'm more than ready for my close-up," she smiled.

Max felt a twinge in his stomach, feeling slightly nauseated. He thought about leaning his head out the window and vomiting. He swallowed some water instead. "Let's go. We've got a movie to make," as he held the car door open for her and they made their way inside.

Max was told to go to the top floor where he would be greeted by the council members. It would be the high priest Mortimer (not his real name, obviously) who would lead the ceremony. Max would give himself over that night following the sacrifice.

As they got off the elevator, Max and Daisy slowly crept down a darkened hall. He wanted to turn back, renege on his promise, but he knew it was too late. They were already met by a council member donning a hooded black cape who escorted them silently to the room at the end of the hall.

The shrouded council member opened the heavy, metal door and led Max and Daisy inside. A small circle of cloaked figures chanted in the center of the room. An altar was at the opposite end where incense and black candles burned.

"So it's a horror movie?" she whispered.

"Yeah. I should've told you. I'm sorry."

Max was deeply sorry. He never considered who the girl might be and what was to happen to her. Poor Daisy. His heart weighed heavy in his chest. The atmosphere was boding evil, so much so that Max was shaking in his shoes.

Daisy surveyed the room. "Where's the camera?"

Max nodded in the direction of the goat's head hanging above the altar. "Right there. It's hidden," he murmured. Daisy squeezed his arm tightly. More out of excitement than terror.

The high priest Mortimer soon entered the circle. He, too, wore a vestment, except on his was embroidered an inverted crucifix. A pentagram dangled from his neck. Max had never seen Mortimer's face because he was always masked. He'd only spoken to him on the phone, but he recognized his voice.

"Council, we are gathered here tonight in order to pay tribute to him who gives joy unto us. Our name is the name of the infernal lord who reigns on earth. Thine is the earth, Lord Satan." Mortimer continued as the other members chanted in what sounded like perverted Latin.

Max glanced over at Daisy, wondering if he should hold onto her in case she was frightened. He did. Then quickly he jumped back.

Daisy's once taut skin appeared to ripple. Her lustrous hair was now dry and brittle and falling out by the handfuls. She released a foul odor that smelled like something rotting.

The stench immediately made Max sick to his stomach. He gagged, looking about the room for a way out only to find none since the room was nearly pitch black except for the flickering candles. He blotted his brow, for the room started to boil. He was dripping in sweat, and at that point everything started to spin.

Max placed his hand on the chair arm to maintain his balance, while Mortimer raised an ornate, golden chalice above his head and carried on with the ritual: "We hold this sacrificial ceremony in its honor, the one we have invoked to bring us earthly riches and power."

Max's heart beat so fast that he felt it might burst through his chest. He had to get out of there. Suddenly, he turned to make a run for it. Two robed members came up behind him, grabbing hold of his arms. Max wriggled to release from their grip. "What are you doing? Let go of me," Max pleaded to no avail. "Daisy, run!"

Alas, poor Daisy was gone. In her place, a demon whose skin seethed, eyes blazed, and claws ripped at what was left of the floral printed dress on its back. A revolting creature straight from the bowels of hell.

After Mortimer sipped from the chalice, he spoke what were to be the last words to fall on Max's ears. "Tonight we provide an offering. And we celebrate. For tonight it feasts."

Max shrieked out, fully understanding his doom was imminent. The demon lunged for him, tearing right into his flesh. Blood sputtered out, and he wailed in anguish. It dug its jagged fangs in deeper, chewing into Max's intestines, internal organs, and bones until there were no more gurglings heard. Only the smacking sounds of the demon's putrid lips, gnawing on what was left of Max's femur.

Mortimer walked over to the creature, pulling back the hood of his robe to stroke the thing's head.

"There, there," he said as the demon licked its bloodied claws. "Foolish filmmakers. They fall for the virgin bit every time. Like they say, this town will eat you alive. If you let it."

And then Mortimer released a shrill, maniacal laugh that was heard all over Los Angeles.

Even in the Valley.

Richard Tanne produced the feature films Mischief Night, *featuring Malcolm McDowell, and* Worst Friends, *for which he also co-wrote the story and starred alongside Kathryn Erbe and Larry Fessenden. He also played a lead role opposite Kristy Swanson and D.B. Sweeney in the Syfy Channel Original movie* Swamp Shark *and co-created and hosts the movie culture talk show* Cinema Cool. *Visit* www.richard tanne.com *for more information.*

THE POWER

Richard Tanne

"MARCIENNE," SAID JAY, "is extremely powerful. She transmorphs before your very eyes into your deepest, darkest fear and allows you to confront it. Head on."

Jay was a struggling Hollywood actor, and Jay was quasi-spiritual. In the ten years I had known him, he had attempted to better his career—and his soul—by trying out yoga, meditation, psychic mediums, crystals, and a host of religions and cults. Now, he was turned onto something he called "transferal projection". Naturally, I was skeptical.

At first it was easy to decline Jay's invitations to visit Marcienne, but the more he saw *me* struggle, the more insistent he became. "Your first draft deadline is only a week away. You haven't written a single word of the script. If you don't deliver, the studio will can you and your agent will drop you."

I hated to admit it, but he was absolutely right. After my first script sale three years ago, I had failed to deliver on my last two gun-for-hire assignments, garnering myself a reputation around town as either a choker, a fraud, or a one-hit wonder. My agent warned that if there was a third strike, I'd be out.

"Any time a person is creatively blocked it's because we

have fear," Jay lectured. "You need to see Marcienne to identify and confront your fear, and then you'll be able write your script."

It was the only alternative to sitting in front of a blank screen. *Why not try something new?*

"Let's do it," I said.

As we snaked our way down Mulholland to find ourselves idling in midday Hollywood traffic, Jay explained that Marcienne was a widowed geometry teacher in her forties. She was not a religious person or a believer in the supernormal, but after the death of her husband a year ago, she sought emotional relief through meditation and had become uncannily powerful. In the last couple of months, people had been visiting her at her apartment in Los Angeles and, in some cases, making pilgrimages from places as far as Arizona and Texas just to consult with her.

Apparently, Marcienne was still grappling with her new role as a sage and worried that her bizarre and mysterious power would not always produce positive results for her visitors.

Jay described Marcienne's remarkable power as "the ultimate trip." It had begun in Marcienne's meditation class six months ago when her classmates had started seeing things. They saw Marcienne change form during meditation: Sometimes her hair was blonde, other times it was red. Sometimes her face was smooth and young, other times it was coarse and twisted. Soon, relics from their lives materialized before their mesmerized eyes. Beloved heirlooms. Faces of dead relatives. Some felt emotions they hadn't felt in years.

Eventually, Marcienne learned to focus her energy to a single person, transferring his or her mental and emotional anxiety inside herself, and then projecting it outwards, onto herself, like a human canvas. The results were astounding.

For one woman, Marcienne shape shifted into a two-foot tall barn spider with black, bristly hair and green-spiked legs. The woman, paralyzed by fear, stood helplessly as the spider scaled her body, lined its genital opening up to her mouth, and dropped hundreds of silky eggs down her throat. Once settled in the woman's stomach, the eggs hatched and hundreds of slimy, molting spiderlings ruptured through her flesh. The woman ferociously stomped on as many of the spiderlings as possible but then, strangely, she began to feel remorse over killing them.

When the vision ended, the woman revealed that her greatest fear was not spiders, but rather having children. Her parents had been unkind to her, and she, in turn, feared being unkind to her own children. The woman came to this conclusion on her own, by virtue of Marcienne's transferal projection. Shortly thereafter, the woman became engaged to her long-time boyfriend, a man whom she loved sincerely but had kept at arm's length because of her then unknown and deep-rooted fear.

Jay personally testified that while he was in Marcienne's presence, everything turned off: The world with all its sights and sounds, his brain with its unending stream of consciousness, and then the entire universe; burning stars and planets all sizzled down, like a cosmic blackout. Jay was suspended in nothingness. For the first time in his life, he felt lifelessness. And when the transferal projection passed, he knew that it was death that scared him more than anything. But he no longer feared it because, "death was quite literally nothing, and nothing felt like nothing." I was still privately skeptical, but decided to go in with an open mind. I had nothing left to lose.

Marcienne lived in a characterless apartment on Wilcox Avenue in a pretty run-down area of Hollywood. It was a sparsely decorated one bedroom furnished with photos of her and her deceased husband. The photos were mostly from vacations, and judging by their generous smiles, the couple had been truly happy. In fact, Marcienne still seemed happy. She had long, straight brown hair, deep green eyes, and a perpetual, sunny smile. It was difficult to believe that such a simple, unassuming, and all-together agreeable person was capable of conjuring up such horrific specters. But Marcienne assured me she did no such thing, her visitors conjured up those specters themselves. She merely tapped into their emotional currents and interpreted their energy. As far as she was concerned, there was no rhyme or reason to it; she had mistakenly unearthed her special power, and imagined that if others explored themselves as deeply as she had, they too might find their own unique powers buried within.

The bedroom was even more Spartan than the living room. Marcienne sat in the corner on the floor and I sat on the bed next to a night stand that was host to a glass vase filled with sun flowers. Marcienne said that all I had to do was close my eyes and let my mind run free. She asked me not to steer my thoughts in any particular direction, to let them flow like a river, and to allow the sound of that river to block out the noises coming from the street outside; the humming engines, the honking, the chatter of the neighborhood bums.

My contrarian mind did exactly the opposite. I tuned into the sounds coming from outside. I didn't plug into my own thoughts until I heard two cars screeching away from near collision. It reminded me of a car accident I was in as a teenager. We were both drunk—Sam drove us home from a party. Donna Goldsmith's party. Sam hit the median. The car flipped. We were thrown eighty yards. I was seventeen years old. It took me two months to recover. During those two months I wrote my first novel. My first novel. At seventeen. I had never written anything other than a school essay before it. I hated school. Except for English. There was nothing holding me back. My compulsion to write was demonic. Fevered. It produced a science fiction book. *What the fuck was it called again? That's right, Dangerous Planet. Of course!* I was inspired to write it after catching a late-night TV showing of *Forbidden Planet,* the 1950s science fiction movie starring Leslie Nielsen. And Anne Francis. Anne Francis as Altaira. A hot little blonde running around in a futuristic mini-skirt. Perky tits. It was the first time I had masturbated since the accident. I did it in the hospital, even stained the sheets. Don't know if the nurse noticed when she changed them the next morning. I've been caught masturbating twice in my life, one of them was last week. Melissa came home in the middle of the day to change before a meeting; I was sitting at the computer, ostensibly writing my script, but was jerking off instead. Avoiding work. I'm always avoiding work. *What else is new?*

"What else is new?" I asked aloud. Surprised by my own voice, I covered my mouth with my hands. I suddenly felt very unsettled. Two questions loomed in my mind.

What had started me on that train of thought? And where was I?

I opened my eyes to find out.

It was the extra bedroom in my and Melissa's apartment, the one I used as my study. The window shades were closed and the room would have been pitch black if not for the numbing blue tint of the computer screen. The computer sat on a desk pushed up against the wall and in front of it was a leather swivel chair that was rocking back and forth. Its springs were squeaking loudly. I approached the chair, in spite of my growing trepidation of whatever was behind it.

As I got closer, the rocking became violent. The foundation of the chair shook. Screws, nuts, and bolts were falling out of place. The squeaking now sounded like pained, human squeals, and soon, within those squeals, I could make out a tiny voice calling for help. I spun the chair around and found a nightmare sitting before me.

It was another me. But the skin on his face was sliding off his bones. His eyeballs were expanding, like balloons inflating. And his right hand was savagely stroking his tattered, bleeding phallus. The squeaks were, in fact, pained squeals. My decomposing double was crying out in anguished horror.

Stroke by stroke, he shaved off more and more skin until eventually he was belligerently massaging a withering bone. When the bone was gone all that remained was a dark, gaping hole in his pelvis. The other me looked down at the hole with curiosity, and seconds later, a geyser of blood shot up, drenched his face, and poured out onto the floor with no sign of letting up.

It was then that I noticed a manuscript resting on the desk.

The stack looked to be about one hundred and fifty pages thick and my title and name were on the cover page. It was my completed screenplay. Inches away from me. It was so good I could taste it. I stepped toward it, my feet sloshing in the now ankle-high pool of blood, but I was stopped by the other me. He placed his skeletal hand on my chest and shook his head "no." I tried to run around him but he clasped my face with his bony hands and brought my mouth down to the hole in his pelvis. The fountain of blood shot through my throat with the overpowering force of a fire hose, pumping my body with enough blood to make me puke. I hit the floor face-first, landing in the pool of blood and vomit. The other me sidled up to my body, flipped me onto my back and fired still more blood into my mouth.

I was now completely submerged. The room had turned into a crimson sea. Resisting the urge to pass out, I opened my eyes to search for a solution. But I saw only two things. The other me, his face now completely skeletal, still heaving a cascade of blood into my mouth, and my screenplay, still resting on the desk, still unscathed. I wanted it. I wanted it more than anything I've ever wanted. I admitted that to myself while simultaneously admitting that I probably didn't have the strength or the will to retrieve it. I was too weak. Too overwhelmed. That's when I noticed a third thing that seemed to have appeared out of nowhere. Perched above me was a night stand host to a glass vase filled with sun flowers. It seemed out of place, but it also seemed familiar, like it was deja vu.

For the first time since becoming cognizant of this nightmare, a voice in my head suggested that all of this might not be real. But the physicality of the event, the blood, the drowning, the desire to possess my script—all of these things were telling me it was real and that I was on the verge of dying. I mustered whatever limited strength I had left, reached up to the night stand and grabbed the vase. I smashed it against the wall and used the remaining glass shard to stab the other me in his gaping pelvic hole. I got on my knees and swung the make-shift knife upwards, slicing into his abdomen.

At that point, I could have grabbed hold of the script but I chose to further disfigure the other me instead. I hacked away at myself until I was sure that the torn, bloody pulp I felt on my finger tips was that of a dead man.

I opened my eyes.

I saw Jay at the bedroom door, confused and pale. And then, I saw that there was no screenplay.

Standing in that tiny apartment, sweating and panting, shivering and crying, I stared down dumbly at the bits of Marcienne's flesh hanging off the glass shard in my hand, and as I heard police sirens in the distance, it was finally clear to me.

My deepest, darkest fear was success. And I had just done everything within my power to ensure that I would never achieve it.

Travis Baker wrote and directed the film Mischief Night, *featuring Malcolm McDowell (and at least one severed head). In crafting his feature debut, Baker utilized all the skills he honed while writing screenplays for producers like Eli Roth and Wes Craven. In 2011, he was a top-30 Finalist for the Nicholl Fellowship in Screenwriting, awarded by the Academy of Motion Picture Arts and Sciences. His writings as a film historian are routinely published with special edition Blu-ray and DVD releases for various studios, including the anniversary editions of* Easy Rider, Dr. Strangelove *and* The Terminator. *His first published short story appeared in—no joke—a defunct Jews for Jesus newsletter. This book contains his second.*

PYRE

Travis Baker

WALT AWOKE WITH A STARTLE and thought for a moment that Maura was sleeping next to him. He moved to place a hand on her fussy-but-lovely morning hair, and remembered that she was gone before his hand landed on the pillow.

Long gone.

He'd awoken suddenly, as if from a bad dream, but his sleep had for quite some time been dreamless. In fact, he awoke because of a harsh burning sensation at the back of his throat, and after realizing he was alone in bed, his mind again revisited that awful burning sensation. He pulled himself from bed and managed to ignore the hideous cracking in his knee joints as he faltered toward the bathroom—the arthritis was a bit trickier to disregard, but he'd trained himself to become quite the mental magician: Now you *feel* it, now you *don't*.

He cranked the sink up cold as it would go, topped off his rinsing mug, and gulped and gargled much as he could to alleviate the burn in his throat. The burning sensation remained, however; impervious to the icy remedy of the cold water. His throat didn't burn because he was thirsty, and he was unsettled, because he hadn't the foggiest idea as to why.

He showered and he thought of Maura. He brushed his dentures, put on his khaki shorts and white undershirt and made his way downstairs, thinking of Maura every inch of the way. When he stepped outside to fetch the morning paper, he found it strange that it hadn't been delivered. Surely no one had stolen it; it would have taken a truly dedicated paper thief to drive roughly two miles of unpaved, twisty canyon road just to steal his paper. Utterly nonsensical. Walt turned to the mountains when he caught a faint whiff of fumes. Dark smoke rose from beyond their slopes in thin, twirling wisps, as if exhaust from a stunt plane. He sighed softly.

His phone was ringing when he got back inside, but he knew who it was and he didn't pick up. Instead, he switched on the television set as the message machine received his daughter's voice. "Hi, dad. I know you're up and at 'em, and you can probably hear this. Have you gone outside yet? Have you turned on the TV?"

Walt cranked up the volume on the television, drowning out his daughter's faintly worried voice. It was a newscast. A woman who was too distractingly good looking to be a reporter reported from a rocky mountain road, firemen in yellow overalls rushing to and fro behind her like bustling worker bees. "...for the last several hours. A representative for the Los Angeles County Fire Department has told us that they are currently at zero containment and that the afternoon winds will determine—" Walt switched off the television set.

After breakfast he went back to work on his hands and knees, hammering and nailing planks of two-by-four redwood to the half-constructed backyard deck. Another six weeks, maybe eight, and he'd be finished. Maura had always wanted a deck overlooking the mountains, and he'd been so Goddamn stubborn about it, raving to her (quite wrongly) that it would cut into their land, and that buyers want *land*, not frills. If the buyers wanted a deck, then by God, they would go ahead and build one for *themselves*. Of course, the mistake in his logic had nothing to do with the needs of prospective homeowners, but instead it had everything to do with Maura's line of thought: She wanted the deck because she wanted the deck, and because this was their *home*, had been so for the last thirty years, and it would be the home that they would die in, buyers be damned. But Walt couldn't see it that way, never could, and so the deck remained entirely non-existent, at least until Maura had passed. How he wished she could see...

Pausing for a much needed rest, Walt poured himself some orange juice from a bottle that was as sweaty as he, and drank liberally. It tasted disgustingly sweet, and did little to remedy his burning throat, but then, whiskey wouldn't have helped much in that department either. And even if it would have, he was about as interested in drinking whiskey as he was in listening to Nancy News Reporter with the taut tits on the tube telling him how bad the fires were, he *knew* how bad the fires were; every year, sometimes twice a year, it was the same story. *Wildfire!* Like the end of days. Like the bomb had dropped. Like Christ climbed off his cross and came home to roost.

As he reluctantly hydrated himself, faint flurries floated through the air, snowing down on his deck, on his shoulders. Snow flurries were utterly unprecedented in August in Southern California, but ash flurries were all too common-place. Walt grimaced at the dark billows of smoke tainting the white clouds above. The winds were blowing to the east, which meant the winds were nudging the fires in his direction. Twice a year, same story.

A sharp honk brought Walt around front, where a police cruiser, complete with police officer, awaited.

"Walt Reynolds? I'm Deputy Mort Hogart, Sheriff's Department. We're making our rounds up here, you know the drill. Evacuation is voluntary right now, but the wind is really acting up, and you just never know. Five firefighters been injured already, and I'm not just talking smoke inhalation, I'm talking *scorched.* Yeah... could be one for the books. Anyhow, you might want to pack your necessaries."

Walt nodded. There wasn't much more to say.

Walt trudged through the cellar and painfully (how his old arms ached) pulled a plastic bin out from underneath some damp cardboard boxes. Inside were ten photo albums stacked in two piles, each album containing roughly half a decade of precious family memories. Walt opened the first album—the early years. Maura's headshots from the time she was a little girl up until she was twenty-five. She had been a cute kid, but as she grew older she grew more radiant, more magnificent. The day he met her was the day he knew he'd found his lass for life.

"Are you alright?" she came over and asked him. A rivulet of blood streamed from his forehead down into his eyes as he looked up at her. He was sitting with the set medic, trying not to focus on the needle and thread that was hastily stitching his skin back together. He couldn't have asked for a better distraction from the pain.

"Crashed through the glass, flipped twice, like the director wanted, landed on the airbag, though it would've been nice if the bastards installed the candy glass instead of leaving in the real stuff. Cut, print, moving on. Yeah, I'm alright, thank you kindly."

She smiled softly. "I'm glad," she said. "It was a really fine stunt." And with that, she turned to go.

"Hey, wait!" he called after her. She turned, and when her eyes fell upon him, he felt more pressure to perform than when the cameras were rolling and he had to prove himself to the world. "Are you the star of this movie?" he asked.

She blushed bright red and let out a hint of a giggle. "I've got five lines and they cut four of them."

"Really?" he asked, and then winced as the medic tugged

on his final stitch. She looked concerned, so he smiled to let her know he was just fine. Then he said the line that earned him her heart. "You sure look like a star to me."

There would be no more headshots because Maura wouldn't be acting anymore. They started their little life together very quickly, and with a little help from their folks, and two banks, they were able to buy their dream house in the hills.

Walt looked at the first page of each of the other albums, but no further. Their wedding, the birth of Jerry, the birth of Susan, the kids' teenage years, the grandchildren. A decade earlier, during another "one for the books," probably the closest call they'd ever had, Maura insisted they organize their photos into one concise and portable location, so that they could grab it and run should the need arise. Walt balked at the idea; they weren't *leaving* to go anywhere, anyhow. The only people who lost their homes were the people who *left* their homes, because the fire spread from embers. And embers could be dealt with on an individual basis. Nonetheless, Maura went ahead and organized without him knowing it. He was, of course, relieved to know that should they ever really and truly *have* to leave, they could take the bin and run, but he'd never let her know that. Stubborn old coot, he was, and he knew it, and so did she, and God bless her, she still managed to love him.

"But memories exist in places other than photos," he said out loud to her, although he, of course, knew she was dead and could not hear. "This house, for instance. Thirty years we've lived here... loved here... thirty years of memories." He left the cellar, leaving the bin of memories behind; this wildfire would be no different from any other: He would *not* evacuate.

The phone rang for the hundredth time since he woke, and at last he answered it. "Hello, dear. And how are you?"

Susan proceeded like a repressed floodgate at long last relieved. "My God, are you watching the news? It's gone national. I know you don't have a computer, but there's images plastered all over the web! We really need to get you a computer, it's got the most reliable, up-to-the-minute reports. Have you heard about the road closures? Practically all the canyon roads from Topanga to *Siam*; they're trying desperately to save all the horses, but I don't know, this one's hitting so hard so fast! Dad, why don't you answer my calls?"

"I'm talking to you now, aren't I?" he said. "Susan, listen, you don't need to worry, I'll be fine."

"Well are you *leaving*? Do you need help? They're saying six thousand acres have gone up already, a lot of houses... do you remember my old friend, Amy Gordon? Her parents' place is gone—they're in Florida, thank God—but their house is *gone*! God help their cat..."

"Susan, please," he said. "We've lived through any number of these scares, as you well know. Your mother and I will be fine right here. It's not bad up here."

There was a silence on the other end, and that's when Walt knew he had put his foot in it; Susan was *never* silent. "Dad... are you alright? You said you and mom."

"Did I? Well you know what I mean," he said.

Susan immediately responded, but her tone was uncharacteristic, she was very tentative, she was obviously very worried. "Dad... I'm... going to call Jerry."

"*Don't*," he warned. But her ensuing silence told him she meant business.

Walt stepped outside and saw that the sky was a deep dark smoldering orange, and that the mountains to the west were on fire; like they were mountains made of charcoal. Bulky aircrafts swarmed over the reaching flames, reminding him of a scene out of *King Kong*; they fought at the fire with flame retardant sand, but their effect was minimal, like trying to cool down a volcano with a cold glass of lemonade. He tasted the smoke in the back of his stinging throat, and swatted at the snowing ash like gnats.

It was time.

From out of the detached garage, Walt emerged with an armful of buckets: three return trips saw him repeat the same. He went back and forth several more times, each time coming back to the front walk, his base of operations, with more supplies. He had six lengths of green garden hose, two of which were coupled together with a brass fastener for greater length. He methodically fixed each hose to its own spigot at various points around the circumference of the house.

He revved up the generator in the work shed and turned on the water pump, which was connected through two hundred meters of underground tubing to a natural stream. It wasn't exactly legal (this being a county where water conservation drew more attention than public school education), but then, Walt wasn't always exactly law abiding. He then filled each tin bucket about halfway (if he filled them all the way, he'd never be able to handle them freely) and placed them at various posts between the hoses. He was not too embarrassed to fill up a bag of water balloons for quick fixes, nor did he see any shame in arming an arsenal of pump-action Super Soakers, which would come in handy if he had to retreat inside. This was war, and a soldier doesn't blush.

Walt sat on his half-completed deck and waited, and thought of Maura. He spoke to her, knowing she could not hear him. "Well there it goes, lass. Your beautiful woods, nestled away in the heart of your beautiful mountains. Ravaged. Where will you pick your berries and wild flowers now? Where will you watch your deer and sparrows? Your loving nature is at war. It wasn't arson that started this, it was a rainless cloud, some dry leaves, and an unconscionably hot sun. But this is our home. And I'll defend it. I'll stand by you, lass. I love you, and I know you know, but I need to say it, now more than ever. Now... just when you can't hear it."

Walt started to well up, but he stopped himself. If things

went down, which, by the look of the black, mid-afternoon sky, they would, then he'd need every last drop of water he had.

A sound of sirens. Walt knew he had to act quick.

He drove his Toyota into the garage and threw a black tarpaulin over it. He grabbed a hammer and nail from his toolbox out back, scrawled three words on the back of a manila envelope, and nailed it to the front door: GONE TO SHELTER.

Walt then went inside, into the living room, and watched his driveway from behind the shades, from behind his couch. The phone rang, Goddamn Susan, and he quickly went around, taking the phones off of the hook. By the time he returned to his post, two police cars were making their way up the drive.

Deputy Hogart stayed in his vehicle and honked his horn as another lawman stepped out of his cruiser and proceeded to the front door. He saw the note, pointed it out to Hogart, then pounded on the door for good measure. Satisfied that no one was still home, and not paying any mind to the bucket of water he nearly tripped over, he returned to his vehicle and headed off. Hogart lingered, watching the house, unaware that Walt was inside, watching him.

"Come take a look inside, you bastard... see what valuables the old man left behind, please, I'd like nothing *better*." Walt gripped the handle of his .45 and curled his lip. "This is my Goddamn house, and I'm not going anywhere." As if hearing him loud and clear, Hogart threw his car into gear, pulled a swift K-turn, and headed back down the way he came. Walt snickered. It was one of the few times in a long time that he legitimately felt like a man.

"You like that, Maura?" he boasted, though he knew she couldn't hear him.

Walt switched on the television, and thankfully, he noted, the reporter was a man this time out. "...receiving reports of sixty-five structures destroyed, including over fifty domiciles, and ten outbuildings—" and then the power fizzled and faded. Walt nodded; it was beginning.

He went to the fridge and poured himself some fruit

punch. The sweetness was sour against his burning throat and he hated it so.

He went out onto the half-completed deck, which was now buried in an inch of ash. The air was markedly hotter and darker; it wasn't difficult to breathe, but his lungs could tell it wasn't business as usual. The fierce flow of breeze wasn't making life much easier, but at least it felt good on his skin.

Not much later, Jerry pulled up in his Bronco. Walt wasn't especially surprised to see him, he knew Susan was going to place the call, and that for Susan, Jerry would come. He was, however, surprised to see that Jerry had grown out a mustache, perhaps to compensate for the fact that he was now totally bald on his crown. Didn't Jerry have a full mop up top last time he saw him? Had it been so long?

"Son," he said, and he gave Jerry a cordial nod.

"You know why I'm here?" Jerry said coldly, eyeing the buckets and hoses and, knowing his father, guessing their purpose.

"Your sister's a worrier."

"You think everyone's a worrier. You thought mom was a worrier when she wanted to take me to the doctor for my heart when I was *ten*."

"How was I supposed to know you had a murmur?" Walt asked. He still didn't understand what a murmur really even *was*, and why it meant everyone had to walk tippy-toed around Jerry like he was a porcelain china doll.

Jerry knew better than to try and answer. The last time they had a conversation that grew heated it ended with Walt taking a swing at Jerry and telling him he never wanted to see him again. That was eight years earlier. "Look. I'm not here to tell you what to do, what you do is your business, and I don't really care either way. Susan asked me to come, I'm here, and I'm planning on leaving real soon. You don't know the shit I had to go through just to *get* up here, alright?" Jerry paused, as if searching for what to say next. "I need a drink, can I have a drink?"

"No drinks here," said Walt. "Unless you'd like fruit punch. Or OJ."

Jerry was noticeably caught off-guard, and upon second thought, he found he didn't believe his father, figuring his father probably just wanted him gone, which was fine by Jerry. He turned back to his Bronco and opened the door, stopping only before sitting. "If she was here I'd take her with me, you know that, don't you?"

"If you're talking about your mother," said Walt, "I'd say you're wrong. I'd say she'd stay right here, with me."

Jerry smiled and shook his head. "You know, you're probably right. She always stood by your side. Like a whipped dog. Except you know what she told Susan, that Susan later told me after mom died? She told Susan that the reason she liked going off into the wilderness everyday wasn't to pick flowers and watch the rabbits play. The reason she'd disappear was to escape from *you*. She always figured one day she'd just keep walking till she found whatever it was she was looking for. And that day... I guess she did."

Walt sighed. On the day he was referring to, Maura went off into the woods as she had everyday for the last twenty or so years, only this time she didn't come back. Several hours later, Walt frantically phoned the police, and with a hoarse, teary voice, told them she was missing. They never found her in entirety, but some weeks later an Eagle Scout troop came upon a lower jaw that was medically determined to be hers. Authorities suspected she got disoriented, lost, and eventually succumbed to the elements, or crossed paths with a bear or mountain lion. The forest scavengers had had their way with her, and aside from an occasional bone in an animal den, that would be all they'd ever find.

"Goodbye, Jerry," said Walt.

"Yeah," said Jerry, and he got back into his Bronco, threw it in reverse, and gunned it away, out of Walt's life, as he had years earlier.

The sky festered, blackened like a cancerous lung with poisonous smoke, and spewed the ash of six thousand acres and sixty-five structures like ticker-tape confetti, like he was on parade, and the whistling wind, and the crying sirens, and the growling flames were the scream of the crowd. Little orange cinders lit up the sky like a cityscape, and were soon finding their way onto his property. Walt got to work.

He grabbed up a hose, fired up the spigot, and let it rip. Earlier he'd fastened a special head to each of the hoses to maximize pressure, and the water came out in a powerful frenzy. Those cinders didn't have a chance. "That's right, you bastard."

The wind picked up and the floating embers danced through the air like dandelion tendrils toward the back of the house. Walt dropped the hose and walked quickly around back, grabbing up another hose and repeating the process. When one ember, larger than all the others, landed in a nearby tree, Walt increased hose pressure to the maximum and gave the tree a thorough dousing. He wasn't concerned with brush, he'd made sure to rake up loose debris as part of his daily routine, it was only a matter of protecting the trees—he knew that if one tree went, others would follow.

That in mind, Walt started to indiscriminately soak all the trees within the reach of the water, why not, it made sense. He dropped one hose, then went to another and followed suit. Then another. "See that, Maura? What'd I tell you?"

But by the time he again reached the front of the house, the roof of his garage had caught fire. "Miserable bastard," said Walt, grabbing two buckets by the bails and running them toward the garage. Around him, embers whizzed to and fro, like a sea of shooting stars, like a migration of muted, docile fireworks. A sudden and sharp pain shot up through Walt's right arm, causing it to spasm. He dropped one bucket and the water seeped into the dirt.

He scowled; even his own body was conspiring against him. "Sneaky bastard," he said, and then he proceeded to ignore the pain and heave the water upward at the burning roof. A direct hit. He managed a smile. The fire that fed off the shingles wilted, as if wincing in pain, and smoke sizzled from its wound, like the outpouring of its blood.

A red glow drew his attention: a tree had gone up. Amidst the madness, he'd forgotten to wet it down. Walt ran to it fast as his buckling legs would take him. He grabbed up the nearest hose and turned it on, twisting his wrist in the process. Walt emitted a sharp cry, then swallowed his pain as he aimed the hose at the tree and beat at that blaze with all his might.

The fire hissed and swatted at the hose, it seemed to groan and shriek as the water battered it back and forth, cheek to cheek. The flames dashed down the base of the tree, as if to escape, but the pounding water was there to meet its every step, somehow cooling it into oblivion. Out of breath and feeling woozy, Walt managed to save the tree.

A guttural chirping sounded from overhead, as if from a dinosaur-sized bird. Looking up, through the dusky haze, that's actually what Walt thought it was, until he realized it was a news helicopter. He raised his arms in triumph. "What now, huh? This is my home!" He turned away from the helicopter, back to the garage, which was now a bonfire, which was now lost. "Our home," he muttered to Maura, though Maura was dead.

Walt ran inside the garage, looking up at the burning ceiling. If the garage was on fire, but still standing, it would act like a trampoline, flames jumping through the air and landing on the roof of his house. The garage was no longer a part of his home—it was a part of the problem. He growled and threw the tarp off of the Toyota. He didn't remember if he had his keys, and was grateful to find, as he reached into his pockets, that he in fact *did*. He closed the garage door and started his engine.

"Not going to make it easy on you," he said as he threw the car into drive and smashed through the garage door. He slammed the brakes, screeching to a halt, and then kicked it into reverse, pedal to the metal, topping sixty when he smashed through the back wall of the garage, which he knew was fairly thin and, thus, breakable. His forehead slammed against the wheel, but there was too much happening at once to feel it, and Walt climbed out of the car, blood dripping into his eye.

As he clamored back to his command post as the garage collapsed on top of itself, mostly, he hoped, because of his ardent action. Now just an unorganized bonfire of timber, he could temper the garage's burning rage, preventing it from harming the house. He grabbed a bucket with his good arm, hobbled back over to the massive fire, and threw the water, bucket and all, into its center. The fire lapped it up hungrily, and Walt found himself irritated by its attitude. "Stubborn little shit..."

Next he knew, the work shed had caught, and the work shed, in addition to his pump, also housed a large propane tank. Walt hosed it as best as he could, but this particular fire was a fighting fire, and it absorbed his blows like a boxer, punching through the roof, powering into the shed, beating him by strength alone to take the shed when the whole thing exploded like a fireball, knocking Walt onto his back. The ember bit at him like mosquitoes. He futilely swatted at them, but they burned through his clothes, into his skin.

Walt struggled to his feet in time to see the western wall of his home ignite in an orange flash, saddening him profoundly. "No," he muttered, and he limped over to a hose and tried to turn it on. But the work shed had blown, and the pump along with it; there would be no more water. Walt shuffled over to his front door, head hung low in defeat. He scorched his hand on the doorknob, but he scarcely cared.

He staggered into his living room, which was now ablaze. Their curtains, their couch, their carpet, pictures of them and their children on the wall, in another life, in happier times. Did such times ever exist? He didn't know. He went to his water guns, but they had melted into a puddle of bubbling plastic pus. He went to his bucket of water balloons, but unsurprisingly the heat had caused them all to pop. He dumped the bucket out, irritating the fire, but there were now several fires, and they were becoming harder to see, the air was so dark.

"Maura," he said, and on his hands and knees he crawled

out back, to their partly constructed deck. "Maura, I'm here," he said, and he laid on the deck, resting his head on the very first plank he nailed in place just after her death. Maura always wanted a deck, but he stubbornly refused, for this reason or that, as he did so often, ignoring her wants and needs as much as he indulged in his own.

The air was so scorching hot he barely felt it. The smoke so thick he couldn't see for more than an inch, but of what he saw within that inch, he saw with perfect clarity. He grew more restful as the chaos of the world around him simplified, and the source of his true pain came into focus.

"Why did you want to leave me, Maura?" he asked, although he knew Maura wasn't there, because he knew Maura was dead. "You were the only one who understood me... even our own damn kids didn't, just you..." He stroked the plank of wood beneath his cheek tenderly, disregarding the splinters that ate into his palm. "Why did you have to try and leave?"

His memory took him back to before, to that morning, the morning Maura told him she had it, that she was going to leave. "Was it the deck?" he wanted to know; if it was the deck he'd consider building her one. Maura was full of spite that morning, she wasn't her usual self. It *wasn't* the deck, it *wasn't* the alcohol, it wasn't even the way he struck her on occasion, it wasn't *even* the cavalier attitude with which he disowned Jerry, their only son, it was *him, him,* and nothing but *him,* and *everything* about *him.* She was leaving him, and leaving him for good.

Walt was beside himself, he wasn't his normal self, it was early in the morning but he'd already taken to the bottle. He grabbed her by the arm, but only because he wanted to talk to her more, and she had turned away. She pushed his chest, and he pushed her back, but only to show her he wouldn't tolerate that. He didn't mean to do what he ended up doing... things just... escalated.

Walt remembered standing over her body, the fire poker in his trembling hand, the blood dripping in beads off of the tip onto her Oriental rug. Walt bellowed a scream so severe, so anguished, it ripped at his throat, it was like he had swallowed fire and the fire had caught in his throat. He could have killed himself for what he'd done, but he didn't. He felt he needed to redeem himself, to prove to Maura that he loved her so, if in fact, she didn't already know it, as she claimed at the end that she didn't. Hadn't he ever told her...? No, no he hadn't. No he hadn't.

Everyone who knew Maura knew of her meandering morning walks through the wild, which at her declining age were increasingly unadvisable. It wasn't so hard to believe that she could just... disappear. Walt took no pleasure in separating her lower jaw from her body with a crowbar, but he knew that if it was found in the woods all suspicions would be put to rest, and he knew of a trail where it would surely be found.

"I love you, Maura," he said, as the fire ate up the deck he'd worked to build in her honor, and revealed underneath the first plank a jawless rubble of bone, the remains of what were once his beautiful wife. He saw her face in the blaze as the blaze closed in all around him, moving in toward him, as if for a kiss. He spoke to the blaze, spoke to her glowing face. "And I'm sorry," he said softly as the fire stripped the flesh from his body, boiled his blood, and vaporized his organs, reducing him to a rubble of bone.

And he meant it.

Sean Yopchick is a writer, freelance editor and Production Assistant. He has written and directed two short films, Fear and Control *and* The Overman, *and has worked on many Hollywood films including* Shutter Island, Inception *and* Money Ball. *When he's not finding ways to cover a bad check or diverting his landlord's attention from the 1ˢᵗ of the month, he enjoys riding his bike. He lives in Los Angeles and is originally from Wakefield, Massachusetts.*

APARTMENT 13

Sean Yopchick

NEON LIGHTS WRAPPED IN liquid darkness. Alleyways sprayed with mystery. Shadows dance in apartment windows. GIRLS! GIRLS! GIRLS! Angelo stumbles through the Sunday night revelers on Sunset Boulevard. Each step is cautious and dedicated. He drags a cigarette from his coat pocket. The words from a bar patron echo in his head: *Sometimes you just need to be honest with yourself... I saw the writing on the wall.* He needs to get home. It's nine pm and he has to work tomorrow. He's the assistant to a big name actor and she needs to be in early for makeup. And it's an hour drive to set.

He turns the key and opens up into the dark abyss of a studio apartment. He turns on a switch and stale light sprays out and over old furniture and scattered headshots. He puts his keys down. He makes his way to the refrigerator. He pulls out a beer and opens it. He takes off his coat and readies for a shower.

In the shower he leans against the mildewed tile. He looks to the clear liquid that spirals down into the drain. The bathroom is fogged by the heat of the water and Angelo takes a moment to fill the deep hollow of his stomach with a daydream: He sits at a desk and answers questions in an interview about his new movie and how much he liked his costars; he's at a party filled with A-listers and he's the most popular one and he raises a glass and laughs; a theatre echoes with applause as he walks down a narrow aisle and he reaches a podium and raises an award and thanks all those who have helped him along the way.

After the shower he makes sure the alarm is set: Four a.m. He sits on his bed. His eyes are blood shot red. He drags his fingers through his wet hair. He takes a deep breath and looks out the window. He sees a billboard: A young girl with dark wet eyes and red lipstick leans seductively on her knees and stares into his room. He looks back down to an aging rug and hopes that one day he will leave this tiny apartment behind. He gets up, takes one more look toward the empty street and shuts the blinds.

He turns on a small fan and shuts off the light. He stares into the swirling midnight that envelops his room. He needs to be on set in just a few hours and the clock keeps moving forward. He turns to his side. His body is filled with alcohol and he feels it swimming in his head. He turns to the other side and then the thoughts come again. The thoughts that only creep in at this hour when the body begs for sleep but the mind is turning and restless and there's nothing left to do but marinate in the black mysteries of the insides.

What's in a room? What lingers there? Angelo can feel it sometimes when he gets anxious like this and can't go to sleep. The history and tiny moments that breathe into the darkness and create stinging sensations that always linger and sometimes penetrate the overall mood and feeling of the morning hours. He closes his eyes again and a network of worries slide into his stomach. *I saw the writing on the wall.* The whirling character of the fan begins to melt into distorted, echoing rhythms. He drifts into sleep.

We want you to join us. Angelo stirs in his bed. The sheets are hot and the blinds are open. He hears the voice again. *We want you to join us, Angelo.*

Angelo gets out of his bed. He pulls the blinds back and peers through the stained glass of his window and sees the billboard. Something is different. Instead of the girl it seems to be a hundred people with blank exhausted expressions staring into his apartment. Angelo closes the blinds. He stands at the window for a moment. Thoughts race through his head as he tries to recognize the sensations of dream. Is it a dream? Then he hears something coming from the bathroom. He looks to the moonlight splashing out over the kitchen. He walks toward it.

I lived here. All of us lived here. And we want you to join us.

He puts his hand against the cheap wood of the bathroom doorframe and peers in. There is something moving in the bathtub. Angelo is frozen there. His mouth trembles with terror. His eyes swell with panic. He slowly raises his hand and turns on the light. No one is there but the bathtub is full of water. He moves toward it. He sticks his hand in and feels the warm liquid against his skin. The water ripples as he removes the plug. He looks and sees the reflection of a young girl. Her brunette hair covers her face as her body molds into waves. He stares into the wall not wanting to look back. He forces his head around. Nothing. The water rushes and spirals into the pipe.

Angelo stirs in the night as footsteps against concrete and couples in arguments and drunkards singing and angry beggars yelling at ghosts infiltrate the visions that come to him in his anxious sleep. He wakes up. He looks at the clock. It's only one a.m. He readjusts and looks toward the window. The blinds are closed. It's still dark out. He rolls over on his back and drags his hands over his forehead. He did not over sleep. He still has three and a half hours to rest. His body is heavy and his mind still knee deep in the remnants of dream. He looks to his clock and lets the red light from the numbers splash over his face.

He remembers his landlord used to talk about a girl who lived here before him. "She was always really busy." He said. "I'd always hear her talking to her parents and she would tell them how many auditions she'd been on and sometimes she was really excited and other times she was disappointed. She used to sing in her house in the afternoons when she wasn't working. I very much enjoyed it. Then the last three weeks she just looked sad. Like she was hopeless. I guess it was all the rejection. And then something happened to her."

Angelo lets the words echo in his head. The fear grows in his stomach. Another failed story in the desert. He can feel it sometimes too even though he tries to push the thoughts away: That all his anxious pursuits are tied up in the crushing waves of failure. And it's around this time when the city is wrapped in slumber and the noises of the house creep into his mind that he feels alone and helpless. He closes his eyes. He forces himself to sleep.

Footsteps echo in the hallway. Angelo wakes up in a panic. He checks the clock. It's 3 a.m. He hears something but he cannot make out what it is. And finally he recognizes it: The soft smooth escalation of a young woman's voice. He looks over and light spills out from the open crack in the bathroom doorway. He sees something: The outline of someone in the darkness. It disappears into the ether and he calms himself by thinking that his mind is just playing tricks on him. But then he hears something crash in the sink. He stays frozen. He grabs a fistful of sheets. He waits to see if he hears anything again. Nothing. He gets up. He moves toward the bathroom door. He peers inside and sees the long flowing brunette hair of a young girl. He looks into the mirror. He sees her eyes: Vicious, tortured.

He hears her whisper: *All I wanted to do in the whole world was what I loved... but then I had to join them and so do you. Sometimes you have to be honest with yourself... I saw the writing on the wall.*

He puts his hand through the thick darkness and opens the door slowly. He hears the movement of someone in the bathtub. He looks inside. He sees her. Blood trickles down the bathtub from her arm. The water—red—spills out onto the cold bathroom tile. Her head leans back and her lifeless eyes stare into the ceiling. Angelo cautiously moves toward the tub as his heart bangs against his chest and his breathing becomes rough and stifled. He leans over. He looks to the face in horror. It's not the girl... It is him. His eyes like dark voids and his skin pale and bloodless. He retreats and stumbles back toward the door. He tries to scream but it comes out as hollow breath. His teeth clenched, eyes wide, chest full of panic.

The ALARM! The ALARM! The ALARM! Angelo shuts it off. He gets up quickly. He puts on whatever isn't dirty and in a foggy haze he grabs his coat and cigarettes and makes his way toward the door.

He turns the knob but it's locked. He reaches for the dead bolt and turns it. He opens the door. He walks through the doorway and fishes for his car keys. He pulls them out of his jacket pocket and looks up. He's still in his room. He looks around. The stale light splashes over the furniture. He opens the door again. He walks through the door. He closes it behind himself and searches for the keyhole to lock it. He turns. He's in his room again. This time at the edge of the room by the closet. The front door seems a mile away.

He runs toward the front door. Tries to open it. He can't. It's locked. With sweat pouring down his forehead he pulls at the knob in frustration. He lets out a primal grunt as he smashes his foot into the door. He presses his hands against the cold wood of the frame and closes his eyes hoping it is just the last stage of this crazy dream. He opens them up again. He sees the aging rug. He looks to the window. He opens the blinds. There's no window. It is just a black wall made of concrete.

There's no escape now.

Angelo turns slowly. He sees the people who were on the billboard. They stand behind the girl from the bathroom. Their faces are all distorted and unrecognizable. The girl stands, hair in her face and water slides over her body and onto the floor. She starts to approach and the others follow her. Angelo turns and tries the knob again. It won't budge. He turns back. The people over take him. He slides down and onto the floor. He looks up to them as they mob him. He puts his hands up and screams. The girl bends down and brushes the hair from her face. Angelo looks into it. But it's not a face it is the images of his daydream: At the party, on the talk show; walking up the aisle and to the podium to accept the award and his face is distorted just like the others in the room.

We're so glad you decided to join us.

The sun is out. It splashes over the door and the number 13. The landlord knocks. No one answers. He turns the knob. The door opens up and the landlord steps into the apartment.

"Hello?" He says as he moves toward the bathroom. He peers in. "Oh my God."

He looks to the bathtub, the floor littered with dried blood, and Angelo, with cuts in his wrists, lies in the tub with his lifeless eyes staring into the ceiling.

Knifepoint Writer/Producer/Director Jed Strahm is not nearly as sick a person as you would expect from his choice of entertainment. He ventured to Hollywood from Oklahoma by way of Austin, Texas, where he weaned his young movie-loving self at the early South by Southwest film festival. He now spends countless hours absorbing horror films from all corners of the world, further twisting his worldview, wrapping it up in tissue paper and blood-red ribbons. Jed's co-writer for this story Ray G. Ing has written a number of Hollywood horror films under a different name, and has also done a few uncredited script rewrites—which is just the way the ultra-reclusive writer likes it.

I'D LIKE TO THANK...

Jed Strahm & Ray G. Ing

THE DOORBELL BUZZED again and again, finally dragging Fiona from her drug-induced slumber. Catatonia was actually a better word for her sleep these days; the older she got, the harder it was to nod off, so she gobbled pills by the handful. And none of the new-fangled pills like Ambien or Lunestra; she didn't trust them and their slick ad campaigns. Nothing but old school downers prescribed to her in bulk by Doctor Havilland graced the dreams of the one time Queen of the Silver Screen.

"Nadia," She growled to her housekeeper. "Answer the fucking door." Nadia didn't answer.

Fiona moaned as she sat up and the late morning sunlight hit her eyes. Louder this time, in case the worthless woman was lounging in the kitchen or somewhere else instead of staying in earshot as she had been told a hundred times: "Goddamnit, Nadia! If you don't get the door, I'll—"

And then she remembered; Nadia had quit yesterday.

In Fiona's version of the story, she had fired the latest in a string of housekeepers, each more lazy and useless than the last. But then reality peeked through her drug addled haze a bit, giving her a ragged glimpse of the woman packing her bags and cursing in Spanish as she stomped down the driveway to her beat up Toyota. Fiona's hysterical screams echoing across the lawn had actually made the neighbors call the police; they thought someone was being murdered. Again. But no, it was just Fiona in another one of her frequent rages, accusing yet another worker of stealing one of her precious furs.

Fiona had patiently explained to the Beverly Hills police officer that she had simply told the worthless immigrant woman to get off her property and never return. And she *had* to scream, as that the only way the woman could understand English. They were *all* that way, these lazy maids. They only understood you if you screamed. The Officers left without making a report, but warned her to do her yelling in the house next time and not bother the neighbors. Fiona thanked them for their concern, but deep inside she had nothing for disdain for them. The police were *little people*, like all servants, and she loathed being near them. But sometimes one was forced to put up with such creatures, and if nothing else, forty years of professional acting had taught her how to put on a fake smile.

The doorbell rang again, dragging her out of her sleepy reverie.

"Fine. I'll get it myself," she muttered to the walls and pulled on a robe. It was pure silk, with soft mink fur on the cuffs and collar, made by a top European designer and bought years ago on a festival trip to the Med. But the now faded colors and worn spots on the elbows echoed the holes in her career.

Fiona actually didn't care that her last acting job had been over three years ago; she had enough money stashed away thanks to smart investing and four epic divorces lorded over by the nastiest lawyer in town. Miles had extracted certain favors from her each time in addition to his obscene hourly legal fees, but it was worth it to watch him squeeze her exes until they cried. No, there would always be money, and another job if she really wanted to do what it took to get it; producers and studio executives, like lawyers and ex-husbands, could always be had one way or another.

But those things didn't matter to her anymore. All that mattered was the phone call she had gotten two months ago. The call she had waited for all her life, and the one she had obsessively campaigned with all her trademark drive to get. The head of the Silver Screen Academy told her she would finally be recognized by the esteemed organization, that a Lifetime Achievement Award would be presented to her on stage at the awards show this year. Tomorrow night, as a matter of fact. It was the crowning achievement in a stellar career, he told her, but of course she knew that already.

She didn't bother raging at him about the dozens of times she had been passed by for the Best Actress award. Her peers were obviously idiots not to recognize her talent, and though they all publicly lamented her losses, she knew that privately they were all consumed with jealously over her talent and voted for others to spite her. But the Lifetime Award was hers, awarded by the Governors themselves, and no popular vote from no-talent cowardly upstart bitches could take it away. All she had to do was put on her dress, walk down the red carpet and onto the stage and billions of viewers would finally realize that she was, indeed, the greatest actress of hers or any generation.

She reached for the front door handle and yanked the hand polished teak panel open. Sunlight slashed in, and Fiona winced before seeing a delivery man standing on the porch. He had a large box under his arm and held out a signature pad.

"Delivery for Ms. Danforth," he said. She noted his generic delivery outfit, gloves, sunglasses, and hat. Like most servants, she would forget him the moment be left. And she pointedly ignored the signature sheet.

"How did you get inside the gate?" She asked him. "You're supposed to ring from the driveway."

"I'm sorry, M'am. But it was already open. And Dominique said to make sure you got it personally."

She caught her breath at the name. He had come through.

Dominique was the most celebrated clothing designer on Rodeo Drive, a man with such exclusive clientele that even the elite celebrities had to make reservations six months in advance just to see him, let alone get him to design their clothes. And his work with fur was legendary. So he was the first call Fiona had made after she hung up with the academy, and she had convinced him to do her dress for the award show. Convinced was a mild word; when Fiona wanted something, she got it, if not from force of will or choice of words then through her legendary unrelenting nastiness. Most people just gave up the moment she called them rather than try to fight back. Dominique was one of them. He even offered the dress for free if he didn't have to personally do the fitting. Fiona agreed, knowing she could take in her own dress far better than any underling, fancy name or not.

And the dress was here, in less than two months. She still had it.

"Don't just stand there, give it to me," She snapped.

The delivery man pushed the signature sheet back at her. "I'll need you to sign here, please," he said. His voice was oddly flat, nearly emotionless. She was used to people gushing all over her in one way or another, squeals of delight at meeting her, then angry curses when she refused to put her autograph on their silly little trinkets or papers.

"I don't give autographs," she snarled, wanting to grab the box from his hands and rip it open to see the dress inside. "Don't you know who I am?"

"I don't care about your autograph, Ms. Danforth. I just need your *signature* to show that I delivered the box."

He pushed the pad further towards her, and the box as well. Fiona's mouth actually started watering when she saw Dominique's gold-embossed logo on the top. That did it; she snatched the pad from the driver and angrily pulled the pen free from its holder.

"Fine. I'll sign your sheet. But I'll have you know, if this winds up for sale on the internet or somewhere, I'll have more than your job. Do you understand me?"

"Perfectly," he said as she scribbled her name.

She started to hand the pad back, but saw he couldn't take it as he now had something else in his hand. It was a palm-sized black box with two metal prongs at the end. As she stared at it, trying to figure out what it was, the delivery man pushed a button and electricity arced between the prongs.

"What do you think you are—" She started, then the man jabbed the stun gun at her chest and her world exploded with pain and fire.

And for the first time in years, Fiona didn't need a pill or drink to fall asleep.

* * *

Fiona woke up hours later, mouth and head full of cotton. At first she thought she was still in bed, but then realized she wasn't laying down, but rather sleeping propped against a wall. She blinked her eyes and forced them to focus, but what she saw made no sense.

She was in a cage.

Not a large cage like at the zoo, but smaller, not tall enough to stand up in or move around much. The kind some-one might put a large dog in. It was hand-made, with thick bars, but welded with great care and skill. Not that Fiona Danforth would notice such details, even if she was not locked inside it and her brain had not rejected its very existence.

Still in shock, she looked to the room beyond. Other cages lined the wall, and just opposite her was one that was covered with a dark cloth. There were no windows, making it feel like a basement to her, though she knew few houses in Southern California had them. A single metal door was to the right of the cage. She tried to stand up, and bumped her head on the cage's low ceiling.

"Goddamnit! Get me out of here!"

There was no answer. She tried again, louder this time,

turning her voice to the closed door. "Do you hear me!? I demand you open this cage and let me out."

There was still no answer. In a fit of rage, Fiona grabbed the bars and began shaking them, while screaming incomprehensibly at the top of her lungs. It was a display of pure, raw rage and frustration, channeling a spoiled infant demanding a toy, or a trapped animal desperately trying to claw its way out of captivity. The high-pitched wail and rattling lasted for close to a minute, then stopped when the door finally opened.

Fiona glared at the delivery man when he walked in, and she quickly remembered he was not a delivery man at all. That had been a ruse to kidnap her. He was dressed in dark clothes now, no disguise, just a man in a basement with a kidnapped movie star in a cage. She wasn't quite sure what label to put on him now.

He looked down at her, face as impassive as ever. He studied her as a scientist would study a bug. Even his voice was clinical, detached. "You're awake. Good."

"There is nothing good about this situation at all. Now, I don't know who you are, or what this is all about, but I demand that you open the door and let me out of this *fucking CAGE*!" She shrieked.

"I'll let you out," he said, but made no move towards her.

"Today!" She demanded.

He pulled a ring of keys out of his pocket and spun them nonchalantly on a finger. "I'll let you out when you make the right choice. It all depends on you."

"What in God's name are you talking about?"

The man eyed her for a moment, then sighed as he began what sounded like a long-prepared speech. "All these years you chose to maim and kill the innocents, you could have stopped. But you didn't. You chose to revel in their pain. And even when you were reminded of the senseless slaughter you helped propagate, you still chose to clothe yourself in the skins of the helpless. You never stopped to think about the consequence of your actions. Now you *have* to think about them."

She stared at him blankly for a long moment, the confusing words sinking into her still-addled brain, then slowly realization dawned in Fiona's mind. She remembered who he was, or rather, *what* he was. She had a label for him now, a category to put him, a lever she could use to pick him apart and bend him to her will like all the others. Sneering with disdain, she growled at him. "You're one of those animal rights activists, aren't you? The self-righteous fur police."

"I'm an animal activist, yes. But you might be being overly dramatic."

"Hardly. You somehow think you have the right to kidnap a human being and put her in a cage just to make a point about killing some brainless rodents. You don't think that makes you self-righteous?"

"This isn't about me. It's about helpless, feeling creatures. Animals have the right to not be skinned alive for human pleasure."

She snorted at his comment. "I supposed it was you that threw the bucket of blood on me at the premier four years ago."

"I was there."

"I'll have you know you ruined a perfectly good mink stole," she smiled.

For the first time, a hint of emotion crept onto the man's face. Anger. "You shouldn't taunt me, you know."

"Why, what are you going to do, kill me? The police will hunt you down like the mad dog you are. I'm sure they have a dragnet out already, turning the city upside down looking for me."

"No one even knows you're gone. And no one cares."

"Of course they do. People will be asking about me."

"Who? The maid you fired yesterday? The ones you fired before that? Your ex-husbands? Hell, your agent hasn't even talked to you for over a year, and you *make him money.*"

"My friends will notice."

"What friends, Fiona? The entire world hates your guts. Don't tell me you didn't think playing the selfish bitch your whole life would drive people away?"

She sobered a little at this. Desperation was sinking in. He wasn't bending to her will like she had planned. "There's Freddy," she said meekly.

"Ah yes, little Freddy. Your worthless son from husband number two. The trust fund brat. When he's not on safari in Africa killing endangered animals for *sport*, he's sitting at the coffee shop on top of Beverly Glen bothering everyone with his babble about being a producer while other people are trying to take meetings or get some work done or just have a cup of coffee. When was the last time he called you? Or when you called him?"

"He... we..." She trailed off as she remembered that she hadn't talked to her son in over two years. And that was when he had called asking for more money. Needless to say, the conversation had not gone well. Still, he was her son, and she *tried* to love him in her own way, but the boy always made it so *hard*. She chuckled bitterly to herself; he was his mother's son, in spades.

The man read her mind. "You reap what you sow, isn't that the saying?"

Fiona didn't have the energy for a comeback. She just looked at the floor in silent contemplation. After a long while, she looked back up at her captor. "Let's get this over with. What do you want from me? A public admission I was wrong to wear fur? Some sick photo gallery?"

He shook his head. "Like I said before, you have a choice to make."

"I don't see much of a choice from in here."

"You will. You see, we are thinking, rational beings. Everything we do in life past a certain, infantile stage is a choice. Some choices are easy and don't even seem like choices at all, like to eat when you are hungry. Others choices are obvious and hard. Do I take the job in Miami, and leave my family and friends behind? Do I date this person for money, or that one for love? Sometimes the choices are extreme; a man being tortured for information may know that he is likely going to die whether he gives up the information or not, but he has the choice to die quickly and painlessly, or slow and hard."

Fiona let all this sink in for a long moment. "So you are going to kill me."

"If you die today, it will be your decision, not mine."

She shook with helpless rage. "Then tell me what the fucking choice is so I can make it!"

The man turned his back on her and walked to the cage opposite Fiona's. He grabbed the tarp covering it and pulled it off with a flourish. She gasped in surprise when she saw what was revealed.

Freddy sat in a cage just like hers. But he was tied up and gagged, unable to make a move or a sound. He had been there the whole time, listening in, unable to let her know he was there. His tear-stained eyes found hers, begging, pleading with all his might for her to help him. But for the first time in her life, Fiona wasn't sure she could even help herself. She looked back to the man.

"You are insane."

"Again, this isn't about me. It's about you. You are in a unique position right now. Most of the choices that cloud your life have been stripped away. You have only one choice left to make."

"Fine. I'll play your game. What is my choice?"

The man smiled again and pulled out a gleaming skinning knife. "How bad do you want your award?"

* * *

The limousine moved slowly. Another ant in the steady march along the bumper-to-bumper, motorcade parade of lavishly priced, mostly rented vehicles creeping through bottlenecked traffic en route to the red carpet, fame, and glory. It pulled up to the curb two blocks away from the designated drop off spot, so at first none of the photographers or legion of fans noticed. A non-descript man in a suit got out of the front, went to the rear door, and helped his celebrity passenger out. He pointed her in the direction of the red carpet and klieg lights up the street, and Fiona staggered off like a moth to a flame.

By the time people started noticing her, the limo was long gone. But no one at the pre-show ceremony cared about that once she stepped into the lights.

The TV Host was startled for a moment when he saw her; the order of arrival down the red carpet was carefully choreographed. But he quickly recovered like the pro he was and smiled at the cameras.

"And here we have living legend Fiona Danforth, star of over 100 films and a link to Hollywood's golden age."

The Host stepped towards her with his microphone, but hesitated when he got a good look at her. Fiona looked drunk, or on drugs, face slack with an odd smile, and she stumbled up the carpet, barely able to stand up. He switched off the mic.

"Ms. Danforth, are you all right?" he whispered to her.

She smiled crookedly, eyes lighting up. "Of course, my dear. This is the greatest night of my life. Whatever could be wrong?"

The Host shrugged and flipped the mic back on, and it was only then that he noticed her dress. It was an off the rack number, and that in itself was odd given the woman wearing it and the important occasion. But what really caught his eye was the red splatters down the front, on both sides, obviously dripping from the ragged ends of the shawl draped around her neck. He thought it was some sort of leather at first, then he realized with growing horror that is was uncured skin of some sort of animal. And the ends were split into five sections that looked like... fingers.

Human fingers.

The Host looked up into Fiona's eyes, and realized suddenly that she wasn't drunk or high; she was stark, raving insane.

"What... what's going on here?" He asked, backing away in shock. Someone in the crowd shrieked. Hundreds of flashbulbs popped and a dozen TV cameras zoomed in to the unfolding live drama, broadcasting the gruesome image to millions of people.

Fiona waved the bloody end of the shawl around like it was a priceless fur as she rambled on. "Why, I made a choice, of course. The man was right—everything is a choice. And poor Freddy thought he was more important than mommy getting her award. But he was wrong. They were all wrong. Nothing is more important than this..."

And as the Host backed away and the photographers rushed forward, she smiled crookedly at the main camera.

"...Nothing."

Paul J. Salamoff has found success as a Writer, Producer, Film Executive, Comic Book Creator, Author, and originally as a movie Special F/X Make-Up Artist. Born in Natick, MA, he was raised on a healthy diet of sci-fi and horror from the age of five and has been obsessed with it ever since. His Film & TV writing credits include The Dead Hate The Living *(co-written with Dave Parker),* The St. Francisville Experiment *and* Alien Siege *for the Syfy channel. He has written the screenplay* Sinbad: Rogue of Mars *for Morningside Entertainment. He is also the author of the novel* The Silent Planet, *the non-fiction books* ON THE SET: The Hidden Rules of Movie Making Etiquette *and* The Complete DVD Book, *and the writer of the acclaimed graphic novels* Discord, Logan's Run: Last Day, *and* Logan's Run: Aftermath.

BAD FIX

Paul J. Salamoff

IT WAS LATE as the Lincoln Navigator pulled up to the curb outside Club Pandemic. Dylan, Anna, Jared, and Veronica slinked out into the cool Los Angeles night, and Dylan tossed the keys to the valet. The air was crisp and bit into Veronica's bare legs, legs that were barely covered by her miniskirt. It might not have been the most practical attire for a January night on the Sunset Strip, but a flash of the flesh or the pink was sometimes helpful for getting through the congested lines outside the clubs.

That had been necessary earlier in the evening when the hipster quartet had bounced from club to club. But now it didn't matter; Dylan had somehow scored four golden tickets to Pandemic—the hottest, and most exclusive club in town. The tickets promised instant access and drinks on the house, VIP treatment all the way.

"Another present from Daddy?" Anna sneered at Dylan.

Dylan's Father was a wealthy man who dabbled in politics. Not of the "running for office" type, but more like the "man behind the man pulling the strings" type. Special interests. Favors back and forth. VIP Tickets to a hot new club? Just one of many perks. And Dylan lived for, and *on* the favors bestowed by Daddy. But apparently not this time.

He sneered right back. "I've got my own sources, you know. I don't need him for everything."

All three of his friends shot him sarcastic looks that screamed "yeah, right."

"I got them from a guy I know," Dylan blustered. They knew he was notorious for dealing weed to a great many big wigs in the Hollywood scene, the type of people who could give a rat's ass about an all expense paid night at Club Pandemic provided that their chronic was high quality and delivered on time. But they were also the kind of people that, frankly, you couldn't trust further than the last drag on the bong. "He says they're for people just like us."

"Assholes?" Jared ventured.

"Not. VIP's. Very. Important. People."

"That's us." Said Jared. "Or me, anyway. You guys are nothing but posers."

Anna cringed at this, but knew he was right. Jared was the quintessential himbo who fancied himself an actor. He took any role offered to him, from unwatchable direct-to-DVD crap to Skin-e-Max spank films, though the only role he was actually suitable for was being the obligatory train-wreck on some sub-par cable reality show called *Dudeswap*. His limited talents even kept him from playing himself convincingly. The show itself was the umpteenth knock-off of who knows how many other low-rent shows clogging up the lesser channels with their bastardization of cinema verité. "Dudeswap" was destined for failure from its first episode, which premiered a month ago to absolute zero fanfare and across the board scathing reviews. So of course, the show had taken off like a rocket, number one in its time slot and making what-passed-for-stars-these-days out of the whole cast, Jared included.

Life, Anna thought, just wasn't worth the effort sometimes. Like most pretty young things in LA, she had stars in her eyes, and was the first to admit it. But unlike Jared and his ilk, she wanted her name up on the marquee but wanted to *earn* it. Fortunately for her she had a modicum of talent to back her dreams up. It also certainly didn't hurt that she had a nice rack and an equally fine rear end to more than stack the deck in her favor. But her aspirations went beyond playing the requisite "hot girl". She promised herself that every role she took would be quality. Something to be proud of, not just gutter trash films to pad out her up to now paltry IMDB page. She had her standards and for now she was pleased with herself to live by her own code.

So moments like this, playing second, third, or even fourth banana to pseudo-celebrities grated on her. But she was nothing if not a good friend; if Veronica wanted to hang out with losers like Dylan and Jared, the least she could do was go along for the ride and make sure the boys kept their hands where they were supposed to be; in their wallets.

Dylan rolled his eyes as Veronica snuggled close to him. "I heard they have some new designer drug inside, supposed to really blow your mind," she said.

"Yeah. It's called 'Feather' or something." Dylan said, staring down her low-cut top and catching a full view of her bulging fake breasts. "Supposed to fuck you up... and down. It's like X on Acid."

"That doesn't make any sense," said Anna, but everyone ignored her.

"Feather. I like the sound of that. I want some." Veronica kissed him quickly on the mouth, tongue darting between his lips. While he was distracted, she snatched one of the tickets out of his hand and slithered towards the club's door with a seductive smile.

"Me too!" Jared puckered his lips for a kiss too, and when Dylan pulled back in disgust, he snatched a second ticket and followed to Veronica to the entrance.

Dylan was left alone on the sidewalk with Anna. "Well?

You coming in, or do you want to stand out here and pout all night?"

She looked at the tickets and said, "I'm not sure I trust your sources. Those might be fake."

"Cut the bullshit. You don't trust *me*."

Anna's face flushed red. He smiled as she fumbled for words to explain herself when they both knew there weren't any. She *didn't* trust him, not with the way he treated Veronica. It wasn't that he was misogynistic; he treated her well, but it was as if he wasn't interested in her as a person, just a living-breathing prop to hang on his arm to prove he was a man. There's nothing new to that story, plenty of women have played that role over the years and Veronica seemed fine with it. Actually, she loved it, but it rubbed Anna the wrong way.

"Look, Dylan..." She started, but be cut her off.

"Whatever. We'll find out in a minute anyway. If the tickets are fake, I look like shit and you go home happy. If they're real, we get into the party of a lifetime. Win win, I'd say. Now come on. The party is inside, whether you like it or not." He waved the remaining golden tickets at her in a teasing motion, then spun around and walked towards the door.

Anna hesitated for a moment, looked around and saw the Valet was long gone and the street was jammed with strangers, then sighed and followed.

She caught up to them at the Door. She saw Jared preening for a low rent paparazzi wanna-be (TMZ must have had the night off or something) and also saw Veronica back in her usual place, in front of Jared and with one of his domineering hands on her shoulder marking his territory for all to see.

The four of them stepped right up to the bouncer, brushing past the long line of miscreants that waited impatiently for access. Dylan whipped out the tickets before the bouncer had the chance to decline them entrance. As the large man inspected them for authenticity, Dylan turned slightly to two girls at the front of the line. He grinned coyly as he looked them up and down. They were just his type. Long legs. Large breasts straining under their tight clothes. Breathing.

The bouncer nodded to verify the tickets, then let the privileged four past the velvet rope. Dylan lingered behind momentarily; slipping two twenties into the bouncer's hand, he gestured towards the girls leading the line. "I think there's room for two more." He said.

With barely a reaction, the bouncer disengaged the velvet rope on the other line and let the girls through. They smiled lasciviously at Dylan as he rejoined his party. Veronica was looking the other way and didn't see a thing. Dylan smiled; the night was still young and there was plenty of time for a proper thank you from the girls later.

The interior of the club was luxurious. It was a convert of a hotel that had known its heyday in the 40's as a hotspot for Hollywood types but had subsequently fallen into disuse and disrepair over the last few decades. That was until it was resurrected from the dead less than a year ago by the reclusive artist "Stefan", a man so well known he only needed a single name, but so private that he was rarely seen in public. Stefan took what was filth and debris and like a phoenix from the ashes, renewed the building to its once past glory. Not much was known about Stefan except that he appreciated how to create a superb nightlife experience and recognized how to treat his clientele. Where he got his money, no one knew or cared.

"They weren't kidding about this place," marveled Jared, trying to take it all in. Populated by a never-ending mass of Adonises and Aphrodites, it was hedonism run amuck. Sweating bodies gyrated against one another on the dance floor compelled by the beats laid down by the rock star DJ.

The bass was so intense that it pounded in Anna's stomach like a fist. "Do they have food here? I need something to eat." she asked.

"Food's for pussies," exclaimed Dylan over the loud music, "We can eat later. Right now we need to find the Feather."

"If it will get me fucked up, then I'm in, Bro," replied Jared merrily.

"I'm in too," replied Veronica waving her arms above her head and keeping time with the mad beat. "What about you, girlie-girl?" she asked Anna. "Everyone's doing it," she added playfully.

Anna threw a weary glance at Jared before turning back to Dylan, "I'm in as long as your boy keeps his hands to himself."

"Do you hear that, Jared? Keep your busy hands off of Anna's ta-tas."

"Does that mean your fine ass is fair play?" Jared asked Anna for clarification.

"The whole package is off limits."

"You're no fun," he pouted.

"We'll see how fun she is when she's floating on air," added Dylan. "Those thighs aren't as locked up as she pretends."

Flipping Dylan off, Anna sidled up to Veronica. "Now where do we get this all-time high?"

Dylan whipped out the golden tickets. "Right this way, ladies and gentleman."

He led them through the crowd towards an ornate staircase behind the bar. At the top of the stairs was a lavish wooden door carved with meticulously detailed engravings. Like the entrance to Club Pandemic, it was also guarded by a large man who looked so similar to the outside bouncer, he could have been a close cousin or even a brother.

The VIP tickets got them instant access, and through the door they went. The upstairs room was more of a den than an office and it immediately reminded Anna of a harem. The place oozed sex.

The room was populated by an eclectic group of men and women of all races. Some were paired off and engaged in copulation, oblivious or just uncaring of prying eyes. Men and women, men and men, women and women, the scene was animalistic and highly charged.

Dylan caught a glimpse of two young women as they broke free from a sensual embrace; it was the two girls from the front of the line. Just his type, he had thought, and apparently each other's type as well. One of them winked at Dylan, but he discreetly turned away from her glance before Veronica noticed.

But not so discreetly that Anna didn't see. Anger flared at him, but then she put it away with a calculating thought. The sooner Veronica discovered what a cheating man-whore he was, the sooner she'd ditch the loser and they could both get on with their lives instead of following him around night after night, slaves to his whims.

"Have you come to soar on the wings of flight?" a voice asked.

All eyes turned to the corner of the room where a giant of a man sat facing away from them in a Victorian-era chair. He faced a roaring blaze in a fireplace the size of a small car.

"We, um, want to try some Feather," answered Dylan.

"Of course you do, my child." The man rumbled.

When the man got up from the chair, he was a lot larger than they first thought. Almost inhuman in many ways. His limbs seemed elongated and silhouetted by the raging flames behind him, his form seemed slightly off. From their vantage it looked like he was stepping out of Dante's Inferno itself.

And as he got closer, Anna thought she recognized his face from a magazine. "Stefan...?" she breathed. The others heard her, and looked closer.

"Holy Shit!" said Dylan. "It's him all right."

The huge man loomed over them. "In the flesh."

"Rather dramatic," whispered Anna to Veronica, who didn't see the humor.

"So you would like to feel lighter than air, with the ability to take flight amongst the Gods?"

"I would, Sir," offered Jared without hesitation.

"Me too," said Veronica.

"Hell yeah!" said Dylan.

"I'm not sure..." Anna said.

Stefan smiled widely down at them, ignoring Anna. "Then you shall have it."

Dylan got down to business. "Enough for all of us. How much?"

"You name the price," said Stefan.

"Is this a joke?" countered Dylan, growing annoyed by the man's cryptic way. "I have money. Whatever it is I'm sure I can afford it."

"Then pay as much as you feel is fair," suggested the giant.

Dylan chuffed as he dug deep into his pocket, "You and I may have a vastly different opinion of what's fair, but try this." Peeling off a Benjamin he slapped it in the Man's massive hand. "That fair enough?"

"The amount is not the point. The willing payment is. And your payment is accepted. Hold out your hands."

One by one they obeyed and each was rewarded with a single black pill about the size of an aspirin. On its surface was printed the graphic of a fancy quill in white; a feather.

"Bottom's up."

Without hesitation, Dylan popped the pill in his mouth and swallowed hard. Jared was next, followed by Veronica. Anna hesitated.

"What are you waiting for, girlie-girl?" Veronica grabbed Anna's cupped hand and forced it up to her mouth. About to object, Anna was interrupted as the pill flew down her throat, leaving her no option other than to swallow it.

"Now we really party!" exclaimed Dylan as he headed for the door that led to the dance floor below.

Stefan took a giant step and barred his exit, "Best you stay up here, amongst friends."

"Get out of my way. I want to dance."

"First time on Feather can be a—taxing ride," explained the man. "So as I said, it's best if you're amongst friends. And you *are* among friends." Stefan gestured, and Dylan looked to see the two girls from earlier. They looked friendly. Very friendly. Forgetting Veronica, he walked over to the two.

"Is there a bathroom?" Anna looked in a rush.

"Down the hall," said Stefan, pointing to a doorway at the far end of the room. Anna was heading towards it before he could finish. Veronica started to follow, "Need a bathroom buddy?"

"No, I'm fine. Just have to pee. You stay here and keep an eye on lover boy."

Speeding towards the rear of the room, Anna passed by a man and a woman masturbating each other on a chaise lounge by the door. In spite of herself, her eyes wandered to the man's engorged crotch as it was pumped furiously by the woman's heavily bejeweled hand. The jewels sparkled from the glow of the fire across the room and created light traces in a rainbow of colors; the Feather was beginning to take hold.

Determined, Anna pushed her way through the door and rushed into the empty bathroom.

Falling to the floor by the nearest stall, she jammed her fingers unceremoniously into the back of her mouth. It only took a few pokes before her stomach vomited up its contents. The sick filled up the toilet with a variety of colors. She stared at the mix in spite of herself, wondering if it was from the Feather or from the toxic blend of mixed drinks she had imbibed over the course of the long evening. Among the cosmic swirl was the remnants of the black pill. She could still make out the half-digested white quill printed on the surface. Maybe she got it out of her system in time.

A little hazy from the trace amount of drug still in her blood stream, she pulled herself off the floor and went to the sink. She splashed her face with cold water and then took a look at herself in the mirror. "Yeah. Fuck you too." she chided her accusing reflection.

Back in the den, Dylan and the others started to feel the full flight of the Feather. It was like nothing they'd ever experienced before. A natural high that made them feel like they were glowing from inside. Glowing like the fire that appeared to expand from the fireplace and lick up the walls with fingers of bright orange flame. The flaming tendrils wrapped around each of them and warmed their soul. It was a comforting feel. An orgasmic feel.

A nearby woman stepped away from the wall and crossed over to Jared. He smiled at her as she approached. She was dazzlingly beautiful. Naked bronze skin. She took him by the hand and brought him over to another woman and a man. They were also naked and motioned for him to join them. He sat down, and immediately felt their hands roaming over his body. Male and female hands, it didn't matter to him as he floated on Feather. Nothing mattered, he thought, and what if it did? He chuckled at the old song, then forgot it as they peeled off his clothes layer by layer.

As Veronica watched Jared surrounded in pleasure, a veritable Adonis of a man joined her in the middle of the room. He leaned in and pecked at the base of her neck with his lips and tongue. His kiss was light to the touch but still wet with passion. Aware that she was crossing the line, she turned to find Dylan expecting his jealousy to flare, but he didn't seem to care that this strange man was kissing her passionately around her face, neck and then her lips. He was too wrapped up in his own pleasure.

The two women that Dylan helped out earlier decided that now was the time to repay that favor. Appearing at his side, they escorted him to a nearby couch and laid him down on his back. He happily let them remove his shirt, then they each started with his fingers and began sucking and kissing them, slowly working their way up his hand, up his forearms and to his shoulders. Dylan was in heaven. He'd never been with two women before especially ones as insanely lovely as these two vixens. Laying still, he happily let them ravage his body.

As Anna emerged from the bathroom, she heard her friends' moans of pleasure coming from the den and stumbled to find them. She already decided she'd fake being stoned until the others came down and they'd be none the wiser. She hoped that this would be the last time she would have to put up with bullshit like this.

As she burst through the door she found faking it a little more challenging than she anticipated.

Jared's skin had been peeled from his upper torso as a blood drenched man and two women ran their tongues around his chest and back lapping up the liquid crimson seeping from the wounds.

Veronica's face had literally been chewed off by the Adonis. The gorgeous, blood-soaked man was currently biting and tugging on her left ear to rend it free from her grinning exposed skull.

Dylan lay on the couch to her immediate right; he was the worst of them. The two girls had gnawed his arms and legs down to the bone but he was grinning wide with ecstasy, as were Veronica and Jared.

Numb with horror, Anna realized her friends were enjoying every orgasmic moment as they were eaten alive.

As Anna backed away, she felt something wet touch her leg. It was Dylan's chewed-up hand. He smiled up at her from the couch while the girls continued their meal, and held out his hand. "You still want something to eat?" he grinned as blood dribbled down his chin.

Anna spun away and vomited all over the floor. As she heaved, she could hear Dylan talking behind her.

"You gotta love the VIP treatment, babe." He chuckled madly.

Anna ran for the exit door that led to the dance floor, but ran full tilt into the massive Stefan, who blocked her escape. He held out another pill to her. A small, dim part of her mind noticed that this pill was red, not black like the first one.

"No, please—I don't want it," she mumbled.

Stefan chuckled. "Yes you do. You know you do." He stepped forward, not touching her, but his sheer bulk trapped her in a corner.

"Please. I can't pay the price," she pleaded.

Stefan nodded back to Dylan, who was gurgling in pleasure

through a throat full of blood. "He already paid. This one's on the house."

Anna couldn't remember taking the pill from Stefan, nor putting it in her mouth. The only recollection she had, which she could not blot from her mind for the rest of her very long life, was the red pill's sweet coppery taste as it traveled down her throat.

It was the exact same taste of Dylan's heart as she chewed it from his heaving chest.

Jamison Rotch knows a thing or two about the horrors of Hollywood, having served hard time in Los Angeles many moons ago. He escaped to Nashville, Tennessee, but nightmares of pointless meet-and-greets with agents, driving a rental truck on the 405 and something called a "Thomas Guide" continue to haunt him. Rotch has been writing and producing for television in Music City, including a recent primetime NBC special for Taylor Swift. He has also written his first e-book, Beating the Spread, *under the pen name J.R. Beckham.*

THE BOX

Jamison Rotch

THE MAN HAD NEVER gotten used to people looking at him. He would have thought after so many years of starfuckers and sheep staring holes through the back of his head, he'd have built up some kind of immunity to it. Or at least a tolerance. But the man still felt eyes on him.

The worst were the people with the balls to come up and just start talking to him. Mostly about his movies, usually beginning a conversation by squawking back their favorite lines with a shit-eating grin. And then there were the pictures. Christ, the fucking pictures. As far as the man was concerned the worst fucking moment in the history of mankind was the day they started putting cameras in cell phones. You never knew when or where the fuck those snapshots were going to show up online.

The confrontations used to happen more often in the beginning, but that was when the man was obsessed with having his off-screen image match what people saw on-screen. He thought he had to be "on" all the time. After all, as people in suits in boardrooms used to tell him, he was a "brand." Like a

Ferrari. Or a box of fucking Triscuits. But about five years ago, during one of his dark periods, he stopped giving a fuck what he looked like in public and the man couldn't help but notice that fewer people were approaching him. Experience and experimentation taught him a few subtle tricks that would bring down the wattage of his look. Inexpensive glasses. Hair parted to a different side. Rattier, loose-fitting clothes. People still thought he looked familiar, but seeing him through a cheaper prism kept most fans from having the confidence to approach. In fact, not one person in the dive bar he was sitting in had any idea it was actually *him* finishing off his third cheap Mexican beer in the last hour.

Well, there was one person.

The bartender. Early twenties. Good looking. The man could tell that he had figured out who he was, but the bartender kept it to himself. The man appreciated that.

"Need another one?" the kid asked.

The man shook his head.

"All good," he answered. He took the last swig and set the empty bottle down on the counter. "You know, I used to work here."

The man was just as surprised to hear the words coming out of his mouth as the bartender was to hear them. The man had no idea why he said it. The last thing he wanted to do was strike up some fucking small talk. But that was exactly what he set in motion.

"You know I had always heard that," the bartender said. He leaned up against the bar as he settled in for what he thought was going to be a conversation he would remember for the rest of his life. "Jimmy, the guy who owns the place, always swore it. Said he worked with you. Do you remember Jimmy?"

The man shook his head, even though he knew well the particular shithead the bartender was talking about. He could feel eyes around the room beginning to find him. To recognize him. Why the fuck did he open his mouth?

"I never believed him," said the bartender. "You hear that kind of shit all the time but it's never true."

As the man reached back for his wallet, he could feel the bartender building up enough courage to ask one last question before he could escape. The bartender leaned in close so only the man could hear him.

"Listen, this is just my day job," the bartender said. "I know you get asked this all the time, but if you have any advice or tips. Words of inspiration. Anything."

The man got up from his stool and did something he had not done to a fan in years. He looked the bartender square in the eye. The bartender, unprepared for the power of connecting to a person he normally saw hovering above him on a four-story screen, took a half-step back.

"Where are you from?" the man asked.

"Venice."

The man shook his head. "No, where are you *from*?"

It took a moment for the bartender to understand the question. When he did, he answered quietly, "Dickson. Dickson, Tennessee."

The man pulled a one-hundred dollar bill out his wallet and set it on the table.

"Keep the change," he said. "And go back to fucking Dickson."

Traffic on the 405 was relatively light for an afternoon, but the man was in no hurry so he decided to take the back roads back to his home. As he was wandering his way through Westwood Village, his cell phone buzzed. He checked the caller ID display to see his agent's name and phone number glowing on his dash. He considered letting it go to voice mail but then pressed the button on his steering wheel column to connect the call.

A sexy, female voice asked him to hold while his agent was put on the line. A beat later, a voice the man had grown weary of hearing overwhelmed the interior of his car. After an exchange of inane pleasantries, there was a subtle change in the tone of his agent's voice. Over the years the man had learned what that tone meant. There was news to share. And it wasn't good.

"So I just got off the phone with Marty," the agent said. "There's nothing final, but from sources I've got that would know, well, there's just no question the studio is looking very seriously at other options."

The man made a right onto Sunset. The traffic was worse here. Red brake lights snaked up into the distance as far as he could see. It was getting dark enough now that some of the oncoming traffic had switched on their lights.

"You there?" the agent asked.

"I'm here," the man answered.

"I just don't understand," the agent said. "This thing was a done deal. And I want you to know, I really busted Marty's balls over this. We even had a meeting over here this morning about getting legal involved."

"There's no need for that," the man answered.

"It's really baffling to me," said the agent. "I really just don't understand why it all fell apart."

The man knew why, but he kept that information to himself.

"Sometimes you just move on," the man said. "What else have we got?"

There was a pause on the other end of the line. The man could picture his agent leaning back in his chair and staring out on to a West L.A. skyline cast in shadows.

"We've got a few things in the works," the agent said. "But listen, I'm going to shoot straight with you on this. This is unfortunate timing. The two projects you turned down last week are out of the picture. Now Marty owes us on this, so there's a future opportunity there. But that's going to take some time to come together. And the other balls we were juggling got dropped a month ago. But listen, I don't want you to worry about this. There's a stack of scripts here. It's just a matter of finding the right fit..."

The man tuned out the agent's pep talk. He always did. His drivel was meaningless. The next project, the one that would keep his name on the front page of the trades, would happen. But it wouldn't happen because of anything his agent, his manager, or anyone else did. No, the man made his own success. He always had. He would be fine. As long as he did what he had to tonight.

The agent finished his speech and was trying to get off the phone for his next call when the man interrupted.

"Did you get the gift I sent?" the man asked.

"Wait. What gift?" the agent asked back. "Hold on a second."

The man was put on hold. He could picture the agent calling in his assistant. After a few seconds of scrambling he would scream at whoever the poor person was who handed him a bottle of scotch worth more than six months of the assistant's salary. Thirty-seconds later the agent clicked back on.

"It was here and no one bothered to *fucking tell me*," the agent said, emphasizing the last three words for the benefit of some underling cowering outside his door. Then the agent laughed. "You son of a bitch. You beat me to it! It's not today though, is it?"

"No, you're right," the man said. The exact date was seared into his brain. "It's tomorrow."

"Well, I want you to know I didn't forget," the agent laughed. "I've got something for you, but it's not going to be delivered until in the morning."

"I believe you," the man said.

"You're not going to believe this, but I just passed that bar the other day and thought of you. It was down there off Olympic."

"Pico," the man corrected.

"Pico," the agent repeated. "Of course. Christ. It seems longer than ten years ago, doesn't it?"

"Some days," the man answered. He had a clear picture of the agent walking through those doors. Cussing and sweating after a blow out on the 10 nearly killed him. It took over an hour for the tow truck to arrive. The man, tending bar at the time, served him three scotch and waters. By the time he paid his tab with a hundred dollar bill, the man had his first agent.

"I don't remember what the hell I was even doing down there," the agent marveled. "That's fate, old friend. Fate."

"It's something," the man said. But he knew fate had nothing to do with it.

Even with shades on, the man squinted against the harsh fluorescent light illuminating the large vault he was standing in. As the bank manager brought him his safety deposit box and set it down on the marble table in front of him, the man tried to remember how long he had been coming here. There was a time, for at least the first five years, when his strategy was to rent out a new box in a new bank every year. The man purposefully chose remote branches scattered all over the Los Angeles area and would wear elaborate disguises to rent each one out and then retrieve what he kept inside. Over the last five years he had gotten more complacent, keeping the box under his name at a bank in Tarzana until finally settling on the branch of a large bank right in Beverly Hills, less than two miles from his home.

"Can I provide any further assistance, sir?" The bank manager asked.

When the man told him no, the manager nodded. "I'll be just outside the door if you need me."

Only after the manager left the vault, did the man lift the lid.

It was there just as he had left it, wrapped in black cloth. He slowly peeled back the corners of the fabric to reveal a wooden jewelry box. Out of habit, the man picked up the box and turned it over to inspect it. Its appearance remained as it had always been for the last ten years; colored a deep, dark brown with the grain of fine wood still viable beneath the stain. The only distinguishing features were two brass hinges and a simple brass clasp. There was no lock.

The man didn't bother to open it. He knew what was inside. And it would be out soon enough.

When he closed the colossal front door of his palatial home, the man stood for a moment in the entryway with the box tucked under his arm and enjoyed something that was a rare occurrence in his life.

Total silence.

With an army of housekeepers, groundskeepers, maids, and personal assistants on the payroll, there seemed to always be some sort of noisy activity around him. Someone coming, going, cleaning or mowing. Day and night. But a little over five days ago the man had given everyone two weeks off. They happily accepted the offer, so the large house was empty and he was alone.

Well, not exactly alone.

After grabbing a beer from the stocked Sub-Zero fridge in the kitchen, the man made his way outside into the warm evening air. It was a spectacular view of the city, not that he even noticed any more. An infinity edge pool gave the illusion that the water was spilling off into the glowing grid of the Los Angeles skyline. As the man scanned the horizon, he could just make out lights of his direct neighbors, partially obscured by well-positioned landscaped walls of greenery. The lights of dozens of other houses glittered in the valley below.

He took a long swig of his beer and began walking down a narrow stone path that lead toward a back corner of his property. This half-acre was much wilder and more overgrown than any other part of the well-manicured compound. This was by design. Adolfo, his landscaper, made sure the area was watered but he was under strict orders to let the greenery grow unchecked. The rest of the staff never ventured near it. If someone new was brought aboard, the man would overhear them whisper warnings in Spanish. *Tierra maldita* they called it. "Cursed ground."

The man took another sip of his beer and plunged into the thick undergrowth.

Less than twenty yards in, he came to a small bungalow that had been completely swallowed by greenery and savaged by the elements. The real estate agent who sold him the place over a decade ago pitched it as the perfect writer's retreat or artist studio. The man nodded in agreement but knew from the moment he saw it what purpose this building would serve in his life.

As he stepped on the small front porch, the man switched the box to his other hand and fished a set of keys from his pocket. He clicked a small LED light attached to the ring. Three gunmetal gray deadbolts glowed bright against rotting wood. Each of the well-maintained locks opened with a gentle click. The man opened the door with a nudge of his shoulder and stepped inside.

The shoebox shaped interior of the bungalow was divided into three rooms. There was a small bedroom in the back, a full bathroom with an old clawfooted tub in the middle and a modestly furnished den with a small kitchenette that the man was now standing in. A narrow hallway located in the back of the bungalow connected all three. The man checked his watch and then used the hallway to walk past the closed bathroom door and check on the back bedroom.

The area had already been prepped. The room was bare. Plastic tarps covered the walls and floor, just in case. There wasn't always a lot of blood, but when there was, it could get very messy. He learned that lesson the hard way.

The man held up the box again and studied it. As many times as he had held it in his hands, it still amazed him that he had no idea how old it was. There were no markings at all on the box. Not a carving, not a pattern, not even a scratch or mark. It looked exactly the same as the day it was sold to him in a handshake deal twenty years ago.

He heard something moving in the bathroom.

Checking his watch again, he set the box in the middle of the bedroom floor and stepped into the hall. He listened for a moment but heard nothing. Stepping forward, he pressed his ear to the thick oak door; there was something there. It was muffled but distinctive. A clinking sound. Metal on porcelain.

The man opened the door and flicked on the light.

The stark light of the bare bulb above the mirror revealed the girl was still in the bathtub, awake but very groggy. She was still dressed in the outfit she was wearing on the street last night. Her feet were chained to the ancient tub's green tinged faucets. Each hand was actually shackled with foot cuffs, the longer linked chains connecting each wrist to two of the four clawfoot fixtures that kept the tub raised above the tiled floor. Her right hand moved and the chain rattled against the side of the tub.

The man leaned in closer to see her eyes were twitching underneath her closed lids. The girl was still heavily drugged but coming out of it fast. There was a chance he got the dosage wrong. Or maybe she had a higher tolerance for it than the others. Regardless, he was running out of time. When they were awake, it was so much more unpleasant.

It was the pain that brought her back. For countless hours the girl felt like she was submerged in liquid darkness, a heavy weight tied to her waist keeping her down. Then there was a sharp sensation, and suddenly the weight released and she broke the surface into consciousness.

The first thing the girl saw, but did not completely comprehend, was the back of a man kneeling in the middle of a small room covered in plastic. As she was trying to make sense of what was happening, she felt another jolt of the pain that had been her salvation. She looked down to find her hands cuffed and her left wrist sliced open vertically to the middle of her forearm. Blood poured out of a thin, elegant cut.

The girl groaned.

The man turned to face her. She recognized his face immediately. She didn't know why she didn't realize who he was before until, pushing back through the fog of her memory, she realized he looked nothing like this when he picked her up. For a moment the girl thought this was a positive sign, then she remembered the bloody cut on her wrist and all the plastic on the walls and knew there was nothing positive about this situation.

"You're awake," the man said, rising to his feet. He almost looked sorry for her.

The girl nodded. Her eyes darted to an object on the floor. It was what the man must have been kneeling in front of....

"I'm sorry," the man continued. "I would go back up to the house to get another dose but—" The man glanced at his watch. "But I'd never make it back in time for it to do you any good."

...it was a box, the girl realized. A small wooden box. With something painted on the top of it?

"I know it's no consolation," the man said. He was sweating profusely. When he wiped his hand across his forehead, it left a streak of blood. "but it won't last long."

The girl realized the man had a cut on his own wrist. It was smaller incision and horizontal, not vertical like her, but it was still bleeding quite a bit.

The girl's eyes darted back to the box.

The man seemed to recognize the girl's interest in it. With a bemused look, he picked up the box, took a step forward and slid it in front of her.

Now she could see clearly what was painted on top. Painted in fresh blood. At first it looked like just a couple of triangles in a circle. She recognized the symbol. She had seen it when she was looking through the books at the tattoo parlor on Sunset just last week. She couldn't think of the name of it but knew from the other examples that were around it, it couldn't mean anything good.

The man kneeled before her. He touched his finger at the blood pouring from her wrist, then turned the box over and redrew the symbol on the blank side. He then set the box in front her.

"Go ahead," he said. "Open it."

The girl didn't move.

The man reached over, lifted the latch and flipped the top open. The girl closed her eyes and tensed up. When nothing happened she looked down to see...

...the box was empty.

"See?" The man said, snapping the lid shut. "Nothing to worry about?"

The girl relaxed. Maybe this was just some kinky fetish thing. She could handle that. She certainly had before. The vampire thing was hot now and she had had her fair share of biters. Fighting through the lingering haze of whatever drug she had been give, the girl tried to speak. But the man, shook his head.

"Just relax. I'll be back in a few minutes."

The girl nodded.

The man checked his watch again then picked up the box and set it back in the middle of the room. He walked to the bedroom door, gave the girl one last reassuring look, then turned the doorknob with his left hand. He was about to walk out the door when he paused, as he seemed to contemplate something. After a moment he nodded to himself, having made a decision. Right before he closed the door behind him, the man flipped off the light.

Sitting on the floor with his back to the closed bedroom door, the man tried to think positive thoughts. He thought about the call from his agent that would come tomorrow with news that the old project that was thought to be dead would find a new life. Or it might be a new deal, a new script, a new opportunity. But there would be something. And it would come tomorrow. As the man had learned over the years with the particular contract he was fulfilling this evening, action was rewarded almost instantly. The agent would once again talk of fate. As always, the man knew better.

He was suddenly overcome with an urgency to remember the face of the man, if he could call him a man, to whom he owed everything he had in his life. But as hard as he tried, the features were just a blur. He was sure he had seen him at countless other parties, awards show and functions. Well not exactly seen. *Sensed his presence* would be a more accurate term. And as he did every year about this time, when he had his back to this door waiting for the seconds to tick away, the man wondered just how many other wooden boxes there were out there in this town.

His thoughts turned to the girl now as he replayed in his mind how he had left the room. It had been so long since one had been fully awake that he felt the need to put her at ease, to show her the box was empty. And turning out the lights was truly a final act of mercy. The girl might not realize it now, but the man had done her a tremendous favor casting her last moments in darkness.

After the very first time, the man became obsessed with seeing for himself what came out of that box. How could anyone not after hearing what he heard? So he drilled a small hole in the door so he could see inside. The second time the man woke up the next morning passed out on the floor. He remembered no specific detail of what he had seen, save for one fuzzy memory that it had the most beautiful eyes. It wasn't until later that afternoon, when he took a shower in his house, that the man realized his hair had turned white.

He heard the girl's blood curdling scream coming from behind the door. He looked at his watch. Right on time, he marveled. After so many years and so many victims, the punctuality of it still impressed him. As her screams morphed into choking, guttural moans, the man took the last sip of his beer and made a note to go to bed early tonight. He would need his rest. He had a feeling he would have a very busy day tomorrow.

The sacrifice ensured it.

Like his cousin Brian, Charles Muir shares a name with someone else he insists is not him on the Internet, a fellow who
apparently teaches Tantric sex in Maui; not a bad gig at that.
But instead of tanning odd body parts (even he considers them
odd) in the islands, our non-Tantric-sex-guru spends his days
writing lame jokes and event listings for a newspaper in the
Pacific Northwest. He has had stories published in small-
press magazines including Cthulhu Sex Magazine (Lovecraft-
ian, not Tantric), Morpheus Tales, Whispers of Wickedness
and the anthology Mutation Nation: Tales of Genetic Mishaps,
Monsters, and Madness. Charles even managed to score an
honorable mention in The Year's Best Fantasy and Horror. His
flash fiction (for lack of a better term) can be viewed under
the pen name George Kuato at www.microhorror.com.

ALONE AND PALELY LOITERING

Charles Austin Muir

THE SIGN SAID *House of Orchids—Thai Massage.*

Stopping by the blackened window, David Knight twitched his mouth in a palsied smile. The indigo neon sculpture
below the lettering looked more like a Jimson weed than an
orchid, he thought, but the flower itself was a fitting, if
unimaginative, choice for the place. In Victorian times women
were discouraged from even setting eyes on it, for the orchid
was a whore, a sexual deceiver that mimicked female insects to
trick pollinators into mating, and, in some cases, wasting
copious amounts of sperm.

Not likely to happen in my case, he thought, recalling his
vasectomy at a time when Eisenhower was still in office.
Bunching his shoulders together in indecision, he ran his eyes
down the sloppy tinting job someone made of the glass door

when a scream sent a mighty shudder through his bowels, as if a mean-tempered hedgehog were trying to shake itself out his ass.

God damn brats, he thought, as an Escalade rattling electronic noise and poorly feigned hilarity Dopplered down Hollywood Boulevard. Then again, it was Friday night, and it was their world, not his. A world of blonde, vacuous heiresses and their abdominal-obsessed male counterparts, rolling from one club to another in a deafening caravan of hypersexual angst toward a mirage of eternal youthfulness. A mirage he, too, had fallen for when it was his foul language, his puke, his angst smearing the streets of this city that had tossed him out of the party several decades ago. Every generation had its "good old days of Hollywood" story, even if his came from a gentler time, a more romantic time.

There was nothing romantic about what he feared he would find in his underwear when he got home.

Brats.

He frowned, shifting his weight from one leg to the other. For he doubted he would find the courage or will to come out again; if he was going to find sex it had to be here, tonight. It didn't look like much. A strip mall containing a sushi bar, a talent agency and an empty space next to this blacked-out door and window advertising Thai massage. Hell, they were all Thai massage anymore. His stomach rumbled. His underwear felt unsoiled. It was this joint or the steak house across the street; marriage had diminished his responsiveness to personal choice. His hand decided for him.

A black maw gaped as the door swung open.

He let himself be swallowed by it, his insides fluttering with each step. Plush carpet reassured him, his bearings returning with visual adjustment. In the dimness, the furnishings of a small waiting area came clear in the feeble nimbus of an identical neon advertisement flickering near the door.

These consisted of a black vinyl couch, a false wooden desk and a card table lined with magazines, presumably promotional materials of the local sex industry. His senses swam in an exquisite floral aroma. It flowed over him like the perfume signature of a demigoddess, though the truth was he had sunken to a standard of strip-mall harlotry on Hollywood Boulevard: a desperate old man eager to demonstrate he could still open his zipper for someone other than a nurse expecting a urine sample.

Sitting on the couch, he stared into indigo-tinged gloom.

It was possible they offered legitimate massage here... he could certainly benefit from it. But glancing at the bikini-topped cover girl on one of the magazines, and catching a faint whiff of French fries, he doubted it, if only because he had never heard of getting a genuine massage at half past midnight. His eyes rested on a ficus plant near the desk, leaves cupping the glow of a bubble-gum pink nightlight strung over a beaded curtain opposite the entrance, but closer to a rear wall beyond view.

Go home, he told himself, *get out of here before you embarrass yourself.*

Then a mirage stepped through the curtain into the room.

She was the sort of feminine vision that would make the poet Byron weep. Or at least reach inside his pants when no one was looking. A woman in her early twenties, tall, shapely, olive-skinned, with lustrous black hair and eyes of a becoming-ly Asian cast. Though Knight's wife was of German-Irish descent, he had always felt drawn to women of mingled non-Caucasian ancestry, however racist that seemed; perhaps owing to tales he heard from his Navy buddies who came back from the Pacific. Regardless, this woman was the finest example of Anglo-constructed exoticism he had ever seen.

"What can I do for you?" she asked, with a smile.

He almost didn't hear her. He was still taking her in. Her white, gauzy garment with the wide V plunging to her navel gave him much to absorb. He was aware of his rude gaze, but in the back of his mind he knew she expected it, invited it... professionally, of course. In the blacklight her proportions swelled and swelled. And in places he forgot existed, things began to stir.

Knight had a friend, a writer, who soared to dazzling descriptive heights when it came to women's breasts. Ample ones, especially. On paper, they quivered and beckoned as a succulent feast of edibles, their "creamy mounds" and "Hershey's kisses" in contrast to Knight's lens-like assessment, all dimensions appreciable in his worldview. The woman before him was more than a feast, she was a gateway to gluttony, her breasts densely spheroid with long, shadowed cleavage lines, mounted over the proud breastbone of a Valkyrie. And hips, high-velocity curves like a wildfire along twin hummocks, hips that blazed their own sexual lights against the bosom's fearful symmetry. A tigress, Knight thought, like that Amazonian knockout in those cannibal horror films he watched with the sound down when his wife wasn't around, he forgot the actress's name just now.

"Um," was all he said, like a child caught off-guard by the teacher, both hands covering his groin.

"Have you been here before?" she asked, her tone honeyed, perfect.

He started to say, he thought so, back when the lot was a YMCA in the '50s, but "Never... in a place like this," fluttered up in broken syllables from his dry throat.

As if a smile could be any brighter, or attempts to describe it any more banal, he thought, steadying himself against her unblinking gaze. Unflappable, she ignored the judgment he might have wrongly implied in his choice of words. "You want to know how it works?"

Her ensemble eliminated any doubts about the nature of services rendered. Still, he hadn't ventured into such territory since 1944, on another continent, and everything had seemed so black-and-white, even the diseases, back then.

His eyes darted to the beaded curtain from which she'd emerged. Not since the war had performance anxiety like this uncoiled through his insides, a hot-cold itch in his loins that snaked out to his extremities and made his teeth chatter (or in this case, his dentures). Then, as now, he'd feared for his body's qualifications for a task not only mysterious but economized in the formula of underground commerce. Was he capable of accepting what this woman offered—and, conversely, could she accept, without visible revulsion, what he offered, smelling of topical rubs and the irreversible locker-room perspiration woven into the fabric of every old man's aura?

What did she see when she looked at him?

So immersed was he in anticipating his defiant enterprise that the thought had escaped him—just how he would look on the other end. Would she scorn him, reenacting the very humiliation that had inspired him to come out tonight?

Just before she took his hand—her grip like pliers, cold as steel—he glanced at the ficus near the curtain, its leaves browned and curling, some scattered at its base. And thought: I'm like that plant, in the wrong environment, in the wrong world even.

An inner voice, one he associated with his wife, shot back, *Poor, poor David Knight...*

Too late to turn back now.

The curtain beads clicked in parting. Darkness again. And again his stomach stirred with that dizzying feeling of physics about to catch up with him. As if sensing this, she leaned her weight into him, filling his nostrils with tropical scent and the backs of his eyeballs with wondrous light. "The door's just ahead," he heard her murmur, as the inner radiance mellowed and his sight adjusted. On his left a door opened, a tall, spindly fellow slinking away from it along the hallway wall in an anonymous manner. It was someone Knight recognized. Yes: the waiter who'd screwed up his order at the deli last week. He'd been too preoccupied in telling Knight of his starring role in the '80s cult classic, *I Guzzle Your Spinal Fluid,* to jot down his customer's craving for a corned beef sandwich.

At the last instant Knight turned his face away, likewise hoping to avoid notice.

The woman pushed open a door at the rear of the hall.

Fluorescent light blinked on industrial carpet. The woman

ushered him toward a folding chair near the back of the room. Facing it, separated by a fiberglass partition wall, a man sat at a work station, his blue-lit visage partially blocked by his PC monitor, goggling unseen data. Knight shot a questioning glance at his hostess, who seemed to have relinquished her role to this new presence. She seated herself on a bench built into one wall.

Time crawled while Knight fidgeted on this office-atoll, straining to make sense of it. It would appear there had been other cubicles in the room at one time. The desk was cluttered with the usual clerical mishmash, and a glass paperweight shaped like the Jimson weed that was meant to advertise sex. The man appeared to be in charge, though of what Knight could only guess. Was he the manager? A plainclothes cop? A host on one of those "caught on video" TV shows? What was going on?

"Welcome," the man said, at last.

He came around the wall, crushing Knight's hand with a plumber's grip. Through a fiery bush of red beard he seemed windblown and ageless, but Knight guessed late thirties, early forties. He wore a black T-shirt depicting a U-shaped serpent's trunk terminating at both ends in a hissing, green-eyed head; the image was repeated in a scaly tattoo spanning both arms, each terminus adorning the webbing of thumb and forefinger.

"I'm Jones," he said, folding his arms in an impressive display of inkwork intended to seem offhand. "And you are?"

Knight blurted out his name, too confounded by developments to think better of it.

"What do you do, Mr. Knight? Or is it more appropriate to say, what did you do?"

"I'm not sure that's your business," Knight heard himself say, "but I was a landscaper."

"Before that."

"What do you mean?"

"I'm assuming you didn't come to Hollywood to become a landscaper."

Knight's shrug came as a frown. "I did a little acting," he said, cautiously.

"Such as?"

"Oh, it was so long ago, before I got married... some teeny-bopper films, usually the high school quarterback swimming in gravy... I was in my twenties, of course. Though once I got to play Guy Davidson's ex-college buddy who turns out to be a hit man—"

"'Bullets Over Bangkok,'" Jones said, "sure... I saw that. You were good, one of the few bright spots in it. Though your eye patch changed sides halfway through."

Knight's mouth dropped. "How could you know that?"

A snake-headed thumb jerked at the workstation. "The Internet, Mr. Knight, is quite an invention. I happen to like old films. And there's an excellent video store down the block."

Last time Knight had been there, "Bullets Over Bangkok" was out of print.

"What's going on here?" he asked.

Jones chuckled.

"Relax. I just like to meet my clients. Quality assurance, as they say. I trust this is all new to you. So much swindling goes on in places like this, a man can leave with his wallet empty and only the vaguest notion he might have been fondled by a ghost."

The woman in Jones's employ was anything but a ghost, Knight thought, but kept mum as the man continued:

"Anyway, I like to know our customers' wants. In most cases they're straightforward. Though occasionally we find someone who thinks more—well, in the long run..."

"At my age there's nothing long about it."

"See, but that's untrue," Jones countered.

Footfalls murmured on the carpet behind him.

"We have options, Mr. Knight," the woman said, "for people like you. People who want companionship and affection but, because of their situation, are denied those needs by tacitly accepted social laws that refuse to regard the elderly as anything but liabilities." Knight blushed. Other than in a doctor's office, he had never heard himself described in such clinical terms.

Her arm brushed past him, perfume trailing over his senses like a silk scarf.

Jones chimed in: "Right. As our bodies advance in years it becomes socially inappropriate to seek sexual relations. As if, in obeisance to some natural correspondence, the time table of our instincts should be fixed by the effects of gravity."

"Say again? You've lost me."

Jones nodded, pacing before Knight, mirroring the woman's movements at his back. Their tag-team interplay was too pat, too smooth, he noted, like a pair of subway con artists. But for what purpose?

Jones continued:

"But when do we experience this mythical dissolution of our psychoerotic mechanism? Why should the most mature members of society forfeit their privilege as sexually loving beings? The standards of beauty vary widely from era to era and culture to culture. Tuberculosis victims, for example, were at one time considered attractive for their frailty, pallor and violent cough."

"But what's that got to do with—"

"It's conceivable," Jones forged on, "that another culture might worship advancement in years as the twenty-first century Westerner idealizes facial symmetry or low body fat. For to maintain supremacy a people must first reject what I call the hegemony of the outer layer—and assign prestige to its greatest citizens."

"The elderly?" Knight asked doubtfully.

"The extremely elderly, Mr. Knight. You might even say, *ancient*."

"This is some sort of joke."

"Not at all. Such a society would find a way to reprogram the encryption of aging. Naturally, the ruling class would consist of those who have put in the most time to develop this capability, those with the deepest accumulated experience. Doesn't that make sense? So then why discriminate against the wise folk, the survivors of untold cycles? Instead they should be rewarded—by extending the organic adventure they've fought so hard to explore, to endure. What do you think of that?"

"I think you're full of..." Knight let the rest trail off unspoken. "I think I should be going."

"Please. I understand your skepticism. What I'm speaking of would appear to be somewhat... extracurricular under the circumstances. I assure you it's the opposite, appearances to the contrary. We want to help people like you, Mr. Knight."

"Help people like me? How?"

"First of all, by convincing you to reject the system that has already rejected *you*. To turn from a doomed society who scorns and oppresses its greatest citizens and embrace the society I've described. Suppose I'm not bullshitting you, Mr. Knight, suppose it's real. If you could join such a community, would you? It would require certain sacrifices. You would have to shed everything you are to give yourself wholly to the ruling class... but in return you would enjoy everlasting health and vigor, the rewards someone of your longevity deserves."

Knees wobbling, jaw trembling, Knight struggled to his feet.

"I've heard enough," he said.

"We can help," the woman spoke in his ear.

"Help," Knight spat. "I came here to get *laid*, to put it bluntly. Since neither of you seems to know anything about tact. Instead you sit me down and remind me how old I am and blather on about prestige and supremacy and sacrifice. None of it makes any sense. At any rate I don't want to try and make sense of it. Maybe you're worried I'll have a heart attack on the premises and you're grasping at some way to sweet talk me out the door. I'm not so far gone as that, you know. I bounced tables once, right out of the service, and I said just about anything to get rid of drunks without having to put my hands on them. I'll make your job easier and show myself out."

But reaching for the door, he stopped.

"You're right, you know," he looked at the woman, "when

you say no one wants to acknowledge what goes on in the minds of the elderly. Society wants to think we're able to store our youthful feelings away like pictures in an attic. I probably thought the same when I was young. But then we're supposed to put *ourselves* in the attic—the attic built for us by our children and our children's children. Grandpa having a trunk full of dirty magazines? Disgusting.

"But I've got that trunk," he tapped his temple, "in the attic inside my head. Everything I ever wished for and wondered about and the few experiences I've built up over the years. You want to know why I came here tonight? Yesterday I was at a strip club getting a private dance. I'd never had one. I figured it was all I'd get, at my age, now the wife is gone. I'll admit it felt strange, wrong, maybe. But then I overheard this young punk at the next table, shouting over the music—awful music, everything 'bitch-bitch-bitch'—shouting at his buddy, as if he wanted me to hear it: '*Look at that old pervert.*' The two started laughing so hard the whole place turned to look."

Knight sighed. "And while they were laughing, I wondered, why? Why was I a pervert? Weren't we all looking at the same naked woman? The way I saw it, the only relevant difference was that I had a closer view because I paid for it. So I decided that if I'm doomed to be a pervert in my last days I'm going to explore the full range of options, and damn what others think. Only I'd hoped when I came here that I could open the trunk in my attic and touch and smell everything in it and not be ridiculed for it... but it appears I was mistaken. Good-bye."

"Mr. Knight," the woman called after him, "we have options—"

And Jones, too, coaxing him in his bedside voice, the words fading like a Doppler effect as Knight's attention telescoped on the doorknob in his hand. The veins and tendons taut with effort, the chrome orb immovable, isometric resistance drawing all his concentration into a pinhole through which his vision dimmed, wrenching him after it, conscious, thinking but disembodied, a lone signal traveling through interstellar void.

Then his senses splashed down, swimming in scents and sights both outlandish and familiar. It was Naples, 1944, Knight an 18-year-old infantryman, wine hangovers splitting his skull and the mothers of daughters barely into their period offering him shelter, rosy-cheeked girls pushing their tits in his face and proposing in breathless English lire amounts for unlimited acts.

He wished it was his sense of wrong that drove him from those apartments, his groin aching from near contact. But it was his nerves blenching, the fight-or-flight response galvanizing him to escape, to tear down his fantasy that he had been picked off the street for a special reciprocity, and that his coin was a mere pretense for this deeper purpose.

But he always came to his senses, snared in the hunger of an occupied city, while war was fought elsewhere and millions were incinerated in camps he knew nothing about; while the sky ran between rooftops like spoiled milk and the gutters filled with tale-swapping, sex-crazed G.I.'s outside the brothels. His only experience a barnyard tryst with a neighbor's daughter (how cliché can you get?), Knight was too timid to try his luck in those establishments. Until one night some drinking mates put enough wine in him, and he did not take flight this time.

He followed her up a humid stairwell, away from the stink of enlisted men's smoke and sweat, into an attic with a mattress in back. In the cloudy light from the window he saw she was younger than she seemed downstairs, perhaps his own age, a nervous, pixie-like creature with bruises on her thighs and a twitch at one corner of her mouth. As Knight neared climax, she observed him with a tenderness that made him think later of a face emerging from dark water... the vulnerability and curiosity of a newborn in her gaze. It made her both prettier and uglier than parlor light had rendered her, detached from the act and even seeming to float in a veiled reality beyond it, as though he were making love to a phantasm. He wondered if his shudders and groans amused her...

And then sound softened again, his animal noises fading into a woman's moans, breath catching in clenched teeth. Not the woman from the bar but the one from House of Orchids, massaging him all right, giving him the happy ending of which he'd dreamed. Only there had been no beginning, no middle. And now, arching with her rhythm, focusing on her heavy bosom and flat belly and swelling hips as she straddled him, he felt the moments slipping away like streaks of maize in an October sunset. When would he ever sleep with a woman this beautiful again? With any woman?

Poor, poor David Knight.

No. His wife was gone, gone into the dark with her many lovers.

It was his turn for a change. His turn now, despite an awkward start. So what if it was over sixty years since he felt a woman besides Esther... as they say, even in Hollywood, it was never too late. This could be the performance of his life. Still, his mind reached back to events before the displacement, the temporal shift. He'd been talking to the tattooed man and this woman... and then... blank. How much time had escaped without his cognizance?

It mattered. Even as the woman rode him, sawing and swaying to his own feeble spasms, it mattered. She must see it in his face, in the confusion of his efforts. He was like a third-string nose tackle tossed into a goal line stand in overtime without warning. Normally he wouldn't lament a lost hour gazing at the TV, but this... it amounted to self-sabotage at its cruelest. It mattered—

"I have Alzheimer's," he confessed.

The words arose without forethought, as though someone else spoke them. Yet they carried back to him in his own voice, and for the first time. They seemed to affirm a growing darkness inside him, a void that was drawing all his being into it, even as, in being spoken, they kept him from being devoured by it. And he saw, by the faintest flicker in her eyes, that she knew.

He had come here, to this shabby storefront flaunting a Jimson weed for an orchid, to shout *screw you* to the punk at the strip club and everyone else who condemned him for having virile thoughts; but behind his defiance crouched his terror of an all too common prognosis, and the gray shadows that threatened to cloud every moment between consciousness and the grave.

The woman grimaced, but said nothing. Through the pressure of her fingertips flowed the urgency to be silent, to allow her to release him from his dirty secret. She would forgive his sagging body, his ailing brain. But she would do more than that. She would cleanse away the feelings of inadequacy that lingered after his wife swore to be faithful—before her second and last fight with cancer—and the sometimes tortured speculations of what his life might have been like had he avoided the altar.

All the sexual encounters he missed were bound up in this woman. The tarts and starlets he'd passed up during his brief celebrity, shying away from their brushes and glances as though Hollywood was but an extension of all the brothels of Naples. Of course it stemmed from insecurity, he was romantically inept. Esther, however blunt, was right about that. But their marriage was over, death and this woman did them part; with her lustrous black hair and night-sparkling eyes, her voluptuous presence that seemed to constantly reinvent itself as though she alternated between satiety and starvation moment by moment.

Let me hold on to this one memory, he prayed to no god in particular, *let me remember this, please.*

Yet it couldn't be real. It was too fantastic, too expressive of his own palliative fantasies. As though a composite of all his notions of beauty and affection had acquired physical form out of an act of will on his part to be soothed, to be congratulated even, for his struggle to face nature's stings to his masculine— hell, his *human*—pride.

And indeed, taking in his environment for the first time since he'd awakened, he glimpsed the impossible: he was surrounded by orchids, rolling starbursts of color as far as the eye could see. Adrift, so his eyes and prostrate body told him, on what felt like a marble slab on a sea of psychedelic botany. And soaring over him a white expanse that stung his eyes to meet directly: A harsh brilliance, as of artificial light. The flowers, swollen and labial in shape, made him think of dreamy flora clinging to a coral reef in a surrealist painting come to life, expressing through their keen, throbbing hues a voracious and inexhaustible hunger.

The dense, meaty odor of the orchids rushed his nostrils as the woman leaned into him.

"Are you willing," she breathed, "to give yourself to the Ruling Class, to sacrifice everything you are in exchange for eternal health and vigor?"

If only you were real, Knight thought, and not an old man's mirage, a medley of sensations mostly imagined, or long since dried up.

Yet the sinews at his fingertips quivered with substance and flexed with intention – and chilled his flesh like the slab beneath him.

His mind flashed on the dancer at the strip club, jiggling her breasts in his face. No such cheap theatrics here. Compassion, a desire to free him, radiated from this woman, this fragrant figment of his imagination.

"Look at that old pervert," he heard the punk say, as he felt himself approaching orgasm.

And thought: *Says you.* "Yes," he croaked, adding, "I'm willing," so the affirmative would not be misconstrued for an ejaculation, in both senses of the word.

Moments later he repeated the affirmative, in both senses of the word.

And then his vitals shut down, and all physical sensation fled.

It was as though he watched everything that formed David Knight—from his organic matter to the patterns of selfhood and experience imprinted in that material—sucked into a black nothingness. Yet out of that enveloping nullity sounded a voice, the only focal point in the absoluteness of the void. It began as an unintelligible whisper, rising in volume and deepening in pitch until the words spun through his emptiness like stars in a universe he had dreamed into creation; and he no longer felt alone but surrounded by listeners like himself, static but attentive in their repose.

Then open sea rolled away from him in all directions, a sea of dreaming faces. Illuminated by the voice's silver light, drinking in each luminous word with hungry, infantile mouths. And his was one of those mouths, a voracious aperture in the mask that was all that was left of him; a mask that with what remained of his consciousness he associated with convolution and vibrancy, as if he was but part of a festival of masks that had abandoned their wearers, masks in the form of brilliant flora displayed in a feverish celebration of gaping lust.

"You are part of our Garden now, Mr. Knight," the voice said, and in its bell-like tones throbbed a multitude of voices, "our garden of need, of self-sustaining promise. For the specimens in our garden, to be satisfied is to wilt and die. Therefore we keep you hungry, in perpetual longing, watering you with vicarious pleasures you once enjoyed, nourished but never sated by the fleeting ecstasies of creatures like yourself, who, if they are fortunate enough to find us, will one day face the choice you've made.

"The last vestiges of consciousness within you struggle to grasp our motives. Understand we do not wish to alleviate or end suffering. Our motives are not cruel, nor are they bene-volent or humanitarian, providing relief, comfort or refuge from pain. They might be characterized as aesthetic: we find beauty in the vitalizing effects of passion on a broken organic system, in watching sad, failing creatures like yourself live on in a state of insatiable desire, sensuous and buoyant for eternity."

* * *

She stroked the plant's pale petals and deposited it in a corner. For an instant, as with every new plant, she fancied she could detect a whiff of the creature from which it had bloomed. Sometimes, as also in this case, she could swear the flowers seemed to be... *smiling*, in their way. After all, Mr. Knight had everything to lose—or had already lost it—and much to gain. Better than the attic, right, Mr. Knight? Better than the attic, certainly.

Before leaving she took a last look around. Knight was the sole botanical occupant in this section, the first to be renovated in the new space. She had argued for a more grandiose architectural statement—to build a sort of overgrown paradise in the mini-mall, hidden amid the city's faded grandeur—than preserving the room's original dimensions, but Jones rejected the idea on the grounds that a dingy semblance was necessary to continue spreading without detection or resistance. From the talent agency to the sushi joint with its regular crowd of out-of-work actors to the bothersome private detective whose office they had just acquired, they would branch ever further into this wilderness of broken contracts and wasted lives until they had transformed it into a lush conservatory of radiant dreamers who, were they capable of self-reflection, could not conceive of coping with an existence outside the perennial comforts of the Garden.

Knight was her first conversion in this dimension and she wanted to honor him somehow. Toward that end she'd put up a framed one-sheet for "Bullets Over Bangkok," knowing he'd have much to feed on under the zipper masks and other barbaric instruments betokening mistreatment, a custom considered a birthright here like the ever-present smoky haze in which the natives suffered their repetitive—yet mysteriously attractive—torments.

Jones glanced up from the couch when she returned to the waiting area. Beside him a new customer sat staring into space. "Too easy," he said, his snake's head pulsing indigo as he passed his hand over the oldster's face. "I can control him like a puppet. Like the last one who came here."

"Knight," she said.

"Yes, Knight. Only more advanced." He looked on as the old man doddered to his feet. "What do you think, Belle? Skip the office and take him straight to the Garden?"

"It's better than the attic," she said.

C. Courtney Joyner has written the screenplays for more than 25 movies, including the cult films The Offspring *starring Vincent Price,* Prison *starring Viggo Mortenson, and the new 3D adventure* Return of Captain Nemo *starring Hugh Bonneville and directed by Perry Tao. He's written extensively about the history of American film and his book* The Westerners *is considered "essential" by Leonard Maltin. The film journalism has led to interviews/commentaries on a number of horror and western DVD's, including the John Wayne films* The Big Trail *and* The Comancheros, *as well as the* Charlie Chan *series. Courtney's western fiction has been anthologized in* Fistful of Legends, Law of the Gun, *and* The Traditional West *among others. His short story "Two-Bit Kill" was nominated as Best Short Story of 2010 by the Western Fictioneers, and his work in the genre was recognized this year by The Western Writers of America who presented him with their 2011 President's Award. His newest projects are the crime anthology* Beat to a Pulp, Round Two, *the film book* Warner Brothers Fantastic *for McFarland, the graphic novel* Saga of Billy the Kid *with artist Mike Gagnon, and the screenplay* Legend of Belle Starr, *which has been optioned by Instinctive Management. Courtney lives in Los Angeles with his fiancé and a ton of movie posters.*

ONE NIGHT IN THE VALLEY

C. Courtney Joyner

"WHERE THE HELL was Charles Bronson?"

Bronson was stubborn in Gyp's thoughts as he maneuvered his primer-orange Rabbit around the taco truck, carefully avoiding turning too hard to the left since left turns always killed the engine. The wheel shuddered in his hand as the transmission cried, but the Rabbit kept running. Gyp will-ed the engine to rev and it lurched to 35 mph. The headlights dimmed until Gyp slowed again, then re-lit his Clove. He liked the way he looked with a cigarette, like Charlie in "Rider on the Rain."

The V.W. shook, then calmed. Gyp knew he had to get his mechanic buddy to check it, but he was working on a "kick-ass strippers vs. zombie script" with a "seriously great" role for Gyp. Besides, he wanted twenty bucks, maybe even lunch, for the job. The repairs could wait; the Rabbit was doing all right tonight, carrying Gyp down Ventura toward Van Nuys Boulevard, where he'd take a right, thank God.

But where had he seen Bronson? Gyp should've remembered, but there was too much in his head tonight; too much history.

Gyp tapped the brakes as he passed Vineland, leaning across the passenger side to check out the backlit dreams in the Porsche dealership because he remembered Charlie in a high-end ragtop. Gyp carefully rolled his Clove against the lip of the ashtray so he could save it for later, and pictured Bronson behind the wheel. No, a Porsche was too dainty; that wasn't the Charlie Gyp knew.

Gyp eased through the yellow light onto Van Nuys, groaning in the curve, and passing the tiny casting office that had hired him for his role opposite Charlie. That was a good day: the parking meter by Star Casting had failed and he'd gotten the part of Security Guard Number Two just by walking in the door. The memory was still warm since Gyp almost had a line in that one. Almost. It was a Cannon flick and the assistant director promised to throw Gyp something but gave it to his fat girl friend instead. Security Guard Number One offered Gyp his sympathy and a pull on his hash pipe, "Tits win."

Still, Gyp got to stand next to Bronson, and when the second-second asked for his name, he said, "Gyppo. Like Gyppo Nolan in 'The Informer.'" The second signed Gyp's time card with a shrug, but Bronson reacted to the reference.

Gyp took the opening, "For some reason my Mom loved Victor McLaglen."

Bronson narrow-eyed the crew, "The bastards always make you wait."

Gyp was sweating for the next thing to say when Bronson turned and left, but he still had his moment with "The Mechanic" himself, and if Gyp had flagged Charlie down when he saw him in that little foreign job, he would have had a second moment, and that was a hell of a lot more than his friends at the breakfast burrito place could say. They spouted about their big roles with big stars, but were always too broke to buy another actor a cup of coffee.

Gyp's feelings were a shout when he punched the gas, pushing past the office where he'd bombed his auditions for "ER" and "According to Jim." He drifted to the left, avoiding the boarded-up entrance to the studio where he'd taped his hair restoration infomercial for Telemundo; the one that was never shown. Each light took Gyp deeper into the muddy neon of the valley as Hollywood's promise receded behind him. The blocks of pawnshops became miles of for-lease storefronts, until Gyp turned onto Sherman Way, jerking to a stop for some bearded rat-bait who was pushing a wheelchair full of trash to the curb.

A tow truck pulled up, blasting its horn, while Gyp waited for rat-bait to pick up some plastic bags stuffed with other plastic bags that were blowing across the intersection. Gyp knew this corner, since he did his first double blowjob scene here in the parking lot behind the La Carnacia restaurant, next to the check-cashing place.

Aziz had called him and challenged, "You're an actor, right? You get paid, right? And the girls, they're—okay. Fifty bucks."

That was the gig that changed everything.

It changed Gyp's name, and what he told his Mom about his career; she always wanted to know when he was going to do another movie with Mr. Bronson, and he'd say "Looks like I'm in the new one," never telling her that Charlie was long dead. It also changed his income, since he was actually banking enough to get him from Tuesday to Saturday and then Aziz would call with another gig. The tow's horn blasted loud again, and Gyp drove around rat-bait, who spit-screamed at him in his own language.

Gyp headed down Sherman Way toward the Van Nuys Airport, passing one location after another: "Catholic Girls Luv Spunk", "Blast My Face #5"; the titles, the girls, the adjectives humping the adverbs, all washed together. He fought to keep from going back in time anymore, as a yellow fog settled on the street, veiling the lights and the moving shapes around the bus shelters.

The valley was miles of empty tonight, and this cruise was a great way to catalog regrets, but Gyp shook it off: He was an actor and this was business; besides he was still doing show-cases for casting directors. Plus, someone had slipped a flyer for extra work on his windshield and you never knew where that might lead. This had been a shitty day, but it was almost over, and he'd start fresh in the morning.

Gyp had a burst of good feeling, sat up straight, angled right by the Korean barbershop and drove down a dead-end side street that ran parallel to the airport runway, before pulling into a low-slung storage facility. Gyp re-lit his Clove, drew long, and sat in front of the rusty office door of the only producer to write him a check in three years. He thought about not going in, but what would Bronson do?

Aziz Abrahamian worked the mint-flavored floss against his incisor, trying to free the last dried bits of his meal that had wedged between his teeth and gums. He spit pink into the sink, and then studied himself in the bent reflection of the paper towel dispenser. Much of Aziz's face was hidden by a growing-wild thicket of black beard, but his eyes still revealed too much about his age, and this worried him.

He ran stubby fingers across his forehead to tame the dyed strands he had dangling while thinking he never should have smashed the damn bathroom mirror. The buzzer rang, and Aziz barely cinched his robe around his pumpkin belly before barking for Gyp to, "Come the fuck in!"

Gyp tried to work the knob as Aziz yanked the door open with, "Turn left and push! You know that."

Gyp hung back, his eyes fighting to adjust to the dim red of Aziz's office, as the huge shape in the robe grabbed his arm with, "We've got to get this party started. Look on the desk."

The desk was a scarred dining room table, covered by a mountain of porn magazines, over-due bills, actor headshots and pizza boxes. The rest of the room was just as random and sad; once-nice furniture from Aziz's mother's house had been beaten by years of spills, cigarettes, the burned plastic smell of cheap meth, and the occasional on-camera sex act. Pillars of Adult Video News and The Hollywood Reporter leaned in the shadowed corners, waiting to be read, while flyers for Aziz's movies hung in honored plastic frames along the windowless walls that continued down a narrow hallway to a small bedroom/studio. The door to the bedroom was barely open, but Gyp could see the halting flicker of a jar-candle. Except for the lit candle, the place hadn't changed in three years.

Aziz belched without covering his mouth, "Right there."

The money order for one seventy-five was on top of a stack of stills of Gyp with four other guys and a Korean girl in pigtails. He turned the picture over, and slipped the third of his rent into his pocket.

"I left the name blank, so you can put in whatever you want. What about tonight? Are you John Long, Brett Steel, or what?"

"I don't care."

"You don't look like John Long anymore. Your hair's gone and your gut hangs over your belt. Remember when we got that letter from that chick who thought you were Kevin Costner? Jesus fucking Christ, we wouldn't get that now, so start thinking. Fuck that, I'll come up with something. This is a new series, and needs a new star. Fat Fred or Aging Arnold, maybe."

Aziz laughed and tossed Gyp a pack of Cloves, "No, I'll

come up with it. Fresh pack. I bet you haven't seen one of those in a while."

"I—I'm doing all right. There's some big things coming up."

"Yeah, like what? What did you do today?"

"Had a meeting with a writer who's got a kick-ass part for me, went to the doctor's, got your call, and—"

"Came running. Good, because this is huge. A chance to make real money."

"This has got to be the last time, man. Really."

"Yeah, yeah, of course. You hear what I said, asshole? Real money."

"Uh-huh. For you or me?" Gyp fingered the stack of collection threats on the table.

"What happened to your trust? I keep my fucking word. Come on, I'll show you."

Aziz gave one of the ad slicks on the wall a gentle pat, "Your fat ass to the camera, because they want to see the girl. But this is different."

Gyp followed Aziz down the hallway to the bedroom, his head and his voice down, "We'll see."

The crimson was always on top, ending in an upward curve around the eye with a softening puff. Blending along the lid was the layer of lavender that washed into light green and then all the colors spread from the corner of the eye in a small burst, highlighted by a tiny kiss of glitter. The make-up was an amazing creation, but Chrystal Catt managed it every time Gyp worked with her. He'd even asked how many hours it took and she just shrugged, "What else do I have to do, Gyppo?"

Chrystal loved calling Gyp by his given name because it made her giggle, just as he always called her Penelope, named for her grandmother. Penelope was lying on the futon in the studio, surrounded by faux satin pillows, dressed only in a man's button-down that was spread open like pinstriped wings. Her left nipple was painted Navy blue, and there was a smear of Navy between her breasts that slopped to her ribs, as if she had lost control while decorating herself. Her eyes were, as always, works of art.

Aziz put a video card into the palm-sized camera, "Bang My Passed-Out Girlfriend."

Gyp ran his fingers across Penelope's purple lips. The color smudged away, revealing purple underneath. Her skin was cold, and getting colder.

Aziz turned on a lava lamp in the corner, then pushed the candle closer to the futon. "We shoot the girls partying, then when they pass out, you fuck 'em and a cream pie. Say, six girls an episode. Depending. And it's uncovered. We're going website first, then our own DVD line. We distribute ourselves; we've made enough money for those pricks, now it's our time, right? Bang My Passed-Out Girlfriend, Number One of who-the-hell-knows."

"But—I like her—I like Penelope."

Gyp cradled the back of Penelope's head, and slipped a pillow behind her. Bits of glitter stuck to his hands as he gently brushed her hair back with his palms. Aziz settled on the futon, bracing his elbows against his bare knees to hold the camera steady, "We got no fluffer, so go in the john and whack yourself. There's lotion and Viagra on the sink. I've got to check focus."

Air caught in Gyp's throat and he tasted the Clove again, "I—I'm an a—actor."

"These little things say you can get close, but it always looks like fuzzy shit. And we got to see you."

"I'm an actor, and she's an actress."

"What the fuck are you on about? I know your credits. Bronson. IMDB."

"Penelope and I did a workshop in Studio City. 'Bus Stop,' and 'Shakespeare in Love' and everybody said we were great. Best in class. There was a junior agent from CAA, and we blew him away!"

"Yeah, I believe she blew him away."

"F—fuck you. What—what did you do to her?"

Aziz's hand was at Gyp's throat in less than a heartbeat, pushing him down on Penelope's body, forcing her to sigh. Aziz's fingers squeezed, drawing a tear of blood around his dirty nails, "I'm the producer, I got her ready for work. Now you've been paid, asshole. Do you want to fuck and live, or fuck and die?"

Gyp gasp-nodded toward Penelope and Aziz took that for his answer. His fingers relaxed, leaving deep ridges on Gyp's throat, like tire-tracks in the snow. Aziz leaned in close, and Gyp could smell rotting meat with each whisper, "I spoke badly. How long have we been working together? This is a chance for a real creative partnership. You and me, yes? Partners? But I need to trust you; I need you to do this thing. Do your job, Gyp. And I'll do mine, and we'll all win, right?"

"She's dead."

"She—slipped away. It's a tragedy, but she was a junkie, so—"

"No, no, she wasn't."

Gyp rolled up the sleeve of Penelope's shirt, revealing a single puncture in the crease of her elbow with just a hint of bruising, and said, "See? This is all you, something you did..."

"Look, you hump cold for a few minutes, then it will make her famous too. And that's what she always wanted, right?"

The shot sounded like someone punching a sack of flour, as it tore through Aziz's middle and out his side, just above his hip. His robe billowed with the exiting slug, as a jet of blood, made sloppy black by the tint of the room, spattered across the wall. Aziz dropped to his knees, panting, and looked up at Gyp who was holding the 9mm with shaking hands.

"Jesus, you—you brought a gun in here?"

Gyp's eyes were more surprised than Aziz's, and his words came slowly, "My Mom's. She gave it to me. I hocked it, but got it out today."

"Why the fuck?"

Gyp sat on the floor next to Aziz, his hand drooping under the gun's weight, but he could still manage a kill-shot if he fired again.

"I had my reasons."

"All you're doing is wasting time, asshole. And she's getting cold..."

Aziz yanked the sash on his robe and pulled the blood-sticky silk away from his body to reveal his belly wound. Surrounded by curly hair, the hole was the size of the tip of Gyp's little finger, while the torn skin fringed back along the edges like delicate, bloody, lace.

Aziz's deep breaths forced air bubbles from the wound and Gyp couldn't take his eyes away from the damaged tissue; beneath the slick of blood, the flesh seemed to be moving and shifting on its own. Aziz grinned as the edges of torn skin came together, melting into a new layer of tissue. He coughed hard, and the little bit of the mended wound stayed closed, "A couple of minutes and I'll be fine. All the stupid shit you did; what did you think you were going to do? Sit and watch me die, then bury the girl with respect?"

Aziz grabbed Gyp's shoulder, and pushed himself to his feet with a grunt. The rupture was almost sealed and his whole body racked with a cough as he challenged, "You're the big shit who knows everything about everything. What do you think I am?"

The gun was heavier now, and Gyp didn't have any words. Aziz coughed again, "Don't say vampire, because that's what they all say."

Aziz picked up the camera and sat on the bed, shoving Penelope's legs aside. He took another deep breath, "It gets harder, after all these years. Anytime something like this happens, a little longer to heal from the inside, but I always make it. And always will, you know why? Because of actors."

Gyp looked up at Aziz from the floor, raising the pistol so it was aimed directly at his bearded chin. Aziz closed his eyes and smiled, "Don't you see? I'm the dream; the hope every actor has of making it in the movies, on the stage, or who knows what-the-fuck. That desire is what keeps you going, and it's been the same for every actor for a thousand years. If I force myself, I can remember riding into a mountain village in a wagon, with my troop walking behind. You rang a bell and people came out of their homes to see the play. Just coins in a hat, but it was enough. And in every place there was a girl with her dreams, so I could always feed. I promised the fame, money, all the wine you could drink, or a name people will always remember. Actors will follow you to the end of the Earth for these things. And the ones I took died happy, because I whispered the right thing as their life was draining away. Hundreds of them."

"You drank their blood...?"

"You're a simple shit. Let's say I took what my casts offered. Of course, when the agents appeared, it made things a lot easier."

Aziz straightened Penelope's body on the futon, oblivious to any threat as Gyp kept the gun aimed at his shoulders and said, "Then—what are you...?"

"It says Aziz Pictures on the door, right? Adult shit? Fifty years ago it was western shit for TV under another name. A hundred years ago in London, it was an office in the West End, fifty years before that I was in Paris introducing the most beautiful women to the world. Who built the first theater, paid actors to speak? We've been here since the beginning, and a hundred years from now, I still will be. That's what I am, and I want you inside the girl, no holding back. You're going to leave something behind."

"Fuck you."

Aziz steadied the camera, zooming in on Penelope's eyes, then widening the shot until he was satisfied. The command returned to his voice, "Yeah, technology has changed every-thing we do. The bitches twitter before they can talk, how can you hide anything anymore?"

Aziz turned the lens on Gyp, "The cops love video. Threat-en me again. You might as well take direction, you're not going anywhere," then lowered the camera, "Why'd you bring that gun, anyway?"

"My process is my own..."

"To kill the one producer who thinks you're worth a shit.

Typical. So now you're Bronson, is that it? You're just another bitch with a SAG card."

Gyp spit on the lens, the gobs spraying Aziz's face. Aziz powdered Gyp's jaw with a single punch that slammed him to the floor and killed all feeling. Aziz grabbed the 9mm, as Gyp's hands blindly found one of Penelope's eyebrow pencils. Gyp rolled into Aziz's knees, and sprang, jamming the pencil through his beard and into his throat. Aziz screamed and a burst of red soaked Gyp, just as he saw the muzzle flash.

The slug hit Gyp squarely in the breastbone, and rag-dolled him across the bed. His body twisted, and came down on top of Penelope as Aziz's screams became hoarse, rough, cries. One of Penelope's arms cradled Gyp as Aziz pulled the pencil from his throat, and dropped heavy onto the futon, collapsing it.

Aziz grabbed Gyp by the hair, pulling his head back so that his neck began to crack, "You're going to keep me alive—!"

Gyp twisted, but Aziz's mouth found the wound, and he swallowed it in a deep kiss, sucking the blood as it pumped freely. Aziz's strength chained Gyp and he shut his eyes tight. He thought of Penelope, and the darkness.

Aziz choked, pushing Gyp away. He stood, his hand clutching the blood-matted hair around his throat. The wound wasn't deep, but the flesh wouldn't knit. Aziz contorted, his muscles fighting themselves, as the pain raced through him like burning gasoline. Flecks of foam ran from the corners of his mouth, and his tongue began to swell and turn.

His words were gargled fragments of sound, "Wha—fu—ck... you... to me...?"

Gyp pulled a folded piece of paper from his pocket, and held it out. It was the results of a blood test. Aziz struggled to read it, as grey fluid flooded his eyes.

"HIV positive and Hepatitis C, thanks to working for you there's no dream. Nothing left to take."

Gyp picked up the gun and pressed it against Aziz's temple, "'Do you believe in Jesus? Well, you're going to meet him.' That's from 'Death Wish II.' I always wanted to say it... and I did it good."

Aziz's mouth sink-holed open as his flesh corrupted from his skeleton. His last sound was an infant's cry. Gyp moved to the futon and covered Penelope with a sheet, then took a small pillow that had "LUV" written across it and held it against the bullet hole in his chest. The thick smell of sex, blood, sweet incense, rot, and gunpowder was dizzying, and Gyp lurched to the door, half-stumbling over Aziz's now-liquid form. Gyp wasn't going to die in that room.

The valley morning was clear and there had been a touch of pre-dawn rain to sweeten the air. Gyp staggered from the storage unit, the pillow clutched to his chest. Blood striped his pants, and he left moist footprints as he staggered to his car, but the air tasted good to him and he swallowed a lung-full. He felt better.

Gyp started to plan his day: there was an emergency clinic on Ventura Boulevard, and he might just make it there, or maybe the burrito place. He could cash Aziz's money order and buy breakfast for his pals. There was a director who hung out there some mornings, and this was a good chance to make a contact. Gyp liked that plan; he tried his keys in the car door, but his fingers couldn't make them fit.

Gyp sat on the curb to get his second wind when he saw Charles Bronson driving by in a 1969 black Jaguar convertible. Charlie slowed, looked at Gyp, and smiled with his eyes before nodding. He raised his index finger like a gun, and dropped his thumb to shoot, then laughed.

Gyp stood, let the pillow fall away, and followed Charlie into the morning sun.

Shane Bitterling is an award-winning artist who turned to writing after feeling that the only thing he could draw was flies. He sold his action-adventure-horror screenplay WitchFinders, *to 20th Century Fox, New Regency and Arnold Koppelson. He wrote the always-playing-on-the-Syfy Channel cult favorite,* Beneath Loch Ness, *the Lifetime Channel thriller* Desperate Escape, *as well as scads of movies he doesn't want you to know about. He has worked with Jon Voight, Jim Henson and many others in positions of script development. He is currently chained to his chair, working on a graphic novel, several screenplays and short stories, as well as a feature film he plans to direct. He lives in Los Angeles with his wife, Agnes, and their scruffy pup, Rodan, and can sometimes be found haunting his blog at www.moonshine frankenstein.blogspot. com.*

THEY GO IN THREES

Shane Bitterling

KALVIN KASH'S FACE looked like a Florida navel gone supernova. It was a combination of far too many hours spent in the tanning bed, years of agonizing jealousy and months of simmering rage. He chewed on his bottom lip, as he always did absentmindedly when he was irked off, ticked off, pissed off or just plain felt clueless to what was going on. His bottom lip got a constant workout these days. At least the gnawing was done by those perfectly straight teeth, the ones Kalvin spent a small fortune on capping. Now they were slightly too big for his mouth, but damned if he didn't know how to flash them. His smile was so big and bleached, sparkling white, a Red bastard could spot him from the international space station without binoculars. And don't even bring up the hair; there's no sense in talking about something that everybody would agree is perfection. It just gets redundant.

Kalvin knew all of this and a whole lot more. He'd spent years and every dime he ever had cultivating his new image. He'd left all of his old friends behind long ago. Hadn't spoken to his family in years, especially the ones who called him out on his bullshit. They all knew where he came from. Not everybody sprouted from Los Angeles or New York, but Kal didn't want to be cornered by any uncomfortable questions where he might squeak out some tasty morsel about growing up with poor people and dirt in Virginia.

For the past seven years, Kal had been a regular contributor to *All Access*, the grand daddy of all syndicated entertainment news programs. In an effort to become hip, the producers had spent millions of dollars to promote a newer and easier to digest moniker; *AA*. The irony was not lost on the public, and certainly not to Kal.

"I'm late for my *AA* meeting," he would shout for all in the restaurant to hear before speeding off in his convertible. He assumed they all got the joke, but he just recently realized that nobody drank in his presence.

Kal had started out doing red carpet interviews of major stars for mega movies, which he loved at first. All the pomp and glam really turned his crank. His gift for bumping gums shined like a nickel. He knew all the inane questions that these people loved to hear and he was able to follow those questions up with something equally mundane like a true pro.

Then reality began to set in. Kal's reality. After a year or so of standing on the sidelines and watching actors, actresses and their spokesholes going into the theater, Kal became aware that he was on the outside looking in. The guy with the microphone never got to go inside. That's where all the action was, and most likely an orgy.

He was later given a promotion, of sorts, and was able to spend more time in the studio. He liked that. He didn't have to go out and personally witness the world passing him by. He could stand inside and view it on a monitor, which deadened the reality of it all.

But how in the hell did I wind up here? he quizzed himself. The sixty-four thousand dollar retort was definitely Lorna Hope. There was no doubt anywhere in the folds of his brain.

Lorna sat behind her desk on the far side of the studio, as she had since the show debuted in 1982. That same place where she had become a staple in American homes. The same place where she had been rubbing salt in Kal's wounds for the past couple years.

Lorna Hope was gorgeous. A true lady in every sense of the word. She was the type who spent hours primping in front of the mirror just to go to the mailbox. Her makeup was flawless and every hair on her head was as organized as a Thanksgiving Day Parade marching band. Her green eyes glinted like royal emeralds, but they were often overtaken by her large, toothy smile. Unlike Kal, Lorna didn't need caps. She may have had braces when she was in piggy tails, but for the most part, she was all natural. That was the smile that lit up a room, as they say. Kal knew that to be literal. At just the right angle, the studio lights would refract off of those pearlies and blind him. It was a perma-grin, but one that came easily and with sincerity. She had a spectacular body that matched her face. A full package. Several years ago, Lorna became her own news story when she had her ass cheeks insured for over a million dollars.

She was in her late fifties now, but you would only realize that if you thought about how long she had been on the show. She didn't look one bit different today than she did way back when. It was the result of good breeding and whatever the hell else she did in private. Not the work of a Beverly Hills doctor, and she was proud of it.

"Good clean living," she always said with a wink.

And she was a dream to be around. It was easy to see why she became who she was. She was as curious about people as she was beautiful. She never phoned in a segment. She treated each story with the same exuberance as she did during her first beauty pageant. She knew the names of everybody on the crew, as well as the names and birthdays of their kids. At least twice a week, she would bring in cookies that she baked from scratch. She treated for lunch and she hosted fabulous parties at her house. She even made her own centerpieces, long before Martha Stewart said that it was in vogue.

Everybody wanted to speak with her, and she got full access to everybody. They clamored for her attention. If you got airtime with her, millions of people would know that you had arrived. She was a consummate professional and everybody loved her.

Except Kal.

"Hurry up, you robo bitch." He wasn't sure if he said it aloud or not, so he looked around to see if anybody had heard him. He seemed safe, but he hoped the control room had his mic off.

As long as she was sitting in that chair, Kal would never be the star of the show. He deserved it. She had her shot. Everybody else had come and gone, so why was she being so damned stubborn? Not counting the occasional vacation, Lorna's million dollar butt had never left that anchor's chair. She was a permanent fixture five nights a week and most weekends for the wrap-up show. It wasn't fair. Kal thought it was criminal. She was spitting in the face of all the rules of nature. There should be some kind of law that says you have to grow old and move on.

Lorna Hope didn't fool him. He knew that nobody could be that perfect all of the time. He fantasized about her leaving the studio every evening and going bat-shit crazy on her kids at home. She would knock those brats upside the head repeatedly and then demand that her husband watch as the gardener plowed that pricey hiney with whatever could be found in the shed. Repeatedly.

Kal tottered back and forth on his heels, waiting for Lorna to pass things over to him. It pissed him off that this was an actual news day, and his anorexic weight loss segment may not air at all. He hated sitting in makeup for nothing. All the fluff that was scheduled to air was taking a back seat because something actually newsworthy happened for a change.

News of the death of one of today's biggest stars, Jerry Michael Lonaghan, rocked the entire world. Earlier that year, he became a household name for his portrayal of the villain, The Whizzer, in one of those superhero flicks that dominated the multiplexes. He was only twenty-seven years old, and the world was about to be his oyster. Talks of an Academy Award were already being bantered about town. Now that he was dead, he was a shoe-in to take home the gold, such as it were.

Lorna gave all the details of Lonaghan's sudden death. A maid found his lifeless body in the bedroom, surrounded by drug paraphernalia. Parting words from friends, colleagues and family flashed in the monitors. All of them expressed that Lonaghan had a lust for life, and none were aware that there was a drug problem.

Kal thought that it was funny that no celebrity ever had a drug problem. It was always played off as some kind of freak accident. Slipping in your shower is high on the list of freak accidents. Or having your arm torn off by a chimpanzee. Not buying heroin, smoking or injecting it and then choking on your own vomit. That doesn't really count in the grand scheme of pulling a boner.

"After the break, we'll learn what police have to say in regards to the investigation, and coming up, my exclusive final interview with Jerry Michael Lonaghan. Only on *AA*."

"Damn it! How in the shit does she do that?" Kal bit his bottom lip.

"How does she do what?"

Kal grimaced as he realized, too late, that he wasn't just thinking what he said. But he was glad that it was only Chloe Steiner that heard it and not the entire control room.

Chloe was an eager beaver if there ever was one. She was very young and very pretty. She started at *AA* in the spring of last year as an intern, and wasn't above doing anything anybody asked her to do. She knew her way around the control room and made coffee like a champ. On more than one occasion, she was allowed to do an on air segment for the weekend show, which was her goal. She wanted to work in front of the camera and thought that by learning everything behind it, she stood a better chance.

She was exactly the type of person anybody would want to have work for them. And Kal thought she was exactly the type of person he could take advantage of. On the last night of her internship, he asked her out for drinks as a thank you for all that she had done. She was putty in his hands. He had her seventeen ways to Sunday, by his count, and it was only Thursday. The problem was that she had done such a great job at the show, the producers decided to put her on salary. It had been awkward ever since.

She never mentioned that night, and she didn't goggle at him with doe eyes. That she wasn't affected at all bugged Kal.

"How does she do what, Kal?" she repeated.

"How does she get those final interviews? It doesn't make any sense. Lonaghan is different, because everybody wants to talk to The Whizzer. But most of them are old coots that no-body's talked to in years. Somehow she gets them to talk to her just before they croak. She always gets the exclusive on these guys. I want an exclusive. She must be psychic or something."

"She's not psychic. She's good. And you're being paranoid."

"Out with it. What've you heard?"

"Nothing unusual. You lost the Dead Pool. Lorna said you have to pay up. Now."

"Why? Who won?"

"Lorna."

Kal cursed as he reached into his pocket and retrieved his wallet. "See? Who in the hell would have Lonaghan on their list?"

Chloe silently shrugged as she held out her hand, waiting for the money. She saw Kal biting his lower lip, which had many connotations. But only one for this situation.

"I'll tell her that you owe her. Again. By the way, Lona-ghan started a new trifecta. Who you think is next?"

"No, he *was* the trifecta. A new round is in play," he corrected.

"The game show host was last week. Next was the old jazzy lady that stroked out."

"That's two," he said, wagging two fingers in front of her face. "Boom!"

"Then some dude from *Love American Style* kicked it last night before Lonaghan. *He* was the trifecta. Lonaghan starts a new round. Boom!"

"Damn. What was his name?"

"Hell if I know. Before my time."

"Why didn't I hear about it?"

Chloe pointed to a series of monitors, all displaying Lonaghan at different stages of his career. "Take a guess."

"That sucks."

Kal made a mental note to never die on the same day that a bigger celebrity decided to check out. It was a sure fire way of being forgotten.

"Sucks for you," she said as she disappeared into the commercial break buzz of the studio.

"What's that mean?" he called, but she was already gone. He thought for a second that maybe there was some resentment after that long ago night. Then he quickly decided against that possibility. Why would it take so many months for the anger to brew?

Kal chewed on his lip with such intensity that his mouth filled with the coppery taste of his own blood. It dawned on him that it was exactly these kinds of situations that solidified Lorna's popularity. She was always the one who delivered the big story. And the final interviews were the icing on the cake. She was a part of the story. She was a name that you could trust. But Kal didn't trust her at all. Even he knew he was stretching for the truth, but blind anger took hold and strangled him. Lorna Hope was a glory whore. She didn't want Kal to be the star that he knew he was. She was jealous of him, so she stole his airtime for herself. He didn't even get to report on the anorexics when they croaked. And Lorna winning the Dead Pool today, again, was her final kick to his balls.

The Dead Pool was always one of his favorite pastimes. It

was an office tradition. At the start of the New Year, players would make a list of actors, musicians or other famous people in the entertainment industry that they thought were sure to die before the end of the year. It is a simple game with a simple premise, but Kal took it very seriously. He put a lot of thought into each of his picks, and he was always the last to turn in his list. The possibilities were endless. Age didn't matter when it came to the business of death. In Hollywood, everybody was a target. Kal liked to study old actors and their ailments. They were always a sure bet and the law of averages were on their side to lose. Young actors with their substance abuse or mental breakdowns were more of a longshot. They had an entire life ahead of them, but their excesses evened the playing field. Never count them out. But the ones that Kal loved were actors on career skids. They were true wild cards. There was no telling what they would get into, or what they would die of. They were the ones prone to freak accidents of epic proportions.

  Kal never officially won the Dead Pool, but he always came in a close second or third. He always had fun coming up with his picks, so the only real losers were the ones that keeled off. He wondered if he was on somebody's list. He *hoped* he was. He was a regular on television, but not quite famous enough to be on the radar, no thanks to Lorna. But sorry for the poor sap who scribbled his name. They weren't going to pick off of his corpse for a very long time.

  A time honored side game to the Dead Pool was the Rule of Threes. Famous people never did anything alone; that included dying. For some unknown reason, they always shoved off in groups of three. That group would complete a trifecta, and then a new one would begin. It was Gospel fact. There may be a spell where nobody died for months. But as soon as that first person dropped, anybody and everybody came into play. Kal loved it. The excitement crackled in the air. If the first one wasn't on his list, he'd have two more chances coming very soon. The deaths usually occurred within two weeks, so it gave him plenty of time to run his numbers and talk about statistics.

But on rare occasion, celebs dropped like flies, and keeping track of the trifecta was difficult.

Kal drove listlessly down PCH with the radio turned off and his hand cupping the wind. Driving along the coast was the one thing that he truly enjoyed. There was no pretense about it. It was just one of those things that people did in Los Angeles to clear the cobwebs from their mind. And Kal's cobwebs were growing thicker by the day. It was as if time itself slowed to a crawl to allow Kal to think things through. He didn't know what he needed to think about. He just needed to do it. Even the setting sun seemed to hang in the air until his gray matter could spit out a plan. For Kal, it was the only time he could be truly alone. People in other cars didn't exist. They were just machines at that point. Nothing else mattered except the way the wind whistled through his fingers if he contorted them in a certain way.

There was always a downside to his occasional jaunts. Kal didn't like to spend too much time with himself in the quiet. That's when the insecurities came rushing at him from the darkness. All of those wasted moments. All of those failed auditions. All of those perfect girlfriends that he pushed aside and treated as one night stands. Everything.

Kal hated those moments. They made him feel inadequate.

He turned the car towards civilization. He had enough of the cool breeze and his whistling fingers. He needed to quiet that bloating cloud in his head before it got black and ugly.

The BMW rolled slowly through the quiet neighborhood with its expansive mansions before coming to a stop just inside the mouth of his favorite cul-de-sac. Kal loved to come down here every now and again. Each of these houses belonged to old money. He felt good about that. If he won the celebrity lottery tomorrow, he still couldn't own a home here. They were unobtainable. The only way to move into this area was for a family member to die and will it to you. That gave him comfort. He could enjoy the view without the envy.

He sat for awhile, admiring the houses with their stately demeanor and clinging vines. It was as if nature were trying to reclaim what was built on top of it. Kal made a mental note to tell Chloe to get him some foliage for his house. Green ones like old money.

He studied the vines a bit longer. He had no idea what they were called, but he was sure they were from Mexico. They undulated against the house, and then creeped to one side.

"Definitely from Mexico," he said aloud as he watched the vines snake outward from the house, then creep to one side then back again. Kal knew he could get Chloe to nab a sampling, but after what he just witnessed, he was petrified. He was sure he could get the non-crawly vines at Home Depot, as they didn't deal in exotic plants.

Kal had enough of the alien scene in front of him. He reached to turn the key to his engine when it happened again. The vines stretched against the breeze and crawled to one side of the house. A light diamonded through his windshield and he turned to it, squinting.

"You moron." His nervous chuckle bellowed from deep within his chest as he realized that the oncoming headlights from a car at the end of the cul de sac were creating the illusion of the vines' movement. At that point, all of his stress was swept away into the drain. Every once in awhile, Kal forgot how erudite and damned serious he was supposed to be, and his true self launched out from hiding.

The headlights were creeping slowly and steadily at him. He was laughing harder than a mad scientist whose creation just came alive. He didn't want whatever neighbor in the car to stop and ask him questions about why he was acting like a pervert. He liked this place so he ducked down in his seat, eyeballs peering out his driver's side window.

The headlights were blinding and he couldn't see the driver. The car revved as it neared, and the beams of light darted from the street to the trees. Kal heard the distinctive screech of metal as the car hit a speed bump a bit too fast. He sucked air through his teeth at the sound. The headlights hit the road again as the car came off the bump and bounced a time or two.

"Shit!" came from the inside the car. A woman's voice.

Kal blinked away the floating dots the headlights caused in his sight, and he got a decent view of the driver. There was no mistaking the gritting teeth and beauty queen hairdo that was bouncing around her head as one tight unit.

It was Lorna Hope.

Kal almost honked and waived at her, but stopped just short of the horn. He didn't want her to think he was spying on her or peeping through her windows. Her car had already peeled around the corner and was out of sight before the notion occurred to him.

"Waitaminute. She doesn't live here."

Kal wondered what she would be doing in this neighborhood at this time of night. Lorna always made it clear that she didn't work late or cover nighttime events for the show, as she wanted to be home with her husband and children.

"The gardener is waiting for you with his long hose," Kal said as he exited his car and hopped onto the sidewalk, sauntering into the shadows as he crept towards the mansion Lorna was parked in front of moments ago. He lost his footing on the sidewalk ledge but recovered nicely, broadcasting it by shoving his hands in his pockets and lightly whistling. He was aware that he was being far too nonchalant about the whole thing. If somebody were to see him, they would certainly call the police. But he was excited, and this was how you acted when you were trying to be stealthy. Like a ninja with carbuncles.

His routine ended at the base of the cul-de-sac where the car was parked. He looked to both sides of the street, trying to decide which house she came out of. He couldn't be positive, but his gut told him that it was the one with a smattering of lights turned on. All of the others were completely dark. Either everybody went to bed early or they were all watching from their dark windows with their fingers itching to call the fuzz.

He threw his head back and half skipped to the mailbox of the lighted house, hoping to glean a name from it, but only came up with numbers. When he committed them to memory, he made his way back to his car.

"Eight six five one. Eight six five one. Eight six fi..."

A light came alive on one of the lawns. He stopped dead in his tracks and clutched his chest. The light shined directly into his face and he didn't know whether to run or move into it and meet God. It took him a few seconds to realize that he was still alive.

"Damn motion detectors," as he made his way to his car and drove away.

Kal was halfway home, but his heart was still racing. He hooted, hollered and pointed out of his car window as if he had just won the Daytona 500. This was the most excitement he'd had in a long time. He wanted to get home and try to fall asleep before the notion occurred to him that he hadn't accomplished a damn thing except to see a co-worker driving down the street.

He'd research the house number tomorrow. That's when the letdown should happen. Tomorrow. He would find out that the mansion belonged to nobody in particular, and Lorna was just delivering her homemade cookies for a friend's birthday. But tonight, he wanted all of the indecent possibilities to swim in his head while he quickly fell into a slumber. Tonight was for winners.

He pulled into his drive and readied the key to his vineless house. He was already smiling at the decadent visions running through his brain. His bed was just a few yards away. Nothing could ruin this night for him.

"Eight six... four? Eight six four? Five? Eight six... five? Eight six—shit!"

Kal's face hurt when he woke that morning. It wasn't that he slept in an awkward position, or that he ate something that didn't agree with him. It was because he smiled all night long. His dreams were so delicious he could practically taste them. He didn't care if he didn't get to air his segment that day or not. Hell, he didn't care what happened at all. He was basking in the afterglow of his night's canoodling. And the morning was so far so good.

And then he reached the *All Access* studio. It was a flurry of hands, feet and faces flying by him. He could tell that something big had happened, because even the Teamsters, lethargic most days, were excited.

"What's going on?" he asked nobody in particular, and got no reply.

His leisurely pace through the studio was out of place to those bustling by. Kal weaved his way to the control room. Chloe should be in there, and she could help him track down the house number that he was after. Meaning, she would do all the work and he would push buttons on the control panel that he wasn't supposed to.

As expected, Chloe was there. Kal made a beeline towards her, still oblivious to the blizzard of activity around him. He put his arm on her shoulder and smiled his biggest, toothiest smile.

"Really busy, Kal," without looking up from her editing bay.

"Maybe I was just going to stop by and see how you were doing."

"You don't do that. You only talk to me when you want something."

"I do do that. I mean, I don't. Not really."

"Yes, really. And I'm really busy."

"Look, when you're done practicing whatever you're doing, I could *really* use your help with... something."

She stopped clicking buttons and glared at him with eyes three days dead. "Kal, I'm not practicing anything. I'm editing a segment that I produced for tonight's show."

Kal couldn't contain his laughter. "Produced? You produced something? Way to go, kid... uh... Chloe."

"Yes, Kal. I produced it. Now I'm editing it. Just like I've
done at least a hundred times before. I've been assistant
producer for segments, including all of yours, for six months
now. I've only been doing your bullshit little errands in hopes
that you would feel like a total ass when you figured it out. Like
right this second."

Kal was aghast, but his smile only grew wider. It hurt. His
cheeks. His brain. His heart. They all hurt. For once in his life,
he was speechless. He struggled for something to say. Anything.

"Way to go... Chloeee."

Giggles permeated the room. Chloe turned her attention
away from him and back to her monitor. Kal sheepishly backed
to the door.

Somebody on the other side of the control room shouted,
"Anybody have that address again?"

Chloe blurted, "Eight six five one Hampstead."

"What did you say?" Kal asked.

"You're an ass."

"No, after that. What address did you just say?"

"Eight six five one Hampstead."

"That's it! How did you know?"

"Know what?"

"The address. That's the address."

"Everybody knows the address. It's all over the news."

"The news? Why?" He looked cautiously around the
control room. Then leaned into Chloe's ear. "Was somebody
found creeping around there last night?"

Chloe looked at him again. This time, those dead eyes of
hers had the twinkle of sweet revenge in them. "Kevin Locke.
The television star."

"What about him?"

"That's his address."

"So..."

"So, Kevin Locke was found dead this morning at his

house. His house at his address, which is eight six five one Hampstead."

Kal's gray matter pounded like a piston. He couldn't control all of the thoughts that were racing through his mind. A typhoon of questions, mixed with his guilty conscience, overloaded his synapses.

Was Kevin Locke murdered? Do they know who did it? What was that TV series he was in? Did somebody catch me on a security camera? Something in the 80s. Who gets the house? Rich people have security cameras! That show where he had the robot daughter? What the hell was it? Mom has a security camera above the garage, and she isn't rich. Will they tear down the vines? Damn, somebody got me on a security camera!

"I'm busy, Kal."

He semi-snapped out of his haze. "Did they find who murdered him?"

"He was drunk and rolled off the toilet. Bashed his head open on the tub."

"Oh. That's good."

"I think he'd rather be murdered than die ass up."

"Different strokes, I guess."

Kal wanted to walk to the door, but he hovered and worked at his bottom lip. His brain was screaming for him to move his legs one in front of the other to close the distance to the door, but the physical act was utterly foreign to him. He could feel his eyes widen. He knew they were maniacally open, but all of the motors, gears and spokes that made those things called legs operate were gummed up and re-routed to his peepers. The more he concentrated on walking, the wider his eyes seemed to get. They were getting dry, but the immediate forecast didn't call for blinking, just a heavy chance of looking like a sex offender.

Chloe stared, mouth agape, then shook her head slowly.

"You want me to do your spot now, don't you? I really don't have the time. Locke's news will be forgotten by tomorrow, I'll slide you in then. Happy?"

Kal blankly gazed at her, an automaton. Finally, "Yes. Happy."

"You have no idea what I'm talking about, do you?"

"No. I don't."

"We're doing bios for the 30th Anniversary show. I've only sent emails for months now. Just little interviews with the cast. How you started. Your favorite stories. What the show means to you. That bullshit."

"Oh. Yes. Bullshit." He vaguely remembered hearing about this months ago.

"Everybody else did theirs weeks ago. Should take fifteen or twenty minutes."

"Great." He stood motionless.

"Busy, Kal."

"Yes." He strained to manipulate his legs to turn him around. Instead, he managed a slow backwards shuffle towards the door.

As he exited, he heard someone call across the room, "Chloe, how many episodes of Ro*becca ran?"

"Ro*becca!" Kal thought as he scooted out of the control room. Loved that show.

* * *

Kal thought about the past few days. Hardly anybody was talking about Locke, but everybody was still talking about Lonaghan. The news was bigger than anybody would have thought. It was a slow week, so they were milking it for all it was worth, and then some.

He eventually sat down with Chloe to do his little spot for the 30th Anniversary show. He had rehearsed it several different ways, and believed that he nailed it in front of his mirror. Chloe thought that he was acting a little too stiff and rehearsed. It took longer than expected, but eventually, they got something they were both happy with. Truth be told, Kal enjoyed working with Chloe that day. He let his guard down, took her direction and she was right on all accounts. Chloe got him to open up about some things he didn't normally like to talk about, like where he came from and childhood memories. Hopes and ambitions. And when the camera was off; desires and regrets. It was fluff, but it was his fluff.

He felt a twang of guilt for not respecting her new position before, although he was still foggy as to what that was. He sincerely, and repeatedly, apologized for how he had behaved.

"Please let me know if I'm out of line, will ya? Thump me in the head or something," he said as he extended a friendly hand.

"Believe me, I'll do more than that," as she ignored his wavering hand and gave him a lung-collapsing hug. "You're a great guy when you get out of your own way, Kal. I kind of like it."

"Thanks, and I'm sorry again."

"And you're cute, to boot." She planted a kiss on his cheek and broke their embrace. He stood speechless, his lips pursing, and she giggled at his awkwardness. "Let's get back to work, goofy."

Kal ordered Thai for both of them and he watched her edit together the piece. He looked good and he thanked her for it. It was a fun night for him, the best he'd had in a very long time. And for Chloe, as well. She was all smiles and teasey. He sat across the room, looking at her in a different light. She wasn't just some doe-eyed notch in his belt, as he thought before. She was a young, beautiful woman with ambitions, and he admired her for it. In a way, she reminded him of himself a few years ago. He wondered if it could turn into anything. This thing with her. She kept looking over her shoulder and smiling at him, but he didn't want to read too much into it. They already knew each other intimately, and he had just spilled his soul to her more than with any other person he had met in Los Angeles. He didn't want to blow it.

As he walked her to her car, she planted another small peck on his cheek. "See you tomorrow, Kal?" It sounded less like a statement than a question. And that answered all the mysteries he had mulled over the past few hours. He planned on being the first person at the office in the morning.

He had such a great time the past couple of days, that he practically forgot about the whole Kevin Locke thing. The rest of the world forgot about it already. He tried desperately to find a copy of Ro*becca, but he was told again and again that it hadn't been released on DVD. And since nobody gave a hang, it probably wouldn't. But one of Chloe's many little surprises, as of late, was scoring him a bootleg copy on Hollywood Boulevard of the entire series. All nine episodes. She had given them to him in a little pink bag with a heart on the front. He thought she was sending him a message, but he realized she had just rehashed a Victoria's Secret bag from her last purchase. The receipt was crumpled in the bottom. She had primo taste in delicates.

He had watched a few episodes at home, and the show was just as hilarious as he remembered it. He almost pissed himself laughing during each episode when they worked in Ro*becca's tinny sounding fart noises and her catchphrase, *"beep... bloop. Sorry. Daddy. It. Was. A. Taco. Malfunction."* He had worked that one into his lunch patter the next day, but most didn't get the reference. He'd made an oath to himself to keep trying to raise that chestnut from the grave.

It was a shame about Kevin Locke. He was only forty-seven. You star in something as iconic as Ro*becca, but the universe has forgotten you even existed. Kal hoped that when he died, he would go out while doing something memorable, or manly like parachuting or a monster truck crash. He would never do such things as he was afraid of heights and monster trucks would place him too close to home. He relished when celebrities got their lights turned out by some incredulous act of clumsiness, but this was the first time that he truly pondered it. The Grim Reaper was a bastard. He didn't have enough courtesy to wait until you wiped your ass and pulled up your Dockers. He was going to come after you no matter what, and he was gunning to catch you at your most vulnerable moment. A man of note shouldn't pass while reaching for a roll of toilet paper. That wasn't how Kal wanted to go out. But he knew that he couldn't avoid the shitter the rest of his life. He wasn't sure if he could avoid it for the next hour. He nervously shifted in his seat.

"*beep... bloop. Sorry. Daddy. It. Was. A. Taco. Malfunction,*" he giggled as the stench filled his car. He had been sitting in the parking lot for almost two hours. He didn't like to be the first one to leave the studio, because it showed a lack of character. He wanted to prove to the producers that he was eager. To a point. He had feigned a blistering headache, which he thought he pulled off with gusto. He repeatedly shaped his fingers as one would a swan for shadow theater and tapped slowly on the middle of his forehead. He simultaneously squeezed his eyes and gritted his teeth while emitting a moan worthy of a grizzly bear in heat. He made sure everybody saw this production at least twice during the day. He looked like a sham diviner at a low rent carnival trying to guess the weight of a country rube. Finally, after a grueling four hours of award winning hypochondria, somebody told him that he should go home and sleep it off. That was exactly the excuse he needed to beat feet towards the exit.

He had been sitting here ever since. Waiting.

That morning, he noticed a Mercedes with an incredible amount of scraping damage on the lower panels. Kal clicked out of the corner of his mouth at the thought of somebody not caring for such a beautiful piece of machinery. The owner was a lead foot, and should slow down when going over speed bumps or driveways.

His memory triggered, and he recognized the license plate. It was Lorna's car. He had been thinking so much about Chloe lately that he had almost forgotten about seeing Lorna at Locke's house, and he got curious as to why she was there all over again.

It had been nagging at his skull all day like a relentless mother-in-law. Kal thought back to when he had seen Lorna last week, when the news about Locke had broken. Kevin Locke died a king on his throne, and there was no reason to believe foul play was involved. His body was found in a compromising position in the morning by the poor maid. Neighbors had offered up information about how they saw him the day before taking out the garbage or fiddling around with his vines. But there was no mention of Lorna at the house the night before, or that she had ever been there. He heard her mention to one of the producers that she and Locke were friends, but people in Hollywood always say that. The producer had congratulated her on Locke's final interview, which was very touching, to be honest. She had thanked him, in earnest, and Kal noted that her beauty queen appearance faded, if even just a little. And just briefly. She dabbed at the corner of her eyes with a tissue and ran it under her nose a time or two. Kal felt sorry for her. He had never lost a friend like this. He had thrown them away or left them behind. But he never truly lost one. Guilt washed over him as he cursed himself for this non-conspiracy that he created to fill his painful days.

He turned to leave, but he caught her out of the corner of his eye. When she was alone on the set, she tossed the tissue under the desk and the beauty queen came back with a vengeance. She beamed. Kal knew that she was a professional. Lorna was able to turn it on with the best of them. She was able to block out her personal life and focus on the job. And her job was to be perky. He had seen it hundreds of times. She would close out a depressing segment about a starlet's cat with a goiter and immediately start the next, which was as saccharine sweet as Wonka's nutsack. It wasn't unusual for her emotional appearance to turn on a dime. She did it better than anybody.

But it was that sideways look she gave Kal that got him to thinking. Those big eyes of hers bored into him for a millisecond, but that was enough to wash away his guilt. Mulling it over, he wasn't even sure she was looking at him. His mind told him that she was making sure nobody saw her cry. But his heart told him otherwise.

That's when he had worked his headache pony show. He had been sitting so long in his car that he talked himself out of what he was about to do. He was bored and his wallet made his ass hurt. He couldn't quite figure what sparked his obsession with peeping on Lorna, but he was going to follow her tonight and see what she was up to, if anything. He hated her for not giving him the limelight he so deserved. But when he cut through it all, he hated himself for hating her. It wasn't her fault that he wasn't as successful as he wanted to be. Who is? Even when you're on top, the top isn't enough. He knew her from work, and could recite odds and ends about her personal life that everybody knew. But he wanted to *know* her. Be personal with her. He wanted to be invited over for dinner on Sundays and get gifts on Christmas from her kids. She was respected, which was something he never experienced. He was a talking head that people liked, but he was just another chatterbox with a smile you could see from space. She was always genuinely nice to him, her cookies were to write home about and, although sex wasn't his endgame, if she gave him half a chance, he would love to slap her million dollar derriere and ride the wave till the break of dawn.

"You're an asshole," he said with shame.

He snapped out of his reverie. The car was heating up, and smelling foul, so he rolled down the window. What he really hated was him sitting in that car for hours on end. It always makes those thoughts percolate and bubble up from the depths. He was bored, his ass hurt and he was lonely.

Tired of waiting, and ashamed of himself for thinking someone as pure as Lorna could be up to something diabolical, he decided to give up on his amateur spy act and reached for the ignition. That's when he saw Lorna approaching her car. She wrestled a large gray, mottled camera case into the trunk then drove off.

"What the hell?"

Kal couldn't believe that he was actually going through with this. If he got caught spying on Lorna, he would most certainly lose his job. He would most likely end up in jail. He was positive that Chloe would bail him out, because that is what not-too-distant future girlfriends do. But it was too early in the relationship, if you could call it that, for that sort of embarrassment. He thought his mom would be the best bet in that situation, but that brought on an entirely new set of issues.

"Dang," he tapped on the steering wheel. "Nobody to bail you out, Kal?"

He convinced himself that he wouldn't be spending any time in the jug anytime soon. Tailing a car came easy to him. He was a natural. He never got too close, nor too far. He stayed a few cars back, but never let Lorna out of his sight. He paid attention to her movements. She wasn't driving too carefully or too erratically. She wasn't checking the mirrors more than average. He knew that his skill at this was enough to make a police chief blush.

At a stoplight, he came to his senses and called off the mission. By the time the light turned green, he talked himself back into it.

"I've come this far. Who's going to get those cookies tonight?"

Kal followed Lorna into a zigzagging residential area. There was no traffic to hide him so he left plenty of room between him and his mark. He turned his headlights off, using hers as a distant gauge. The houses here were opulent, and grew larger and more spacious with each turn of the wheel. During the last few zigs, wrought iron gates had sprung curbside like black fingers of guardian giants hiding the master's homes from prying eyes.

At last, Lorna's brake lights burned red; demon eyes floating through the inky darkness. They hovered momentarily and Kal pulled to the curb, under cover of ancient oaks. He strained to see, but could only make out the two lights, until an even blacker darkness enveloped and winked them out.

"Shit, gates," he mumbled as he chewed on his bottom lip.

Shoes on the ground where they belonged, Kal gagged down some air, which had become a thick, salty soup. He couldn't believe that he had managed to heave and grunt his way over the stone wall. Adrenaline overload made his eyes bug out of his skull, but it helped to get a sense of his surroundings. The driveway wound lazily around more of the oak trees, which were popular around here, and ended in front of a mansion. In the dark, the place resembled something straight out of a Dracula movie. In the daylight, it was probably just another Spanish style villa. The lawn was massive, and he could make out some kind of topiary in the center of it. It could have been a fountain, but his pounding heart would have drowned out the noise from Niagara Falls.

He picked an end point, a beacon light inside the mansion entrance, and began his slow and silent trek.

Lights flashed from behind him, projecting his shadow all the way up to the house. He froze. Motion sensors never entered into his plan, until now. He fully expected spotlights from guard towers, alarms, Nazis with machine guns and dogs with heads the size of Volkswagens any second, but they didn't come. He slowly realized that the lights came from the street, accompanied by the sound of an idling motor. Just a car.

He pushed his feet through the dew-coated lawn and made it to the window just left of the mansion entrance. He pumped his fist in pure exhilaration. He had done good.

Shrubbery leaned against the entire front of the house. It would provide cover for him and he applauded the owner's choice of foliage. Vines wouldn't have worked well for this operation.

Rising from a crouch, he peered inside. The view was that of a giant foyer. The décor was elegant, but indistinguishable. He couldn't surmise who lived here, and that was bugging him.

There was a massive staircase in the center of the room. The kind that flared out towards the bottom. This worried him.

"Please don't be upstairs," he begged. He needed whatever that was going on in there to be on the bottom floor. If they had gone up, his entire night was bust and he was nothing more than a degenerate peeping tom.

"Yes," he said as a man doddered his way down the stairs. He was a short, squat old man, but still too far away to tell who it was. He took the stairs one at a time, knees quivering like picnic gelatin with each step. He clung to the railing in a death grip and slid one, then the other hand, slowly down in sync with his feet.

"Hurry the hell up." Kal strained to identify the man, and felt that he, too, would be on his death bed before he could. The descent down the stairs was taking an eternity.

A man of this wealth and ill health should invest in an elevator, Kal thought.

Several minutes later, the man reached the ground floor. Both he and Kal let out an audible sigh of relief. The man teetered before finally getting his footing, then palmed the sweat from his brow. He shuffled around the side of the stairs and disappeared into the back recesses of the house. That had to be where Lorna was.

Kal retreated from the bushes and made his way around the side of the mansion, keeping low so he couldn't be seen from the windows. He stopped briefly when he heard faint rustling by the topiary. He waited, holding his breath. He focused his nervous attention on the movement of the leaves swaying in the breeze. He was thankful for the easy wind, as sweat was beading off of him.

Seeing no further movement and satisfied that the topiary would not attack, he made his way to the rear of house. As with the front, bushes created excellent cover near the windows. There was much concrete back here, which led to the pool area. The windows were much larger than in the front, giving him a better view, but there was more of a chance of being seen. The doors were large panes of sliding glass.

He heard Lorna's voice coming from within.

"...and what was it like that day? Tell me about it."

"I felt like a million bucks," the old man croaked. "I was on top of the world. I was just a kid from the Bronx. Not even in my wildest dreams," the old man said.

"And the rest was history."

"A lonnnng history. I never stopped working until just a few years ago when I retired."

The conversation continued, and Kal thought it was strange for friends to speak to each other like that. It almost sounded like an interview. Gulping courage, he poked his nose over the windowsill and gazed inside. He saw Lorna and the old man, sitting across from each other, as formally and comfortably as their patter.

His instincts were correct. This was an interview. Next to Lorna was a camera, pointing at the old man. A small red light showed it was recording. A quick survey of the room revealed the gray camera case that she hefted into her trunk. A medium sized leather bag sat next to it.

He still couldn't tell who the man was, as he could only see a three quarter view from behind a reclining chair. Mostly, he saw a pudgy arm moving to the rhythm of his labored speech.

"Damn it," he whispered. "Who are you?"

"It stopped being fun," the old man went on. "All of my friends from those days are gone. There's nobody to play with. The Big Gold one can't bring them back."

"Big Gold one?!" Kal hoped he shouted only inside his head. "Give it up! Who *are* you?" He intently scanned the dark, cherry wood shelves. "Bingo!"

There, just over Lorna's shoulder, front and center of all the other antiquities was that golden ticket to fame. The Grand Puba of awards. The one that everybody in Hollywood wanted to place on their mantle. Big Gold. Kal ruled out that the old man was a producer or a director. He had to be a star. Otherwise, Lorna wouldn't be here at all.

This was driving him mad, and he had to stop himself short of breaking the glass and screaming at the old fool to reveal himself. Whoever he may be, Kal felt sorry for him. The man was a huge star at some point, maybe even before electricity. From the looks of his palace, he lived a life that most couldn't even begin to dream about. He outlived his friends and loved ones, which left him all alone. And Kal knew how that was. Not the old part. He knew how the mind played cruel games with you when there was silence. When there was nothing to fill the void of loneliness. Kal thought it must be torture to be elderly like the unknown man inside. When he heard the distant gallop of insecurities coming, he was able to ward them off with a trip to a favorite watering hole or dinner at the loudest restaurant he could find. But when you aren't mobile, your only option is to sit and ride the memory trail. Kal had just over thirty years to contend with. Living to be over eighty, like this man, hundred had to be a grueling experience. The Grim Reaper may rob you of your dignity, but God was a true sadist.

"Are we done now?" Kal heard the man inside question.

"I think we got everything we needed."

"That's it then. Let's move on to the second act," he said, rubbing those pudgy hands together.

Lorna's smile grew from ear to ear. She stood and turned the camera off.

"I'll be right back. I need to freshen up." She turned her back to the old man, picked up the leather bag and trotted towards the far door. She turned to the old man and winked before disappearing from the room.

"Second act?" Kal wondered. "What in the shit is going on?"

The old man stood from his chair, still rubbing his hands together as if warming them. Kal leaned through the bushes, desperately trying to see his face. The man turned and looked straight in his direction. Kal's stomach lurches; he knew the man, had seen him a thousand times.

Willy Bartling.

Bartling was a bonafide Hollywood legend. He was the biggest child star of his day, but unlike most, he kept getting work as an adult and transitioned his early success into a flourishing career that lasted decades. Kal knew that he had over two hundred credits to his resume, but none were as famous as a long string of films in the 30s and 40s, where he played a precocious street urchin named Willy, no less, who solved crimes on poverty row. The crimes were always just some kind of misunderstanding, and the movies always ended with him getting some kind of punishment like painting a fence. Kal saw them all when he was a kid and loved the way they spoke in that old lingo. But he watched them mainly because Willy had a hilarious black man who played his side-kick by the name of Montague Moorhouse. He was one of the greatest scaredy cat types of the silver screen. Kal stifled laughter as he remembered that guy's bugging eyes when he screamed, "Mistahh Willeeeeeeeeeeee!!" Pure comic genius. He made a mental note to see if Chloe could find those movies for him.

Not wanting to play a kid forever, Willy Bartling chose a serious role to tackle, and it paid off the first time out. He won the award, Big Gold, which was sitting on the shelf on the other side of the room. He continued on in countless other roles for the next several decades. None that were memorable, but his place in history had long been solidified.

Although Willy was older than Noah, he still had a child-like appearance. This was surprising since he was also a legendary drinker. He was short and a good few over two hundred pounds. Basically bald, but with a few strands of hair looped from one ear to the other. Despite hearing about his dearly departed days, Kal still caught a twinkle in the man's cataract-filled eyes.

Willy shuffled to the glass sliding door, fanning his head with those fat little hands of his. A smile plastered to his face, he cackled like a loon as he slid open the door. Kal pushed himself further into the bushes, so as not to be seen. He knew if Willy looked his way, he would be caught. Willy's face had turned an unattractive red, and Kal wasn't sure if that was due to his apparent hot flashes or the thousand plus years of boozing.

"Hot dilly," Willy shouted to the yard between bouts of spastic laughter. Kal almost gave himself away when he heard the icon utter his catchphrase, but he managed to clasp his hand over his guffawing mouth.

Willy buried his head into his double chin and started working at his belt. He battled with it for a moment, then finally freed himself of the buckle. He ripped at the Velcro closure of his waistband and dropped his pants around his ankles. Kal guessed that people with money could pee wherever they wanted to. But the only thing Willy relieved himself of was his boxer shorts. He pulled them all the way down then carefully stepped out of them, using the door jam as a brace. His gut hung out of the bottom of his shirt and created an awning over his stubby penis. His shriveled testicles were as hairless as his head. His legs were stocky, and were adorned with elastic garters at the knees to hold up his socks. His wrinkled ass drooped and disappeared into his thighs, and Kal thought he looked like a deflating balloon that was once the shape of a turkey.

Kal absolutely loved this. To think he had almost gone home and missed all of the action. His only regret was that he wouldn't be able to tell anybody about it. And if he did, nobody would believe him. Lorna was prudish, and this old lecher's saggy balls were bound to give her a heart attack right here and now. Kal could hardly contain himself, waiting to see the look on her face. He wished he could get to that camera inside and record this. *Ro*becca* failed in comedy comparison.

"Are you ready?" Lorna called from inside.

"Yes, ma'am," Willy shouted as he turned in military attention.

Both men turned their gaze to the far side of the room, where Lorna stood. Kal's mouth dropped, and his eyes bulged as if he were auditioning for Willy's sidekick. He was confused to the point that he wasn't sure if he was still on planet earth.

Lorna had traded her conservative blouse and skirt for scanty lingerie. It was corseted blue, and sculpted her amazing body. Like Willy, she wore garters, but Kal could easily pick the winner in this category. Lorna took a couple strides, then turned, bounced her hips back and forth, and stopped. She placed one hand on her hip and let the leather bag she was carrying dangle off of her index finger. She had not let her beauty queen training get rusty. She was a knockout, especially for a woman in her mid-fifties.

She tossed the leather bag next to the recliner and gave Willy a come hither in one fluid movement. She was a pro in all regards.

"Get over here," she cooed.

Willy laughed like a gold crazy prospector as he scooted his feet towards her, his tallywhacker pecking around like a baby bird in search of food.

She took one of his hands and seductively spun him into the chair she was sitting in earlier. Lorna pranced around the recliner before bending over, palms flat on the floor, giving Willy a full view of her insurance dividend. She took a small vial out of the leather bag without losing her balance. Willy licked his lips and slobbered, which Kal found disgusting, even from the distance. On any other normal day, he would have been aroused, but this was no normal day.

She stood, snaked her panties slowly around her ankle and kicked them into the corner of the room. She then assumed her bent position once more. Kal got firsthand proof that the million dollar policy on her ass was not a publicity stunt. It was worth every penny, and should be considered a national treasure.

"Oh boy!" Willy gasped as he bongoed his hands on her cheeks. She opened the vial and tapped white powder onto the small of her back.

"You like that candy, do you?" she purred as Willy buried his moon face. Kal could hear the slurping from where he stood, and it turned his stomach. Willy came up for air and glubbed for breath, puffing a cloud of cocaine from his nostrils like a defeated dragon. His tongue lolled helplessly around that pumpkin mouth of his. As stomach churning as he looked, Kal knew that Willy was having the best night of his life, and wondered how many hundreds of others he had just like this.

Willy started for another round, but Lorna spun on him, pushing him back into his chair.

"It's your turn," she breathed as she got on her knees and tapped the remainder of the snow onto Willy's stump.

"Hot dilleeeeeee," he said as his eyes rolled into his head.

Lorna's perfect hair bobbed slowly and rhythmically like a bee's nest on the end of a long stick. Willy pumped the air with his fists before resting them on her head.

"Don't fuck up my hair," she warned before slapping him across the face with the back of her hand. Willy wiped a droplet of blood from his livered lips, then licked it with his strangled eel of a tongue.

"Let's get to the good stuff, baby! I want the good stuff! Let's get on with it! Stop foolin' around." The blow had taken effect, and he launched out of the chair, knocking Lorna to the ground. "Are you sure this is the way to do it?"

"I'm positive."

"Then grab that bag of yours and do it to it!" He snatched Big Gold off of the shelf and goose stepped through the door.

Lorna's eyes sparkled as she plucked the leather bag from the floor and followed bouncing Willy out of the room.

Kal moved to the sliding glass for a better vantage point. He saw Lorna and Willy further down the hallway. They stopped at a room, and Willy military turned inside. Lorna took some kind of black cloth and what looked like rope from her leather bag and disappeared within.

"You sick old prick," Kal uttered in disappointment. The show was over. He had a full view of the hallway, but not inside the room. Whatever was going on in there was something that could not be missed. He had no idea what the good stuff was Willy spoke of. But what he had already witnessed was no less than superb. If Lorna was saving the good stuff for last, then it must involve a fireworks display and a trained kitten.

He moved from window to window, craning his neck to get a view. All he could see were shadows spilling into the hallway. He raised his hands in despair, spun around and clicked his tongue in disbelief as if somebody turned the channel on him just before the winning touchdown.

That's when he realized that the sliding glass door was still standing open.

Kal stood in the center of the living room, listening to the domineering tone of Lorna Hope and the muffled panting of Willy Bartling down the hall. His imagination raced as to what was happening behind that door, but a horrendous unease came over him. Not at what he, himself, was doing, but in regards to the sheer kink that he was unable to witness. Nor did he want to anymore.

The sounds agitated him for reasons unknown, and his disdain for the woman turned his stomach. It was people like those in the next room that kept Kal at bay, never sharing what it was they had, and not inviting him to the show. As usual, he was on the outside looking in, and it just wasn't acceptable to him anymore.

It came to him all at once, in a haze of red rage. It frightened him that he had reached this point, but it also fueled his decision. He had never before achieved this monumental lack of control, and it was not something that could be calmed on a long coastal drive. The beast had to be satiated, and Lorna would be the sacrifice.

He grabbed the digital camera that Lorna used to record the interview off of the tripod, turned it on and stormed down the hall. He saw the shadows poking out from under the door, but they weren't enough. He needed to see it all. He kicked the door in.

"Jesus Christ!" bellowed from Kal's lungs as he took in the scene.

Lorna kneeled next to an open closet, where Willy Bartling hung from the pole in a kneeling position. His knees swung just inches from the floor. Kal recognized the pieces of cloth Lorna retrieved from the bag as silk neckties, expertly knotted for added length. One used for a blindfold, several for the hanging rope and another to tie his arms awkwardly behind his back.

Fully undressed, he had what some would call an erection, and Lorna was on her knees, tugging at it. Willy swung back and forth to the rhythm of her hands.

"Who ghat?" Willy said through the gag. His head looked ready for NASA countdown. It was a deep red, and the veins on his neck were set to pop. It was clear that he was close to losing consciousness.

"Kal!?" a shocked Lorna spun from her position. "What the fuck are you doing here?!"

"Who ith Kahhh?" Willy croaked.

Kal had heard of autoerotic asphyxiation before. And he knew that it was the single most embarrassing way for a man to die. Way further up the scale than reaching for a roll of Charmin. Many famous men had gone out that way, and all of their accomplishments in life were forever overshadowed by a final act of sleaze.

"Jesus Christ!" Kal repeated.

Lorna bounded to him. "It isn't what you think."

But he knew that it was always worse than what you think. "Jesus Christ!"

His face went red hot and it took him a moment to register that Lorna had slapped him. Dazed from the open hand and the image of Willy, he looked at her with listless eyes.

"Did you like that? I can do it again." she asked.

He didn't, and he wouldn't let her. She swung with a fist, but he was able to knock the blow aside. She pulled at the camera, but Kal clenched it with a death grip.

"What do you plan to do with that? Give it to me."

"You're not getting anything. Not anymore! No more breaking news! No more exclusives! No more expensive gift bags! No more final interviews!" Kal stomped the floor, spittle flying from his mouth. "It's my turn. I want it. I deserve it! And this tape is my ticket to it!"

"That's what this is all about? You don't feel like you're getting enough time in the sun?" Her smile widened. "Kalvin, all you had to do was say something to me. That would have been a lot easier than all of this, don't you think?"

"What'thhh goinnnnnngah?" Willy panted from his closet perch.

"Hush up, Willy. We already did the interview."

"Get him down from there, He's going to die!"

"Yeaghuh," Willy strained. Drool cascaded over his chin.

Kal was thunderstruck. "Final... interview?"

"Yes, Kal. Now why don't you put down the camera and let Mr. Bartling go in peace."

"Guhng peakhhh?!"

"How is *that* going in peace? He doesn't want to die."

"It's the best way for him. He hasn't been news for a long, long time. Years have gone by, and people have forgotten him. This will get him a lead-in, and he'll be remembered forever. Isn't that right, Willy?" She went to him and caressed his purple head.

"Ungh-ughh. Noh."

"You just hang tight. It'll all be over soon, dear." And with that, she put her full weight on his shoulders. The gurgling rattle that emanated from within Willy's gut turned Kal's.

"Cut him down! You're killing him!"

"It's what he wants. Isn't that right, baby?"

"Fughh nogh..." Willy's red mottled head darted back and forth. He strained against his ties.

Kal searched inside but couldn't find his will to act.

"Now let's talk about what Kal wants." She slinked to him and ran a finger from his lips to his crotch.

"How many times have you done this?" he asked with an uneasy step backwards.

She pouted her lips and shrugged her shoulders. "I don't keep score. But they're not all like this."

"It's all murder, isn't it?"

"Not if they want it. Not if they need it. I call it one hand washing the other. I'm doing them a favor, and in return, they give me..."

"Their final interview. Some favor. This is how you've been able to stay on top all of these years. You don't wait for the news. You create it."

"Kal, there's a lot you need to learn about this business. I saw an opportunity and I took it." She led him out of the room by the arm. "Now let's let Willy do his thing and stop talking about the past. Let's sit down and talk about the future of Kal Kash."

Kal glanced over his shoulder at Willy, whose body had begun to convulse. He knew that he had to help the old man, but his mind had severed all ties to his body.

"Wuhhait... wuhhere you gung?"

Kal sat nervously in the recliner and Lorna stood behind him, her hands rubbing his chest. His blind rage had dissipated and turned to horror when he viewed Willy hanging in the next room. Lorna cooed sultry into his ear, but he could not relax his racing heart. It didn't help that Willy's breathing became labored and erratic, bouncing along the wood paneled hallway, and it pummeled into Kal's ear like a derrick.

"I've been doing this so long, Kal. It doesn't get any easier. I'm not young anymore. It might be nice to have someone younger, stronger, to help me. There would be... *rewards*. On the air, and off."

Kal gulped as she licked her lips. Even with a tied-up slobbering octogenarian hanging in the next room, Lorna was devastatingly sexy. And appealing to his ego was a sure-fire way to talk Kal into anything. But still, his brain was screaming that this was all wrong.

"Lonaghan?" he asked.

"What about him?"

"Did you kill him?"

"No, I didn't kill him. Drugs are the easy way out. I gave

him some super special cookies and Lonaghan took care of himself. It's the ones like that old bastard in there that are hard to pull off."

"Oh," he uttered as if understanding.

"It's the perfect time to turn the reins over to you. You're right. You deserve everything that you want. Just do me a little favor, huh?" Her hands slipped off his chest.

"What's that?"

"I mean, I'll mentor you for the first few, but don't forget me. Give me a little taste now and then, won't you?" Her voice hitched.

He knew something was wrong, as if anything had gone right tonight. His heart beat into his throat, and he found it increasingly difficult to swallow it down.

Willy began to scream in the other room. It was deafening. A heaving gasp, then a guttural scream. One after the other. There was banging and knocking and crashing and more heaves and screams. It overtook Lorna's low, sensual voice, and even Kal's own inner critic that was yelling at him to get out of the chair and call the police. Willie's screech consumed every thought that Kal had. Nothing else existed at that moment. Kal had never been witness to a man's death rattle, but something in his bones told him that this was not that sound. The cacophony in the next room was that of a man who wanted to survive.

"Don't pay any attention to that silly old Willy. He can't do for you what I can do for you." She pulled his head back by the hair and covered his mouth with hers. It was a moment that he had always dreamed of. But it wasn't sitting right.

"Kevin Locke?" Kal asked.

"That one was fun."

It was all Kal could take. He pushed her off of him, purged himself of the chair and rocketed down the hallway to save Willie.

"Kal," Lorna shouted, and he turned to her on instinct. He knew that he would see her running after him, pleading. The last thing he expected was to see her swinging the tripod like a club. But like everything else today, nothing was as Kal expected.

He didn't know how long he was out, but he was sure it was only a few seconds. An eye squeaked open, but everything was filtered through cobwebs. A large baby lumbered by his blurry frame and crashed into the wall. It spun around, and ran wildly out of view. His other eye fluttered open, and the vision was much worse. Lorna squatted directly over him, strangling him with the tripod. Somehow, she had managed to fill his arm with concrete, because he could barely lift it to slap her. He managed less than a love tap, and it didn't even mess her hair. He knew in that instant that he was a dead man.

He closed his eyes so that he could imagine something far better than the deranged green ones that bore into his. He gasped for air, but the tripod forced him to choke it back up. He heard crashes and wild screaming elsewhere in the room, and he blessed the naked baby who was voicing what he could not.

It wasn't true what they said about your life flashing before your eyes, he thought. The only snippets that flickered by were that of failure. Kal thought it was all a sick joke. It was too hard to concentrate on the happy memories when your brain was on fire and there was shrieking in your head that wasn't yours.

The bawling screech grew louder as the giant baby neared, and Kal figured that this was as close to an angel's trumpet as he was going to hear.

I'm dying, and some asshole still has to steal my thunder, he thought. Kal felt a lurch in his chest, and he wondered how long these death throes would last. He waited for another one, but it didn't come. Lorna's weight shifted away from him, and he was able to swallow a breath. He creaked his eyes open, and blinked through the haze. Lorna was in a tumble several feet away. The careening baby hulked over her, slapping and pulling and she kicked it away.

It stumbled by Kal, and he saw that it wasn't a leviathan infant after all. It was Willy, who had somehow managed to escape the closet. The neckties were dangling from his neck and wrists, and he looked more like a derelict marionette escaping from Gepetto's work shed than a human being. Kal lifted his head and followed the pinballing spectacle with detachment. He had wondered where Big Gold had disappeared to, and there it was, sticking out of Willy's ass like a balloon knot.

"Sweet Jesus," Kal mumbled.

Willy bounced off the wall gut first and with a wail. The pressure from the contact was enough to dislodge the statue, which rocketed out with a thunderous fart.

"beep... bloop. Sorry. Daddy. It. Was. A. Taco. Malfunction," rolled through Kal's head, but this time, he couldn't laugh.

Willy spun out of control and cried his way out the sliding door and into the pool with a splash.

Kal's body reminded him to breathe, and he did with a choke. He managed himself onto his elbows and saw that Lorna had done the same. Her teeth gritted and her hands still grasped the tripod. Sheer insanity widened her eyes and she clawed her way to him.

He didn't see the tripod strike him, but he sure felt it. The blow spun his body on the floor and all he could think was, "What next?"

Lorna used the tripod to gain her footing. She stood over Kal, raised it over her head and was set to impale him with it.

It was too ugly for him to look at. Big Gold glinted into the corner of his eye as it finally rolled to a stop. Kal turned to it, and thought it was the most beautiful thing he had ever seen. It was the embodiment of all of his fantasies. He placed a hand on it, and set it upright and respectful, like it deserved.

"You little bitch!" she shouted, and he hated that those were the last words that he would ever hear. He closed his eyes in preparation and heard a dull thud, followed by a slippery crack.

After a moment of nightmare silence, he peeked through his eyelids, and just as he thought, there was Lorna. Only she wasn't looming over him anymore. She had somehow fallen to the floor and was laying face down. The electricity had gone out of her eye and her open smile was condemned. Blood streamed from the back of her perfect hair and down her face like fast growing roots. Somehow, Lorna had fallen and taken possession of Willy's Big Gold—Smack dab through her eye and out the back of her head.

Her body lay lifeless on the floor as Kal's began to rise. His soul was taking flight, but he didn't think it would be this slow and rough of a ride. He jostled quite a bit as he looked down to see his body next to Lorna's but it wasn't there.

"You gotta help me, man."

He thought that was a funny thing for an angel's greeting, but he would take what he could get. His body turned, and he realized that it was his favorite angel of all.

"Chloe?"

She put his arm around her shoulder and hefted his weight into the recliner, which enveloped him with warmth and a feeling of safety. He let his eyes drift close, and his body collapsed with relief.

"I'm so glad you came. How did you know I was here?"

"I followed you all night. I thought you saw me by the topiary earlier."

"I *thought* somebody was there. Hey, this shit is really crazy, isn't it?"

"Yup."

"I can't believe that Lorna. What a bitch."

A noise sounded in front of him, a ripping sound, but he was too tired to open his eyes to see what it was.

What's that?" he asked dreamily.

"Don't worry about it. Just relax."

"Ok. That poor giant baby. Is he dead?"

"Willy? I pulled him out of the pool. He's going to be great."

"Good," he slurred as he tried to raise his eyelids but only managed to lift his brows. "I really thought I was a goner. I was almost Lorna's trifecta. I thought I was number three."

"Hush, Kal. You'll always be my number one."

He forced his eyes open so he could look at the other most beautiful thing he had ever seen, but Chloe wasn't there. He tried to move, but couldn't. He looked down, and saw that his arms and body were wrapped in duct tape.

"Chloe?!" he called as he heard her footsteps clattering away.

He struggled to free himself, but couldn't get leverage. A shadow lumbered behind him.

"Willy? Thank God you're ok!"

The shadow encroached and Willy's pudgy hands came into view. One took hold of an end of the dangling necktie around the other's wrist....

"Please... please help me out of this."

...the necktie twisted around Kal's neck...

"Please, Willy. I'm a big fan."

...and pulled.

"Sorry, buddy. That gal offered me a hot dilly."

* * *

News of the bizarre events fueled entertainment programs, late night talk show comedians and celebrity disaster seekers for weeks. But it was the new *All Access* anchor, Chloe Steiner, who led the charge in breaking the story and all of the latest developments. It was the kind of story that jumpstarted a career, and Chloe learned from the best on how to keep a good thing going.

"I still just can't believe what happened," said the makeup woman as she dabbed foundation on Chloe's forehead.

"I know, right?" Chloe said with shocked delight. "But that doesn't get you out of it. Cough up the goods." Chloe held out her hand. The woman chuckled, reached into her brassiere and slapped a twenty dollar bill into the waggling fingers.

"I never win this stupid thing. Why on earth would you have Kalvin Kash on your Dead Pool?"

"Lucky guess. Everybody goes sooner or later."

"I'll get that twenty back some day. Just you wait."

"I'm not going anywhere." They shared a smile and the woman disappeared with her makeup bag into the fray of the busy studio.

Chloe turned in her chair and beamed as the camera closed in on her. She heard the three, two, one countdown from a stage hand, and her face turned from elation to mock earnest before the light on top of the camera turned red.

"The death of an American sweetheart. The latest on the salacious sex crimes and shocking murder of *All Access'* very own Lorna Hope by the hands of her jealous co-worker and deranged killer, Kalvin Kash. Check your local listings for our special one hour tribute to the life, loves and legacy of Lorna Hope. We'll miss her very much.

"What sparked the horrible events leading up to this international tragedy? We'll speak with family and friends from Killer Kal's bitter past to try to get some insight into the mind of a jealous psychopath.

"Later, we'll hear directly from everyone's favorite perpetual child star, living legend, award winner and now, media darling, Willy Bartling, and his heroic role in this torrid love triangle. He'll recount his futile attempt to save Lorna's life. And how he bravely faced off against the disturbed Killer Kal, and brought him to vigilante justice. Willy will also tell us about another new role that he'll be tackling, besides being a national hero; that as the oldest contestant on the new season of *CelebriDance!* Such a cutie.

"We'll have all of that and more coming up right after the break, including my very own *All Access* exclusive, Kalvin Kash's final interview."

Star Wars *fans take note: Brian Muir, a.k.a. Domonic Muir, did* not *sculpt the Darth Vader helmet. He did, however, invent the furry little aliens known as* Critters *in the eighties cult classic of the same name. As a screenwriter he followed that early success with over two decades of film work ranging from Jet Li action/ adventures to Garfield animated features, and sharing credit for the acclaimed indie "neo-noir" film* Broke Sky. *An Elmore Leonard fan, he hit his stride as a crime writer as well, thrilling readers of* Ellery Queen *and* Alfred Hitchcock *mystery magazines with many tales revolving around a female private detective set in his home-town of Portland, Oregon. He was a two-time cancer survivor who died of complications of a brain tumor in 2010 at age 48. He leaves behind four novels, dozens of short stories and a large body of film criticism. You can read more at* www. squidoo.com/BrianDomonic Muir.

NOT ELVES

Brian Domonic Muir

SNORTING, THE OLD MAN AWOKE, with the back of his hand wiping drool from his mouth. He rattled in his seat, the row empty but for him. The plane. Yes, now he remembered. Cabin lights dim for the nighttime flight. The few others aboard asleep or reading or talking quietly. A flight attendant stood near the curtain to first class, scowling.

The old man turned to look out his small window. Nothing but dark greyness out there. A blinking light on the wing tip fought to show its brightness through the soup of passing clouds. Ice crystals sparkled on riveted metal.

He tilted his watch to glance at its face, but time meant nothing to him. He couldn't recall when the flight was scheduled to land, his memory not what it once was, his brain atrophied like his sinew, once firm and strong.

He turned his head and, drooping his chin on his shoulder, was asleep again in moments.

"What's the matter with you?" his legal aide said when she saw Bill grinning to himself and staring at the lights of Los Angeles sweeping away from his office window.

It was Merrilee that caused him to daydream so. Thinking of her often made it difficult for Bill to focus on the case files stacked high on his desk, though in court he never faltered. Imagining Merrilee watching him from the gallery, he preened and strutted, owning the courtroom, engaging the jury with his commanding closing arguments.

Whenever the judge's gavel signaled recess, Bill couldn't wait to call Merrilee, to see her, to kiss her sweet lips and hug her so hard he might crush her petite form, feeling every inch of her body against his, smelling lilac in her brown curls.

On Saturday evenings, Bill went to Mass with Merrilee. He couldn't think of not going—just to spend time with her— though sitting in that dark ornate church brought him discomfort; the hymns sung by those gathered, rather than a calming peace seemed to exude sadness. For until Merrilee, Bill had not been inside the walls of a church since he was nine years old.

His mother had taken him to Midnight Mass that Christmas and he'd been embraced by the love of those gathered, heart lifted by their song, warmed by Father's sermon of Christ's open arms and the comfort of God's heaven waiting for them beyond this life. But driving home that dark Christmas Eve, a young caroler dressed as an elf had darted across the street in front of them. His mother swerved to avoid him, skidding on black ice, rolling the car. She'd been ejected through the windshield glass. Unhooking himself from his seat belt, young Bill had rushed to her side. The group of carolers costumed as elves watched from the curb, stunned, their long ears pointed skyward. The words of Father's sermon meant nothing to Bill at that moment, cradling his mother's head in his lap, her tender neck twisted and sliced like fresh beef, blood steaming on the frigid air. Bill felt no warmth in the thought of Christ's open arms nor the comfort of heaven welcoming his mother, only the sharp freeze of black ice and earth beneath him.

They'd met Karchi one night as they emerged from church, Bill and Merrilee with arms wrapped around each other, she kissing his cheek, teasing him that he should have listened instead of stroking her leg while the priest was sermonizing.

Karchi marched briskly past going the other way and Bill didn't give him a second glance, seeing out of the corner of his eye the rags of a homeless person.

"Good work the other day, counselor," they both heard him say behind them.

They turned to see him grinning wide. His homeless rags were in reality a three hundred dollar pair of jeans extending on long legs out from under an Armani overcoat, a Kangol perched crookedly atop a mop of stylish curls. And, as improbable as it seemed, a skateboard tucked under one arm. Bill recognized him: Karchi, one name only like Moby or McG, the hottest filmmaker in Hollywood. Known for his eccentric behavior and flighty tendencies, he surprised everyone with the *Ahriman* trilogy, a sort of mashup of "Gangs of New York" and the Book of Revelation that earned an Oscar for Best Film Editing and seven total nominations, including Best Picture.

He held out his hand, "Karchi. You're Rettig, right? Bill Rettig? I saw you in the paper last week."

Bill shook Karchi's hand, introducing Merrilee.

Karchi's teeth sparkled like ice. "It was great you putting away Tarling like you did."

Bill blinked. Karchi was referring to Stephen Tarling, who'd stolen a hundred million dollars in a stock scam; Bill had spoken to the press after successfully convicting him. It seemed a random subject for the director to bring up in a chance encounter, but then Karchi was noted for his randomness. Perhaps he was interested in turning the story into a film.

Karchi shifted his skateboard under the other arm. "Scum like him fascinate me as you might have guessed—I assume you saw the first 'Ahriman'?"

Bill shook his head, embarrassed.

Karchi laughed. "All the better, to know someone utterly unimpressed by my *oeuvre*. Say, how 'bout I buy you two a drink?"

Merrilee sipped her white wine, one hand on Bill's knee under the table, listening as the two men engaged in spirited debate.

"So you're saying it's not because Tarling was ripping off thousands of investors that you're happy I put him away, it's because he stole money from two of *your* investors."

Karchi's grin hadn't left his face since they'd entered the sports bar, "Got to look out for number one, baby."

He raised a tall wide glass, draining the last of his dark ale. Catching the cute server's eye, he ordered another for himself and Bill.

"And here I'd pegged you for the altruistic type," said Bill, not without a note of bemusement.

"Look at it this way, counselor: I've worked hard, building a business from the ground up, my number one goal: To make myself rich. In doing so, I've created hundreds of jobs, entertained thousands of fans and added depth previously missing from the angels-versus-demons genre, at least according to the critics who think the rest of my stuff sucks. That benefits society, brother, not just yours truly."

Bill asked, "So when I put away a child molester, are you happy I've rid society of that menace, or happy because it protects your children, assuming you have any?"

Karchi shot back, "Answer me this, honestly. Every time you put away one of those scum are you telling me you're not thinking about improving your conviction record, upping your paycheck, greasing your path to the District Attorney's seat? That's not completely altruistic, is it?"

Karchi grabbed a handful of Spanish peanuts from a bowl and popped them into his grinning mouth one by one.

Bill often contemplated going into private practice where there was more money and less stress, especially now, with his increased workload at the D.A.'s office. Crime in the city was on the rise; violent, often unspeakable crime, and many of those cases fell on his desk. What he saw in evidence photos and heard in court testimony turned his stomach and hardened his heart.

He and Merrilee talked often of marriage and eventually having children, but to raise those children in a world with such darkness frightened Bill to the brink of tears.

Merrilee would comfort him, holding him close in their bed, "It's not so bad, honey."

"You don't understand the things I see. The things people do to each other."

"I know," she pulled him to her breast. "I know."

In an orange jumpsuit, wiry Isaac Szardo right-angled the defendant's table, shackled wrist to ankle. His public defender sat next to him, quivering, mopping his forehead with a handkerchief.

Szardo fixed dead black eyes on the county Medical Examiner foxholed in the witness box.

At one time an aspiring actor, Szardo was playing up the homicidal maniac with Ed Harris-like intensity, the ferocity in his visage like a fist poised for the solar plexus. Though everyone in that courtroom knew the trail of carnage he'd left since going insane was anything but scripted. Word was even Manson, to whom Szardo had written several letters since his capture, found the murderer repugnant.

Bill stood next to the jury, all of them peering at the blown-up photos perched on the easel, several jurors quickly looking away from the horrific images.

As the M.E. recounted technical details of the family murder scene—briefly, so as not to repulse the jury more than necessary—Szardo turned to view the disturbing images with absolutely nothing on his face.

"Thank you, doctor." Bill finished his line of questioning and returned to his table.

The judge turned to the defense. "Counsel?"

The public defender glanced at his client shackled next to him, Szardo still staring at the crime scene photos of the dead infant.

The lawyer swallowed once, "No questions at this time, your honor."

"Very well. Will the prosecution call their next witness...?"

As Bill stood to address the court, Szardo spoke up, his voice scratchy and dry, "Your witnesses are unnecessary."

The judge scowled, "Will defense counsel please tell your client to be quiet? If he wants to testify he can do so on the stand."

"Of course, your honor, I apolog—"

Szardo interrupted, "Soon, you will all bear witness to what is about to happen."

The judge white-knuckled his gavel, "Be quiet, sir. Or I will hold you in contempt."

Szardo's clipped, sour laugh was the first emotion he'd shown since the proceedings began. "Contempt? You're pathetic, clinging to these archaic rituals of civilized jurisprudence. You think you have the right to judge me?"

"Keep talking and I'll have your mouth taped shut, and don't think I won't do it."

Szardo stood from his chair, chains rattling. A rumble went through the jury box. Two court bailiffs stepped forward, hands on pistol-butts.

The defense attorney leapt backward to get out of the way, clutching briefcase to chest like a shield.

At his table, Bill froze as Szardo locked onto him with those black shark eyes.

"It's happening all around you. Gathering those in prominent positions to the cause. Preparations for the return of the Great One, so he can once more rule the Earth..."

The judge slammed his gavel, the sound startling as an M-80. "Get him the hell out of here!"

The bailiffs each grabbed one of Szardo's arms. He offered no resistance, staring at Bill as he was dragged away: "He will vanquish love and turn the Earth to ash..."

Then Szardo was hustled out the side door and down the hall, where he could no longer be heard.

The judge tossed his gavel clattering to the bench. "Recess until tomorrow morning at 9:30." He jabbed a finger at the frightened young defense counsel, "And you'd better be able to control your client, or I'll hold *you* in contempt."

With a sweep of dark robes, he disappeared into his chambers.

Bill heard none of this, still haunted by Szardo's words, and those dark dead eyes.

Though it was six weeks before the world turned, it took less than six hours for Bill's life to unravel.

He let himself into the apartment, tie loosened, jacket draped over one arm. He tossed his case on the couch and spied a stack of envelopes on the table.

He sniffed the meaty aroma, "Smells good, hon, whatever it is."

He'd riffled through all the mail before he realized she hadn't answered him.

He poked his head in the kitchen.

Empty.

He opened the stove. Two Cornish game hens cooked, juices crackling in the pan, the skin too dark, too crisp.

He opened the fogged microwave glass to find a bowl of green beans, heated but already cooling.

"Lee?"

He strode through the front room, past the bathroom and

office—all empty—steps quickening as he approached the bedroom at the end of the hall, the door ajar.

Bursting inside, he saw the comforter strewn on the floor, as if torn from the bed. The window pane was busted in a gaping maw of jagged glass teeth.

"Lee!" Bill leapt to the open window, stuck his head into the cool evening air. The paint on the vacant fire escape peeled like a sunburn.

He heard the *shoooosh-slam* of a cargo door sliding shut, cranking his head to spy a mud-colored van pulling out of a parking space, nudging the bumper of the Toyota in front of it, sending the car alarm bansheeing as the van growled around the corner and out of sight.

"Leeeee!"

There was no one to listen but for the neighbors, who chose not to hear.

The police questioned the creep, a natural path in the course of the investigation, but he told them he would talk to Bill only.

So now Bill sat across from him, the man chained to a steel bench, a rabid dog on a short leash.

"What is it you wanted to tell me?" the question had trouble rising from the sour pit of his stomach.

Szardo stared at him, unsettling, then turned his gaze upon the prison guard at the rear of the cell.

Bill understood and to the guard he said, "Would you please leave us alone?"

"I'm afraid I can't do that, sir. You aren't his attorney and you know the regulations."

"Please. Leave."

The guard contemplated the pleading in Bill's eyes and seemed to consider the gravity of the situation, a woman's life at stake; and empathy with Bill's plight, the guard with his own young wife and newborn at home. Then he turned and left the cell, locking behind him the stone door with the tiny barred window.

Leaving Bill alone with the multiple murderer he was working so hard to convict.

"Where is she? Where's Merrilee?"

Szardo didn't smile, didn't grimace, showed no feeling at all as he answered, "You'll find her in the place she feels most comfortable, the place she brought you back to after so many years away."

Bill avoided looking into those dead eyes, running through his mind all the places he'd been with Merrilee.

"She's crying right now," continued Szardo. "She's thinking about you, frightened she'll never see you again, praying for you and not herself."

Yet still Szardo showed no emotion, big-knuckled hands interlaced in his lap. Like coiled sleeping vipers, his chains made not a tinkle of sound.

St. Agatha's quietly dominated the corner. Bill stood for minutes, wondering if this could be it. It made no sense to him. But as Szardo had intimated, the large church was certainly a place where Merrilee felt comfortable, a place she re-introduced him to, so many years after his dark Christmas Eve at another church so far away.

During his short discourse with Szardo the inference had been clear: No police. So Bill stood alone in the street gazing up at the dark cross topping the tall brick house of God, the place less inviting than it had ever seemed. He caressed cold steel in the pocket of his windbreaker but it failed to fortify him as he stepped off the sidewalk and up the front steps.

The doors were unlocked and he entered undisturbed. The pews were empty, not a worshipper in sight; no one kneeling with head bowed, thumb ticking off rosary beads; rack of votive candles lining the vestibule unlit, nothing but cold white wax.

The doors to the confessional booths were closed. Bill watched them for a moment, thinking he'd heard mumbling inside one, waiting for the confessor or priest to exit. But the doors did not open.

The mumbling emanated from elsewhere, below his feet.

His shoe soles shushed along the carpeted aisle as he made his way to the nave, softly opening the door to the sacristy. There he found the changing room for the priest and altar boys, coat hangers empty of cloaks and vestments. Through another door was father's small office; a framed print of Christ with glowing heart above a desk cluttered with letters and receipts.

The mumbling swelled to a chant as Bill found yet another narrow doorway at the rear of the office. Stepping through it he stood atop a claustrophobic stairway that dropped into a basement. Flickering shadows cast by candlelight on the wall below beckoned as the chanting pulsed with deadly rhythm.

Each footstep grew heavier as he descended the stairs, the steel in his pocket a lead barbell. His heart rabbit-thumped in his chest, lungs chuffing like broken bellows. His tongue clicked dry as he swallowed.

He stepped off the bottom stair onto concrete so cold he could feel it through his shoes. The chanting bounced off the walls and warped his ears, his view blocked by white altar boy robes hanging wet from clotheslines, glowing yellow from candlelight behind them as if afire, shadow-forms weaving side to side as if in chorus, distended and distorted.

Bill pulled the pistol from his pocket, a snub-nosed .38. He'd never fired it at another human, couldn't even imagine it, but if there were a time to do so it was certainly now, if poor Merrilee was down here in this cold church basement amid whoever was chanting in twisted Gregorian plainsong, the Satanic rumble cutting through to his marrow and vibrating his very soul.

He brushed aside heavy wet robes with the back of his hand, the pistol barrel leading him deeper toward the source of that incessant unharmonious verse.

He discerned another sound amid that rumble, the sound of Merrilee whimpering softly.

Bill swallowed a lump of emotion as he brushed through the last layer of hanging vestments to encounter the backs of a ring of people swaying to and fro, humming that horrific chant. All were dressed in everyday clothes, jeans and blouses, t-shirts and business attire; no black robes, scarlet hoods, or pentagrams hanging from chains, nothing out of a silly B-movie, which made them more real to him, more frightening. He couldn't see past or over them, but knew that Merrilee was somewhere in their center.

No one had seen him yet. They couldn't hear him over the noise they were making. As he clicked back the hammer of the pistol, the sound went unnoticed.

He considered the smartest course of action, feeling it best to go on the offensive, as he did in court when backing defense counsel into a tight corner.

He lifted the barrel toward the wood-beam ceiling and pulled the trigger. As if a one-eyed giant clapping great calloused hands, the loud crack caused some of the worshippers to flinch. All stopped their chanting and turned toward the source of the sound.

Bill cocked the pistol again, pointed it at the closest row of people staring at him.

He shouted, "Get back!" and knew it sounded stupid the moment he said it, but he could think of nothing else.

A few of the chanters shuffled their feet but didn't perceptibly change position.

"Lee!" he yelled into the now quiet basement.

"...Bill..." came the response, weak and tentative, as if her mouth were somehow restricted from free speech.

He shoved through those before him, pushing and prodding with the pistol barrel. A woman stepped in front of him, twentysomething grin malevolent behind hair that hung dirty in her face like old bootlaces.

He pressed the pistol to her chest. "Get away."

"You can't have her. Not yet," she grinned.

"Get back!" he shoved her with the pistol, but she wouldn't move.

So he shot her.

With a warm splash, her blood coated his knuckles; the ball of his thumb ached with the gunkick; the wince of barrel-smoke stung his nose.

Her head drooped, looking down at the hole in her chest, spreading crimson across her shirt. Then she raised her face and smiled, her eyes onyx marbles, black goo dripping from her lips.

Stunned, he raised the gun to her forehead to fire again, but was instantly swarmed by those around him. He struggled ineffectually against them, muscles straining to fight them off. They tore the pistol from his clawed fingers and it went off again, the bullet harmlessly *thwocking* a ceiling 2x4.

"No" and "Let me go" bellowed through the press of chanters who strong-armed him toward the center of the base-ment, where finally he beheld his beloved Merrilee, laid out on an altar of sorts crudely formed of sawhorses and a length of wallboard barren of ornamentation.

"Lee!"

Held down by an old man with dockworker's forearms and two young women restraining her legs and feet, she could only shake her head, wet eyes brimming with love and hope-lessness. Mascara ran down her cheeks in black rivulets.

He tried to reach her but couldn't, held back by strong arms a dozen in number.

Emerging from behind a damp-hanging priestly robe, making an entrance that appeared dripping with practiced theatricality, though one which he pulled off with casual aplomb was Karchi, his smile wide and arms open.

"Bill. Glad you could make it. You got my message from Szardo, I take it?"

Bill's mouth dropped open as if to catch a fly, too stunned to speak.

Karchi flicked his hand, a gesture telling those surround-ing Bill to release him but not relax their vigilance as they shouldered him on either side. Bill attempted no heroics as Karchi approached.

"What's going on?" he asked, almost too quiet to be heard.

"It's what Szardo said in court the other day. I didn't want him to be so public about it, but turns out nobody paid him any attention."

"What he said...?" Bill tried to recall.

"About the return of the Great One. You know who I'm talking about."

Bill looked at the grinning chanters surrounding him, their smiles void of warmth; then at Merrilee, still pinned to that altar of sorts.

"You can't be serious."

Karchi nodded, "Mmm-hmm. Right now it's all about gathering followers, especially ones with skills or social prominence. Somebody like you, an up-and-comer with the D.A.'s office who can help us grease wheels when we need to, like with our boy Szardo. We need him out from behind bars. He's a help to us."

"You're nuts if you think I'll help you get him released."

"Get him released? You're going to throw the case. And after tonight, you'll do it willingly. Because tonight you become our bitch, Billy Boy... you'll do whatever we want. We're going to doll you up nice and pretty, with pretty red paint to go on those pretty lips, so quick to turn a pretty phrase for the common welfare." And though he was smiling, the next words came like a growl from the back of his throat: "And you'll serve in that capacity until we're through with your earthly husk."

Bill shook his head like one would at a child after they'd pulled a prank that turned nasty.

"It's true," Karchi insisted. "I've got bigger plans than acting like some douchebag movie mogul skating about town in Keds with designer jeans. If you'd bothered to see the *third* in the *Ahriman* trilogy you'd have some notion of what I'm talking about.

"Except in real life it starts in the City of Angels, with all the smog and the traffic and those young fellas who shoot at eight-year-old girls from passing cars because they can't aim straight. With all the spoiled twats and shitbirds in their daddy's Jeep Wranglers and the hordes of delusionals who think they've got what it to takes to walk the red carpet for weeping in some shitty movie that supposedly says something heavy about that most pathetic of delusions, *the human condition*. It starts with one known for passing off such a shitty movie – three of them, in fact, all grossing over 800 million – building up an empire in the midst of this, forming networks, winning converts, among the most powerful and influential members of society.

"But we don't exclude the silent majority who are secretly ready for a change, a big change, a takeover. We've got more followers than that asshat on Twitter. And when we're done recruiting, then the Great One's minions will come to the surface – crazy little bastards, a real kick; wait till you meet 'em. And they'll make the world ready, and the Big Guy himself can take over."

"The Big Guy? The Great One?" a laugh of incredulity escaped Bill's lips.

"Oh yeah, the red-skinned wonder himself. He's real, believe it."

Held down by the dockworker, Merrilee finally spoke up, still with fight left in her soul, "If he's real, then that means God is real too."

Karchi regarded her with half a smile dimpling his cheek, "You really think He gives a shit about what happens to all of us down here? If He cared, He would have stepped in a long time ago."

Disbelief crumpled Bill's brow.

"I know it's a lot to process, Bill. But it'll get easier for you, after tonight."

"How do you figure?"

"Well, it's kinda hard to explain. But it involves the incanting of some Aramaic words, or maybe they're just backwards, like the ones on those old LPs spun in reverse. I don't know, I just say 'em like they're written down and they seem to work." He jerked a thumb over his shoulder at an old yellowed tome splayed atop a steamer trunk.

Then from a back pocket, Karchi produced a curved knife, its handle worn dull and blade nicked. "Along with the chanting and this special knife... blah-blah-blah... You get the idea."

Karchi tilted his head to those at Bill's side, and Bill was once again held in an octopus grip of iron.

"It's all about the heart," Karchi continued, "or maybe it's the soul. I don't know. But for our purposes, it's the heart. Transferring it from one who's good..."

He tipped the knifepoint toward Merrilee, "Like your girl... to one who can be turned."

Locking upon Bill's frightened eyes, Karchi stared without hint of playfulness or amity.

Bill heard the words but didn't want to believe them. He read the intent in Karchi's dark eyes, but didn't want to think it real, the whole thing now truly like something out of a horror movie, a lurid tale with a bad ending.

He lunged for Karchi, but his body could only strain against those holding him, muscles popping cord-like under his skin.

"No!" he shouted ineffectually as Karchi stood over Merrilee with the dagger. She tried to kick, to yank her arms free, but to no avail.

Accepting what was to come, she stopped struggling against the arms pinning her, looking not at Karchi or his looming blade, but shaking her head at Bill, the simple motion asking him not to be sad. He saw not hopelessness in her eyes, but confidence, an electric undercurrent of optimism, an assuredness that she would soon be with her Lord and Savior.

Those gathered began once again to chant, as Karchi tore open Merrilee's blouse, laying cold metal to warm breast. He joined in the chant, the dark chorus thrumming church basement walls.

"...lee..." was all Bill could say, his eyes not as hopeful as Merrilee's as he saw her lips form the silent words: *I love you.*

Then Karchi shoved the blade into her chest, leaning on it with all his weight to drive steel through breastbone.

If she made a sound Bill didn't hear, for his voice burst on the air with bestial rage, the wail of an animal crying for its dead in the wilds of a new world.

Merrilee's head dropped back, her eyes dying but open.

Then Karchi began to saw with the blade and Bill closed his eyes to the horror, thankful for the loud chanting which masked the sounds of human butchery.

After a time, the chanting ceased, leaving only a quiet mumble, a breaking of still air that indicated the presence of other bodies around him.

Crying, he soon felt something warm and wet press against his quivering lips and instinctively opened his eyes to see redness filling his vision.

Before him, Karchi held aloft Merrilee's heart, a blue-veined lump of muscle, slathered with slick blood like a scarlet glove dripping off his hand.

"Eat it," Karchi grinned.

Bill slammed his eyes shut once again, clapping his lips together like a child warding off a plate of fetid peas.

He felt the warm gristle pressed against his mouth, some of the dripping blood finding a way between his lips, touching his tongue with the tang of a filthy penny.

He heard Karchi say, "Eat it, Goddamn you. Eat it."

With strong hands holding his head in place and Merrilee's dead flesh smashing against his mouth, eventually he had to submit.

And sobbing, he bit into it.

Snorting, the old man awoke, with the back of his hand wiping drool from his mouth.

The plane was quiet, its rumbling ceased.

He sat up in his seat, lower back protesting painfully. He saw a passenger carry a tote bag up the aisle toward the front of the plane.

The scowling flight attendant came up behind the old man, looming over, startling him.

"We've landed," she said, impatient.

The old man glanced out the small window to see it was gloomy outside. He checked his watch. 4:17 p.m.

As he got off the plane and walked through the nearly empty terminal, he had trouble reading the signs for Baggage Terminal and Ground Transportation, the arrows guiding him; trouble reading not because of failing eyesight, but because of an enveloping dimness, as if the airport were on emergency power, lights weak and pulsing.

Trudging the concourse, he saw through large wide glass, the sky dense with charcoal clouds, source of the gloom. He hoped that meant there would be snow. He loved snow at Christmastime; at least he had a long time ago.

He exited the airport to the smell of exhaust. Grimy taxi-cabs and other cars picked up the scattering of passengers. It was warmer out here than the old man expected, nothing like winter at all. And there was no Santa Claus ringing his charity bell over a red metal basket near the doors; he'd always liked hearing those bells.

Flakes fell from the dark grey sky and he stepped out from under the overhang, holding out his palm to catch one. It was large, a light fluffy wisp of grey, like a torn corner of tissue paper. Strangely, it didn't melt from the warmth of his hand, instead blowing away on the breeze.

Suddenly, the strong sweet scent of lilac overpowered the stench of exhaust. The smell made him smile but he couldn't remember why and it brought pain to his heart. Then just as quickly the smell was gone, blown away by a gust of exhaust and air too warm for December.

He carried his single bag across four lanes of paved road to the parking structure across the way, climbing concrete steps to the second level. At the top he snatched up a scrap of paper, a burnt remnant of a brochure it looked like, showing part of a city map and the broken phrase "*ILLS STARS.*" He started to crumple it up, then stuffed it in his pocket. Through the dark rows of cars he navigated toward the far side of the structure, where he could rest his arms on the safety railing and look out the open walls.

Gazing past the lower-level parking lot he saw the great, sprawling city. Like the scent of lilac it stirred buried memories, a pang of belonging, as of homecoming. Only his "home" was engulfed in smoke, dense, billowing clouds of it rising from blackened buildings, orange flames spitting and fluttering, sometimes flaring high and long before being quelled, as if a controlled burn.

And on the distant hills a fiery gash, something up there manmade but unlike the other burning structures. It must be huge to be visible at that distance, he thought, a modern-day idol turning to cinders, its looming skeleton mere bonfire kindling now.

He stuck his hand out over the safety railing and caught another snowflake, observing with growing dread as it crumpled to dust between his fingertips.

Not snow. Ash.

That's why there had been no Santa ringing his bell. That's why it was too warm for December. Because it was June. How he could forget that, he didn't know; but there were many things he often forgot. Like his destination, the town he and his beloved had called home, perishing in flames. It was all coming back to him now, though.

Movement caught his eye in the distance, at the edge of the nearly empty lower-level parking lot, where dark people far away shoveled ash from the pavement, piling it high as mountains.

The snow shovels they were using almost made the old man doubt his tenuous mind again, that it really was Christmas and not June, and that it was snowing in L.A., incredibly, and they were shoveling snow and not ash.

But no, he remembered, there was no Christmas, not anymore. Not since the world turned what seemed like ages ago.

As he watched the dark people shoveling that ash, he realized that they weren't so far away as he'd thought, reduced by distance like the blazing sign, but rather they were very small people, their sharp ears pointing skyward, as if dressed like little elves for the holidays.

But it is not Christmas, he reminded himself.

It is not snow they are shoveling.

And no, they are not wearing elf costumes.

They are what they are.

Not elves at all.

FADE TO BLACK